THE IDENTITY THIEF

Alex Bryant

K & M Books

HI, HELLO, WELCOME TO MY BOOK

The Identity Thief is the beginning of the God Machine series. To get the inside scoop on how the saga is progressing, visit **www.alexbryantauthor.com** and join the Readers Club! Club members also get a free copy of *I'm Nobody*, a follow-up novella that delves into the backstory of *The Identity Thief.* (Whatever you do, don't read *I'm Nobody* first. That will ruin both novels for you at once.)

If you have opinions you'd like to share, you can find me all over the place:

Goodreads: **/alexbryantauthor**
Instagram: **@alexbryantauthor**
Facebook: **@alexbryantauthor**
Twitter: **@alexbryantauth**
Email: **alexbryant@km-books.com**

TRIGGER WARNINGS

The Identity Thief contains numerous upsetting, unpleasant, and downright unnecessary themes. Sensitive readers, and anyone under the age of 12, are advised to take a look at the trigger warnings: **www.alexbryantauthor.com/the-identity-thief-tw**. Don't say I didn't warn you.

FUN FUN BOOK FACTS

First published in Great Britain in 2020 by K&M Books

First edition.

ISBN 978-1-913571-00-9

CONTENTS

ONE

DANGEROUS WORDS

Every word that follows is false.

It's strange how quickly a life can unravel. Only a few minutes ago, the father had been woken up by shuffling sounds coming from his study. Against his better judgement, he'd gone to investigate, fearing burglars. But what he'd found was far worse: his own daughter, sitting on his desk chair in her nightie, her hopelessly frizzy hair falling into her eyes as she bent over his book.

It was a chapter of his life that he'd tried to keep closed. But it had opened of its own accord, in the middle of the night, and once open it wouldn't be easy to shut again.

"Where did you get that book, Sophie?" he asked.

It was a stupid question that could only have one answer. His daughter pointed shyly to a gap on the uppermost bookshelf on his office wall. The spot where the book had been resting, untouched, since before the girl was born.

"How did you reach that shelf? You didn't stand on the chair, did you? You know that's very dangerous."

The daughter shrugged bashfully, not wanting to admit anything.

But that didn't matter right now. All that mattered was getting his daughter away from that book.

The key was to act normally. Not to overreact.

"Never mind. I'm not angry. Let's just put that book away and go back to bed. It's two o'clock in the morning!"

"I *knooooow*," the daughter replied. "But I couldn't sleep, Daddy. There was a monster in my bed."

"Aren't you a bit old for monsters?"

"That's what I said to it. But it wouldn't listen."

The father drew the sash of his dressing gown tighter. "Well, I'll come with you, and scare it away."

"But I'm not sleepy now." The daughter pointed to the book's title.

Η ΡΗΤΟΡΙΚΗ
ΤΟΥ ΑΡΙΣΤΟΤΕΛΗ

"Why do these letters look funny?"

"It's Greek. Some of the letters in their alphabet are different from ours."

"Why do you have a Greek book?"

"It's, uh, it's something I was interested in a long time ago. But not anymore."

Underneath the title was a small but immaculately drawn torch: a slender stem topped with stylized fire. Thankfully, his daughter didn't ask what it was. Her eyes had returned to the strange handwritten message. *Every word that follows is false.*

"Who wrote that?"

"I don't know, honey. It doesn't matter."

"You're not supposed to write in books."

"You're not supposed to be reading this book in the first place!"

With a forced laugh, the father pulled the heavy leather book out from under his daughter's curious gaze, snapped it shut, and returned it to its place on the uppermost shelf. He'd hoped it would stay far from prying eyes up there. How stupid he'd been, leaving something like that out in the open. He should have got rid of it years ago. And now it was too late.

"Why can't I see it?"

"It's…it's not a good book for children to read."

"What does it say?"

"It's very boring, I promise you. You wouldn't want to know. Why don't we find a book in your room, and I'll read that to help you fall asleep?"

"But I want that one," the girl whispered, gazing up at the top shelf.

The father had always been proud of his daughter's bottomless curiosity about the world around her. As soon as she'd started speaking, she'd been relentlessly asking him questions, determinedly unpicking the world around her. She was never happy with easy answers – she'd just keep asking new questions until she was satisfied. Questions he needed like a hole in the head.

"Please, Sophie. I'd rather we didn't think about that book anymore. And I'd rather you didn't talk about that book to anyone at school." The shadow of a headache was beginning. A guilty pulse behind his left eye.

"Why, Daddy?"

The daughter's face was all wide-eyed innocence. Her guileless gaze tore a hole straight into the world that he'd kept hidden for so long. But if he tried to fob her off with an excuse, the hole would only get bigger and bigger, until his entire life fell through.

He should have just ignored the book. He should have just steered her straight out the room and not looked back. He saw that now. But it was too late. His daughter knew there was something not quite right about what she'd found, and she'd keep drilling into him until she found something resembling the truth.

The father took a deep and measured breath. "Some people think that these kinds of books are dangerous. And they think that people like me shouldn't have them. So if anyone found out I had them here, I could get in trouble."

"What kind of trouble?"

"Very bad indeed. I could even be sent to prison."

"What? Are you a criminal, Daddy?"

Yes.

"No. Of course not. It's just that...some people would get the wrong idea if they knew about this. They'd think the worst of me."

The daughter's brow wrinkled in confusion. "How could a book be so dangerous that you have to go to prison?"

No matter how he turned it over in his mind, the father couldn't find a way to answer that question in a way that wouldn't destroy his family's lives. The headache wasn't helping, lancing from his eye to the back of this head. All he could offer was, "Because it contains dangerous words."

The daughter's brow stayed wrinkled. He was going to be answering questions about this for days, perhaps weeks. But as long as his daughter was only asking him those questions, and not anyone else, they'd be OK. Tomorrow morning, he could gather up all the books on his top shelf and take them far away. Burn them. Drown them in the ocean. Whatever he had to do, he'd do it. And before long, his daughter's curiosity would alight on something else, and this episode would be nothing but a long-forgotten nightmare.

"Now, I think it's time to go back to bed, don't you? I'll read you any story you like. Even one of my incredibly boring ones." He turned to the opposite wall and tugged a book off the shelf at random. An edition of *Crime and Punishment* with one of those classic book cover designs that went out of its way to be ugly. "Hmm?"

The daughter bit her fingers and shook her head. "No. I want this one." She held out a dusty leatherbound book.

The father suppressed a scream. It was the same book, the book he'd put back moments ago. Its spot on the top shelf was somehow empty. "How the hell did you get that down?"

The daughter quailed. "You swore!"

"I'm sorry. I didn't mean to. I'd just rather you didn't touch that book." The father snatched the book away and rammed it back into place. He grabbed his daughter by the wrist and pulled her out of the room, slamming the door shut behind them.

"Ouch, you're hurting me!" the daughter said, pulling her arm away.

"Sorry, honey. I just don't think we should be in there right now. It's very late, and that book is…that book is not for children. OK? Let's go back to your room."

"I don't want to. There's a monster in there!"

"I'll fight it for you. I'm not afraid of monsters." He'd gladly take on any number of monsters, rather than stay a second longer in the same room as that book.

"Don't do that! It might kill you."

"I'd like to see it try."

"OK, fine," his daughter continued. "I can go to bed by myself."

"Don't be silly! We have a monster to slay."

"But my room's really messy."

"Ah, so *that's* why you're so keen to keep me out? That I can believe. But don't worry, I'll let you off just this once."

The daughter's bedroom door was tight shut. The father opened it into total darkness. He fumbled across the room, his bare feet landing on a plastic bow and arrow, and turned on the bedside lamp.

In the bed, sound asleep, was a young girl. Her blanket knotted tightly under her chin, her hopelessly frizzy hair fanning out on her pillow. His daughter.

The father leaped away from the apparition, his mind blank with terror. His headache was a white hot nail, driving straight through his left eye and all the way through his brain. He turned to face his daughter, his other daughter, standing in the middle of the bedroom, fear in her eyes.

"See? I told you there was a monster, Daddy," said the daughter. "You should have listened to me."

"Wh-what's going on, honey? Who is this?"

"Shhh! Don't wake her up!" the daughter whispered. "It's worse when she's awake."

The father's eyes leaped from one version of his child to the other, praying for one of them to disappear, for the horror to unravel. But it did not. Both children remained stubbornly solid, certain in their own reality.

The father placed a hand on the sleeping daughter's head. The warmth of her skin through her hair was unmistakeably real. So was her gentle, slow breathing.

"What's going on, Sophie?" the father whispered, either to the sleeping child or to the one still standing behind him. He couldn't be sure anymore.

"I said, don't wake her up," the standing child said, with a new edge to her voice.

The father turned back to her. She had picked up her toy bow and arrow from the floor and pointed it at him. A strange solemnity had settled into her. One eye was squeezed shut, the other staring directly down the arrow shaft.

"Who are you?"

The plastic bow hardened into wood. The arrow grew a razor sharp tip.

"Me? I'm nobody. Night night, Daddy."

The daughter released her bow. The arrow ripped through the father's eye and hit the back of his skull. He spent his last few moments of consciousness praying only that his daughter would not wake up to find him like this. But the prayers of a man like him, he knew, would not be answered.

TWO

THE CEMETERY INCIDENT

It was one of those awkward moments when your eyes meet across a deserted cemetery. You know who he is, and he probably knows who you are, but you'd still never say 'hi' if you passed him in a school corridor. You're not really in the mood to talk to anyone, and obviously neither is he, and you think *perhaps if I pretend I haven't seen him, he'll pretend he hasn't seen me and we'll simply glide past each other and pretend this never happened.* This is never going to work, for at least two reasons:

A) By the time your brain has got that far, you've enjoyed at least 3 seconds of silence, and by that point it's too late to do anything but admit that you've been staring awkwardly at each other.

B) He's in literally all your classes, so whatever you do now you're going to be bumping into each other again. And then there'll be that moment when you next make awkward eye contact and think *So…do I mention the cemetery incident? Or would that make it more awkward?* and in the time it takes you to think that, he'll obviously be thinking the exact same thing, and then you'll both realise that the other person is thinking the exact same thing, so you'll have no choice but to mention it. In which case, you may as well just get it over with now and say something.

But what can you even say? You could go for "Hi, Hector!" but that would give away that you know his name despite having never officially met before, which would look really stalkerish. It's bad enough that you've been following him through a deserted cemetery in broad daylight. If you turn around and admit that you know his name, he'll probably run away screaming, sending the Awkwardness Quotient off the charts, even if the only reason you happen to know is because Jess keeps muttering it darkly whenever he shambles past.

But you've got to say something, so you say, "Heya! Almost didn't notice you there."

Your words come out painfully loud. There may as well be a miffed corpse popping up somewhere to say "Don't you know this is an ancient place of inviolable sanctity?"

But he's not listening anyway. His eyes have drifted away from yours and are tracking around the cemetery clearing, as if looking for something just beyond the trees. Fear and panic is eating up his face. He raises both hands in front of him. He mutters something harshly, which from where you stand sounds like "Back!" but really could be anything. He takes a small step backwards, into the shadow of an enormous stone head, which glowers down onto the clearing from the top of a pedestal.

"Back!" he's saying again, more clearly now, choking on the word. "Back!" His whole face screws up around his lips as they squeeze the word out, again and again. His arms, still stuck out in front of him, are clutching at something out of sight, each time he says the word. He looks like a video loop repeating itself pointlessly, jerking back to the beginning every two seconds.

"Back!" But this time, the word gets trapped in his mouth, slurring into a low, strangled moan. His throat bulges and tenses as if swallowing down something twice its size, blue veins popping out of his skin. His outstretched hands are twisted backwards into claws, tracing a wide circle around his body as they're pushed backwards. He hovers for a second, his body knotted and doubled over, before he collapses to the floor with a sound like ripping wood.

A moment of silence. Then he's thrashing wildly on the ground, kicking up brown leaves and dirt around him. His face is contorted in the same grimace he was wearing when he fell, his jaw clenched up and his eyes squeezed shut. Muffled moans force their way past his locked teeth.

It dimly occurred to me that I should do something to help him. But I didn't move. I didn't know how. I just wanted someone to tell me what to do. But the cemetery stayed as empty as ever. It was just me, Hector, and that giant stone head, who'd done nothing the whole time but point his beard ferociously at the scene unfolding beneath him.

By the time I remembered how to walk again, Hector's face had become strangely peaceful. His breathing lengthened out into deep, tranquil sighs. He could have been lying there for hours. His golden-brown skin matched the colour of the leaves piled around him perfectly. He looked just as small and fragile. There was a little clump of bubbles on his lips. As I watched, a renegade batch broke off from the main cluster and slid down his pudgy cheek. Then, his eyes fluttered open.

I knelt down next to him. If my hair had still been long, it would have been brushing against his face, but I'd cut it to shoulder length just before the start of Year 8. I was starting to shiver. It was the kind of day where if you stopped moving for too long, the chill started to soak through your clothes. But Hector didn't seem to mind. Nor did he mind the earth and wet leaves that were steadily caking themselves into the back of his jacket and head. His eyes circled gently around the small patch of sky above our heads, before they drew back to find me leaning over him.

Hector opened and shut his mouth a couple of times. Then, he drew a deep, rattling breath and wiped a long stream of spit off his chin. "Well," he said after an uncomfortable pause. "This is awkward."

You may be wondering – you may even have been wondering for some time – what exactly I was doing in the cemetery. Your immediate reaction was probably, "*What's a girl at the tender age of twelve doing, following people around cemeteries in broad daylight? Doesn't she have homework to be getting on with? Huh?*"

Well, you're right. I didn't really have a good excuse. But the bottom line is, it was all Jess's fault.

Hector had joined Whittington School a couple of weeks ago, at the start of Year 8. There was nothing that made him stand out, nothing interesting enough about him to make an otherwise non-stalkerish girl in his year follow him through one of London's weirdest tourist attractions. He definitely wasn't hot, if that's what you'd crassly assumed. He was kind of short, kind of chubby, and obviously Greek. Not that there was anything wrong with that, but you know.

It had been Jess who'd narrowed her eyes at him, the first time we'd walked (early) into our English class and spotted him hunched by himself on a desk in the corner, reading. As we'd sat down on the other side of the room, Jess had muttered to me, "I think that's the guy. He's one of the River People."

"River people?"

Jess nodded grimly. "They came back. They're living in that weird house in the cemetery. Mum told me to watch out for him. Your mum must have done too, right?"

I shook my head. I'd completely forgotten about the River People. I thought they'd just been a ghost story that Jess made up years ago. And Hector may as well have been a ghost, for all anyone noticed him. Nobody talked to him, or even looked at him, as he drifted from lesson to lesson. He had a hunched-up way of moving, like he was trying to make himself as small as possible, trying not to be seen. And he was fantastic at it, most of the time. It was just me that started to see him everywhere I went. Gobbling his food down, alone, in the cafeteria. Doing his homework on one of the picnic benches in the playground. Reading in the corner of the locker room.

The day of the awkward cemetery incident, I'd been walking home from school when I decided to swing by to visit Dad. This was a weird habit that I'd just taken up. Mum didn't like visiting Dad – thought it was mawkish. But over the summer holidays I'd seen a film which started with a family crying and laying flowers on their father's grave, and it seemed like the kind of thing I ought to be doing. So I snuck down one day on the way to see Chloë, and stood for a while at Dad's grave, and waited to see if I'd cry. I didn't.

There'd been a bouquet of flowers leaning against his headstone. Not wanting to be outdone, I picked some wildflowers from nearby and laid them on the grave. And immediately realized they'd looked much nicer growing than they did slowly dying in my father's honour. I felt kind of depressed about the whole thing and left. Then a few weeks later, I felt bad, and come back to see if things would feel any different. They didn't.

So that's what I was doing in Highgate Cemetery – feeling bad about not feeling bad about a dad who I didn't remember. That's when I'd seen a flash of purple through the trees. The exact shade of the Whittington School jumper.

I looked up and saw Hector marching away. His shoulders were hunched, his hands dug deep into his pockets, and he had a rucksack that looked heavier than him dangling over his bum. His face was scrunched up, like he was plotting the end of the world.

I didn't decide to follow him. I just sort of did.

Hector turned onto one of the tiny pathways that led deeper into the heart of the cemetery. It threaded narrowly between enormous trees with shattered gravestones cradled in their roots. I wasn't looking, though. I still had Hector in my sights, his shiny black hair poking out from a jacket too big for him.

It wasn't that late, but the cold had driven all but the most hardcore tourists away on that particular day. The sun was out, but it didn't help much – the trees hung so thick and heavy over every path that it felt permanently like dusk in there. I was sure Hector would hear me eventually as I trod on the occasional leaf pile or stone, but he was obviously too wrapped up in whatever it was going on in his brain that made his face scrunch up all the time.

The deeper we journeyed into the cemetery, the more epic the tombstones got. We passed stone columns reaching up into the tree canopies. Stone urns overflowing with stone flowers. Stone angels draped despairingly over stone beds.

We stumbled out onto one of the main pathways, in front of a mausoleum that looked like a temple. It had a metal door in the middle. A woman and a man stood on either side wearing togas, holding up the two front corners of the temple roof with their heads. I didn't have time to stop and read the inscriptions covering every flat surface – Hector had turned right and continued into a clearing. It was only when he'd reached the other side of the clearing that he'd stopped and looked around for the first time. In front of, as you may recall, a huge stone face doomed to an eternity keeping watch over this corner of Highgate Cemetery, who was clearly regretting that decision more and more with each passing moment he was forced to spend with a couple of annoying Year 8s.

Me, a few minutes later: "Hi. My name's Cass. Welcome to Whittington School."

There – this was turning almost into a normal situation. Sure, I could have picked a better time to welcome him to my school – that one time Jess and I turned up to an English lesson early, for example, and he was the only other person in the room. Not now, while he was nestling up against a big bearded monument, his breathing still a bit too loud.

Hector still wasn't in a talkative mood. He kept drifting in and out of focus, his eyes stumbling around the edge of the clearing as if they'd lost something. "Hi," he said, not looking at me.

"You looked like you were being...I don't know, *attacked* or something. It was awful. What happened to you?"

Hector shook his head woozily. "Don't remember."

My thoughts chilled. "What if it was sorcery?" I tried to summon up all the wise advice I'd been given over the years about recognising sorcery. But my mind was blank. "This might be serious. I should call the police. Or maybe even Mum."

"Don't do that. I'm fine," Hector slurred. He was getting sharper now, beginning to squirm into a more comfortable position, looking at me carefully. "It couldn't be sorcery. This is consecrated ground."

"Consecrated?"

"Consecrated means the cemetery's been blessed."

"Yes, I know what consecrated means," I replied, irritated because in reality I'd only been about 70% sure what consecrated meant. "You're telling me that the blessing would stop sorcery from working?"

"Yeah."

Mum had never mentioned anything like this to me. And she normally told me everything there was to know about sorcery.

"OK, if you're sure. But whatever just happened, you look terrible. What about an ambulance?"

I put a hand on his arm. Hector pulled back in shock, like I'd just electrocuted him. "What are you doing here?"

"Me? Oh, I just came by to see Dad."

"Does he work here?"

Oh, the poor guy. The poor, stupid guy. He'd walked right into what was probably going to become the most awkward moment of his entire life to date. I thought for a second whether there was any way I could save him – even wondered whether I should just lie and say Dad was the Official Gravescrubber or something – but ultimately, I knew the only thing I could do was come out with it.

"No. He's buried here."

Now, I've had to deliver the bad news about Dad plenty of times to randomers or forgetful teachers or whoever, and one thing that always gets me is the way they say "I'm sorry," and try to go all downcast, as if they'd known Dad for years. Some of them would take it upon themselves to deliver a short speech on the subject of Death, like "That must be so hard," or "I knew someone who died once. It was terrible."

But if I got chewed up every time I had to tell someone about Dad being dead, I'd be a nailbitten wreck by now. The only difficult part about saying it, for me, is knowing about the upset and awkwardness I'm causing the other person. Especially on a day like this, where, as you've probably noticed, the Awkwardness Factory was paying all its workers overtime.

Hector wasn't hit quite as badly as most people are. He just blinked confusedly and said, "Oh. That's a shame," as if he'd broken my favourite pencil.

I offered him a hand up, but he didn't take it. Instead, he spent about three hours slowly and dazedly clambering to his feet while doing everything he could to avoid my outstretched hand.

"Could I just. Say something." Hector stared at the ground again, his mouth twitching as it tried to hold in something it didn't want to say. For a second, I thought the whole thing was going to happen again. He turned to Big Stoney Face for support, but only got an especially fierce mouthful of beard in return. Then he looked somewhere past me. "Please don't tell anyone about this. I was hoping that nobody in Whittington School would find out."

"Sure. I won't tell anyone."

For the first time that day, Hector's face unknotted. "Thank you, Cassandra. I just…don't want anybody to know."

"You can just call me Cass."

"OK then, Cass. Thank you. I'd better go home now."

Hector turned and drifted away abruptly. So abruptly that it was only when I reached the gates that I wondered why he hadn't come back with me – why he'd turned and carried on walking deeper into the cemetery.

The London Press

BELOVED TEACHER AND FATHER OF TWO NYXED IN BRIXTON HOME

Joost Meyer

A family home in Brixton has become the site of a violent assault. This crime is the latest in a string of similar magically aided attacks taking place around London.

The victim was Frank McPhearson, a much-loved teacher in a local school.

The police took an emergency call from McPhearson at 2:13am on Wednesday morning. He reported that someone had broken into his house and was trying to gain access to his study.

Police arrived on the scene to find McPhearson in atroposy (magically induced unconsciousness) in a bedroom. He was brought to hospital, where he is currently in a stable condition. He has no recollection of the break-in or subsequent assault, suggesting that he was nyxed at the scene.

It's not currently clear what the assailant's motivations were. It may be that the assailant was surprised by McPhearson in the middle of a robbery, although nothing has been reported stolen from the house.

This is the sixth similar attack to be reported in the last month alone. In each incident, the victim has reported a break-in while it was underway, only to be found unconscious by the response team, with no sign of the perpetrator. In each case, there has been no reported theft, and no other clear motivation for the break-in or attack.

A Sorcerer Investigation Department (SID) spokesperson said, "While we can confirm that the assault was magically aided, there is currently nothing linking this incident with previous magical attacks on individuals in their homes. We don't wish to speculate about the assailant or assailants' motivations at this time."

However, what we do know is that following a gradual decline over the past decade, the incidence of magical crime appears to be rising sharply. Sorcerer networks appear to be recruiting young men and women in increasing numbers, inducting them into a lifetime of sorcery from which it is almost impossible to escape. London's hospitals are reporting an ever-growing surge of patients showing signs of magical violence.

One thing is clear: the threat of sorcery is rising, and sooner or later it will impact all of us.

10 steps you can take today to make your house magic-proof p. 37

THREE

SPIDER'S WEB

This story isn't really about me. If someone were to come along and turn it into a documentary or something, they would cast Cuttlefish as the villain, the deranged criminal who nearly fools the world. Mum would be the hero – the detective who refuses to give up until she brings him to justice. I'd be that adorable child who the detective tucks up in bed, saying "Darling, I promise once this case is over, you and I are going to spend a lot more time together." (Just so you know, Mum never actually said that, or even tucked me up in bed for that matter, but the documentary writers would have to give Mum's character a bit of popular appeal somehow.)

But I can't tell you the real story, I can only tell you the part I saw. It's kind of a different story, one that didn't make much sense to me at the time, but I can't help that. I'm the villain more often than I'm the hero, and the bits where I'm the hero are basically flukes, but I can't help that either. And my story starts two weeks into Year 8. It starts with Hector wandering in, having a tonic-clonic seizure, then wandering off again before I've had a chance to work out what's going on.

That's what it was, by the way. A tonic-clonic seizure. He told me the next day. Like this:

"It was a tonic-clonic seizure."

He had the exact same tense expression on as he'd had in the cemetery, although the classroom lights made his face look paler, the colour of the toasted parts of very slightly toasted toast.

Actually, that hadn't been the first thing he'd said. The first thing he said, when I sat down next to him at the beginning of English, was:

"It's not important. It doesn't matter. It was nothing."

I didn't know much at the tender age of twelve, but I knew what *nothing* looked like, and it was a lot more boring than whatever had happened to Hector in the cemetery. I told him so. He didn't come quietly, twisting away from my glances and murmuring "It doesn't matter!" a few more times. But eventually, he owned up.

"It was a tonic-clonic seizure. Can I have my phone back now?"

I stretched Hector's phone even further out behind me. "Only if you tell me what a clonic-tonic seizure is."

"It's just one of the things epilepsy can do." He made another grab for his phone, but I didn't budge. "I take medication to stop them happening, but sometimes they happen anyway."

"But *why* do they happen?"

"I don't know. There can be a lot of reasons. Like being tired, or being bugged the whole time by someone who promised they weren't going to talk about it."

"Hey, I said I wouldn't tell anyone, and I didn't. I just want to know what happened."

"Can't you just look it up online?"

I'd already tried, last night, but I hadn't got anywhere. "Fine. I'm just trying to be friendly. But I can leave you alone if you want."

I dropped his phone on the desk in front of him and left him sitting alone, in his favourite seat in the corner. I was just in time – Jess came in moments later, along with the rest of the class. (I'd come early from break because I knew I'd find Hector sitting by himself as usual.) And that was the last time Hector and I ever spoke.

I wish.

That lunch, things started to go wrong. Really, *properly* wrong, not just tonic-clonic-seizure-in-a-cemetery wrong. It all boils down to table design.

In Whittington Junior School, they set up picnic tables in the sports hall every day for us to sit at. Each table could only fit four people, which worked out perfectly for Jess, Tori, Chloë, and me. But the senior school had its own cafeteria, which was for nothing but eating. It was high-ceilinged, and full to bursting with light and noise and speed. Everything was futuristic and glistening new. There were four glistening food counters, where you got served your heart's desire by four glistening chefs. The only catch was, it had long tables for us all to sit together, meaning for the first time in our lives, we were forced to eat food in the presence of randomers in our year. Normally, the music crowd ended up sharing a table with us, but that particular day, they were nowhere to be seen.

So there we all were, huddled at the end of a long table. Little did we know what foul fate was about to befall us. Tori was waving her fork at Chloë's stuffed pepper.

"How *is* that for you?" she asked.

"Not bad," said Chloë.

"I meant the whole vegetarianism thing. I was thinking of becoming a vegetarian myself. It's meant to be really good for you."

"Really?" said Jess.

"Yeah. That's why all the models do it. Look at Chloë. She's really slim."

Chloë looked down at herself guiltily. "Am I?"

"Don't be silly, Chloë. You've got a *gorgeous* figure."

Chloë had been my best friend in primary school so I'd known her the longest. I could tell from her blank stare, cheeks chipmunked with rice, that she'd never thought about it before.

Jess appraised Chloë. "You do," she said. Since Jess had started wearing glasses a year ago, she managed to make everything she said sound like an expert opinion.

"Thanks," she said mushily.

"That's why you do it, right? Why else would you? Unless you, like, really cared about animals or the environment or something."

Chloë shrugged. "It's just a Chinese Buddhism thing. Actually, just a general Buddhism thing. No-one in my family eats meat. I don't think I'd like it that much."

"How do you know you don't like it if you've never tried it?"

"I once had some lamb by mistake. It tasted like a nosebleed."

As Chloë was talking, I happened to glance up at the buffet line. And guess who was standing right there, tray in hand, lasagne on tray, glancing forlornly back at me?

No really. Guess.

I'll wait.

OK, well done, it was Hector. The moment was so breathtakingly awkward, it would only have been slightly worse if he'd dropped his tray and had another one of his tonic-clonic seizures, right there in his lasagne. (By the way, you could tell he was new here by the way he'd chosen the lasagne. Nobody chose the lasagne more than once.) He was gazing around the cafeteria forlornly.

The cafeteria was one place I'd not noticed Hector before. I think he tended to grab his food and then slink away somewhere else. But not this time. Now we locked in a staring contest that had already gone on for untold aeons, and would perhaps never end.

Needless to say, Jess was right there to point out the obvious. "Oh my God, Cass... Is Hector *staring* at you?"

"That guy is *such* a freak. You were right about him, Jess," Tori chipped in. Then she patted me on the wrist. "Cass, if he starts trying to talk to you or anything, just move away. Or the next thing you know is, he'll be following you around everywhere."

Jess nodded wisely in agreement, one finger curling through her brown ringlets.

Tori was a full head taller than the rest of us – lunch was the only opportunity we had to look her in the eye. And it wasn't just height which Tori did better than anyone else. Her caramel hair always looked like a shampoo advert. She only ever wore clothes that clung to her skinny waist. She basically looked like someone's big sister who was being forced to babysit us the whole time.

She didn't just look the part, she played it too. She had not one, but two older sisters giving her the cheat sheets on everything you could ever want to know. How to ignore guys so that they won't talk to you, vs. how to ignore them so that they *will* talk to you. What to do when you have menstrual cramps in an exam. How to avoid sweating. None of this information had ever come in handy, but Jess and I could tell it was going to one day. That's why when Tori spoke, we listened.

Chloë, not so much. You could rely on her to space out whenever the conversation got too teenagery. She didn't even know there was more than one way to ignore a guy. She'd stopped paying attention when we started talking about Hector, just smiling at her stuffed pepper like it was better company than us. She chose that exact moment to look up and say, "He's coming over."

We all did our best to look at him while not looking like we were looking at him. None of us succeeded.

Tori: "Chloë's right. What's he doing?"

Jess: "He's probably just on his way to another table."

Tori: "He's still doing that creepy stare at Cass though."

Tori was right. Hector seriously needed to practise using his face in a mirror before he brought it out in public. It was sending out all the wrong messages.

Jess looked at me with concern. "You haven't *talked* to him or anything, have you? Like, why would he think it's OK to just stare at you like that?"

But luckily I didn't get a chance to answer the question, because just then Hector banged his tray down at the empty space next to us and dove into his lasagne, like it was the kind of thing he did every day.

The rest of us all tried to see who could pull the most aghast expression. Tori won by a long way.

Chloë completely failed to realise how shocking this was. She just turned to him and said, "Hi. I'm Chloë," reaching through my Chicken 'n' Chips to shake hands with him. That was typical Chloë, to casually introduce herself as if Hector were a normal person.

"I'm Hector. Hello," he said to her stuffed pepper. He looked around the rest of us furtively, then carried on inserting mincemeat into his face.

The rest of lunch was one of the quietest meals I can remember. Quieter than the time Tori had gone through her devout religious phase just before her Bat Mitzvah and taken a vow of silence. (The devout religious phase had lasted three days and the vow of silence three hours, not including the bit during lunch she explained all the devout religious reasons she had for taking the vow.) The only highlight I can remember is Tori leaning over Jess and saying "So, Hector, huh? That's a weird name."

Hector said nothing, so Chloë turned and said, "What school did you used to go to?" in her most grandmotherly voice. Chloë was the kind of girl who you could tell would make a fantastic grandmother one day. She had big misty eyes that would look way better with a pair of half-moon reading glasses. Whenever she laughed or smiled, she got these enormous creases, kind of uber-dimples, across her cheeks, that were just biding their time until they became epic grandma-wrinkles one day.

"I've been homeschooled," Hector said.

Jess: "Homeschooled? What's that?"

"It's where your parents teach you everything at home."

"My parents were thinking of homeschooling me for a while," said Tori, to everyone except Hector. "But they decided I'd do better with a *real* education, you know? Meeting *real* people." She smiled benevolently down at the rest of us.

Nothing else was said until Hector scooped the final renegade pieces of meat into his mouth and stood up, saying "It was nice to meet you all." Then he scuttled off – unfortunately for him, in the wrong direction, making him double back past our table one last time then out of our lunchtimes for good. Needless to say, he never tried to sit with us, or anywhere in the cafeteria, again.

"I just don't get it," Tori mused after he'd gone. "Why would he just come and randomly sit with us? What kind of a person even *does* that?"

"Maybe he was being friendly," said Chloë.

Tori and Jess stared at her. She went back to her stuffed pepper.

Each strand of the spider's web is invisible. It's only when you draw back that you can see the pattern. If you're already trapped, there's no pattern to see.

FOUR

FOOLPROOF

It was hard to tell where the canal stopped and the towpath began. Roiling mist carpeted both. The streetlights in the distance didn't dare make their way down this route, consigning it to darkness every dusk.

Understandably, almost nobody came this way once night had fallen. It wasn't a useful way to go at the best of times. It led to nowhere but a disused car park around the back of some warehouses, empty except for a weatherbeaten van with SISKOS ELECTRICAL stencilled down the side. The only people who even knew of this car park's existence were joggers and dog walkers, for whom the vegetation crawling out of the cracks in the cement provided the closest thing they had to greenery. But in the darkness, the place had nothing to offer but fear. Fear of the kind of people who'd want to come to a place like this.

People very much like the dealer, in fact, who came here precisely because of its ability to repel everyone else away. It was a perfect arrangement for everyone concerned: no respectable person would want to get mixed up with the likes of him, and he certainly didn't want to get mixed up with respectable people. He leant against the side of his van, gazing at the ember on the end of his cigarette. Whenever people told him cigarettes were going to kill him, he'd say he'd taken care of the problem by becoming morbidly obese instead. "There's not a chance in hell lung cancer is going to get me first!"

The dealer dropped his cigarette to the ground when he saw another figure emerge out of the darkness, the mist carpet parting around his feet. The newcomer didn't seem nearly as comfortable as the dealer to find himself here. His hands were clenched deep in his jacket, and his eyes darted nervously into the gloom on each side of the car park. With his close-cropped charcoal hair and glasses, he looked exactly like a respectable businessman who'd badly lost his way. Which was true, the dealer reflected to himself. They'd both lost their way a long time ago.

"Evening, Frank!" the dealer said, trying to put the newcomer at ease. "Me favourite customer. Long time no see."

"Listen. Something awful has happened," said the newcomer abruptly. "I was attacked. In my house. He stole all my books. My – you know, my grimoires."

"All of them?"

"Every last one. But thank God it *was* every last one. The SID turned up before I knew what was happening. If they'd found even a single dodgy book, that would have been it for me. My life would have been over." The customer hadn't stopped walking since he'd arrived. He continued to pace in circles in front of the van, as if his true destination was somewhere far out of reach.

The dealer nodded sagely. "Guess it could of been worse."

"He was wearing my daughter's face, George. My own daughter! Do you have any idea what that's like?"

The dealer shook his head sympathetically. "Can't imagine how horrible that must have been for you, mate."

"And then she – or he, or it, whatever it was – killed me in front of her. While she slept. What if she'd woken up? What if she'd seen the whole thing? She'd be traumatised."

"Mimesis must be a horrible thing to see first hand."

The customer's frantic pacing stopped briefly. "Mimesis?"

"Identity theft. Changing your appearance to match someone else's. A lot of sorcerers like to mess around with their looks, of course, but a proper mimetic can imitate someone else precisely. It's only an illusion, of course, same as any kind of sorcery. But if they're good, it'll be an illusion strong enough to fool anyone. Even friends and family. It's advanced magic. I've never seen it in real life."

"Yes. That's exactly what happened to me. I should have realised something smelt ratty. But when I saw them both together, my mind just froze, I couldn't think straight."

"Don't worry, you're not the first person to be taken surprise by a sorcerer. The good news is, you're here, you and your daughter are fine, and if you want to avoid anything like that happening again, you've come to the right place!"

The dealer flung open the back doors of his van. The customer peered inside, his forehead furrowed with confusion.

"What am I supposed to be looking at, George?"

The dealer glanced inside. The sides of the van were lined with shelves, piled high with unprepossessing pieces of electrical equipment: rolls of wire, toolboxes, safety signage.

"Hang on a minute," said the dealer cheerily. He slammed the van doors shut again. "Ἀποκαλύπτω!" he whispered, once more turning the handle and swinging the doors back.

The dusty equipment was gone. In its place were equally disordered piles of considerably more interesting items. Jewellery boxes, overflowing with chains and trinkets. Crystals and polished gemstones arranged on velvet trays. Rows of wands clipped into a display board.

"That's more like it, wouldn't you say, Frank?" the dealer said, unable to keep the pride out of his voice.

The customer's eyes lit up with amazement as they took in every plush surface, every gleaming treasure.

"Yeah, I've done a little bit of renovation since you last saw this," the dealer said. "Had a friend install that enchantment on the lock, to keep away prying eyes. You just never know nowadays when the SID might show up." And all it would take was one visit from the wrong person for his life's work to go up in smoke.

The dealer heaved his round body into the van, followed by the customer.

"Close the doors behind you, would you? Don't wanna risk someone strolling past and having a look inside."

"But what about that...*enchantment* thing? Won't it trap us inside?"

The dealer suppressed a smile. No matter how long he'd been in this business, he was still amazed by the weird ideas some people had about sorcery. "That enchantment is just a trick of the eye, Frank. No way it could trap us anywhere. It's the antitheft enchantments you want to watch out for. If anyone comes in here without my say so, their bodies will get stuck to any surface they touch. And if anyone tries to take something out, it explodes in their hands! Foolproof. You can't be too careful nowadays."

As the customer closed the doors behind him, the dealer plucked a couple of necklaces from around the neck of a wooden head. "Does your daughter like jewellery? If so, I have a number of very fashionable pieces here that just so happened to have been enchanted by professionals. They'll keep her well protected from any malicious magic, night or day. And don't worry, I've got plenty of stuff that can be worn by a man like yourself without attracting any strange looks. How about a nice watch, for example? Or these cufflinks?"

The customer looked despairingly at the items in the dealer's hands.

"If it's the price that is worrying you, don't worry, for an old friend like yourself I'm sure I can cut you a deal. Especially if you're looking for a few things today."

"What if a teacher at school decides to take a close look at the jewellery that my daughter's wearing?"

"Oh, this is totally undetectable. Untraceable. At face value, there's no way of seeing a difference between this kind of amulet and the cheap stuff that you can buy in any corner shop. Only difference is, this has been *properly* enchanted, like. So it's guaranteed to do its job. Of course, when I say that, no amulet is foolproof, and a very powerful or determined sorcerer is likely to get round it eventually. But this is the same merch that I use myself. See?" The dealer tugged on a chain hanging around his neck, revealing a golden ankh from under his shirt. "It's kept me safe from my more...*volatile* customers all these years, so I'm sure it'll keep your daughter safe too."

The customer shook his head. "I don't feel comfortable with this. She's only seven. Too young for jewellery."

"Not a problem, not a problem." The dealer tucked his ankh away. Then, with considerable difficulty, he lowered himself to his hands and knees and pulled a tightly sealed glass jar from underneath the shelving. "If you'd rather have a solution that you can install and then not worry about, how about this? All you need to do is pop this jar into the foundations of your house – not as hard as it sounds – and the entire building is protected. Any sorcerer entering the premises will find their powers weakened or vanished completely."

"What on earth is in there?" said the customer, staring nauseously at the jar's murky contents.

"No need to worry yourself about the fine details, Frank. Like I say, this is a plug and play job, no thinking required."

"It looks like... Is that a *heart*?"

"Well spotted, sir, it is indeed a heart," the dealer admitted. "Only a cat, mind, nothing weird. Died of natural causes, in case you were wondering. None of my products involve cruelty to animals, and that's more than you can say about most people in my line of work."

"Are those... Are those *nails* sticking out of it?"

"Only put in after the cat was dead, needless to say."

"Why does it look like it's been set on fire?"

The dealer shoved the jar onto a bottom shelf, next to the rabbits' feet. He'd had the stupid thing for years and never been able to sell it. "I can see you're not a huge fan of the cat heart, sir, but not to worry. As it happens, something's just come in which might be more up your street." The dealer rummaged excitedly through a cardboard box. "Not even had time to inventory this thing yet, sir, that's how fresh it is. Aha!"

The dealer held a thick golden ring up to the customer. Its ruby glinted under the spotlights. "Now, isn't that a beauty? Just you wait until you see what it can do."

The dealer forced the ring onto his index finger. He backed towards the front of his van, taking the customer with him, then pointed at the cardboard box perched near the door.

"Καίτε!"

A stream of flames shot out of the ruby, following the line of his finger, and washed over the cardboard box. The thing erupted into flame. At once, the van filled with smoke and noxious fumes, as the packing material inside the box burned to a cinder.

"Course, this is just an illusion," coughed the dealer, his eyes streaming, "so don't worry about the fumes or anything. Not at all harmful."

The customer squeezed past the dealer, threw the back door open and tossed the box outside. Realising that this did nothing to dispel the heavy smoke that was in the air, he jumped out of the van too.

"If all this is just an illusion," the customer rasped, "how's it going to protect me?"

"An imaginary fire can still cause an imaginary death, Frank! If you point this baby at someone, they'll go up in flames. They'll be in atroposy – totally out of action – for a good few hours. Plenty of time to call the police." The dealer was forced to break off in a fit of hacking coughs.

"Atroposy. Magical death. That's still quite dangerous, isn't it?"

"Well, now, people have different opinions on that. A lot of people insist that getting nyxed does bad things to your brain. The human mind isn't designed to experience its own death, they say. And it's true, people occasionally wake up from atroposy a little…unhinged. Some people never wake up at all. So I definitely don't advise going around nyxing people willy nilly."

"I'm not sure about this," the customer said as they both waited for their lungs to stop hurting. "Seems like too much of a risk."

"If you ask me, if someone breaks into your house and threatens your family, then getting nyxed is the least they deserve," retorted the dealer.

"What if someone finds it and turns it on me? Or my family? What does atroposy do to a child's brain?"

The dealer was getting tired of this. The fire ring was probably the best thing he had in his van. He'd spent most of the day playing with it inside one of the warehouses nearby. "Well, if even this doesn't take your fancy, and I can't imagine why it wouldn't, then I'm running out of ideas! Do you know what it is you had in mind when you came here?"

"Yes. I heard you might have some Daedalus books."

"*Daedalus* books? What would you want with those?"

"To save myself."

The dealer lowered his voice. "I've got a couple, sure. They don't come cheap, though."

"I know."

The dealer turned to the top shelf of his van, where a line of leatherbound grimoires were packed like a dark rainbow. "Here we are," he said, extracting three volumes. "I've got an *Ars Magna*. Latin, 19th-century edition. *On Tragedy*, Ancient Greek but with an English translation, you'll be pleased to hear. And *The Sixth and Seventh Books of Moses.* Of course, there's the usual disclaimer: I've done my best to check this stuff over, but it's your responsibility to protect yourself from any curses that may remain."

The dealer passed the three heavy tomes down to the customer, who was still sheltering outside, away from the fumes.

"But with all due respect, Frank, this is pretty advanced stuff. Someone like yourself is better off using ready-made equipment like this ring, rather than getting stuck into magical theory. You don't really want books like these."

"It's not about what I want. It's about what *he* wants."

"Eh?

"The person who attacked me. He wanted my book because it came from the Daedalus Set. He was looking at the symbol when I walked in on him. I think he's trying to track them down."

The customer was behaving just like he had when he first arrived – pacing around fearfully, casting glances in every direction. But now, he was holding the dealer's highly illegal wares out in the open, where anyone could see. Shouting his wild theories out into the night.

The dealer stumbled out of the van. The car park was as grave and silent as ever. Only the distant hissing of bus brakes cut through the fog. "If that's true, he won't be the first to try. But he's got his work cut out for him. Daedalus books have been trading hands for over a hundred years. They're all over the bloody country by now. If not the world. I myself have sold dozens over the years. And that's just me."

"Dozens? To whom?"

"All sorts. A lot of Lyceum members, of course. Or people claiming to be academics. A few people who were basically mad. Anyone with deep enough pockets, really."

The customer stopped to stare over the canal. Mist coiled over its black depths. "He'll find them all anyway. You'll see."

"Maybe he will, maybe he won't. But if you're right, then this guy has already taken everything he wants from you. At least you're safe from him now!"

"You don't understand. Nobody's safe from him."

"Frank, whatever's on your mind, let's talk about it inside, okay? Somewhere where we're not going to be overheard."

"No. I can't. You don't know what he's capable of. You don't know what he did to me."

The customer turned around. The light coming from the back of the van just barely illuminated his face. But it was enough. Enough for the dealer to see the mottled blood that streamed down its left side, seeping into his jacket collar.

"He's more powerful than you can possibly understand," the customer said. "I couldn't stop him. And neither can you."

The customer took a step closer. The dealer could dimly see something sticking out of his left eye.

"What did you do to you, Frank? What did he do?"

The customer tugged an arrow out of his eye socket. Blood glistened down half its length. With a tormented cry, he flung the arrow at the dealer. Missing its target, it punched through the side of the van with impossible force, leaving only its feathers sticking out of the metalwork inches from the dealer's waist.

The sequence of events unfolded too quickly for the dealer to understand, let alone to respond. His heavy body jerked sideways, realising epochs too late that it was supposed to be dodging the attack. But luckily, the golden ankh hanging around his neck must have been paying more attention, causing the arrow to miss him.

"Who are you?" he yelled, as if that was a remotely relevant question to be asking.

"Nobody," replied the customer. Without the arrow to staunch it, flesh and blood pumped from the customer's eye socket and streamed down his face.

How are you doing that? the dealer wanted to ask next. But the answer to that was obvious. Those books. The dealer had handed this man the most dangerous weapons in his collection, stupidly thinking he wouldn't know how to draw on their power.

But the dealer had been wrong. And now, a shattered monstrosity stood before him, books clutched tight to its chest.

"You're not getting anything from me," the dealer said.

"You've already given everything to me. Your foolproof security didn't seem to account for that."

Rage burned through the dealer's flesh, turning his fear to ashes. Who did this guy think he is, messing with someone like Giorgios Siskos? He may have been able to trick his way through all of his magical defences, but the game was up now. He was not getting away alive.

"Whoever you are, you shouldn't have tried to steal from me," said the dealer, pointing his ruby crowned finger straight at the thief. "Καίτε!"

It turned out that the customer's arrow hadn't been aiming at the dealer after all. His arrow had landed exactly where it had been intended, in the van's fuel tank.

Had the dealer been playing closer attention, he'd have noticed the petrol trickling steadily down the shaft of the arrow and forming a puddle at his feet.

The dealer would also have done well to remember that his ankh could only protect him from other people's magic. It would not stop flames that he himself created.

Sadly, the dealer didn't have time to consider either of these two crucial facts before summoning his deadly flames. And he certainly didn't have time to consider them once his van had detonated, leaving nothing of him behind but a ruby ring, a golden ankh, and a coil of irate ash dissipating into the night.

FIVE

THE RIVER PEOPLE

I was seven when I first heard about the River People.

Like I told you, it was all Jess's fault. The River People are actually the whole reason I ever became friends with Jess in the first place. In Year 3, Jess and Tori swooped into Whittington from their Jewish primary school, surgically attached, full of grace and beauty and private jokes involving Judaism. I didn't talk to them much at first, partially because Chloë and I were Best Friends and I didn't see the point in getting any more, and partially because, well, they seemed too graceful and beautiful to even notice I existed. But one day in Year 5 Jess came up to me and said "You live near Highgate Cemetery, right?"

"Sort of," I said. I walked past it every day on the way to school, so I suppose that counted.

Jess's eyes widened. "Then you must know about Omphalos."

I did. Omphalos was a mansion at the bottom of Highgate Hill. If you walked past it quickly – and it was the kind of place that everyone walked past quickly – you could easily think it was part of Highgate Cemetery, which hemmed it in on all sides. It hid behind a tall, dark hedge, overlooking a mini roundabout. Just like the rest of the cemetery, its bricks were grimy and flaking away, and it seemed to be trapped in its own personal bubble of perpetual twilight. There were never any lights in its tall, rounded windows. Yew trees from the cemetery reached through its tall black railings, trying to tickle its walls. I wouldn't have been surprised to walk past one day to find that it had given up and let itself be eaten by the woodland on all sides.

"Could you take me there?" asked Jess.

"Why?"

"Mum told me I couldn't go anywhere near it. But I can't not go anywhere near it unless I know where it is," Jess explained.

So I took her. She went right up to the front gate (the hedges blocked the view from anywhere else) and stared up at its dark windows.

"So why aren't you allowed to go near it?" I said. "It's empty, isn't it?"

"Empty? Of course it's empty," Jess breathed. "It's been empty for years. But…you never know." One of her fingers was threading through her ringlets. (She's had that habit the whole time I've known her. To be fair, it's extremely fun.)

We both stared up at the house this time, looking for something. I don't know what. For one of the curtains to twitch, maybe?

A crow screamed somewhere inside Highgate Cemetery. We both jumped back from the gate.

"You never know *what?*"

"When the River People will come back," said Jess, with a delicious shudder.

"Who are the River People?"

"Mum wouldn't tell me. She said, maybe she'd tell me when I was older, and until then, I should stay as far away from Nightingale House as possible. Do you think this gate's unlocked?"

It was. We crept up the moss-tinged gravel path to the front door, looking furtively around the front garden in case the River People jumped out.

"Doesn't seem so spooky, does it?" said Jess. "From the way she was going on about it, you'd think there were vampires living here. Or sorcerers."

I couldn't tell if she was joking or not, but I shook my head anyway. "Well, it's definitely not sorcerers. It's my mum's job to catch them."

"What, does she work for the Sorcery Investigation Thingy?"

"Department," I said. "Yes."

"That's amazing! Mum's always saying how grateful we should be to people like that for keeping us safe. Om…"

I turned to look at Jess, trying to figure out why my mum's job had made her spontaneously break into chanting. Turned out she was staring up at the front door. It had round columns on either side, and a triangle shape like a roof over the top. On a flat section just below the roof bit, there were letters engraved:

ΟΜΦΑΛΟΣ

"What do you think that says?" Jess asked, pointing. "Om…"

"Omphalos?" I guessed.

Jess smiled at me. "Man, you're clever. No wonder you're in the top set for everything. What do you think it means?"

I shrugged. "No idea."

Jess took a fearful step closer. "What if it's a hex? Sorcerers can put enchantments on whole buildings, you know. To protect them when they're – Aaaaaaaaaah!"

Jess had climbed into the porch, not noticing the huge spider web that stretched from one column to the other. Or the huge spider squatting in the middle. One of those fat round ones with faces so big that you can see every one of its eyes and fangs staring back at you. Jess pulled her hand away, dragging the whole web and spider with her. She panicked and flicked the remains of the web off her hand. The spider panicked too, and launched itself away. All the panicking made the spider swing round and hit Jess square on the head. Jess screamed again and tangled herself further in the spider's web. Still trying to flee, the spider tangled itself in Jess's ringlets. Both of them got steadily more upset until I got a moment to pluck the spider out by one of its wriggling legs and fling it away.

"It's gone," I said a few times, until Jess stopped screaming long enough to hear.

"What? Did you just pick it up *with your hand*? How could you?"

I shrugged. "They're not that bad really."

Jess looked at my hand with disgust. "Wow. I guess your whole family are pretty brave." Then she scoured the patch of scrubby lawn where I'd thrown the spider.

"Don't worry, it's probably running away as fast as it can," I said.

"I'm not taking any chances," she said, stalking her way through the lawn after it. Then – "Aaaaaaaah!"

With a noise halfway between warcry and police siren, Jess stamped down hard enough to make the whole garden shake. "Serves it right," she said darkly.

Jess turned out to be a better friend to me than to that spider. From that day on, we were inseparable. And given that Tori and Jess were inseparable, and Chloë and me were inseparable, before long we were all – well, you get the picture. We didn't go back to Omphalos again, though. We didn't even go near it.

At least, not until one fateful day three years later, shortly after the Cemetery Incident.

It started when Mum got home, earlier than usual. "So! Sounds like you've been making new friends!" she said brightly, putting her laptop bag down in the hall.

I'd been on my way to my bedroom when she'd walked through the front door. "What?" I said.

"I got a call from another parent. Persephone Skeuopoios. Apparently you've been getting to know her son. Hector?"

Tori had been right. I'd literally talked to the guy three times – only once deliberately – and now he thought we were best friends or something. This is what I got for trying to be nice.

"Yeah. I've met him, I suppose. Why?"

"I thought it might be nice to pay them a visit one of these days! They've just moved back into the neighbourhood, you know. I don't think they know many people yet." Mum took off her green jacket and hung it on the end of the banister.

"I...don't think that's a good idea."

"It sounds like you have a lot in common with him. You're in the same year at school, you're both...you know, only children, and… I just think it's important to do the neighbourly thing once in a while."

I should have smelled a rat there and then. I should have stopped to count on my fingers the number of times, in my twelve years of knowing her, how many times Mum had done the neighbourly thing, and realized I was holding no fingers up. But I was too wrapped up in trying to stop this terrible idea to ask myself why she'd come up with it in the first place.

"Mum, we can't visit them. Those are the River People."

Mum's lip curled, as if I'd just said the W-word at her. "The…*River People*? What's that supposed to mean?"

Strictly speaking, I had no idea. "People think they're sorcerers," I said instead of a proper explanation.

"I see. Who said that?"

"Everybody at school!"

"Like who?"

"Jess's mum."

"Fair enough. Jess's mum probably knows more than me. It's not like it's my job to catch sorcerers or anything."

Mum's sarcasm was cutting enough to take down a hardened sorcerer on its own. Mum's friends from work always jokingly ask me if it's scary being the daughter of the glamorous and terrifying Detective Chief Inquisitor Helen Drake, and at times like this I get what they mean. DCI Helen Drake's default expression is "I've got *real* issues to worry about." It's a serving of "I'll do whatever it takes" with a side helping of "Stop wasting my time". Normally, I don't have to deal with DCI Helen Drake, unless I walk in on her working from home, or I do something stupid enough to deserve her full professionally-honed scorn.

People say I look like her, which is half true. We have the same straight hair, the same high forehead, the same precise features. But our colour schemes are completely different. She has green eyes, mine are dark. She has blonde hair, mine is almost black. Her skin has a healthy glow, mine makes me look like an alien from some barren, sunless planet. But other than that, sure, we looked the same.

"Ha ha," I replied.

Mum walked away in triumph. I'd not managed to come up with a withering retort, so she must have won the argument. Classic Mum logic. "Let's find a good time say hi," she called back to me as she headed to the kitchen. "You can find out what they're really like, and then tell Jess she must have made a mistake."

To tell you the truth, I didn't actually think the River People were sorcerers. The situation cut way deeper than that.

Let me explain.

I'd been friends with Chloë since forever. Or at least since Year 1, when I'd found out her real name was Zhou Qing, and 'Chloë' was just an alias she used to blend in with white people.

Then when Jess and I had become friends in Year 5, Chloë came along for the ride. Neither Jess nor Tori were really sure about Chloë at first. Chloë had always lived in her own world, and never seemed to care or even notice what other people thought about her, so I could see where they were coming from. Eventually, Jess accepted her as one of our own, but Tori could never quite bring herself to do the same.

So when Hector arrived at the start of Year 8, the scene looked like this:

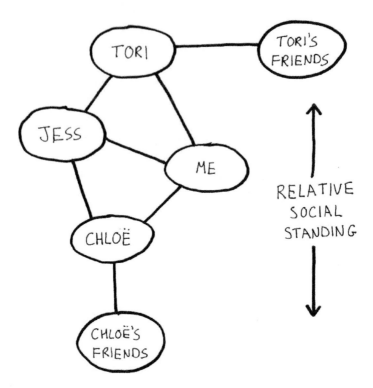

Jess and Tori were made of the purest helium. Nothing could really touch them. Chloë was like a three-day-old balloon, just about able to hold her own weight, so I didn't need to worry about her too much. The main problem was that for some reason, Chloë also spent a lot of time with these slightly strange friends which she'd made last summer who were dragging her down a bit. "But they're really nice people, once you get to know them!" she'd say, every time Tori or Jess questioned their reasons for existing.

Things looked pretty neat. I was happy where I was. The trouble was Hector. I couldn't let Hector tie himself to me, or before long the scene would have ended up like this:

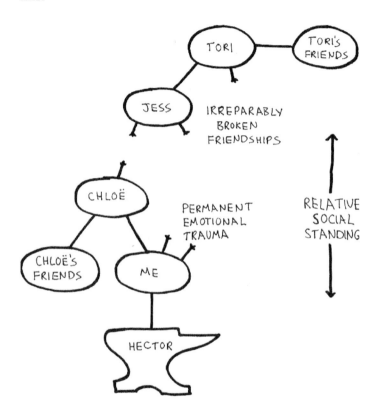

The guy was a walking anvil. Jess and Tori would have happily cut me loose, rather than risk being dragged down with me. Chloë would have stuck with me – she's stupid like that – so Jess and Tori would have had no choice but to break ties with her too. But I would have been left forgotten in the soot, among the broken horseshoes.

But did Mum understand any of this? No. Did she care? No. Did I even try to explain? No. Instead, Mum came home a few days later, grabbed a packet of crumpets with one hand and me with the other, and dragged us all down to Omphalos.

SECTION 6: MIMESIS

Mimesis is the mimicry or impersonation of a subject, to the extent that someone genuinely appears to be that subject. It is often, confusingly, known as 'identity theft' in English-speaking countries, although identity theft is of course a much broader crime that can take many non-magical forms. Mimesis is exclusively magical in nature, as it involves creating a living, breathing illusion that one is someone else.

Mimesis is often classified as an area of sorcery in its own right, alongside rhetoric, enchantment, alchemy, and so on. However, it could more accurately be considered to be a subcategory of conjuration, as its methods and results are largely the same. Conjuration (Section 5) refers to any illusory manipulation of the physical world: making objects appear, changing the appearance of existing objects, and so on. Mimesis only differs from this in that the sorcerer him- or herself is the target of the illusion; mimesis involves the changing of the sorcerer's own physical form, rather than something in their environment.

14.1 The Origins of Mimesis

The Ancient Greeks, from whom we get the word 'mimesis', did not appear to distinguish between mimesis as we now think of it and conjuration. In fact, they confusingly referred to both branches of magic as 'mimesis' (ΜΙΜΗΣΙΣ). The word is derived from ΜΙΜΕΙΣΘΑΙ, to imitate, which is in turn derived from ΜΙΜΟΣ, a mime. Mimesis, that is, the physical change in appearance to someone else, is thought to have been one of the most widespread forms of sorcery in Ancient Greece. It was commonly used on the stage, to allow actors to play multiple roles. A 'persona' or mask would be worn to ease the actor into adopting a new character via mimesis, though as mimesis became better understood, many Greek actors no longer required the masks to achieve this effect. It's from this practice that we get the word 'persona' in the psychological sense, to denote a social role played by an individual, as well as in the magical sense, to indicate a particular appearance adopted via mimesis.

There are no accounts in Ancient Greece of mimesis being used for anything other than harmless entertainment. Though it seems surprising to us today, it may simply be that the dangerous potential of mimesis – to exploit people by impersonating someone they know – simply wasn't considered. Much like the Chinese used gunpowder to create fireworks for centuries before its deadly potential was realized, it seems that the Ancient Greeks simply didn't contemplate using mimeses off the stage; perhaps because it was too closely linked to the use of stage masks and other theatrical devices.

Aristotle's accounts of mimesis, in both *On Comedy* and *On Tragedy*, are generally considered to be the definitive texts on the subject. His works only consider mimesis in a theatrical context, and elide the creation of personae with the creation of anything onstage: objects, scenery, even weather (illusions that we'd today consider to be acts of conjuration). He also draws an interesting comparison between the evocation of false emotions in oneself with the evocation of powerful emotions in the audience; the technique of catharsis, that in this treatment we group under rhetoric (Section 8.3).

SIX

OMPHALOS

Winter was only just arriving for the rest of the road, but it had never left Omphalos. It squatted on its mini roundabout, as dark and brooding as ever.

Mum pushed the front gate open with an eerie squeal. (From the gate, not Mum.) The gravel path leading to the door was lined with shrubs. A scarecrow stood smiling dustily in the middle of the front lawn. None of that had been there last time I'd visited with Jess, two years ago.

"How lovely to see you both. This must be Cassandra," said the smiling scarecrow. It turned out it wasn't a scarecrow at all, but an actual human woman. She was wearing an enormous floppy hat, earth-streaked overalls, and elbow length gardening gloves. She pulled one glove off and held out an earth-encrusted hand to me. "I'm phoney."

I squinted at her. "What?"

She put her hand away again when she saw I wasn't going anywhere near it. "Sorry. Persephone. Foni for short. Sorry if that sounds *phoney* to you. Or perhaps it sounds *funny*?"

Foni wheezed to herself. At the time, I had no idea what was going on. Only much later, after many more traumatic encounters with Foni's sense of humour, did I understand that she'd been making a series of puns based on her own name, and then laughing at them. But because of her weird accent, which I assumed was Greek, I couldn't even tell she'd been trying to say a different word each time. Her voice was dry, like an old woman's, the sound of someone who spent all day inhaling dust from old books. (Which is exactly what she did, I soon found out.)

Foni didn't go up to the front door. With its columns and mini-roof, it looked like the entrance to some dark and ancient temple – too dramatic to actually go through. Instead, she scuttled around the back of the house. She paused to crouch in a flowerbed for a while, like she was trying to disguise herself as a mushroom, then led us onto a veranda. She tapped the back door open, carefully brushing earth from her overalls into the carpet. "Sorry for the state the house is in. There's still a lot of work to do." She led us through a dark kitchen into the large, empty front room. The bright daylight that had felt so nice outside made the room feel like a hospital, picking out every crevasse in Foni's papery face and turning her fading brown hair grey. "We just haven't had much time to mingle, what with all the housework we've been doing. And Hector has been so good, helping me all the time, haven't you, Hector?" She tilted vaguely in Hector's direction.

Hector. I hadn't noticed him when I'd looked around the first time. But there he was, sitting on a wooden chair in the corner, reading soggily to himself. He hadn't looked up once since we'd arrived. "Hector, why don't you show Cassandra around a bit? I'm sure she'd love to see the house."

Hector looked up at his mother, then back in my direction, kind of over my shoulder. His face brightened and he started twitching like an excited puppy. He lowered his book carefully onto a rickety table and shuffled over to the hallway, waiting for me to follow. I pretended I couldn't see him. But Mum pressed a hand on my back and said, "Go on! Or you'll be stuck talking to us for hours."

Which was definitely the better out of two appalling options I had, but it didn't matter. Mum's hand on my back told me it wasn't actually an option to stay.

Hector led me up a huge flight of stairs in the hall and along several neverending corridors. I realised that I wouldn't be able to find my way back if I needed to escape quickly.

We finally reached what Hector said was his bedroom, though the only sign of recent human habitation was a cardboard box sitting in the boarded-up fireplace. Everything else – the bed, the wardrobe, the child-size desk – had a layer of grey age on it, like they'd been abandoned here years ago. The walls had little hot air balloons floating serenely across what was maybe once a cheery blue sky, that years of neglect had turned dark and stormy. It must have last been the bedroom of a toddler.

"When are you going to redecorate this place?" I asked, trying not to imagine the fate of the young kid who had slept in this room before Hector.

Hector looked at me like I'd asked something stupid. "Never," he said. "I like it like this." Dust billowed around Hector as he collapsed onto the mattress, coughing wetly.

"Really? It looks horrible."

It was the worst wallpaper I could have imagined. Each little hot air balloon had a tiny family waving out from it. A mother and a father. A boy and a girl. All with identical grins, wherever I looked. The one I was closest to seemed different. Darker than the rest, like the wallpaper over their faces had been stained. As I stepped closer to figure out what was happening, the father leapt suddenly out of the basket and plummeted through the open air…

"Urgh!"

I reared backwards in shock. My entire body sung like it had just been plunged underwater.

"What's the matter, Cassandra?"

The father hadn't really moved. Obviously. But there'd been a huge spider sitting directly over the little family, like it was deliberately trying to disguise itself. As I'd got closer, it had made a bolt for safety across the open blue sky.

Hector saw it crawling down towards the corner. "Are you afraid of spiders?"

"No," I said firmly. Mum had never allowed me to be afraid of spiders. "That one just gave me a shock."

"Oh. Sorry."

Hector cupped both hands over the spider as it scarpered across the wall. It crawled out from underneath them, onto his wrist. He hurried over to his window, opened it, and pressed his arm against the outer windowsill. The spider crawled gratefully to freedom. Hector shut the window.

"This house is full of insects. Bugs, I mean. Spiders are technically arachnids, not insects. I don't mind if there's just a few, but they're everywhere. Every day, I have to put more outside. Do you want to see some books?"

I'd stopped listening, so it took me a moment to notice Hector had asked me a question.

"They were in the basement when we got here. My mother said I could keep them." He opened the cardboard box. He padded across the room and placed a book at my feet quickly, before retreating again. I saw the word ALICE IN WONDERLAND on its green cover. I stared back out the darkly stained window, where there was a bus driver getting into an argument with someone on the pavement.

"It's an early edition. It's over one hundred years old. It's probably quite valuable. My mother doesn't really care though."

I'd thought it had been the effect of the seizure, but Hector still had a voice like a broken printer, full of breaths and long silences. And whenever he managed to get any words out at all, they came too fast, in a flat jumbled spew. I could see why he didn't talk much in school.

I noticed, out of the corner of my ear, that he was still talking. "My mother says, she'll bring up one of the empty bookshelves from downstairs. But she hasn't found anyone who can help her yet. Then I'm going to arrange the books in chronological order. Do you want to smell them?"

Hector got on his hands and knees and stuck his face into the box, making a muffled snuffling noise. His buttocks rippled with happiness.

I thought about making a bolt for the door. But then I remembered the winding corridor we had come down to get here. There was no hope of finding my way out. I'd probably get lost forever, become another ghost howling from one of Omphalos's windows. Instead, I waited. Waited while weird grunting/gulping noises started coming out of the box, as if Hector was trying to eat his precious books whole. While he told me how many books he had counted so far in the library in the basement, while he recited the Greek alphabet, while he rocked back and forth on his bed.

I held out as long as I could. I really did. But when I saw the sun starting to set outside, I finally snapped. "I need to, er, ask Mum something. Can we head back?"

Hector broke off in the middle of whatever boring fact he was telling me. "Oh. OK. They're probably in my mother's study."

Foni's study was all the way back at the front of the house, just across the hall from the living room. It looked a lot like Mum's, if it had been abandoned for a hundred years. Every wall was lined with bookshelves. But even that wasn't enough – the books spilled out of the shelves and formed little piles around the edge of the room. The ancient desk had a green leather surface, covered in ink stains. It looked like it wanted to hold a little inkpot and quill, perhaps a pile of bound scrolls, but all it got to carry was an asthmatic laptop and a few more books. Mum was sitting at Foni's desk, while Foni leant over it. The only light in the room came from the laptop screen, giving both of their faces an eerie underlit effect. Their muttering stopped as we entered the room.

"Hello there, Cassandra! Hector!" Foni said jovially. "I hope Hector's being a good host?"

"Yeah," I lied, picking up a small golden dagger from Foni's desk. It wasn't as sharp as it had looked from across the room.

"That's a letter opener!" Foni said. "Antique. Well, I suppose all letter openers are antique to you, aren't they?"

Foni talked to both of us like we were seven years old. In fairness, if she only had Hector as an example of what a normal twelve-year-old acted like, then I couldn't really blame her.

"We've just been having a look at some of Foni's books," said Mum. "*So* fascinating. And very important for my work, funnily enough. Foni's a doctor!"

"Not a medical one! Just a fusty old academic. I'm a history professor. Ancient Greece," added Foni.

"I showed her my books upstairs," Hector said. He turned and stared at my shins. "You know, you can have as many as you like. I don't mind."

"Wonderful! I knew you'd get along. Cass gets on with everybody," Mum said, looking straight at me. She was – was she? – yep, smirking right at me. Smirking. Did I really deserve a full-on, no-holds-barred *smirk*? Right then, I was so sure she'd done it all deliberately. Really. Turning her own daughter into an outcast of society was probably her idea of a joke.

"I have a riddle for you, Cassandra," said Foni. "Who was the first Drake at Omphalos?"

Foni waggled her eyebrows at me.

"I don't know."

"The Python!" Foni smiled delightedly at all of us. Only Hector smiled back.

"Sorry? Was…that a joke?" It came out as cutting, but I'd meant it as a sincere question.

"Perhaps it would help if I told you *Omphalos* means 'belly button' in Ancient Greek. And *Drake*, as I'm sure you know, means 'dragon'. It's almost the same in

Ancient Greek. *Drako.* So what I'm really asking is…who was the first dragon in the belly button?"

I had a vivid premonition that Foni's riddle would not only be painfully unfunny, it would be a slow-burning nightmare with no escape. I turned out to be exactly right.

"Right. Right," I said, with the tone of voice I'd use to soothe a confused but potentially dangerous animal.

"You don't have to wonder why someone might get given the surname 'Dragon'," Foni continued, "especially not after meeting your mum! Eh, Cassandra?"

Mum laughed weakly. I didn't bother.

"But why would someone want to name a house 'Belly Button?'"

Hector's hands fluttered with excitement. He knew the answer already. But he was waiting for his mum to reveal it to Mum and me.

"Well, in Greek, *Omphalos* has a bit of a grander meaning than it does in English," Foni explained. "It meant both the centre of the body, and the centre of the world. The Ancient Greeks believed that the world's *Omphalos* was Delphi, where the god Apollo bestowed the gift of prophecy to humanity at his shrine…"

I wondered which god had bestowed upon humanity the gift of boring others to death. And if Foni and Hector had a special shrine to that god in their cold, dusty house.

"…guarded since the beginning of time by the ancient dragon-god Python. It was only after Apollo slayed Python that the ancient oracles began to worship him at Delphi. And *that's* why the first Drake at Omphalos was Python!"

Hector started rocking delightedly at the punchline, if that's what it was. I waited, too afraid to speak in case I set Foni off again. Mum laughed.

"You certainly know your Greek myths!"

Foni smiled modestly. "That's what the university pays me for, after all."

"Well, anyway…" I said, looking at Mum forcefully.

Mum refused to pick up on my hint. Luckily, Foni did. "Got things to be getting back to? Don't let us keep you!"

We finally stumbled, blinking, into the light of day. Foni paused to show Mum the doorway, complete with the engraved house name. "An interesting example of early Neo-Classical architecture," she commented. "Stylistically a total mess, of course. They've paired Corinthian columns with a Doric architrave. Can you imagine!"

I certainly couldn't.

Hector turned to me. "This house is very important, architecturally," he added.

Once Foni and Hector had finally allowed us to escape into the road, Mum turned to me and said, "So! What did you think!"

The smirk hadn't left her face. It was official: she was doing this on purpose. Maybe she was punishing me for leaving the fridge door open that one time.

"Foni's a very interesting character," she continued, "very interesting. She's done a lot of very innovative work on Ancient Greece. I'm sure Hector's an interesting guy too, once you get to know him."

"You can drop the act now. I don't think they can overhear us."

"What act?" Mum said firmly.

"Those were about the most boring people I've ever met."

"Oh, come on, that's a bit harsh!" Mum smiled Mumfully. "Foni told me that Hector came home from school gushing about you. So you must have made an impression somehow!" She caught a glimpse of my horrified expression. "I mean, she didn't say *gushing*. That would be weird."

The road got darker as the trees from Highgate Cemetery stretched out to cover it. Not a sound could be heard. Especially not from my mouth.

Mum threw herself into the silence.

"We ought to go again sometime. It'll be nice. I don't think they've made many friends in the area yet."

"Mum, we've done the neighbourly thing now. I don't see why we have to go back."

"I want to make sure they're settling in OK. It must be hard for them."

"OK. You can do that if you want. Why do I have to be dragged along?"

"Don't you think it would be a bit suspicious if I went back alone? Hector might think you didn't like him."

"Maybe it's best he finds that out sooner rather than later."

Mum vanished. Standing in her place was DCI Helen Drake, SID. "What exactly is your problem with him?" she said, her voice like polished glass.

"I don't have a *problem* with him, I just think he has…social issues, OK?"

"Oh. OK." DCI Helen Drake didn't sound upset about this, or surprised. DCI Helen Drake just tucked her blonde hair behind her ear and filed my testimony away for later. "Well, that's fair enough. It looked like the two of you might have found common ground, but maybe I was wrong."

"Yeah. You were wrong."

"Well, would it kill you to give him a chance? He's been homeschooled for a while so he's probably having a hard time adjusting to being around lots of people."

I was running out of comebacks fast. I had only one move left to make.

"If Dad were here, he wouldn't still be trying to decide my friends for me."

TRIED AND TESTED WAYS OF SHUTTING MUM UP

1. "If Dad were here…"
2. A storm of bullets

By the age of twelve, I didn't know about the second option, so really I had no choice what to do.

I mean, obviously, I had no idea what Dad would do if he were there because he never was and never had been. But that wasn't the point.

Look, I couldn't go back to Omphalos again. I had to make Mum realise that I was desperate. And back then I didn't know exactly what I was saying, exactly what effect it had on Mum. It was just something I said to get what I wanted. OK? It worked almost every time. So you can't blame me for using it. What do you expect, that I'd have worked out a rigorous moral code at the tender age of twelve?

For a while, it looked like it was going to work this time as well. DCI Helen Drake was gone. Mum's eyebrows quivered slightly, and she blinked a few times. She took a deep breath and turned to face up the road ahead. Then, just as we were reaching our street, she said, "If you really don't want to be friends with Hector, fine. But it won't cost you anything to be nice to him."

And that was it. We stopped talking about the River People, and for what it's worth, we stopped talking about Dad too.

SEVEN

COLLECTOR'S PIECE

"You shouldn't be here, Mr Siskos."

If the dealer was offended by this abrupt welcome, he didn't show it. "I know. But I don't have a choice, do I?"

The collector's well-fed armchair let out a snort as he squeezed himself back into it. "You shouldn't even know where I live. How did you know where to find me?"

The dealer had so far declined to sit down, despite the range of collectible antique furniture available for this purpose. Instead, he plodded erratically around the collector's drawing room, occasionally fondling the collector's prized possessions.

"Look, in my line of business, you got to keep records on who you deal with. You never know when one of them will try to doublecross you, and when they do, you need to know where to find them. I'm sorry, but that included you."

The dealer had not aged well since their last meeting, over ten years ago. He'd managed to become even more overweight, looking ready to burst any second out of the seams of his jacket. His face had sunk into itself, leaving dark bruises around his eyes. His expression was permanently shadowed, as if some terrible weight were hanging over him.

Then again, the collector had not aged well either. He'd finally let his hair go grey, while his body was beginning to give up the pretence of strength and settle into elderly frailty.

"So you found out my address? You've been keeping it all this time?"

The dealer nodded, gripping the back of an antique sofa. "I would only have used it in a life in death situation. But that's what we're in. I was attacked at my van a few nights ago. By a guy pretending to be another customer of mine. He nyxed me and stole my Lyceum books. He ignored everything else." The dealer's eyes roved across the many wondrous treasures on display in the collector's drawing room; from the shotgun hanging over the mantelpiece to the grand piano in the bay window. But his gaze seemed fixed on something altogether more distant.

"So the rumours are true."

"I've seen him with my own eyes. There's no mistaking it. Cuttlefish has returned."

A dramatic clash of notes rang out from the grand piano.

The collector jumped in his armchair. "Can you not play that right now?"

The dealer got up from the piano stool. "Sorry."

The collector's thought returned instantly to Cuttlefish. "I'd heard all the rumours, of course. I heard that he'd been killed by the police. Or sent up the river. Or gone insane. Or simply vanished into thin air."

"All true," the dealer said gravely. "But that was a decade ago, Mr Foley. A lot has changed since then. Cuttlefish has changed."

The collector glanced upwards. The ceilings in this wing of his house had always been too low for his liking. The ornate rose in the centre of the drawing room ceiling no longer held a chandelier like it used to, but nevertheless seemed to be dangling something else right over his head. Something invisible, but no less heavy.

"Well, he didn't find me last time," the collector said. "Even if he has somehow returned, there's no reason to think he'll come looking for me."

"Funny you should say that," said the dealer despondently. "That's exactly what I thought. And then…he came."

"I keep my books hidden behind state-of-the-art security systems."

"So did I."

Gleaming black dread descended onto the collector. "Why are you so sure he's going to come here, anyway?"

"He's a collector. Just like you. But the only thing he's collecting are grimoires. Not just any grimoires, either – he only cares about books from the Daedalus Set. He wants every last one."

"Every last one? But there are hundreds, scattered all over the country. The world, even. Some of them have been lost for centuries. That's totally insane."

"It is. But so is he."

The dealer accompanied this announcement with a demonic chord progression on the piano.

"Stop that! The piano is a 1901 Steinway Model A. The most expensive thing in this room, and incredibly fragile."

"Is that so? My bad." The dealer's chords trailed into a quiet and melancholy coda, each one pressing the collector further into the ground.

"You're saying it's only a matter of time until he shows up?"

"Exactly. In fact, you may already be too late."

"Ridiculous. He can't have been here already. I can see my collection from this chair, and I can tell you with absolute certainty that nothing is missing."

"So they're nearby, are they?" The dealer glanced around the room's many treasures with newfound interest. "You must keep them well hidden."

"Of course I do. The only way he could find it is if he demolished the entire house and picked through the rubble piece by piece."

"I wouldn't tell him that if I were you. You might give him ideas."

"You think I'm scared of him?" said the collector, wondering if he was convincing even his 200-year-old sideboard that he was unafraid. "Because I'm not. Whatever bag of cheap tricks he has up his sleeve, they won't be enough to break through my security."

The dealer shook his head sadly. "He won't need to break through your security. All he needs to do is break through your mind." The dealer tapped the side of his skull. "Just like he did to me. He's a mimetic, see. An identity thief. He'll convince you that he's the only person you can trust. By the time he's done with you, you'll be handing your books over to him willingly. And thanking him for taking them off your hands."

A shadow passed over the collector's head. "Then what should I do? How am I supposed to defend myself against the likes of him? I'm not a sorcerer. I never get mixed up in that kind of thing."

"For a start, you've got to get your books out of this house. And you've got to do so straight away."

"Where could I take them? There's nowhere I could put them that's more secure than inside this house."

The dealer shrugged. "Anywhere is more secure, as long as you yourself don't know where they are. Otherwise, Cuttlefish will find a way to trick the information out of you. He always does."

"I need to hide my books from *myself?* That's insane."

"It is. But so is he."

The collector stood up, his mind somersaulting with fear. "I refuse to let my life be dictated by this...this *maniac,*" he shouted.

"You're only saying that because you haven't seen what he's capable of," the dealer whispered.

"Sorcery is nothing but illusions and trickery. All in the mind. I'm not afraid of it."

"All in the mind. That's right. But pain is only ever in the mind, Keith. You must know that. Doesn't matter whether it comes from a real wound or an imagined one. It hurts exactly the same. And believe me, Cuttlefish can make you feel pain. Pain so much worse than anything you've experienced in reality."

The dealer almost seemed to be enjoying himself. Revelling in the collector's visible horror at the thought of unending magical tortures.

"Have you ever been nyxed, Keith?" the dealer went on. "It might not sound so bad. Waking up a few hours later, no memory of anything. But somewhere deep inside, you *do* remember. The experience of death leaves its mark. You're never truly the same again. Some part of you is lost forever."

"Alright," the collector exploded. "Point taken. I'll find a way to deal with this Cuttlefish problem."

"There's another option, of course. You could just hand your Daedalus books over to him without a fight."

"What? You know full well how much I paid you for those grimoires. I would never let that monster have his way so easily."

"You're a rich man. Are a handful of books really worth losing your mind over?"

"It's not the money. It's the principle. I have never, in my life, bowed down to threats and extortion. I'm not going to start now. I'll...I'll find someone to look after my grimoires for a while, if that's what it takes."

"Good luck." The dealer's pudgy face broke into a sinister smile.

The collector mentally ran through a list of his closest friends. Friends who knew about his little hobby, who'd be willing to help him out. Friends who he trusted not to spill the beans or double cross him.

There was nobody on the list. He had no options. Except for...

"You. You need to sort this out. This horrible mess you've got us both into. Take the books out of the house. You'll do that for me, won't you? It's the least you could do, quite frankly."

"Me?"

"You're the only person I can trust right now. You're used to handling sensitive material. You could keep them hidden for a little while. I'll pay you for your trouble, of course."

The collector got up before the dealer could respond, and snapped through a pair of glass doors into the central atrium. He'd had the space completely remodelled a couple of years ago, when he'd retired. He'd knocked through both floors down the centre, and built an extravagant cupola over the top. The space was now an enormous cylinder, lined with precisely 88 bookshelves.

The crown jewel of the atrium was the fountain in its centre. It consisted of eight thick granite slabs, cut to crystal perfection straight out of the Alps and stacked into a gracefully tottering tower. In the collector's eyes, they resembled nothing more than a pile of old books. The surface of each was gently concave, allowing water hewn from Alpine glaciers to collect, trickling from pool to pool in a haphazard-looking but carefully controlled way.

The dealer had followed him into the atrium. "I don't know about this. I don't want to risk him coming to find me again."

The collector brushed off this complaint instantly. "I'm sure we can come to an arrangement we're both happy with." The collector pulled a first edition hardcover copy of *The Fountainhead* off one of the 88 bookshelves lining the walls. His hand flopped thirstily in the space where the book had been, until it clamped down on a switch.

The fountain in the middle of the atrium delicately unfurled. Each granite slab swung outwards in sequence, emptying their pools in a sudden rush. Through the middle of the cascading water rose the 89th bookshelf in the atrium, its priceless contents emerging from behind their liquid curtain without getting wet.

It was like magic.

The dealer whistled. "You were right. He would never have been able to find your collection without your help."

The collector scanned his beloved titles. "Here." He tugged *On Becoming and Unbecoming* (a nineteenth century English translation) off the shelf and placed it on the rim of the fountain.

The dealer flipped it open to its title page. There he found Daedalus's torch insignia, the symbol capable of trebling the price of any book it was found in. He nodded to himself and closed the book.

The collector pulled another book, *Herbarium Apuleii Platonici*, from the shelf. A fourteenth century edition in its original leather binding, containing errata that had been amended by an unknown eighteenth century sorcerer. A small black torch, of course, adorned the title page. He stacked it on top of *The Book of Abramelin*, followed shortly by *The Key of Solomon* and *Theatrum Chemicum*.

"That's all of them. Now get them out of here until this all blows over."

"If you insist, Mr Foley."

As the collector watched the dealer heave his books into a bag, the weight over his head seemed to lift higher, higher, until it was just a speck hovering high in the atrium dome. "Thank you, Mr Siskos. Thank—"

His thanks became caught in his throat. *You'll be handing your books over to him willingly. And thanking him for taking them off your hands.*

The collector's bones splintered under the weight of his mistake. An urge to charge at the dealer, to knock him into the fountain pool, to pummel his face with his fists, gripped the collector. But he was an old man. No match for the dealer at all, even without the use of magic.

He had a chance, now. A window of opportunity before the dealer realized he was rumbled. His only chance to bring this smug dealer to his knees.

The collector stole away furtively into his drawing room. Its low ceiling bore down on him, squeezing his life away. His eyes flicked across his expensive furnishings and decoration. Mounted in the doorway was a panic button that would bring the police. But that was suicide now, with his collection of illegal books displayed for the world to see. He had to salvage this situation without destroying himself. There had to be another way...

"You've had your fun, Cuttlefish," announced the collector a few moments later, storming back into the atrium. "Now get the hell out of my house."

The dealer looked up to see what the collector had brought back with him.

"This is another collector's piece of mine," the collector snarled. "The Purdey over-and-under shotgun. 1913. Customised three-inch magnum chambers. Very rare."

The collector raised his antique shotgun to his eye and stared down its sight, wishing he had decided to collect some bullets as well. Surely, the dealer would see through this trick. But miraculously, he seemed to listen. He slowly raised his hands, revealing a rope held tight in one fist that rose up into the atrium.

A dark shadow fell over the collector. The world became shrouded, silent. Against his better judgement, the collector followed the rope upwards, along a series of pulleys mounted high on every wall. At the other end of the rope hung a polished black monstrosity, directly above him. Its shape was familiar, yet so out of context that it took a heartbeat for the collector to recognize it.

"The Steinway Model A grand piano. 1901. An even rarer collector's piece," said the dealer. The alarm on his face was replaced by a gleeful grin.

"You're insane," the collector whispered.

"I know," said the dealer, letting go of the rope.

A shriek of pulley wheels. A heavy groan. The collector's world turned black.

EIGHT

I DON'T KNOW WHO YOU ARE

In the olden days, it must have been much easier to put up with someone like Hector. No matter how many weird glances they threw you during lessons, no matter how many times your own mother forced you to visit their house on some demented neighbourly crusade, at least you could shut yourself in your bedroom at the end of the day and be safe from them for a while.

But that was before the Age of Agora.

In the Age of Agora, there was no escape. You carried your friends and your enemies with you wherever you went. They watched you on the toilet. They watched you as you slept.

I suppose I could have just left my phone somewhere else every now and then, but I wasn't *insane*. Those seventeen new photos of Tori weren't going to give *themselves* kudos. So, as usual, I was lying on my bed, dutifully swiping and tapping at my screen. That's when he struck.

Hector Skeuopoios wants to be your friend. Accept?

Hector's picture was absolutely iconic. He was smiling stickily into the camera from too close up, his hideous hot air balloon wallpaper dimly visible in the background. Everything was in shadow. You know what – just google 'smiling sloth' for an exact representation of the photo Hector had run with.

I accepted and had a look at his profile. He had one other photo, which was almost identical. Nobody had commented on either. He had a couple of other friends – Whittington School's other total recluses. That was it. I can't say I was surprised. And I soon realized why – he'd created his profile only a few hours ago.

Now, does that strike you as weird? For a twelve-year-old boy to have only just made an Agora profile? If he hadn't been on Agora until now, what on earth did he spend his evenings doing? Surely there were only so many times you could reorganise your vintage book collection.

All these questions were pushed to one side by a message popping up on my screen.

Hector: Thanks for accepting me

See what I mean? No escape.

Cass: Sure

Hector: Do you think I can ask everyone to be my friend on here? I'm not sure how Agora works.

Cass: If you've talked to them then yeah sure I guess

Hector: How much?

Cass: what?

Hector: How much should I have talked to them before I ask them to be my friend?

Cass: um I don't know. Like at least one proper conversation I guess?

Hector: How do you know if a conversation's proper or not?

Cass: how should I know? Use your common sense

Hector: Sorry

Hector: Sorry if these questions are annoying

Hector: Are these questions annoying?

Another notification came up. **Hector Skeuopoios has commented on your profile picture!**

NO ESCAPE.

I went to my profile picture. It was a pretty old one, from the summer, when I still had long hair. But it had got 37 kudos, which was almost a record for me, so I didn't want to change it. (If one of Tori's profile pictures ever got below 40, she deleted it out of shame. But still.)

And there was Hector's sloth smile, below a long list of girls I never spoke to lying to me about how pretty I was. **This is a very nice picture, Cass!**, he'd written.

As I watched, my kudos count went to 38.

His comment had already been up for ten seconds. In another ten, Jess and Tori would be guaranteed to see it. In about a minute, everyone who'd commented on the photo would have taken a look too. The clock was ticking.

Cass: sorry would you mind deleting that comment on my photo

Hector: Sorry

Hector: Very sorry

Hector: I thought that's what you were supposed to do

Cass: right now, please

Hector: I'm very sorry

The comment disappeared.

Cass: thanks

Hector: I didn't mean it to sound creepy

Hector: I just thought it was a nice photo

Cass: It's not that, it's just we don't know each other very well and you're a guy so it's a bit weird

Hector: Sorry, I didn't know

Hector: I won't do it again

Cass: thanks

Hector. Whose photos should I comment on?

Cass: probably nobody's

Cass: no offence

My kudos count slid back to 37.

Cass: You can give kudos if you want. That's fine.

My kudos went back to 38. Good.

Hector: Why is that?

Cass: I don't know

I did know. Let me explain.

In the olden days, children must have only been able to guess how popular they were, based on how everyone treated them. The poor, ignorant things. In the Age of Agora, your popularity had a precise numerical value; the number of kudos your photos got. The only way you got kudos was from your faithful Agora friends, and the only way to be sure of keeping them faithful was to give their photos kudos in return. Which is exactly what I was busy doing that very moment, propped up on my elbows in bed, between replying to Hector.

Obviously, at the tender age of twelve, I didn't know much about statistical analysis yet. But if I did, I could have told you that the weighted average of Tori's photo kudos was 52.4, and mine was only 27.1, making her almost twice as popular as me. Jess's was 34.0, which might sound bad for me, but only if you didn't take into account the confidence intervals of 3.2 and 5.9 respectively, which once computed, revealed that there was no statistically significant difference between our level of popularity.

Chloë's average kudos, outrageously enough, was 39.6. Not significantly higher than Jess's, but significantly higher than mine, which was the greatest insult imaginable given how Chloë didn't even check Agora more than once a day, or add photos more than once a week. But this was only the result of a confounding variable – Chloë's two parents, two step-parents, seven grandparents / step-grandparents, twelve aunts and uncles, and basically infinite cousins all went on Agora, as far as I could tell, for the sole purpose of showering their darling daughter / stepdaughter / granddaughter / niece / cousin with kudos every time she so much as farted online. She even had a whole wing of the family tucked away in China, dedicated to her cause.

Look, I'm getting sidetracked. All I'm saying is, I was unjustly trailing in the rankings, so I couldn't exactly afford to turn down a free limitless +1 boost to all my future kudos. And it might make Hector happy to feel like we were hanging out on Agora, too, which I guess was nice. It's just what Mum would have wanted.

Hector: Should I give kudos to the other friends I have?

Cass: Boys, sure. Girls, no. Unless they're a proper friend of yours.

Guys had their own kudos scale, way below any of the girls. They weren't a threat.

My friends were the only threat.

Hector: Really? But I can give you kudos?

Cass: yep

Hector: OK! Thanks, Cass!

Cass: no problem

It was a win-win. He got to interact with me on Agora, sort of. I got to inch closer to Jess in the kudos league table.

It only took thirteen hours for that dream to unravel. Only thirteen hours for me to realize what I'd said.

It was morning break, the next day. We'd just got outside. Hector was sitting on a picnic bench by himself. The same bench he always sat on. But this time, as soon as he saw me, he stood up, his whole face trembling with excitement. He bounded up to me, his rucksack lolloping up and down heavily on his back.

"Cass! Hey! Cassandra! Cass! It's me! How's it going! Hey!"

Etc.

Even when he was in good mood – and right then he was in the best mood I'd ever seen him – his voice had that strange habit of stopping and starting, and going up and down, at weird times. I wondered if it was to do with him being Greek, but Foni didn't talk that way at all.

When he reached me, he realised he couldn't run any further so he kind of bounded up and down on the spot, staring over my shoulder. He flapped his hands by his sides, like he was doing a bee impression.

Tori was standing right next to me. She looked at him and raised her eyebrows. "Um…yes?" she said. "Can we help you?"

"Oh, I just wanted to talk to Cassandra," Hector said brightly.

"Well, Cass doesn't want to talk to you, thanks," said Jess. "And as far as I'm concerned, people like you should be…" She turned to me. "What's that word that means kicked out of the country?"

"Deported?" Hector suggested.

"Yeah. Deported."

Hector's forehead drooped down over his eyes. His bee impression came to a tragic end.

I've been putting it off as long as possible, but this is the point where I have no choice but to introduce Baz's crew to the story.

Baz and his crew weren't really individuals, just a single unit of horror. All their names sounded the same, Gaz or Waz or Taz or something. They all looked like they'd crawled out of a swamp, they all smelt like cheese-flavoured snacks, and they spent every break spitting on each other and giving themselves grazes. The loudest, swampiest, and cheesiest of them was Baz, which I suppose was why he was in charge. Just then, Baz called: "Check it out! Hector's making a move on the *lay-deez*!"

Shaz and Faz laughed. Hector didn't turn around. He just stared at the ground.

"I didn't know you were such a player!" said Chaz. They all laughed louder, and punched each other on the arms.

Baz started in with another line, but was cut off when Hector wheeled around, wobbling with fury.

"Look, I'm just trying to talk to my friend, OK?"

I had a sudden sinking feeling, and began creeping backwards, pushing Jess and Tori and Chloë in front of me.

"You don't have any friends," Phwaz pointed out.

"Cassandra is my friend! We talk on Agora. We do all kinds of things together. So shut up!"

Baz's crew oohed loudly. Luckily, they were too busy making fun of Hector to take what he was saying seriously. But Jess was staring at me with newfound concern. I would be able to explain things to her later, so I was still just about OK as long as Hector stopped talking.

But why on earth would he have done that? I mean, that would have been almost sensible.

"Right, Cass?" Hector stared straight at me. All my friends skittered off to the side before they got hit by his toxic gaze, leaving me standing speechless in the middle.

Wow. This was all happening the exact way it did in my worst nightmares. Word-perfect. It was spooky.

An enormous space had cleared around Hector and me, as if we were about to start dancing. Off to one side were all my former friends, their eyes melting the back of my head. Off to the other side were Baz and his cronies. And there, in the middle, Hector, holding his sticky hands out in front of him like a leper.

It was bad. How bad? This bad:

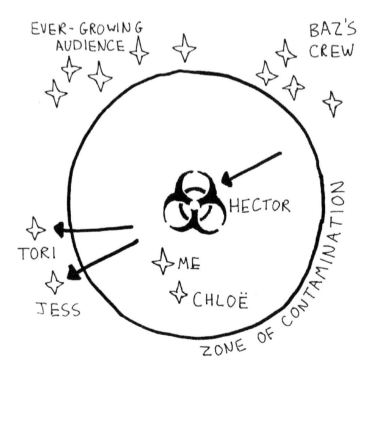

Everyone waited to see who would make the first move.

I did.

"I... I... I don't know who you are," I said. I scrambled to join Jess, who was leaning on one leg with her arms crossed.

It was a good look. I did the same thing.

Hector froze, mouth open, one arm in the air. "Uh... Uh... Uh," he said.

Baz's crew exploded. Baz himself was laughing so hard that he'd lost control of all his limbs and had collapsed into someone else. McDaz was saying *I don't know who you are!* in a high-pitched voice, which was stupid because he'd made no attempt to start puberty and his voice was higher than mine already.

Tori and Jess just stared at me, waiting. I took a breath and said, "Mum forced me to go round to their house. She said it would be nice. She's really stupid sometimes."

There was a pause while they digested this story. They already knew how stupid Mum was sometimes, because I'd told them. Then Tori smiled down at all of us from the top of her neverending legs. "What a total pain. That must have sucked."

Jess agreed. "I'm sorry, Cass. That sounds horrible."

Chloë hadn't been listening to my explanation. She was staring at Hector and biting her lip. "Guys. I think something's wrong with Hector–"

"If he says anything else to you, just ignore him," interrupted Tori. "That's the only way to deal with those kinds of people."

I was saved! I leant back and felt the wind on my face as Jess and Tori airlifted me to safety. From this distance, Hector already looked like a tiny, tiny crawling insect.

"Uh... Uh... Uh," Hector said, mouth open, one arm in the air.

"Guys, look at Hector! Something's happening to him!"

This time, Chloë managed to make us look. Hector hadn't moved. He'd just been making a low, choked sound, over and over again.

Baz's crew had noticed too, and one by one, stopped laughing. One of them, Jason (OK, I knew his name, but only because he was the only one of them who was in the top set with me), stepped forward and said "Dude? Are you OK?"

"Uh... Uh... Uh," Hector said. His eyes tracked through the crowd, seeing nobody, until they stopped.

On me.

Pain flashed through my head. Not pain, exactly – more a sense of wrongness, a shudder like there was a spider crawling across my skin. It was the first time ever that he'd looked me in the eye. Looked anyone in the eye, as far as I knew.

I flinched away immediately. But it was too late.

My chest froze. I couldn't breathe. My hands went to my throat, but I wasn't choking. I wasn't suffocating either. My muscles had just stopped. My lungs were still.

Agony mounted in my chest and spread to the rest of my body. Not agony, exactly – more that same creeping sense of wrongness, as my body weakened and failed. I couldn't shout, of course. My body was too weak to move. So, not a single person noticed as I slowly began to die. They had all turned to look at Hector.

"Uh... Uh... Uh," Hector said, his body as twisted and stiff as an old tree.

Then every muscle in his body spasmed, and he fell to the ground.

I gasped. My lungs filled with sweet, beautiful oxygen.

The whole crowd jumped back from Hector. Jason flinched, and then took another step closer. "Dude? Hector?"

Hector moaned, and his arms and legs began to thrash back and forth. His school uniform grated against the stone floor. His face was clenched tight, a constant choked screech forcing its way through his locked teeth. Jason stood helplessly over him, occasionally trying to reach in and stop his head from smashing against the ground and getting nothing but a slap in the face from Hector's flailing hands. Everyone else just looked on.

Ever since Hector's first outburst, the crowd around him had silently grown. By the time Hector stopped thrashing and fell silent and still, half the school must have been gathered round. I'd come back to life, too, shaking the last of my dizziness out of my head.

"OK. Stand aside, everyone." Ms Zima, our tight-bunned form tutor and chemistry teacher, strode into the middle of the circle, brushing the crowd aside with her cold eyes and crisp Czech accent. "Hector, can you hear me?"

Ms Zima knelt at Hector's side, and then flinched away from him with a grimace that she was too late to suppress. The crowd peered forward to see what had happened.

Ms Zima's knee had landed in a dark puddle that was spreading slowly away from Hector's limp body. We all knew immediately what it was. We'd all seen the disgust on Ms Zima's face.

"Miss, has he... Has he *peed himself?*" yelled Baz, his face lighting up with pure joy.

"That is not your concern. Could all of you please disperse so I can help Hector." It wasn't a question. Ms Zima took a subtle step back, out of the way of the spreading puddle.

"I can't believe it! He's peed himself! He's actually peed himself!" Snorts of laughter spread through the crowd.

Hector sat up. He stared down at his wet trousers, saying nothing.

"Urgh! I can smell it from here!" Baz's cronies shuffled backwards. As soon as Baz had said it, I swear I could smell it too. A tinge of bitter dampness on the air. I wrinkled my nose.

"If you have nothing useful to say, any of you, please leave," said Ms Zima through gritted teeth.

Baz's crew turned and fled from Ms Zima's furious glare, doubled over with hysterical laughter.

"The same goes for you, girls," said Ms Zima. "Don't you have somewhere more important to be?"

The four of us hurried away, leaving Ms Zima crouched over Hector. I couldn't shake the feeling that Hector's eyes were still burning into the back of my head. It stayed there even after we'd turned the corner and gone out of sight.

RECLUSIVE MILLIONAIRE, 66, LEFT FOR DEAD BY SORCERER IN KENSINGTON MANSION BREAK-IN HORROR

Vinh Nguyen

- Unknown assailant leaves wealthy OAP fighting for life
- Police stumble into grisly magical murder
- No suspects have yet been identified

A usually idyllic mansion enclave in South Kensington became a nightmarish hotpot of magic and violence yesterday evening. Retired banker Keith Foley was found crushed underneath his own grand piano by police responding to an emergency call. Once they ascertained the gory accident was magical in nature, they rushed Foley to hospital where he awoke from atroposy several hours later. He is said to be making a good recovery.

The SID believe Foley was nyxed by an intruder to his house. There were no signs of break-in, indicating either that the sorcerer was known to Foley, or duped Foley into letting him inside via magical means.

Police are on the lookout for a man of stocky build with a Mediterranean complexion who neighbours reported seeing hurrying away from Foley's house late in the evening.

The People's Voice

WHEN IS LONDON GOING TO WAKE UP?

Freya Hardlin

So. Another day, another grisly news story dominating every channel, station, and website. Half of us are bored out of our minds while the other half are beside ourselves in terror. I have to admit, I spend a lot of my time sympathising with both of these positions at once. And then I remember: *we shouldn't be accepting this at all.*

This time, it's a retired banker. Last week, an electrician. The week before that, a schoolteacher. All of them, as far as we can tell, nyxed with no clear motive. It's little wonder that so many of us are worrying that next week, it could be us. Or our family.

Fifteen years ago, Prime Minister Paul Gilchrist promised to the nation to declare 'war on sorcery' and spent millions expanding the SID. Since then, they've mounted one high-profile campaign against Cuttlefish (remember him!?) that ended in disaster, won a few victories against minor sorcerer gangs, and otherwise failed spectacularly to stem the rising tide of magic in Britain, particularly our capital city. Magical crime in London is in fact at a ten-year high, and opinion polls show that fear of sorcery is its residents' number one concern.

True, most magical crime remains sorcerer-on-sorcerer. Rival gang members attacking each other in the streets, or sick 'duels' taking place under cover of darkness in shady establishments. But in light of recent events, the age-old argument – if you're not an aggressor, you won't be a victim – just doesn't wash. London's law-abiding citizens risk suffering any imaginable suffering or even a magical death at the hands of sorcerer cabals such as the Lyceum who *de facto* control our streets.

While magical injuries might be nothing but illusions, science has shown that the long-term trauma they cause is real. Getting nyxed leads to psychosis, PTSD, and many other long-term mental health issues. Why should we be expected to accept this risk every time we step out of our front doors?

Giving the SID extra money and resources didn't work. What they need is *power* – a meaningful, legally-backed mandate to clear up our streets once and for all. We need a new raft of anti-sorcery laws allowing the police and SID to act forcefully to eliminate the sorcerer threat wherever it springs up.

What's more, Britain's Greek communities need to take a good, hard look in the mirror and start clearing out their house of magical extremism. The SID might be too afraid to tackle sorcery at its source, for fear of being branded "racist" – but moderate Greeks could be doing more to resist magical propaganda that starts in their communities. Together, it's time to show sorcerers that we mean business.

NINE

THE LIBRARY

Hector was stupid, but he wasn't *that* stupid – he didn't try to talk to me again in school. Ever. When we saw each other, he would stare at the ground even harder than usual and scurry past me.

It was for the best. I couldn't have helped him – he was too far gone. If I'd tried, he'd have just pulled me down with him. Then we'd both have been miserable.

I wasn't completely heartless. It's not like I went out of my way to make Hector miserable, which was what Baz's crew seemed to do. After Hector's seizure, the whole group would hold their noses whenever he walked past, although after five seconds would be snorting with laughter too hard to keep it going.

Some of Hector's shame soaked into me too. From that day forward, Baz started calling me "HECTOR'S GIRLFRIEND!" whenever he crossed me in a corridor. It took one of Tori's weaponised glances to make him stop doing it unless he caught me alone.

But I didn't see the point in making Hector feeling miserable for no reason. He was miserable enough as it is. In fact, I messaged him the day of the seizure to see how he was doing. **Sorry about what happened today. Did you have another tonic seizure?**

I checked back later. He'd seen it, but not responded.

Cass: I think you might have got confused. when I said we could be friends, I meant friends on Agora, not FRIENDS friends.

Seen.

Cass: look, I just don't think it's a good idea for you to talk to me in school. People might get the wrong idea.

Hector: OK

That was the last thing he ever said to me on Agora. His smiling sloth face didn't bubble up on my feed ever again. He didn't even give me that kudos he'd promised me next time I changed my profile picture.

I met up with Tori and Jess after school. We headed to Hampstead Heath, the park around the corner from Whittington School, for a bit. (Chloë was never allowed to come. Jess had told her to pretend she was going around to Jess's, but she refused.) About half the school wandered over there every day, for an hour or two, before heading home. Mostly so they could slope off into the trees to smoke or make out or both. But the three of us just grabbed a park bench and gazed out over London's skyline for a bit.

I decided it was time to explain what had happened to me during Hector's attack. It didn't take long.

"Sounds scary," said Jess when I was finished, her eyes wide behind her glasses.

"I mean, it could be nothing," I said. "It could have all been in my head. But I stopped being able to breathe the *moment* he looked me in the eyes."

"Still, you should say something to the school," said Jess.

Tori snorted. "They can't do anything about it. There's not enough evidence."

"Even if they don't do anything about it now…maybe something else will happen. Or maybe something else already *has* happened which we don't know about. It'll all help the case."

"What case?" I asked.

"Oh, you know. The case against the River People. I'm not saying there's going to *be* one, but…my mum's been worried about something like this happening for a while. Look at all the stuff that's happening in the news – Wait. Cass, I think one of Baz's friends is looking at you."

"What?" Tori pulled herself upright and looked over my shoulder. "You mean Jason?"

I shuffled in my seat.

"*Don't* turn around, Cass, whatever you do," Jess said sharply.

"Are you sure he's looking at her? That doesn't make sense. Maybe he's looking at me." Tori tipped her head back and looked at him through her nostrils.

"No, it's only Cass he's got eyes for. I caught him doing that during English as well. You know, Cass, you don't really strike me as the *type*."

"What type?" I asked, wondering if I wanted to know the answer.

But Jess didn't reply. She just tilted her head and said, "He's not actually bad-looking. What do you think, Tori?"

Tori squinted at him for a bit before giving us her expert opinion. "Yes, in a way. But I'd give him a few years."

"Er… Cass?"

It was Jason. Somehow, Tori and Jess had both forgotten to tell me that he was actually walking over to us. I jumped around like I'd just been electrocuted and looked up at him.

"Hi...Jason?" I pretended I'd only just noticed him.

"Could I ask you something really quickly?"

Jess and Tori both started visibly vibrating next to me. It's like they'd both just overdosed on drama and were going into some kind of shock.

"Sure." I left them both on the bench to recover in peace. We found a spot where none of the clusters of pupils would be able to overhear us.

"It's about the other day. What happened with Hector."

"Oh. Of course."

I hadn't been expecting Jason to ask me out then and there. I really hadn't. I wasn't even sure I wanted to start seeing anyone anyway, not after my first "relationship" which took place almost entirely on one of the benches in this exact park. His name was Lukas, and he'd told me he loved me three weeks in, and I'd said it back, although even at the time I suspected that the feeling I was calling "love" was actually just smugness that I'd managed to land a semi-hot boyfriend before Jess. Not before Tori, of course, whose full-time hobby for the whole of Year 7 had been breaking Year 8 guys' hearts.

"Thanks for trying to help Hector," I continued. "That was...nice."

Jason shrugged, and wiped his hair out of his eyes. "I didn't really do much to help."

"You did more than anyone else did."

"Anyone else would have done the same thing."

We silently contemplated the falsity of this statement for a while. Then it suddenly dawned on me that Jess had been right. Jason was actually quite hot.

OK, that's not entirely true. I had noticed this important fact about Jason before. He'd been in the top set with me since the start of Year 8. But because he'd made the terrible life choice of hanging around with Baz's crew, it had never really mattered much.

He looked Middle Eastern. He had big, serious brown eyes, kind of like Hector, but unlike Hector, his face had an actual shape. His jaw was straight and just the right level of sharp. He had eyelashes six times the length of mine. He had shiny black hair that was always flopping in his face, which is why I'd never really noticed it until now. His lips were...

"Cass, did you hear me?"

I blinked. "What?"

"I said, what was Hector saying to you before that thing happened to him?"

"Um...to be honest, I can't really remember." *Cassandra is my friend!*

"I was just trying to figure out whether something made it happen, or whether that kind of thing just...happens...on its own."

"Oh, it was a seizure. He gets them from time to time. I don't think they're caused by anything." *I... I... I don't know who you are.*

"Oh cool, did he talk to you about it, then?"

"No!"

I don't wear much jewellery. Just a silver ring, a tiny snake wrapped three times around my finger with its own tail in its mouth. It has an emerald for an eye. I got it when I was ten, and thought it was the most badass thing ever. I still secretly thought it was the most badass thing ever. I fiddled with it whenever I was nervous. Just then, I was fiddling with it so hard that I had to sit on my hands to stop.

"Then how do you know so much about it?" Jason asked.

"Oh. Well... I suppose he *did* tell me about it. Just quickly. After it happened."

"OK. I keep wanting to ask him how he is, but...he'd probably just think I was playing some trick on him. My friends are being such jerks to him right now."

He turned to look back at the others dejectedly. We'd broken away from the purple-uniformed huddle completely. We were almost at the border of Makeout Forest.

"Yeah, they are. But that's not your fault."

"Isn't it? I feel like I should stand up to them more, but when I say something, they just ignore me."

"Well, you've done the best you can." I felt a bit sick, for some reason.

"Like...is there a *reason* everyone picks on Hector? Is there something I'm missing? Or is it just because he's Greek?"

"What? No," I said unhelpfully.

"Oh, come on. He's the only obviously Greek guy in our year, and you think it's just a coincidence everyone picks on him?"

"I don't think it's *that*, I think it's just...the general way he is." It wasn't the best line I'd ever come up with. *Just the general way he is.* I noticed my hands had snuck back together again, so that they could twist my ring back and forth.

"I get that he's strange, the way he talks and stuff, but... there's a few other guys like that in our year, and we just let them be. But Baz seems weirdly obsessed with making Hector's life hell. He says Hector's a sorcerer. And I don't know why anyone would think that unless they were just being racist, basically. Which is stupid. Baz is Indian, Yaz is Middle Eastern, they should both know better than to go around accusing all Greek people of being sorcerers. You know?"

"You really think that's why?" I'd never thought about that before. I'd just assumed it was because Hector was weird.

"Could be. I'm half Greek, you know. It's fine for me, I take more after my mum, who's Iranian, but my older brother – he looks properly Mediterranean. And he has a Greek name. He's had people say nasty stuff to him before. He's had people calling him a *wi–* you know, calling him the W-word in the street."

"Jason, that's...horrible. Who'd use the W-word on a teenager?"

"Yeah, well my parents wised up after they had him, so they gave me an English name. Named me after a character from some Ancient Greek thing. Kind of pretentious, but at least it blends in."

"Still. Baz must know you're half Greek, right?"

"Sure."

"And he's friends with you. So he's not being like that to Hector just because he's Greek."

"It doesn't work that way," Jason said abruptly, and looked away like I'd said something wrong.

I turned away too, to find Jess and Tori on their bench. Neither of them were looking at me. In fact, they were doing an especially good job of not looking at me. They were looking at each other so intently, it's like they hadn't even noticed the two of us standing on the edge of Makeout Forest.

Jason continued, "Like…when people know you're Greek, they just look at you differently. They don't do it on purpose. They just can't help themselves. And the second you do anything wrong, *bam*! All their worst suspicions are confirmed about you. You know? You have to *prove* that you're not secretly a sorcerer, that you're just an average person like everyone else. I saw this article the other day basically saying that it was all Greek people's fault. Like, even if we're not sorcerers ourselves, it's our job to stop other Greeks from becoming sorcerers… It's just stupid. Really stupid."

"I'm sorry, Jason. I didn't realize it was like that."

"I'm sorry too. I didn't mean to sound so angry. It's not like it's your fault. Anyway, that's all I wanted to say. Better get back to your friends before they assume we've got married or something."

I tried to laugh, but all that came out was a long, old-man "Haaaaaa!"

Jason backed away with a nervous smile. "See you around!"

"Hope so!"

Hope so? Really?

He was already out of earshot. Hopefully, he hadn't heard.

I didn't tell Jason about the weird breathing thing that had happened to me. But I told Mum all about it that evening, when I got back from Hampstead Heath.

DCI Helen Drake nodded at me very seriously from across the kitchen table while I provided my witness testimony. "God, poor thing," she said when I'd finished. "Foni told me about it earlier. Epilepsy can be a really tough condition to live with."

Typical Mum. Caring more about some weird guy than about her beloved only daughter. "What about me?" I asked. "It felt like he was *doing* something to me. I couldn't breathe!"

"Yes," Mum said, clearly as an afterthought. "That must have been quite upsetting too. I'm not sure what happened there."

"Could it have been sorcery?"

"That kind of thing is *possible*, yes. But the much more likely explanation is that you had a strong emotional reaction to the situation, which affected you physiologically."

"What? You're saying it was all in my *head?*" I was outraged.

"Not necessarily. But I don't think it will do anyone any favours to speculate about sorcery. Not with all the nasty rumours already circulating."

I snorted. "But that's the whole point! What if the rumours are true?"

"It seems to me like we need to clear the air. How about we visit them again soon?"

"What? No way. What if Hector hurts me?"

"Hector is *not* going to hurt you."

Mum's voice had changed completely. Polished, but full of jagged edges. I looked up at her. Yep – it was DCI Helen Drake, her green glass stare leaving me nowhere to hide.

"Kid, I've been held at wandpoint more times than I can count. I've been burnt, shot, electrified, and nearly drowned at the hands of violent criminals. I know a dangerous sorcerer when I see one. Hector is not one of them. But don't worry, I'll be there just in case I need to protect you from him."

This is how DCI Helen Drake trapped you. If I said no to the visit, I'd look stupid. And that's how the two of us ended up returning to Omphalos, a few days later.

Once again, Foni was outside on her hands and knees, wearing dungarees that were at least twice as old as me, and gloves down to her elbows. When she saw us, she stood up, brushing earth off her groin. "Helen, the winterbloom is beginning to turn. I must show you."

"Fantastic!" Mum said, and followed her to a particularly damp and earthy corner of the front lawn to inspect a quailing shrub.

Mum had never once shown any interest in gardening before meeting Foni. Our own garden looked like the set to a film about aliens exterminating all known life-forms on Earth, leaving the last traces of humanity to crawl pathetically around in the mud searching for nutrition in that stack of plastic flowerpots that never got used.

"Hector's over there," Foni said to me, pointing one begloved finger to the path round the side of the house.

Hector was waiting in the shadow of Omphalos. He smiled at my shoes when he saw me. "Do you want to know a secret?" he said.

I had no idea how sinister that sentence could sound.

"Sure?" I replied.

Hector led me to the edge of the garden, where one of the black railings was missing. "I use this to sneak in and out of the cemetery. It's a great shortcut from school."

"Great," I said. I didn't mean to sound sarcastic, but of course I did. Luckily, Hector was oblivious.

"Do you want to explore?"

I contemplated the prospect of running around the rapidly darkening cemetery with Hector. "I'm OK, thanks."

I needed to distract Hector with a change of topic. But the only thing I had to say to him was hard to say. I decided to just drop it straight in, cutting Hector's bizarre train of thought off.

"Hector," I said, "I think you did something to me while you were having your seizure. It felt like I couldn't breathe."

Hector's face fell further. "Oh." No shock in his eyes, no confusion. Just sad acceptance.

"Do you know what that was?"

"No. I don't remember what happened at all."

Oh, yeah. Hector didn't remember his seizures. How convenient.

"I'm sorry," he continued. "I didn't mean to do anything."

"So you *did* do something?"

"I don't know."

"Well, what could it have been? It felt like you did something with your eyes."

"I don't know!" Hector was staring fixedly at a sickly-looking worm on the lawn. "But I'm sorry. And I'm sorry for talking to you in school. That was stupid of me."

"That's OK."

We sat in silence for our next three lifetimes, with only the writhing of the worm to mark the passage of decades.

"I would never want to hurt you," he said at last.

"I know."

"Can I show you another secret?"

"Sure."

Hector took me into Omphalos, through the kitchen door and into the front hall. He opened a door, hidden in the panelling in the side of the staircase. Behind the door was a much smaller staircase than the one directly above it, turning steeply to the right. Hector had already disappeared down it. I scrambled after him, suddenly feeling tiny and alone. Without daylight and the sound of the city outside, I lost my bearings in time. The walls of the basement passage were lined with books that looked like they hadn't been touched for centuries.

It was like we were reaching the core of Omphalos. The strange musty smell that filled every room intensified down here, like we were approaching its source. Feeling my way through the near-darkness, I bumped into Hector with his arm deep inside one of the shelves, making an odd grunting noise.

At first, I thought Hector was having one of his weird Hector moments with the books. But then a muffled click came from somewhere inside the wall, and with a soft hiss, the entire shelf swung open. I could see nothing behind it but blackness, but a waft of dry warmth told me that Hector had just opened the door into an enormous space.

It was the most amazing thing I'd ever seen.

"My mother said that I couldn't tell anyone about this room. But I want you to know that I'm sorry about everything. I really am."

Hector shuffled forward and found a light switch. A cobwebby chandelier blazed into life in the distance, showing me the room he'd just opened stretching out beneath us. It was enormous. I could barely make out the walls, they were so far away, each lined with floor-to-ceiling shelves. The shelves were almost all empty, just rows of dark cavities like an abandoned insects' nest. The walls were much higher than the passageway we were standing in – the room sank down into the earth below us. We were standing at the level of a gallery that wrapped around the outside of the room, letting you reach the top half of the bookshelves. To get to the floor below us, you had to take a tiny spiral staircase.

Hector was already bustling down this staircase, making it groan uncomfortably. I followed him past ancient-looking pieces of furniture: an armchair piled high with linen, an ugly sofa bed. In the back corner was some huge machine, tightly wound up and completely still, like a gigantic millipede. The shelves behind it were the only ones that contained any books, a flickering tapestry of leather spines and gold writing.

Hector had buried himself in a cupboard in the other corner, his pudgy legs flailing. On top of the cupboard was an old-fashioned gramophone, with a massive horn at least the size of Hector's face.

Hector held something triumphantly above his head. After a second, I realised it was a vinyl record in a faded purple sleeve.

Hector took the record out and placed it delicately on the gramophone. A woman's voice, scratched and desolate, filled the room. The song sounded old, the kind which women in glittering dresses crooned from the corner of smoky underground rooms in between sips of cocktail. I couldn't make out the tune because the record kept jumping backwards and forwards, making dusty coughing sounds. Hector was looking at my chin now and swaying slightly, his doughy eyes containing two tiny chandeliers.

"Hector," I asked, "why do they call you the River People?"

Hector smiled in my direction. His sticky, secret smile. "I don't know," he replied, swaying slightly.

He didn't seem to mind at all. I guess some bizarre nickname was the least of his worries.

Hector's swaying took his body over, and his feet scrubbed across the worn floorboards around me. Somewhere beneath us, the woman's voice cracked and repeated, as if she had some secret she was building up to, but couldn't bear to say.

I'm not sure what Hector's dance would be called, if it had a name. It was a swooping and weirdly elegant dance, like a waltz for one person. He swivelled and glided around me, smiling to himself as if I wasn't even there. Every time the record skipped, his body would jerk and change direction, like that had been his plan all along. Against all the odds, he actually managed to make it look good. He'd managed to reach depths of absurdity so ridiculous, so humiliating, that it looked somehow graceful again.

I can't actually remember how this scene ends. Nothing seems to happen afterwards – it just goes on forever. I think that somewhere, the twelve-year-old Hector is still spiralling merrily around that room, while the twelve-year-old me watches him, squirming with embarrassment, almost jealous of his freedom. A little slice of us trapped in time.

How to...

Say No to Nyxing!

Would **you** know what to do if you encountered someone who'd been nyxed? It may seem unlikely, but one day, you could be the first person on the scene of a magical death, so it's essential that you know how to respond.

❖ The first step is to check for danger. Are there sorcerers or magical artefacts in the area? Get yourself to safety before trying to help others.

❖ Next, **call 999**. Be sure to tell the operator that you suspect magic is involved. All paramedics are trained to deal with magical injury and death.

If you're early to the scene of a magical assault, you may encounter **gruesome and upsetting injuries**. But don't panic! All you're seeing is a **residual**

magical illusion. This will only last a few hours. All you need to remember is:

> ➢ Don't try to move the victim out of danger. Remember, no long-term physical harm can come to them. Letting the victim heal in their own time reduces the risk of psychological damage.

If you're late to the scene of a magical assault, the illusion may have worn off, leaving behind a victim who appears **sleeping or unconscious**. This state is called **atroposy**, and it's nothing more than an unusually deep sleep that lasts for a few hours. Almost all victims of nyxing wake up from atroposy on their own. But here's what you can do to help someone in atroposy:

○ Check that they're still breathing. Very deep atroposy, caused by the strongest magic, can lead to **respiratory failure** and even **death**!

○ Don't try to wake them up. The mind is most likely to heal from magical trauma when it's given time to recover.

And that's how to **SAY NO TO NYXING**!

TEN

IRRELEVANT CHAPTER

This chapter is completely irrelevant to the story. Sorry about that. If you want to skip it, go right ahead. You won't miss anything important. The only point of it is to explain how and why Jason and I never become a *thing.* So if you thought that's where this story might be leading, think again. It doesn't. It never does. And now that you know that, you can skip straight to Chapter Eleven.

It happened because of my old friend, Judaism. Ever since I'd known them, Jess and Tori had liked to bunk off school on various shifty pretexts, leaving Chloë and I to struggle through school as usual. At first that had seemed a fair enough exchange for not being able to celebrate Christmas. Then I'd discovered that they got *more* presents than me over the Christmas holidays, making Judaism objectively better than Christianity on every possible count. Then, after Tori's ridiculous Bat Mitzvah, where no fewer than three godlike dancers sprayed us all with UV paint, leading to the sexual awakening of at least half the class, I'd snapped and asked Mum how hard it was to convert to Judaism in time for my twelfth birthday.

"Very," Mum had replied, not looking up from her computer. "At the very least, you'd probably have to believe in God."

"No problem," I said. "All my friends do anyway." My eleven-year-old self wasn't big into theological questions.

After a couple of days deciding whether I could be bothered to believe in God, I'd come into Mum's study again. "Mum, why don't we believe in God?"

"Because She doesn't exist," Mum said, still not looking up.

Mum wasn't big into theological questions either. My dreams of converting to Judaism died quickly.

Which meant, as usual, I ended up stuck on my own in English, while Jess was off all day eating bagels in a shed. **Who am I supposed to sit with?** I asked her on Agora just before the lesson started.

Why don't you ask Jason?? came the instant reply, along with a picture of Jess's family grinning at me with bagels in their mouths.

Thanks. I said. As I was punching in the sarcastic full stop, a shadow passed over my screen. I looked up. My face collided with Jason's. We both screamed silently in horror.

"Oh, hi, Cass," he said, like he hadn't been peering at my phone's screen moments ago. Had he seen Jess's last text? I didn't know. "Mind if I sit here?"

I nodded. I put my phone away, just seeing Jess's final Agora message. **Just remember: he's more afraid of you than you are of him!** I snapped my phone away before Jason had a chance to read it and looked back up, to find his thoughtful gaze pointed my way. "There's something I should probably tell you," he said reluctantly.

But I didn't find out what it was. At that moment, the door burst open and all 12 of Mr Kaplan's elbows and knees burst into speech.

"Destiny!" he said, his face buzzing with excitement in the afternoon sun. Mr Kaplan's classroom was always sunny. "What does it mean to you?"

Like with most of Mr Kaplan's questions, we were all too asleep or confused or afraid to answer. Mr Kaplan didn't mind. He never did. "An interesting word, destiny. I've always preferred the Turkish word for destiny, *kismet*. Destiny is something you can't escape from, right? The more you fight to overcome it, the more it'll trap you. But *kismet* is more like…your starting hand in a game of cards. You could get bad luck, a bad *kismet*, and still be able to overcome it. But both the Greek word and the Turkish word originally meant the same thing. Portion. Like the servers in the cafeteria. They hand you your portion, and either you accept what you're given or you get out. You wouldn't dare ask for a bigger helping, or somebody else's meal. That's just your *kismet.*"

As Mr Kaplan talked, plonking a pile of folders onto his desk, a strange lilt crept into his voice. It was the barest traces of a foreign accent, hot and earthy. As if the word *kismet* had reminded him that he was Turkish.

"We all get served different *kismets*, but the question is, what do we do with them? That makes the difference. Not destiny. Choice! Choice is the icing on the coffin."

"Icing on the coffin?" someone asked.

Mr Kaplan broke off, confused. "It was just a turn of speech."

The more Mr Kaplan talked about *kismet*, the more I thought about Hector and his cold lasagne, that time he'd tried to sit at our lunch table. He hadn't chosen to be born awkward. Or overweight. Or Greek. But that was his *kismet*. Cold lasagne and cold stares.

The right side of my head felt slightly warm for the whole lesson, like Jason had quietly caught fire beside me. When it ended, he followed me out.

As we reached the staircase, he said, "Hey, Cass, do you mind if I talk to you?"

"You're already talking to me." I probably thought I was being sassy, or something.

"Yeah. I meant, alone. Not...*alone,* alone. Just so nobody hears."

I eyed up the window quickly – double glazed, and probably made of child-resistant glass. There was no way I would be able to break through that sucker. And even if I could, we were three storeys up.

Jason took a deep breath. "You know I don't like you, right?"

Such a charmer that guy was. No wonder he'd won Tori over so easily.

"I mean, I *like* you just fine, as a person and everything. I just don't *like* like you. You didn't think I *like* liked you, did you?"

I shook my head. "Why did you think I would?"

"Just something Tori said. It got me worried. I don't like people saying stuff about me that's not true. Especially behind my back."

"Right. Well, that's just her," I said, really hoping that he hadn't seen Jess's messages. I realised we'd somehow stopped moving, making us the only pupils left behind in the building. I gripped the banister and started sliding tensely down the stairs. The sooner I was out in the sunlight, the sooner this awful situation would be over. He followed me, step for step.

"Are you sure?"

"Yep. It's just a joke Tori and Jess have. I don't think they're serious. Just ignore them."

Jason softened. "OK. Fine." So he *had* seen the Agora message, otherwise he wouldn't have been worried about Jess too. "Because, I was worried you'd get the wrong idea, or whatever, if I talked to you. And I'd like to talk to you, sometimes, because I do like you, you know, as a person as everything, just not in *that* way." He suddenly looked horrified. "I'm not calling you ugly or anything, I mean, you're not that at all, I mean, there's nothing *wrong* with you – I mean, you're not *at all* unattractive in any way, and I'm sure lots of guys *would* like you in that way, but just not me. But I do like you, you're one of the nicest, I mean, one of the nic*er* people I've met here."

Wow. It was as if Jason had been going to an after-school class on social skills, run by Hector.

"So, what did Tori say?" I said, ignoring his whole Confession of Like, or whatever that had been.

"Oh, nothing much. It was just…you know she asked me out, right?"

I definitely did not know that. But I nodded anyway.

"And you know I said no, right?"

I nodded, a bit harder than last time. This was beginning to get interesting.

"Well, she didn't really get it at first, when I said no. She was like, I mean, we should go on a date sometime, and I said, I know that's what you meant, but sorry I'm not interested, and she was like, what do you *mean* you're not interested, and I was like, I just don't think that would work, and she just kept staring at me like I'd punched her in the face or something, then eventually she was like, everyone knows you're in love with Cass anyway and she stormed off. And I was like, is *that* what everyone thinks?"

Somewhere in the middle of that speech, Jason had turned into a runaway train (Next Stop: Gossipville). He wasn't even done.

"Because, you know, I'd like to get to know you better–"

I cut him off before he started all *that* again. "So you didn't like Tori either? In that way, I mean?"

"No, not really. Is that such a big deal? Are all the guys meant to have a crush on her or something?"

I shrugged. "How should I know? I don't talk to any. Do they?"

"I don't know. But Tori must think so. She was very sure I did, anyway."

There was a little ring in the way he said that that made me turn to look at him again. He was staring straight down as he clipped his way carefully down the stairs, his lips slightly apart, swallowing back something else.

"Really?" I said.

"Yeah. It's like–" Now he was breaking off, and looking at me. I smiled back. "It's like, does she think every guy's going to feel the same way about her? Can't we have our own opinions? When I said I wasn't interested, it was like she didn't *believe* me. Like, I don't know, I was playing hard to get or something. Or that I was so hopelessly in love with her that I hadn't even realised yet, and it was her job to help me see the truth."

I let out a tiny snort. It was so true – I hadn't thought any guy in the world would be able to turn down Tori. But here was Jason, making it sound like it was the easiest thing in the world. He'd spent only about five minutes with Tori and he somehow knew her better than I did.

Jason was eating his lips, trying not to laugh. "I'm sorry. You must think I'm a terrible person now."

"That's not true." (Other way around. I'd realised that he might have his upsides after all.)

"You're not going to tell her any of this, are you? I don't want to upset her or anything."

"Of course not. I'd never tell Tori." Jess, on the other hand, *needed* to know. It was my duty to inform her. I was already writing the message in my mind. Just enough of a hint what I'd found out to make sure she couldn't concentrate on her endless supply of delicious bagels anymore, but not so much that I'd have nothing to tell her when she came back to school. **It's about Jason. Can't talk here. I'll tell you everything later.** Perfect.

Jason stopped on the landing just below a poster screaming SAY NO TO NYXING! "Year 8's been so weirdly stressful. All my friends have become total morons. And I'm spending my whole time worried I've hurt everyone's feelings by mistake."

"Oh, don't worry. Tori doesn't have – I mean, Tori didn't seem upset to me."

"Really? What did she tell you?"

"Not very much, actually. She just said that she didn't think it was going to work out after all."

"Oh, right. Because obviously, she never wanted to go out with me in the first place. Just as well I turned her down."

We both laughed. Jason held open the door, and we stepped into the sunlight together.

And that's how and why Jason and I never became a thing.

See? I told you this was an irrelevant chapter.

ELEVEN

READY OR NOT

The detective was easy to spot in the crowd. While everyone else jostled through the British Library's atrium, their eyes wide with curiosity, the detective stood stock still, deadpan, her eyes already focused on the Head of Security as he approached. She seemed totally unaware of the tide of humanity washing around her. She was in plainclothes, but her height and close-cropped black hair lent her a natural air of authority.

"Detective Inquisitor Jamila Khan. Security expert with the Sorcery Investigation Department," the detective said by way of introduction, flashing her badge.

"Ahmed Kalat," said the Head of Security, flashing a reassuring smile. He knew that his humongous bald head, not to mention the earpiece he was wearing, made him intimidating to most people, but the detective clearly didn't feel this way. No doubt she'd seen much worse.

"Thanks for agreeing to see me at such short notice," said the detective, her words as sharp and punchy as gunfire. "This appraisal really can't wait. I'm sure you've been seeing how Cuttlefish's attacks are becoming more and more extreme."

"We appreciate your input," said the Head of Security. "I'm sure there's a lot we can learn from someone like you. I think you'll be pleasantly surprised by the measures we have in place already."

The pair didn't bother to keep their voices down as they strolled through the atrium, and up a wide, rolling flight of stairs. The conversations all around them multiplied into a background ringing that made it impossible to make out the words of someone standing even six feet away. There was no real danger they could be overheard.

"How much do you know about Cuttlefish?" said the detective.

"Not much, I'm afraid. I know he's some kind of identity thief. Impersonates other people so that he can steal stuff. He was big news, what, 10 – 15 years ago? And now he's popped up again."

"That's about right, yes. But what's less well known is that throughout his career he's only ever been after one thing: sorcery books belonging to the Daedalus set. I assume you know about the Lyceum?"

"The Lyceum? They're basically some kind of magic Mafia, right?"

The detective winced. "Something like that. They're behind a lot of the organised sorcery in the UK. They've been been around for centuries. Two hundred years ago, one of the Lyceum's major players was known as Daedalus. We don't know a lot about him, but we do know that he devoted his life to some project that even the rest of the Lyceum thought was a terrible idea. To this end, he built up a large collection of sorcery books which he marked with a burning torch symbol. Then, one day, he vanished. But he left his grimoires behind. Today, those sorcery books are very highly prized not just for their contents, but for their talismanic properties."

"Sorry. *Talismanic*?"

"They're capable of enhancing the sorcery of their users. They make it possible to conjure up more powerful illusions, or ward against another sorcerer's magic. That kind of thing. And, perhaps for this reason, or for another that we don't yet understand, Cuttlefish seems to have made it his life mission to collect as many Daedalus books as possible. Naturally, this means most of his victims are sorcerers themselves, or at least sympathisers. However, we're worried that sooner or later he's going to target the British Library."

"Right. I think I see where this is going."

The pair had arrived at the top of the grand staircase. Most of the tourists had been diverted into the British Library's main exhibition space, with its reverentially displayed artefacts, leaving them in the company of only the most intrepid academics. Their conversation paused as they headed through a reading room.

"First security barrier here," the Head of Security pointed out, holding his card to the scanner by the door.

"How many staff have access?"

"Here? All of them. About 2000-odd. The next doors we pass through are more selective, limited to specific departments or senior staff."

The detective nodded and stepped through the door, without giving away her opinions on this.

"You'll see video surveillance actually continues in here, as well as the thorough coverage we have in all the public areas," the Head of Security said, pointing out the periodical cameras down the corridor. "Monitored 24/7."

The detective instantly shot him down. "That's not good enough."

"Can't do better than 24 hours a day, love!"

"Cuttlefish's specialty is mimesis. Adopting the appearance of other people. He'll be able to fool anyone looking at him – even if they're sitting on the other side of the TV screen. Do you use facial recognition software?"

"Not routinely, no.

"That's going to be essential. No matter how talented he is – and believe me, he is talented – Cuttlefish won't be able to fool a computer programme. The trouble is, even facial recognition software is only useful if it knows what it's looking for, and right now we have no leads as to Cuttlefish's true appearance or identity."

The Head of Security reopened the previous conversation as they walked on. "So you're thinking Cuttlefish is going to come after the sorcery books stored here. In particular, the ones that have this torch symbol in them."

"Exactly. It seems that a handful of Daedalus books have been added to the British Library's collections over the years. I'm not entirely clear why. If you ask me, the safest thing to do would be to store all of your magical material in a maximum-security facility. Or better yet, just destroy it."

The Head of Security scoffed. "You probably know what I'm going to say to that. This is a debate we have fairly regularly. These books you're talking about aren't just dangerous weapons. They're a vital part of our cultural heritage, they're very important to historians and academics of all kinds, and to make them totally inaccessible, or worse yet destroy them, would be truly criminal. And it's not like the books we house contain any information that sorcerers nowadays can't just find on the Internet."

"True. But when a grimoire is made, the pages, the binding, even the ink is enchanted for the sake of enhancing the sorcery it's used for. And the older the book, the more enchantment it soaks up, and the more powerful a weapon it can be in the wrong hands."

The Head of Security snorted. "That's just superstition, isn't it?"

"Most sorcerers would disagree with you. Cuttlefish would certainly disagree with you. And ultimately, that's the only thing that matters right now."

"Well, I assure you, there's no need to worry about Cuttlefish breaking into this facility. Our security has been designed to keep the nation's most rare and valuable written material safe, and so far we've done a bloody good job."

The detective narrowed her eyes. "We'll see about that."

They stopped in front of a metal door. A sign overhead read MAGICAL MATERIALS DEPT. AUTHORISED PERSONNEL ONLY.

"All right, this is it!" The Head of Security said proudly. "The inner sanctum. Reinforced walls, floors and ceiling. Only two entrances, both of them blast proof. So if Cuttlefish tries to blow a hole anywhere..."

The detective shook her head impatiently. "Cuttlefish can't do that. He's a sorcerer, not a demolition expert."

"Sorcerers blow stuff up all the time, don't they?"

"In appearance, not reality. Yes, if he wanted to, he could probably find a way to make these doors *look* like they'd been destroyed, but he'd still be incapable of going in. So you have nothing to worry about there."

"Right. Yes, of course, that was stupid of me. Anyway, the tech we've put on these doors is state of the art. Combination code which changes monthly, and a fingerprint scanner. Both of them mandatory."

The security here was similar to the security in place around dozens of other rooms in this building. The security elsewhere protected books from the dangers of the outside world. The security leading to this room had the opposite purpose: to protect the outside world from the dangers of these books.

"Equipment like fingerprint scanners are your best line of defence against Cuttlefish," the detective said. "No matter how easily he can trick a human, he'll never be able to trick a machine like this. However, this equipment only works if you use it strictly. From now on, I recommend everyone entering this area is required to scan themselves in separately. That means no guests, and don't even bring another authorized member of staff with you unless they prove they can get past this scanner. Even if they're your most trusted colleague. Remember, that colleague could be Cuttlefish."

"Right. That makes sense," said the Head of Security, punching this month's combination code into the keypad. Then he placed his thumb on the scanner, and the blast proof metal doors slid open.

Stepping through the door was like travelling 500 years back in time. They were transported from dull clinical corridors into a wonderland of ancient books. It was the smell that always struck the Head of Security first: that dense and venerable combination of leather, dust, and wood. In this airtight space, the smell was more overwhelming than anywhere else in the library.

Looking around, it would be impossible to guess that the books in this room were any different from the thousands of other ancient tomes kept safe in this building. It was hard to imagine the pain, the suffering these books had wrought for hundreds of years, before finding their way to the British Library. To the institution burdened with preserving the nation's words, no matter how dangerous those words might be.

The detective looked around, her expression not betraying any sense of wonder at her surroundings. "This is a lot of books. Tell me, how would Cuttlefish be able to find what he was looking for?"

"Our cataloguing system has just been upgraded," said the Head of Security proudly, heading to a computer terminal. "You can now search through everything stored in here on all kinds of parameters. Including, I think, whether the books come from the Daedalus collection. Yeah, here we go!"

The Head of Security printed off a list of titles in a flash and handed it to the detective. Eight books in total, together with their shelf mark.

The detective raised her eyebrow at the piece of paper. "I'm sure that's very useful, but all you've really done is hand Cuttlefish a list of the exact books he intends to steal."

The Head of Security's face fell for a moment. But he quickly recovered. "Of course, the terminals are password protected."

"That's not going to help if an authorised staff member simply retrieves the information and gives it straight to Cuttlefish," she fired back.

The Head of Security guffawed. "That's not going to happen! Our staff are very well trained. There's no way they'd just hand that information over, under any circumstance."

"How about the books themselves? How are they protected?"

The detective turned her attention to magnificent bookshelves in front of them. Referring to her sheet of paper, she located the first of the eight Lyceum books on the list.

"There's no security on the books per se," admitted the Head of Security. "It's hard to do without damaging the books."

"What? No tags? No sensors? So if Cuttlefish wants to take a book from these shelves, it's as simple as *this*?" The detective pulled a grimoire off the shelf.

"Yeah. But he'd have to get all the way in here, and then all the way out again."

The detective shook her head impatiently. "I feel like we're running in cycles here. I've seen hundreds of cases of magically assisted theft, and it's always the same thing that lets down a security system. The human element. As soon you have humans involved in the process, you have a weakness which any good sorcerer can easily exploit. No matter how hi-tech your security, all Cuttlefish needs to do is convince an authorised staff member to bypass it on his behalf. And believe me, he'll find a way to do that easily." By now, the detective had located and retrieved two more books on the list.

"Don't worry. There's only a handful of people with clearance at this level, and they all answer to me. So it'd be me in the firing line if anything happened."

The detective nodded. "That's good. Keep it that way. And pay very close attention to anyone – I mean *anyone* – who approaches you try and get information about your security. No matter how good their credentials are, no matter how well you think you know them. Cuttlefish could strike at any time. And he could be *anyone.* He may be in the British Library as we speak. In this very room. He may even be having a conversation with you at this very moment. Is that clear?"

The Head of Security nodded enthusiastically. "Yes. Don't worry, we're ready for him."

The detective found the last book on her list and brought it back to the central desk to join the others. "Look at this! A copy of Shakespeare's First Folio." She opened it disbelievingly, but sure enough, there was the torch symbol on the title page, just like all the others.

"What's that doing in here?"

"The Lyceum are far older than Shakespeare. You'd be surprised what ancient books they have in their collection. But to be honest, I'm alarmed by how easy it would be for Cuttlefish to stroll in here, collect up all these books, and stuff them into a duffel bag, much like the one I have here." The detective began packing the books away. "I'd recommend training your staff to be as suspicious as possible. Challenge everyone, even people you recognise and trust. Even if Shakespeare himself turns up and asks to see his work. In fact–" the detective caught herself and stared thoughtfully into space for a moment, " – *especially* if Shakespeare himself turns up. You get the idea?"

"This all seems a bit far-fetched to me. But your advice is appreciated."

Clutching awkwardly onto her heavy bag, the detective made her way out of the room and back down the long, narrow corridors to the public space. The Head of Security followed suit.

As they returned to the high-vaulted atrium, the detective's eyes lit up. "Ah. You didn't mention that there was a café."

"What's the relevance of that?"

"Let me explain. Other than the Daedalus connection, we're struggling to spot any trends in Cuttlefish's criminal behaviour. But one fact we can't ignore is that Cuttlefish loves nothing more than a post-robbery snack." The detective stopped and pointed at a colourful cake display. "If I were you, I'd seriously consider upgrading the security measures in place in and around your food service areas. Take this exquisite-looking cake selection, for example. If I know anything about Cuttlefish, he'll be unable to resist the temptation of a blueberry cupcake. But currently, I'm worried that you're making it almost too easy for him to help himself to whatever he likes." The detective's voice was muffled by crumbs. "Do you want something, by the way?"

"Me? No, thanks."

The detective sat at one of the café's metal tables. The Head of Security, not knowing what else to do, sat opposite her. A robotic voice coming from a walkie-talkie alerted them to a pair of guards approaching the table.

"Ma'am, could I take a look inside this bag?" the nearest guard said.

"Be my guest."

The guard inspected the haul of ancient grimoires inside the duffel bag. "Ma'am, can I ask under whose authority you have these books?"

"There we are!" the detective said to the Head of Security, gesturing emphatically at the guard. "This man is the first to question me or what I'm doing here since I walked in. This is the kind of protocol you all need to follow if you want to have any chance of stopping Cuttlefish. However, if Cuttlefish has already acquired the books he's looking for – namely, the ones in this bag – he's going to be a very significant threat."

"Excuse me, ma'am? I do need an answer to my question," insisted the guard.

"Great job persisting," the detective said. "Always be suspicious of anyone who seems to be evading your questions. But as I was saying, Cuttlefish is a mimetic, only able to change his appearance. But once he gets hold of books like these, he's able to conjure up significant illusions, capable of nyxing people. We've seen the same pattern in every single one of his crimes."

"Significant illusions? What kind of thing do you mean?"

The detective picked up the duffel bag. "Oh, this kind of thing," she explained, drawing her pepper spray and firing it straight into the guard's eyes. He let out a guttural screech and retreated, clutching his face. The detective twisted in her chair and did the same thing to the second guard before he could turn away.

The other café guests shrieked and fled, knocking metal chairs and tables to the floor in their haste to get away. The chefs dived behind the counter. A piercing alarm ripped through the echoing hubbub of the atrium.

"The more books Cuttlefish manages to steal, the greater the illusion he'll be able to create," the detective shouted over the relentless sirens. "If you catch him early, he won't be a threat. But if you leave it too late, it will be child's play for Cuttlefish to dispatch your security team, in a manner such as this." The detective fired her taser over her shoulder into the heart of a stealthily approaching guard. He screamed and fell to the floor, twitching uncontrollably.

"I see," said the Head of Security.

"These cupcakes are disgusting, by the way. They're almost entirely icing. I may need to speak to your catering team about this. They're likely to make Cuttlefish angrier and more dangerous to the public." The detective threw a stun grenade across the café. It exploded at the feet of another couple of guards, sending them tumbling across the floor.

"I'll pass that message on," said the Head of Security, shuffling in his chair.

"I should probably take off before the situation gets any more out of hand," said the detective. "But before I go, this one final thing you need to understand about Cuttlefish's modus operandi. He tends to nyx each of his victims. So be on the lookout for anyone who seems to be have suffered a magical death."

"Magical death, huh? What does that look like?"

The detective drew a pistol from her utility belt. "Like this." The detective shot the Head of Security through the heart. "Any questions?"

The Head of Security thought for a moment, then slowly shook his head.

"Good. Just remember, Cuttlefish could strike at any time, whether you're ready or not." The detective emphasised her words with a couple more gunshots across the room, then took a final bite of her cupcake and hurried away with her duffel bag under her arm, her gun and taser knocking down anyone who stood in her way.

The room went dark. No – wait – that was just the Head of Security's vision, narrowing and blackening in an almost dreamlike way. He was so tired. But he wasn't worried. If Cuttlefish ever showed his face in *his* library, he'd be ready. Oh yes, he'd be ready, alr -

TWELVE

CENTRE OF ATTENTION

Mum's what Tori calls a 'workaholic'. Tori's parents were definitely the worst on that score. I'd almost never met them, and sometimes I wasn't sure Tori had either. But Mum's workaholism came in bouts. Sometimes, she was already home every day when I got back from school, and other times she'd disappear for days at a time. The notes left on the kitchen counter each morning were the only reason I knew she hadn't been kidnapped by sorcerers.

Mum had been busier than usual since the start of term. It hadn't occurred to me to ask why. But after the British Library attack, after the name Cuttlefish started to appear everywhere, she went into full-scale bout mode. As soon as she got home from work each day, she disappeared into her study for the whole evening. I fell asleep and woke to the sound of her keyboard clacking above my head. If she ever slept, she was doing a good job hiding it from me.

Mum's study had started as a small room next to my bedroom, but a few years ago she moved her bedroom next to mine, and turned the whole top floor into her work lair. Every time I went up to give her a mug of tea and look at her balefully, DCI Helen Drake would be lodged behind her computer screen or propped over a damp-looking book, her face pasty white, her tongue sticking out. Don't ask me what any of those books could have had to do with her job. Most of them were history books with tiny letters swarming across their pages, ones she'd borrowed from Foni. And from the looks of it, she picked up more with every visit. Piles of books sprung up around her desk and started to spawn baby piles. It was like the room had caught some nasty infection from Foni's study.

One morning, during one of my baleful tea deliveries, I found DCI Helen Drake pacing up and down in front of the enormous TV screen she'd had installed on her wall. "How was school?" she asked, temporarily stopping her pacing.

"Mum, it's Saturday. It's also 8 o'clock."

Mum just looked at me, confused, wondering why I hadn't just answered the question.

"In the morning."

Her face cleared. "Oh!"

"Would you like some French toast for breakfast?" I asked, balefully. That was the reason I'd come up to her study – to balefully ask her if she wanted breakfast. I always hoped she'd notice the heavy layer of balefulness in my voice, remember that she was supposed to be the mother, and spring downstairs to whip up breakfast for me. This had never happened. But a girl can dream.

This morning, I could tell it was more of a lost cause than usual. Mum had completely forgotten that I was her beloved only daughter, and instead thought I was DCI Helen Drake's young and especially dim-witted junior detective. She launched straight in:

"Seriously, what on *earth* could this guy be thinking?"

I followed Mum's gaze to the TV screen, where a reporter shivered miserably in front of the British Library. "Who?" I asked. "Him?"

"No. Cuttlefish."

"Oh." Since the attack, Agora had been filled with Cuttlefish articles. I'd ended up reading a really long thing on *Exposé* so now I was an expert on him.

"Up until now, he's had a simple modus operandi. Keep a low profile, sneak up on his targets, nyx them to leave them no memory of what happened. So what would possess him to burst into the British Library in broad daylight?"

DCI Helen Drake looked at me, hard. I opened my mouth to answer, but she cut me off before I could. Turned out that she'd been asking a rhetorical question.

"Think about it. He's a *mimetic*. An identity thief. Whatever he's trying to do, surely there's a million easier ways he could be doing it. If *you* wanted to steal some books from the British Library, and you were able to steal the identity of anyone you wanted to, how would you do it?"

Mum looked at me again. I looked back expectantly. But she said nothing. Turned out that this time, it wasn't a rhetorical question.

"I don't know, I'd...pretend to be someone working there? Someone who was allowed to take the books?"

"Exactly! Ten years ago, last time he was active, that's exactly what he would have done. Back then, he used mimesis to keep himself as hidden as possible. He nyxed all the witnesses just to cover his tracks. It took us years to even spot the pattern between his crimes – to realize he was always stealing Daedalus books. And I wouldn't be surprised if we still didn't know about half the books he'd stolen. But ever since he's come back, he's just stopped caring about staying hidden. If this guy had wanted to, he could have stolen these books out of the British Library without anyone noticing. Instead, he starts a shootout in a public area and causes a mass panic. Why?"

I had no answer this time, which was just as well, because this turned out to be another rhetorical question. Mum ploughed straight ahead without allowing me or her to answer it.

"And that got me thinking about all these other possible attacks. Every time, it's been the same pattern. The victim's called the police to report a break-in. The police have rolled up to find the victim nyxed, and the assailant long gone, with no obvious motive for the attack. We think the assailant's been stealing Daedalus grimoires, but the victims have been unwilling to report that to us, for obvious reasons. But then why have they been calling the police at all?"

DCI Helen Drake sat back in her desk chair and triumphantly folded her hands behind her head. I tried not to rise to the bait, but eventually had to ask. "I don't know. Why?"

"They haven't! I went over each call to the police, and found that each time, the victims made them *after* they were nyxed. In other words, the calls didn't come from the victims at all. Cuttlefish is stealing his victims' identity and then making the calls himself! He *wants* his crimes to be discovered. But why could he possibly want that? Thanks to his tipoffs, we've got several candidate fingerprints and DNA samples–" Mum broke off and looked at me in alarm. "You're not going to tell anyone I said that?"

"No."

"Good, because that's all highly confidential, and I should never have told you, etc., etc. You know the drill."

I did know the drill.

"Wait," I said. "If Cuttlefish is always disguised as someone else, won't the fingerprints and DNA and stuff be wrong? Won't they match whoever he was impersonating?"

It took about 28 milliseconds of DCI Helen Drake's withering stare for me to realize what a stupid thing that was to say.

"What is sorcery, Cass?"

"An illusion," I muttered. "Yeah. I get it."

"That's right. And that goes for all sorcery, no matter how realistic it seems. This identity thief might be able to fool anyone looking at him into believing he's someone else, but there's no way he could fool our forensic software." Mum patted one of Foni's books affectionately. "It works just the same way as conjuration. The Ancient Greeks actually called it by the same name."

Conjuration, I knew about already. It was probably the most famous type of sorcery. It was the type that involved making stuff appear or disappear or move or start talking or whatever, which is why crime movies always involved a lot of it. It was the most exciting. Most people – most people who weren't sorcerers, anyway – didn't know there were different names for all the different types of sorcery. But that was just one of the life lessons Mum had given me for free.

"In fact, Aristotle, who was the first to write about mimesis, seemed to think it was the same thing as regular acting. This was back when sorcery was all totally legal, of course. The Ancient Greeks used mimesis when they were performing on stage. They'd use it to turn into different people, or animals, or even gods. It must have been incredible to watch." The excitedly factual tone of Mum's voice reminded me of the way Foni spoke. It was like the books she'd borrowed had infected her with whatever disease the River People had. I shuddered.

"But it was still sorcery, wasn't it?"

"Oh, of course. Of course," said Mum, becoming grave again. "I'm not saying it was a good idea. People still magically hurt and killed each other, and I'm sure that *did* have real, lasting effects on victims' minds, just like it does today. I'm just saying, you know, it was a very different time. Different culture. But that's the world that sorcerers today still believe in, which is why it's so important to understand it."

"So what was the point of becoming a sorcerer back then? Was it just for display?"

Mum shrugged. "I suppose that's one way of putting it. Doesn't seem worth it when you put it like that."

"I don't know. Some people would do anything to be the centre of attention."

Mum stood up like she'd just been set on fire. She slammed her TV off and stared at me, her eyes wide. "You're right!"

I hadn't thought it was that profound. I'd just been quoting our Year 4 form teacher, when she'd found out about Baz taking his trousers off during maths and hurling them out the window. But whatever I'd said had been enough to make Mum vanish on the spot, leaving behind DCI Helen Drake whispering to herself and staring at the ceiling like she'd just had a religious awakening.

"You were just a toddler when the Cuttlefish saga ended, so you won't remember. The first few years he was operational, nobody had heard of him. But eventually, the SID realized we were on the trail of a master thief, and before long the rest of the world did too. The press loved him. By the time it was all over, he was almost a celebrity. *That's* why this guy is calling in all his own crimes. *That's* why his attacks are getting bolder and bolder. He wants the Daedalus grimoires, sure, but he also wants the glory! He wants the world to know that Cuttlefish has returned, and he's stronger than ever. Do you see?"

Mum broke off and scribbled furiously on post-it notes for a while. I took a sip of her tea while I waited.

"OK. All I need to do is make one small trip today, and then who knows? I may even have dinner ready by the time you get home from school."

"Today's Saturday."

"What?"

I sighed and started to explain. "I'm not *going* to school. In the UK, and most of the rest of the world, there's this thing called a 'weekend'. It's traditionally a time when parents and children rejoice, because they get to spend all day with each other. You may not be familiar with the concept–"

"If you feel so strongly about family values, want to come to the British Library with me? It's re-opened to the public. I bet we could sneak you into their new exhibition while I talked to a couple of people."

Before we go any further, let's quickly recap what was wrong with that plan.

NORMAL PARENT: "Hey, Kidz! Want to come to Adrenaline Heights with me? I bet we could sneak you onto their death-defying new rollercoaster, Warp Drive. It goes at three times the speed of light!"

KIDZ: "Yaaaay! We love you, Normal Parent!"

Exactly.

"Sounds great!" I said, fiddling with my ring. "Oh, but I think Jess wanted to go to Camden Market today. I'll just check."

Can I come round? I asked Jess.

That's how I ended up having second breakfast at Jess's house.

Jess's house was basically my second home. It's where I went whenever I knew Mum was getting back late from work, i.e. during bout season. I even had an unofficial bed there, which pulled out from underneath Jess's. Tori had once tried to claim it was *her* unofficial bed, but we both knew it wasn't true. Once, Mum had figured out how much time I was there, and got all funny about it. She'd even tried to offer Jess's mum money for all the dinners I was having there, if you can imagine something that awkward.

As usual, Jess's mum whipped up a feast of epic proportions, then vanished without eating anything while the rest of us tucked in. Jess's dad asked me jovial questions about school, while Jess's brother devoured unholy amounts of turkey bacon. I was just mopping up the last of the maple syrup when I heard Jess's mum: "Cassie! Come quickly!"

Jess's mum was standing in the living room, wrapped in several towels. Her freshly scrubbed face was a slightly softer and wearier version of Jess's, with thicker-rimmed glasses. She was wielding a remote control in one hand and a cushion in the other, as if the TV were a mighty dragon she was trying to slay. It was on the same channel as in Mum's study.

"Your mum's on telly!" Jess's mum said with a tragic attempt at cheeriness.

"The SID remain at a loss to explain these horrific events," the glum reporter was saying. A mixture of bright wintry sunshine and rain was hitting him repeatedly in the face.

In the background, Mum was strolling across the plaza, gesticulating at someone. But then the TV cut back to the anchor saying, "It sounds like no news is definitely bad news for the SID today. Just how was Cuttlefish able to walk so brazenly out of the front door, carrying a bag full of highly restricted material? It's a question, I'm sure, that the British Library security team will be asking–"

Jess pulled the remote out of her mum's hand and turned the TV off.

Jess's mum stared strickenly at the black screen for a second, clutching the Star of David pendant around her neck. "Don't do that!" she gasped. "What if something else happens?"

"You're not even supposed to have the TV on, Mum."

"You're going to start caring about the Sabbath *now?* You've been on your phone *all morning!*"

Jess put the TV back on, muted. A terrified-looking old woman was drowning in a red anorak, waving her arms frantically in front of the reporter. "Mum, you're over-reacting. It's no big deal."

"You're only saying that because you're too young to remember what Cuttlefish can do. He's a *monster*. He's left hundreds of people brain-damaged for life. Cassie, does your mother tell you anything?"

I shrugged. "Nothing special."

"Yes, but you know how it is, she must have to be so careful with what she says in public. Perhaps she tells you, you know, her hunches?"

"She doesn't really tell me anything about her job."

"What about the River People? Has she told you anything about them?"

My face became hot. *How did she know?* It must have been obvious that we'd visited them. Maybe that horrible damp smell, the old books and rot, had seeped into my skin, and now I stunk of it too.

But no, Jess's mum didn't know a thing. Her face was just blankly worried.

"River People?" I asked, in the world's worst impression of forgetfulness. "Oh…you mean Hector and his mum?"

"Yes. The Ski – Skewer – oh, God knows how you're supposed to pronounce it. But you know who I mean. Is someone investigating them yet?"

"I…" I stammered, wiggling my snake ring back and forth. "I really don't know much about them. Mum's not mentioned them to me…"

"I see. Well, for what it's worth, I don't understand how your mother, *of all people*, can turn a blind eye to what's going on down there. We have Lyceum vermin infesting the whole of London, Cuttlefish openly committing sorcery, and she's not even looking into them? What about that thing Hector did to you?"

"Mum–" Jess said, giving me an embarrassed look.

"It's fine if you don't want to talk about it, Cassie," said Jess's mum. "But Jess told me about that incident at school. How he did something funny to your breathing."

"Oh…that," I said. "To be honest, I'm not sure if that was real or not. I might have just been imagining things."

"Never think that!" said Jess's mum. "That's how they win."

Jess tried to divert the conversation again. "Can we just-"

"Sorcery *preys* on our imagination. It makes us see and believe things that aren't there. So just because you think you're imagining things, that's no reason not to take it seriously. *You never know.*"

"That's not what I meant," I said.

"I know what you *think* you meant. But you could be closer to the truth than you realize. First, these people make you doubt yourself. Then, they make you doubt reality. And once you're doing that, they've already won."

"Mum, this is literally so embarrassing."

"I know you think I'm being overdramatic," said Jess's mum. "But I've been saying it for years. Haven't I? If this kind of rot isn't stamped out early, it just keeps spreading. Now, I don't know for sure that the River People have done anything wrong. I'm just saying it's a risk we can't ignore."

"Mum, *please.*"

"Fine. Don't believe me. But Cassie, let me tell you the same thing the same thing I told Jess. Stay away from that house. And stay away from the River People."

EXPOSÉ

CUTTLEFISH: THE WORLD WAKES UP AT LAST

FOR YEARS, THE MAINSTREAM MEDIA HAS BEEN TELLING YOU WE NO LONGER HAD ANYTHING TO FEAR FROM CUTTLEFISH. DON'T WORRY, DARLINGS, YOU WERE TOLD. CUTTLEFISH HAS DISAPPEARED FOR GOOD. YOU CAN ALL SLEEP EASY IN YOUR BEDS AGAIN.

ONLY WE MAINTAINED THE TRUTH. CUTTLEFISH HAD NOT BEEN KILLED BY THE POLICE. WHILE INNOCENT LIVES WERE LOST IN HIS NAME, HE WAS OUT THERE, SOMEWHERE, STILL BIDING HIS TIME. WHILE MAINSTREAM JOURNALISTS MOVED ONTO REPORTING HEALTH SCARES AND DIET FADS, OUR REPORTERS RISKED LIFE AND LIMB TO UNCOVER THE TRUTH BEHIND CUTTLEFISH'S SUDDEN DISAPPEARANCE.

WE MAY NEVER HAVE DISCOVERED WHERE CUTTLEFISH WAS HIDING ALL THOSE YEARS. BUT FINALLY, THE WORLD HAS BEEN FORCED TO ACCEPT THAT WE WERE RIGHT ALL ALONG.

FOR MONTHS, THE PAPERS HAVE BEEN FILLING WITH SINISTER STORIES OF PEOPLE BEING NYXED IN THEIR OWN HOMES FOR NO APPARENT REASON, BY AN UNKNOWN ASSAILANT. SINCE THE VERY FIRST OF THESE STORIES, WE REPORTED THAT CUTTLEFISH WAS BACK, JUST LIKE WE KNEW HE WOULD BE. AND NOW, IN THE WAKE OF A DEVASTATING DAYLIGHT ROBBERY FROM THE BRITISH LIBRARY, IT SEEMS IMPOSSIBLE TO DENY. CUTTLEFISH HAS RETURNED. AND HE'S MORE DANGEROUS THAN EVER.

THE CUTTLEFISH OF TEN YEARS AGO OPERATED IN THE SHADOWS. HE'D DISGUISE HIMSELF AS A LOVED ONE TO WIN YOUR TRUST. HE'D BREAK INTO YOUR HOME WITHOUT YOU EVEN REALIZING, BEFORE HE'D NYX YOU IN COLD BLOOD. AND HE'S STILL DOING THAT, TO BE SURE. JUST ASK KEITH FOLEY. GORGIOS

SISKOS. FRANK MCPHEARSON. ALL HOSPITALIZED IN STATES OF ATROPOSY, FOLLOWING POLICE CALLOUTS.

BUT HIS ATTACK ON THE BRITISH LIBRARY IS LIKE NOTHING WE'VE SEEN BEFORE. HE WALKED BRAZENLY INTO A PUBLIC BUILDING AND NYXED TWELVE MEMBERS OF STAFF IN FRONT OF HUNDREDS OF WITNESSES. THE OLD CUTTLEFISH USED MIMESIS TO STAY OUT OF SIGHT. THE NEW CUTTLEFISH, HIS DEADLY SKILLS ONLY ENHANCED DURING HIS YEARS OF SILENCE, DOESN'T NEED TO HIDE ANYMORE. HE KILLS IN BROAD DAYLIGHT. HE LEAVES A TRAIL OF MENTALLY SCARRED VICTIMS IN HIS WAKE.

WHILE HIS METHODS MAY HAVE BECOME MORE DEADLY, IT SEEMS HIS MOTIVES REMAIN THE SAME. GRIMOIRES. BOOKS OF SORCERY. ADMITTEDLY, THIS HAS ONLY BEEN PROVEN IN THE BRITISH LIBRARY ATTACK. NONE OF HIS PREVIOUS VICTIMS HAVE CONFESSED TO HAVING ANY GRIMOIRES STOLEN. BUT THEN AGAIN…WOULD YOU CONFESS TO A THING LIKE THAT?

OF COURSE, WE AREN'T ACCUSING ANYONE OF HARBOURING ILLEGAL MATERIALS.

BUT DON'T SAY WE DIDN'T WARN YOU.

THIRTEEN

FLESH AND BLOOD

I never stopped to ask myself why Jess's mum hated the River People so much. Like everything I'd grown up with, it seemed so normal to me that it was completely invisible. It's not like there were a shortage of reasons to dislike the River People.

And I was an expert in all of them. Mum's efforts to 'do the neighbourly thing' had swelled into a demented crusade. Once a week, without fail, she dragged me down to Omphalos to spend more quality time with my best pal Hector. It was easy to spot the visits coming, from the creepily upbeat smile Mum would greet me with when she got back from work. Every time, I tried to wriggle free, but Mum always found a way to trap me. Told me how much my visits meant to Hector, said he was having such a hard time fitting in, made me feel like a terrible person for refusing to go.

After a few more weeks, I even found myself starting to accept my fate. I managed to live with the sight of Hector's big grinning face, staring out the window like it was trying to get satellite reception. I could switch off while he was giving me a guided tour of the new skirting boards, or trying to guess how many books he could fit in his pillowcase, or telling me the names for things in Ancient Greek. It was like going to the dentist – just one of those terrible things life has in store for you. Some kids had asthma, or diabetes. I had Hector.

"Don't you find it weird being underground so much of the time?" I asked him once while we were in the basement library, wrinkling my nose at the damp air. The more time I spent there, the more I realized Belly Button was the perfect name for the house – weird looking, and full of grey dust.

Hector shrugged. "I love being down here. It's the only place I know that's completely quiet. Of course, my mother comes down here sometimes. But not very often. She says it's too depressing. Most of the time I can pretend that nobody else exists."

I'd never tried to pretend that nobody existed before. I shut my eyes and imagined it. What would it be like to wake up one day and find Mum vanished, the house empty, every other house empty too, Whittington School quiet and dead, and nobody else but me wandering around the planet?

I quickly shook my head clear of that idea. It was too horrible to think about. But I guess Hector saw things differently.

Another time, looking at a fly bumping against his bedroom window, he said quietly, "I think my favourite time of the week is when you come over. I don't really have anything else to look forward to."

Only ol' Hector knew how to drop something like that into the room, as carelessly as spilling salt, his face a pudgy shrug, not caring if I was listening, without looking up. And as soon as he'd said it, he looked like he'd forgotten. I was the only thing in his life that he had to look forward to, even though he knew I hated him.

I nearly cried. Not out of pity for him. More out of sadness that the world contained kismets like Hector's, and that people like him just had to grit their teeth and swallow them, whether they were enjoying themselves or not. It didn't seem fair.

As Mum and I were pushing ourselves home through an icy wind, she said, "Foni's made us a very nice offer!"

Mum's bouncy voice told me straight away that I would hate Foni's offer, whatever it was, and that she knew I'd hate it, and that she knew I knew she knew I'd hate it, but that she was still going to pretend I'd like it because that was the only way she could let herself torture me week after week with these stupid visits.

"What?" I said.

"She wants us to spend Christmas with them!"

The icy wind ripped through my jacket, my skin, and my very soul. "No."

Now, Mum knew I'd hate the idea, and she knew I knew she knew I'd hate the idea, so obviously she was ready with three billion reasons why it was a great idea, and not a terrible one, as it in fact was. She hit me with them all at once, not bothering to wait for me to reject each one, as she knew I would if she gave me a second's opening. "We've always spent Christmas alone. Wouldn't it be nice to change things up a little bit? After all, most people have big families that get together every year, but we don't, so... And neither do Foni and Hector! It'll be just the two of them otherwise. And what do we even do on Christmas anyway, that we couldn't do down there? We could cook a turkey, for once! And–"

"Mum, I'm not spending Christmas in their damp, stinking, dark house."

"OK, then! Let's invite them around to ours instead," she said, as if she were agreeing with a suggestion I'd made, which, needless to say, I hadn't.

"I can't."

"Why can't you just give the idea a little thought before you tell me what you think?"

"I don't *need* to give the idea some thought. I *hate them*, Mum. Why don't you ever get it?"

Mum slowed down and looked at me. I sped up. I just wanted to get away as quickly as possible. From her gloomy face, from the River People, from everything.

I left her there. I got home without her and went to my room. I heard her a few minutes later, turning her key quietly in the lock and heading into the kitchen without calling up to me. I just didn't get why Mum was so desperate to 'do the neighbourly thing' that she was willing to ruin her Christmas and mine.

Of course, I should have done. It should have been obvious who Foni really was. And what she was trying to do to us.

I found out the truth next time Mum and I went down to Omphalos. If I'd known it was going to be the last of our horrible trips, I might have been a bit chirpier at the time. It started out exactly the same as every other time: Mum and I standing stiffly in the living room, Hector grinning out at me sheepishly from behind his mum, before one of the adults said, "Hector, why don't you take Cass somewhere else?" Anything to get us out the way.

Something was different about Hector this time. He was humming with some quiet energy. He had that look in his eyes, the look he sometimes gave me in school when we passed each other, that sly sideways glance and furtive smile like we were both in on some nasty secret. He led me, without saying anything, up into his room.

I blinked around in confusion when I saw it. I thought he must have moved into a different room, but no, it was the same room, with the same darkly tinted windows overlooking the front garden. Same box of mouldy books in the fireplace. There was just new wallpaper: huge, pink roses linked by thorny spirals, flouncing repulsively down every side of the room.

"You were right," Hector said proudly. "The old wallpaper looked horrible. So I asked my mother if I could change it."

"What? I never said that."

"Yes you did. You said it the first time you came here. You said, my room looked horrible. Do you like it better now?"

I didn't think I was capable of lying about something so monumental as this. But if I said no, he'd probably change it to something even more hideous. So I swallowed back my rising vomit and said, "Sure."

And the weirdest part of all is, he seemed to believe me. His face blossomed into a chubby smile. "We had the wallpaper left over from the hallway. Roses were my father's favourite flower."

"You have a *father?*" Don't get me wrong, I knew that Hector technically had to have a father. But I'd never really thought about it before.

"Of course," he said. "That's why we're friends. Because we have so much in common. Our fathers died."

"Hector, we don't have *anything* in common."

Hector's face fell. "Don't we?"

"No."

"But our parents are dating! That's something that we have in common."

Hector glanced at my stomach, bringing a nest of worms to life inside it.

"*What* did you just say?" I asked him.

"People only go out with each other if they have things in common, don't they? Although people also say that opposites attract. So maybe that's why you're here."

The worms slithered through my guts. "Hector, are you joking? Our mums aren't *going out with* each other. Do you have *any idea* how stupid you sound?"

Hector's face fell. Don't ask me how it managed to fall again, without having picked itself up from the last time. But it did. "Oh. I must have made a mistake. Sorry."

"Why would you even *think* that?" My mum didn't date women. Especially not dusty scarecrow women stuffed with rotting paper.

"I don't know." So typical. He was shutting down, avoiding my questions as slimily as he avoided my gaze.

Silence. I wanted to ask him more, just to prove how wrong he was. But another voice in me was starting to ask questions of its own. A colder, more rational voice, churning through all the ways Mum had acted strangely since meeting the River People...

"Let's go to the library," Hector said, trying to change the subject.

I followed him downstairs. "I'll see you in there," I said as we reached the hall. "I need the toilet."

I let him disappear down the basement stairs before I turned towards the study door. It was closed, like it always was. I could hear Mum and Foni together on the other side.

My hand was on the doorknob. The worms that Hector had brought to life chewed through my intestines. All I could hear was faint murmuring. No words. But even through the door I could make out something in

Mum's voice I'd never heard before. It was high-pitched, singsong, like it was on the verge of breaking into giggles at any moment.

I opened the door.

Mum was sitting on the edge of Foni's desk, her blonde hair loose around her face. Foni was leaning back on her chair with her hands behind her head, the kind of pose Baz threw when he thought he'd made a good joke. She was telling Mum something. I never caught what it was, but it definitely wasn't Ancient Greece facts. Mum was hanging on her every word.

Mum's feet –

She'd taken off her shoes. Her feet were resting in Foni's lap.

Her *lap*.

They stopped talking and pulled away from each other the moment I walked in.

Foni saw me first. She pushed herself backwards on her chair. "Hellooo there, Cassandra!" she said. "Everything OK? Hector's being friendly, I hope?"

Mum was slower to react. She straightened up and muted her soppy teenage grin into her normal smile.

The worms inside me chewed through my lungs and replaced them with a stack of Hector's books.

"Yes," I said. "I was just going get a drink."

"Hector didn't offer to get it for you himself, eh?" Foni said, laughing awkwardly. "I do try to teach him some manners, you know, but he never seems to get the hang of them. Make sure he's doing something you want to do, won't you?"

I nodded and left. I shut the study door on the monstrosities within.

I sat in the entrance hall, slumped against the panel door to the basement. How had it taken me so long to realize? Mum didn't keep forcing me to visit the River People out of some deranged two-month-long attempt at neighbourliness. Mum wasn't there just to admire Foni's home-made bike rack, or exchange opinions on the late Athenian democratic model. Mum was there for Foni herself. Mum *liked* Foni. No: she didn't just like Foni, she *like-liked* Foni. Perhaps she *loved* Foni. My twelve-year-old brain couldn't wrap itself around the idea that *anyone* could love Foni, let alone my actual mother. This had been going on since the beginning, and Mum hadn't told me, because she *knew*. Knew it would make no sense to me. Knew I hated the River People's miserable guts. Knew it would sicken me to my core. So that's why she was trying to reel me in slowly, tangle me up tighter and tighter in Foni and Hector's lives, until I was trapped, wriggling, in the centre.

I opened the basement door and walked down those narrow stairs. Light from the open library door carved a slice out of the gloomy corridor.

I looked down into the library. Hector was lost in a book at the back of the room. Perfectly happy. Why wouldn't he be? This was his dream life. Alone, underground, surrounded by books.

"How long have you known?" I called down to him. He looked up in surprise, with clearly no clue what I was talking about or why I was about to collapse from fear and rage. Of *course* he had no clue. He never had a clue. When it came to other people, even people he was closest to, he couldn't read between the lines, he couldn't join the dots. He just stared up at me, waiting for me to spell everything out like I always did.

But I couldn't this time. I couldn't bear to look at his squidgy sloth smile a second longer. Not this time, when on top of all the other humiliations he'd heaped on me, he'd been *right*.

"You know what? I'm completely done with you. Do the world a favour, stay down here, and never come out again."

It's not like I had the idea in advance. It was one of those ideas that I didn't know I'd had until I'd said those words out loud. I stepped back and swung the heavy door shut. The handle made a satisfying grinding sound as I turned it down, the door bolts sliding smoothly into place.

I paced up and down the basement corridor. My mind took off on a dangerously careening minecart. Mum's horrifying Christmas idea was just the beginning. What would she say next? Glimpses of the future swarmed in front of me. "Have you ever thought how nice it would be to live closer to school? Because there's so much spare room in Omphalos, it seems a pity not to use it... Didn't you used to tell me you wanted a brother or sister? Because Hector feels the exact same way!"

It all made total sense to Mum, of course. She'd been seeing things totally differently. She looked at us and the River People, and saw a kind of beautiful symmetry. Instead of a horrifying eight-legged monster, she saw two tragically broken half-families that needed to be united. *These are our two children. Cassandra and Hector Drapoios. Hector and Cassandra Skeuopake. What's that? They look nothing alike? True, but they're still flesh and blood!*

Flesh and blood. Blood and flesh.

Flesh. And. Blood.

I checked my phone. Almost half an hour had gone past.

Feeling dizzy, I looked along the bookshelves for the hidden door handle. It took me a bit longer to find it than I was expecting – the book titles were hard to read in this grimy light – but eventually I cranked the hidden lever open again.

Everything in Omphalos squeaked and groaned the second you started looking at it. But the library door, even though it was thicker and heavier than any other door in the house, made only a soft hiss as it glided open, quieter than the rush of air through the widening doorway.

It took a while for my eyes to adjust to the light of the chandelier. But I still couldn't see Hector anywhere. The room was silent and still. I could have been the first person to discover this room after hundreds of years.

"Where are you?" I called.

I blinked, and realised he'd been sitting in my view the whole time. He was curled up in the corner, his back pressed into a bookshelf on the far wall, staring at a book. He looked like he was trying to squeeze himself out of the world. I went down the spiral staircase to join him.

"I was going to leave you down here, but then I realized you'd probably die before anyone came looking for you," I said. I meant it as a joke, but Hector didn't laugh. Didn't do anything, actually. I stood in front of him, placing him in my shadow.

"You think my mum's going to fall in love with Foni? You think they'll get *married*? Is that what you want to happen? It's not going to happen," I said. I was calmer now then I'd been before. I was able to spell out my feelings with icy precision. "You make me sick."

That probably sounds cruel. Let me explain. In the time I'd been pacing the corridor outside, I'd realized that pretending to be friends with Hector was the cruellest thing I could have done to him. I'd let him believe that we could hang out like this all the time. He'd told me himself; my visits were the highlight of his week. He probably couldn't wait for us all to move in together, so that every day was like this.

So I had to stop lying to him. I had to be cruel to be kind.

It didn't seem to be working, though. Hector stared at his book, his forehead furrowed, his eyes not moving. I may as well have not been there.

"*Look* at me, Hector!"

He didn't, of course. His lips moved silently as his eyes stayed fixed on the page. He'd somehow hidden himself away somewhere where nothing could reach him.

I wrenched the book out of his hands and ripped the central pages out. The book was ancient. They came easily.

"Look at me!" I commanded.

I tore more pages out. Each filled with thick Greek letters. I dropped them into Hector's lap.

That's when he started screaming.

Up until that exact moment, I knew Hector was capable of a lot of weird things, but I'd never really had him down as a *screamer*. When it came to weird character traits, Hector had always done just fine sticking to the constant whispering under his breath, the rocking back and forth, and the book collection he carried everywhere, without ever wandering into out-and-out screaming territory. But now it turned out that all the noise he should have been making his whole life hadn't just gone away – it had piled up somewhere inside him, waiting for this moment to come exploding out.

At the time, it felt like it was the noise itself that sent me tipping backwards, the back of my head jarring on the wooden floor. But it must have been him, moving so quickly I didn't have time to notice, because the next thing I can picture clearly is Hector's face, all red and puffy, blotting out the light of the chandelier above me. He was everywhere at once, kneeling on top of me, screaming through clenched teeth, his fingers jamming into my eyes and nose and mouth, clawing and scratching in rage. My lungs deflated and my ribs splintered under his weight.

I might also remember Foni, first as a muffled shout underneath that constant scream, then as a pair of hands appearing behind Hector, wrenching him off me. And maybe Mum as well, upside-down, standing in the black doorway, both hands over her mouth. Mum told me later that I'd fainted by then, that I'd had both eyes closed by the time they'd come into the room, and I didn't wake up until Foni had Hector sobbing in one corner and Mum had propped me upright. Other parts of the memory are confused as well, like whether anyone tried to say anything to each other, or whether Mum and I just upped and left, leaving the River People huddled in the corner of the library. I have a memory of Hector's voice going "Sorry! Sorry! Sorry!" over and over again like a jammed photocopier, but that sound isn't attached to anything in particular. It just drifts there, like a fragment of a dream. It could belong here, but it could belong to hundreds of other moments as well, just like the image I have of Hector's wet, panicking face folding in on itself with guilt and horror.

All I know for sure is that I never had to visit the River People again.

FOURTEEN

BEAUTIFUL MAN

He was waiting for her inside her office.

He looked and smelled like a cornered animal. His bony forehead glistened with nervous sweat.

"Cuttlefish is here," is all that he said.

The manager put down her bag. This was not the start to the day that she'd wanted. She hadn't even had her morning coffee yet.

"What? Have you called the police?"

"No. We can't do that yet. It's too risky."

"Pat, if there's any chance that a sorcerer has broken into this property, we've got to report it!"

The night warden shook his head. "You don't understand. He's not broken in. He *lives* here. Cuttlefish is one of our tenants."

Now the manager understood why restless fear had infected the night warden. Whatever he knew – whatever he had discovered during the last night shift – must have shaken him to his core.

"Okay," said the manager with a sympathetic smile. "Let's sit down and talk about this."

The manager's office was small but smart, laid out with the tight efficiency of an engine. It was bare except for columns of filing cabinets up against one wall, and the desk butting up against another. It only had one small window, looking out onto Browning Court's courtyard. The manager let the night warden take her single chair.

Normally, the night warden was an intimidating guy, large in every direction. He was the type of man whose bulk could equally be made up of muscle or fat, or a dangerous combination of the two. Today, he was trying to shrink. Hiding in this room that was too small to contain him, staring out the window every time a solitary figure crossed the courtyard.

"I've stayed up all night thinking about this," said the night warden. "Haven't been able to sleep."

"Isn't it your job to stay up all night?"

"I've had my suspicions for a while, of course, but last night it all came together. You know a guy called Lukianos Zopgraphos?"

"Yeah. Quiet guy. Lives on the fourth floor."

"What do you think of him?"

The manager shrugged awkwardly. "Don't know. He keeps himself to himself. Don't think I've ever talked to him."

"But you've seen him about, right? You must think *something* about him. What are your first impressions?"

"I've never seen him do anything suspicious."

"Look, this is between you and me. No need to be politically correct, or whatever. You can be honest. What do you think of him?"

It was the manager that was starting to feel trapped. Trapped by these questions, questions too big for the tiny room, filling it up until they were both drowning.

"I don't know anything about him!" she pleaded.

Of course, that wasn't quite true. The manager did know something about this particular tenant, something that was obvious at first glance. She wouldn't normally give that fact a second thought, of course, but if the night warden had seen something suspicious – well, there was no point ignoring the fact that this particular tenant was Greek.

"Fine," the night warden said. "Guess I'll be the one to say at first, then. Lukianos Zopgraphos is a very ugly man."

"*What?*"

"You don't need to keep playing deaf with me. It's what we're both thinking. Lukianos is one of the ugliest guys you've ever laid sight on. Admit it."

"Look, I don't know what you're trying to say here."

The night warden chuckled sarcastically. "Come on, Fehime. Just answer this one simple question. Do you think Lukianos Zopgraphos is an ugly man? Yes or no?"

Desperate to change the subject, the manager said, "I thought you were trying to tell me that Lukianos is Cuttlefish. What's that got to do with it?"

"Isn't it obvious? Ugly people are suspicious. Nobody trusts an ugly man unless they have no choice. So what's your opinion?"

Of course, the manager had been secretly agreeing all along. She'd always found the tenant's appearance hypnotizingly monstrous. He had a face like a car crash, all pockmarked greasy skin. She remembered how uneasy she felt, the one time they'd ever spoken; when she'd brought him into her office to sign some paperwork. As if his ugliness were unhygienic, as if it would rub off onto the pen he'd borrowed. She had to open a window after he left to clear the stuffy room of his traces. But none of this, she knew how to say out loud without sounding insane.

"I don't want to answer that question, okay? It doesn't seem right."

The night warden smirked. "You know I'm right, but you don't want to admit it. I'm sorry I'm upsetting you, Fehime, but this is a life in death situation. We can't afford to ignore these kinds of suspicions just because they might offend someone."

"What suspicions? What's behind all this?"

The night warden patted a parcel on the manager's desk. "This arrived for him late yesterday evening. Would you like to guess what's inside?"

"Pat, have you opened a resident's post? That's completely illegal!"

"Yeah, I opened his post, all right? When you're dealing with a man as ugly as Lukianos, you have to bend the rules a little. And it's just as well as I did. Look!"

The night warden tugged at one end of the parcel, allowing a hardback book to slide out. He used the manager's ruler to flip the cover open. Under the title, *The Key of Solomon*, was a symbol of a flaming torch.

"It's one of the books he's stolen," the night warden explained. "A grimoire. A book of magic. Don't touch it! Don't even go near it! A book like this could have all kinds of deadly spells woven into it. The people who make these kinds of things are dangerous criminals."

"I still think you shouldn't have opened his post. But you're right. This looks serious."

"Yeah. We need to get into his apartment straight away. Find the other books he's stolen. Then we'll know it's him for sure."

"We can't do that, Pat! We should turn this book into the police, and let them decide what to do."

"What? Cuttlefish is a mimetic. If the police show up, he'll just transform that ugly face of his into someone else's and disappear without a trace. No. It's down to us. We need to investigate him right now."

"That's too dangerous."

"You think I'm afraid? Of a man as ugly as Lukianos Zopgraphos?" The night warden launched a defiant belly laugh and stood up decisively. "No. I'm going up there. I'd have gone there straightaway, except his apartment key was missing from your set."

"Really? That's not right." The manager felt strangely attacked, like the night warden was criticising her key management system. She was incredibly careful, loaning out the office's spare keys only under the strictest conditions, and they never went missing.

The manager dialled a number into a safebox hanging on the wall. Inside hung a set of keys for every apartment in the building. With a quick glance at the tenant database, she found the tenant's room keys, safe and sound.

"No, they're not missing. They're right here!" she said triumphantly.

"Good. It's time to get some answers." The night warden snatched the keys out of the manager's hands and strode out of her office without looking back. The manager had no choice but to follow him. He stayed three steps ahead of her as they crossed the courtyard and climbed four flights of stairs.

A strange smell hung in this corridor. It seemed to seep out of the old carpet and the decaying walls. The forest fresh scent of the carpet cleaner was draped over it like icing on a turd.

"For the last time, we shouldn't be doing this," the manager hissed as they stood outside the tenant's door.

"He's not home right now. This might be the best chance we get," the night warden said firmly, as he turned the key in the lock.

The stench from the apartment crashed over them the moment the door was open. The miasma of a thousand forgotten takeaway containers, piled up at the sides of the room and left to fester. The manager gagged and drew back. But the night warden had already plunged in.

Just like the manager's office, and indeed every room in this building, the tenant's apartment was small. Suffocatingly small. But while most residents dealt with this by using their space as neatly and efficiently as possible, this tenant had clearly given up many months ago and settled for living in a garbage compactor. Dirty crockery spilled over every surface in the galley kitchen. Old newspapers and cardboard boxes were strewn across the living room floor. You could tell at a glance exactly how this tenant spent his time, from the select few spaces that had been left clear. A single space on the sofa. A narrow path connecting that seat to the bedroom door, the bathroom door, and the exit. And the coffee table, which was bare except for a careful array of items.

"My gods," said the night warden, in unison with the manager's thoughts.

In the corner of the table was a crystal ball. Just below it was a book, opened to a diagram of concentric circles, linked into a hexagonal web and marked with sinister runes. Next to it was a piece of papyrus with the same diagram daubed onto it in what could only be lamb's blood. And lying across the parchment, an extra strut to complete the picture, was a slender branch, stripped of its bark.

A wand.

But the night warden seemed less interested in this unholy weapon than in the book which had helped its creation. *Petit Albert.* He turned to the front page and nodded grimly. "Knew it. This is a Lyceum book. Cuttlefish is here, no doubt about it."

The manager picked up the crystal ball and stared, entranced, at the light refracting through its depths. "You were right," she said.

"You shouldn't be in here."

The manager's blood turned to stone. The words had come from the doorway to the bedroom. Standing the darkness was a rat-faced man in a stained dressing gown. His expression was a mixture of shock, fear, and hatred. But his voice was terrifyingly calm.

The manager hid the crystal ball behind her back, embarrassed by her snooping. But the night warden had no such shame or fear.

"Well, well, well. Good morning, Mr Zopgraphos. Or should I say…Good *Cuttlefish?*" said the night warden.

"You shouldn't be in here," said the rat-faced man again, gripping the door frame.

"You had a good run, Cuttlefish, but the game is up. I suggest you come quietly."

"It's not what you think," said the tenant, his eyes darting frantically between the two intruders. "I'm not Cuttlefish."

"Oh yeah? What are you doing with a magical weapon on the premises, then?"

"It's not a real wand. It doesn't do anything."

The night warden picked the wand up and twiddled it between his fingers. It coughed up a cloud of purple smoke. The night warden jumped in alarm. The wand interpreted this as a signal to eject a stream of silt across the coffee table.

"Not a real wand, eh?" concluded the night warden.

"I was...holding it for a friend," the tenant stammered. "All that stuff. I have no idea what it is."

"Do you think we're stupid? A man like you doesn't have friends, Mr Zopgraphos," the night warden sneered. "And that's even if we overlook the small matter of your other suspicious behaviour."

"Suspicious behaviour? What are you talking about?"

"I'm not going to mince words with you. Let's just come out and say what we're all thinking. You're an ugly man, Mr Zopgraphos. A very ugly man indeed. Even you have to admit, that makes you incredibly suspicious."

The wretched panic on the tenant's face intensified. But his voice remained strangely calm. "What do you mean?"

The night warden shot an incredulous smile at the manager. "I don't think I could make myself any clearer," he said with mock patience. "It's impossible that a man as ugly as you could have come this far in life without at least some basic awareness of his own repellent appearance. What about school? Weren't you ever bullied? You must surely have been bullied."

"I don't understand."

"Oh, really? I suppose next you'll be telling me you're not even Greek."

The manager decided she'd heard enough. "Pat, I know you're under a lot of pressure, but just listen to yourself! If you're not careful, you could end up saying something offensive." She turned to the tenant and explained, "This has nothing to do with your ethnic background."

"And everything to do with your repulsive appearance," the night warden concluded. "But you can explain to the SIDs yourself how you came to look that way, once we've shown them this evil book of yours."

The tenant stared at *Petit Albert*, lying open with its torch symbol exposed. "Of course," he whispered. "I've been so stupid."

"Yes," the night warden magnanimously agreed, "you have. But come quietly, Cuttlefish, and this doesn't have to be hard."

"Fehime, you have to go and get security!" the tenant gasped.

"My dear Cuttlefish," said the night warden, "I *am* the security. And I'm holding you here until the SID arrive."

As if in support of this plan, a small fireball erupted from the wand in the night warden's hand and exploded against the ceiling. Everyone in the room reeled back in shock.

"Can't you see? This is Cuttlefish!" the tenant pleaded, pointing at the night warden.

"Oh, so now *I'm* Cuttlefish?" laughed the night warden. "What an original comeback. But we both know which one of us is Cuttlefish, and it's you." The night warden waved the wand threateningly at the tenant. A jet of light shot past the tenant's head and hit the microwave, turning it into a deeply confused otter.

"Fehime, don't you realize what he's doing?"

"All Fehime can see is a pack of lies coming out of an ugly face," sneered the night warden. A steady stream of butterflies were emerging from the end of his wand, fluttering valiantly towards the window, and dying. "Face it, Luk, you've been cornered in a web of your own lies. Trapped like the rat you so closely resemble."

With a howl of despair, the tenant flung himself at the night warden, seizing one end of the wand before the night warden could react. Another jet of light hit the otter just as it was making good its escape, turning it back into a microwave. A different brand of microwave.

The manager would have thought that the scrawny tenant had no chance of holding his own against the burly night warden. But desperation had given the tenant a mindless ferocity which the night warden could barely resist. The two of them tussled, doing their best to land punches and kicks on the other while keeping a firm grip on the wand. With each blow, the wand blasted substance after unsavoury substance across the walls of the tiny apartment. The manager backed into the kitchen, dodging each stray attack.

The tenant clamped his teeth around the night warden's arm. The night warden gasped and let go of the wand. "It's all over for you now, Cuttlefish," the tenant hissed, backing away with his wand aimed at the night warden's throat.

There are moments in life when the fate of the world seems to hang on a split-second decision; when doors to every possible future open for a heartbeat. This was one of those moments. Spurred into action by the call of destiny itself, the manager darted up behind the tenant and swung the crystal ball overarm into his head.

A sickening crunch bounced back and forth in the tiny room.

The bloodied crystal ball tumbled to the floor.

The tenant fell into the night warden. His wand let out a final spark which changed the colour of the night warden's shirt, then fell from his hand.

The night warden clutched onto the unconscious tenant, cradling his lolling head. "What have you done, Fehime? What have you done?"

"He was going to nyx you," the manager said, clammy shock settling over her skin.

"So you responded with…with *this?* More violence?" The night warden lowered the tenant tenderly onto his sofa, pulling his feet up so they dangled over the end. "Fehime… your own tenant! A member of your own flock!"

Blood oozed through the tenant's hair and soaked into his sofa arm. The manager placed some old newspapers under his head.

"I…I panicked. He seemed dangerous."

"Why? Because he was Greek? Is that it?" The night warden drew himself up. "I've heard enough of your prejudiced bile this morning. You, of all people, should know better. And now, your prejudice may have cost the life of an innocent man."

The blood was coming thicker and faster from the tenant's head. The newspapers were already soaked through, and dripping onto the floor.

"Pat…something's wrong. We need to call an ambulance," said the manager. Her lungs filled with cold panic.

"You're too late to call an ambulance. Your crimes cannot be undone."

What had she done? She'd broken into the apartment of her own tenant and bludgeoned him to death. How could she ever explain it? How could she ever live with it?

The pentagram of blood was getting thicker, wetter. Blood blossomed across the parchment and dripped onto the floor. In response, blood pumped ever faster from the tenant's head, spreading across the carpet to meet it.

The manager drowned in misery, guilt at everything she'd seen and done. "We should never have come here," she said. "We made a terrible mistake."

"*You* made a terrible mistake," pointed out the night manager. "And this poor, beautiful man has paid the price."

Blood pooled across the floor, spreading around empty pizza boxes, under scrunched up tissues, towards the manager's feet. She couldn't breathe. "I can't. I can't!" she gasped, making a break for the door.

As she turned the handle, the door was blasted open by a wave of blood, knocking her back into the centre of the apartment. She flailed around among floating garbage, gagging and gasping, until she managed to cling to something solid which turned out to be the night warden's leg.

"Help!" she retched, her eyes screwed shut, the taste of blood in her mouth and nose.

"Your sins have caught up to you," the night warden said. "Blood to wash away blood."

The night warden let the manager fall beneath the roiling surge of blood. There was no floor to stand on, no surface to break through; just an endless suffocating darkness from which there was no escape.

FIFTEEN

PSYCHO

Mum had never been the doting kind of parent. Whenever I'd fallen ill as a kid, she'd feel my forehead and make sympathetic murmurations, then disappear for work after asking a neighbour to feed me regularly like I was a cat. Nowadays, I didn't even get that treatment, just a few snacks left in my room if I was lucky.

This time, it was different. This time, she sat me in front of the bathroom mirror and carefully put a plaster over each of my scratches. The worst one was down the side of my face. I looked like I'd got into a fight with a badger. Then she looked at the bruises blooming on my neck and pursed her lips.

"There's only a few days left until you break up from school," she said. "I think it's best for you to take them off. You won't be doing any important work now anyway, and this way you'll have from now until the end of the Christmas holidays to rest up. What do you think?"

Now, as I may have mentioned, Mum had never been the doting kind of parent. She'd also never been the type to let me take a day off school unless I was unable to climb out of bed, and even then she'd force me to try as hard as she could while she watched. So it was a bit weird that Mum was suddenly letting me take three whole days off school just because I had a couple of scratches and bruises.

"I'll be OK," I said.

Mum pulled the close-up mirror out on its arm and aimed it at the scratch on my face. "It could become infected," she said. "You might end up needing to take antibiotics. Or even getting a scar. You don't want everyone at school to see you like this, do you?"

She shouldn't have said that. I immediately worked out what was really going on.

"*You* don't want everyone at school to see me like this."

Mum's Doting Parent act died. Her I-Know-What's-Best-For-You act carried on as normal. "I just think there's no point in you spending all of tomorrow having to answer questions about what happened to you."

"Why? Because you're worried about what I'll tell people?"

Mum pretended to admire a framed oil pastel drawing of a fish that I'd done when I was four.

I pushed on. "You don't want anyone finding out what Hector did to me."

Mum effortlessly switched her plan of attack. "You know how sorry he is for what happened. If people at school see this, he could end up in even worse trouble than he already is. Just imagine how you'd be feeling if you were him."

"If I were him, I wouldn't have beaten up a girl for no reason at all," I snarled.

"Can't you show him *any* sympathy?"

"And when are you going to show *me* some sympathy? Why do you care more about Hector's feelings than about mine? All you can do is stand there and tell me I should forgive Hector straight away, that I should cover up what he's done and pretend it's not happened! Why? So that you and Foni can carry on…can carry on…"

My ribs hurt from where Hector had sat on them. The faster I breathed, the worse it got.

"I'm sorry you found out that way, Cass," said Mum. "Foni and I were going to tell you. There was just never a good moment."

"How the *hell* could you want to…you know…" I couldn't even bring myself to say the words to her. They sounded surreal in my head. Like a bad joke.

"To see Foni?" Mum asked.

I nodded.

"I know this must feel completely out of the blue for you," Mum said. "But…I've dated women before. If that's what you were wondering."

"I wasn't," I spat, although of course a bit of me was.

"Well, I can imagine the thought of me dating a woman might seem a little weird to you."

"It's not about that," I shot back, although of course a bit of it was. "It's about *her*. How could you possibly want to date such a boring–"

"She's a history professor! Maybe you don't–"

"…old–"

"Only seven years older than me, you know–"

"…crazy woman with a messed-up sorcerer for a son?"

Mum shut up at last, at least for a few seconds. The lights above the bathroom mirror made her skin look thin and delicate. I'd never noticed how big the bags under her eyes had become. Or how many grey hairs she had woven through the blondness.

"Is that really what you think?"

"I don't know. But I don't want to think about him at all. I just want him out of my life." I'd not talked to Mum like this since I was about six and having a temper tantrum. I heard my voice getting higher and higher but I couldn't stop. "I never wanted to go down there, and you forced me to. You said it would be fine. I trusted you. And Hector nearly killed me. Even if he's not a sorcerer, he's a psycho."

Mum's mouth tightened. She stared emptily over my shoulder, at another one of my masterpieces on the wall. Then she walked out of the room.

I ran after her as she was climbing the stairs to her study. "I'm going to school tomorrow, Mum. And if anyone asks what's happened to me, I'm going to tell them the truth."

The door to Mum's study clicked shut.

Hector didn't come into school the next day. Or for the rest of term. Anyone would have thought that *he* was the one who'd been hurt, who needed time to recover. But I was stronger than him. I walked into school with my head held high, not caring about the eyes following me across the playground.

Jess, Tori, and Chloë were the first to know. They were waiting for me before registration. I'd sent them a photo on Agora the night before, but judging by their faces, the reality was much more gruesome.

"Oh…my *God*, Cass," breathed Jess. "I can't believe he did that to you. You're so brave to be even coming in today."

"Does it hurt?" asked Chloë, poking the plaster on the side of my face.

I told them everything. They'd thrown endless questions at me last night, but I hadn't wanted to go into it. But now I told them everything. I explained how Hector had screamed and pinned me to the ground before I knew what was happening, how his mum had had to pull him off me. I had to leave out the fact that we'd been at his house, otherwise they'd have asked what I was doing there in the first place. So instead I said that it had happened on the way home from school.

"You're going to tell the school about this, aren't you?" said Tori after I'd finished. "Seriously, this is very disturbed behaviour. They need to know."

I didn't have to wait long. Ms Zima asked me to wait behind after registration. "As your form teacher, I am responsible for your pastoral care," she said, with a voice empty of all emotion or empathy or belief in the concept of pastoral care. "Do you mind if I ask how you got those injuries?"

Ms Zima nodded briskly as I repeated my story. "Thank you for telling me. We will need to report this to the head right away."

I had to go through the whole thing again in the head's office, as I steadily pulled my ring on and off my finger. Mrs Olufunwa's soft face got tighter and tighter as she listened. About halfway through, she put her reading glasses on with a pained expression and started taking notes on a pad of paper.

Mrs Olufunwa has the inexplicable power to make anyone fall instantly silent by raising her palm to them. It's called the Hand of God. Normally, she only deployed the Hand of God during assemblies, but as I went through what had happened, she flashed it at me to make me pause while she caught up on her notes. When I was finished, she stood up and glanced nervously out of her window.

"As it's so close to the end of term," Mrs Olufunwa said eventually, nodding to herself, "I think it's best that we review the situation over the holidays before taking any kind of action."

Mr Kaplan found me next. He popped up in the corridor, his rubber face twisting into sympathetic winces and gasps when he saw my face and neck. "Do you mind if I have a quick word, Cass?"

"She's already missed half the period," Mrs Olufunwa said on my behalf.

"Exactly! It'll be far too late to catch up now," said Mr Kaplan, winking at me.

"Very well." The head pursed her lips and retreated back into her office. Mr Kaplan led me into the nearest empty classroom and perched on the edge of a desk. I did the same, facing him.

"I heard you had a pretty nasty experience, Cass!" Mr Kaplan began delightedly. And so I told the whole story again. I was getting so tired of the whole thing that I mixed my story up, saying Hector had attacked me on Hampstead Heath, but I got the idea across.

Mr Kaplan was the first teacher who remembered to care about me. As I talked, his jovial reaction faces gave way to a serious squint. After I was done, he asked me questions. "Had you seen him at all that day?" or "How does he normally act around you?" I answered as best I could, getting more and more confused between the real parts of my story and the adjusted parts. If it weren't for his deep-set eyes staying firmly on compassionate mode, I'd have thought he was cross-examining me. He paused in his questioning, before finally asking, "Cass…what are you trying to cover up?"

His words hit me in the stomach.

"What do you mean?"

"I'm not an expert, but I can tell when someone is holding back on me. Are you trying to protect someone?"

"No!"

Mr Kaplan nodded gravely, like that was the answer he was expecting all along. "I don't mean to sound like I don't believe you. I just think there's more to this story than meets the eye. Do you have any idea what I'm getting at?"

I shook my head.

"Well, let's start with the background. You're saying that you and Hector have barely ever talked. But Hector told me that you've been to his house several times." Mr Kaplan let out a tiny shrug, as if to say that he couldn't be sure whose side of the story was true, though we both knew that the concept of lying was beyond Hector's grasp.

"That's different," I shot back. "I don't go there as his *friend*. My mum makes me go."

"Righty. And you'd rather people at school didn't know about it." Mr Kaplan didn't sound judgmental. "Well, that's neither there nor here. It's more important that we figure out *why* Hector might have done something like this. Can you remember anything – anything at all – that might have triggered what happened?"

I fiddled with my ring. "Nope. Nothing at all."

Mr Kaplan uncrossed his gangly legs and leant forward casually. "And how is your memory of the whole thing? Does any of it seem…unusual to you? Disjointed, maybe?"

"How do you mean?"

"Nothing really. If you knew what I meant… Never mind. I think I've kept you long enough, Cass, and…"

"You think he might have committed sorcery." Suddenly, one of Mum's many lessons on the subject of sorcery came back to me. *Sorcerers might try to make you forget what you've seen, leaving you with blank or jumbled bits in your memory.* And that moment *did* seem confused, more like a series of faded photographs than a video... And had I fallen down before or after he pushed me? I'd told so many slightly adjusted versions of what had happened that pinning down the truth was like trying to grab hold of an eel in a dark cave. Soon, it had wriggled into a pitch-black corner where I couldn't follow.

Mr Kaplan shook his head and lurched onto his feet. "That's not what I meant at all. I'm just looking out for you. Him. Everyone. I don't suspect anything else."

It was pretty obvious Mr Kaplan wasn't telling me the whole truth. "But what if he *has* been doing sorcery? It would explain why he's so–"

"Please, Cass. I would much rather we focused on the facts of this situation rather than any speculations that could do a lot of damage."

"Don't you think he's done enough damage already?"

"I *do* think a lot of damage has been done here, but I'm afraid of something far worse happening. I've seen what these kinds of suspicions can do to people, and it's not something I ever want to see again."

I thought I knew what Mr Kaplan was talking about. I thought he meant the way my story evolved and spread like a virus through the school, faster than I ever could have carried it, occasionally returning to me in raw and mutated forms. *Hector attacked Cass. Hector strangled Cass. Hector tried to kill Cass. Hector's a psycho.*

But all of that? It was just the beginning.

The London Press

CUTTLEFISH BEHIND BARS?

Joost Meyer

A Greek immigrant, Lukianos Zopgraphos, 24, was arrested at his home following a violent altercation with the manager of his residential building, Fehime Khouri, 31.

Ms Khouri called the police to Mr Zopgraphos's apartment in Browning Court, Lewisham, at 7:04 am yesterday morning, claiming that she had discovered Cuttlefish. When they arrived on the scene, Khouri was in atroposy and Zopgraphos was unconscious. Many magical artefacts were discovered inside the apartment. It's thought that Zopgraphos nyxed Khouri in order to cover up evidence of his magical activities, but not before Khouri or some unknown assailant had attacked Zopgraphos in self-defence.

Since then, numerous residents have stepped forward to suggest that Zopgraphos is Cuttlefish, the sorcerer responsible for a recent series of magical attacks in London. "Heard SIDs say they've finally got their guy today!!" one resident posted on Agora during yesterday's investigation. "Can't believe Cuttlefish was living here! Never trusted that guy, he was quiet but there wasn't something quite right about him," posted another.

Zopgraphos was not known to authorities at the time of his arrest, but the London Press can reveal that he has been claiming jobseeker's allowance for the past two years.

Only two weeks ago, Cuttlefish joyfully ate a blueberry muffin as he unleashed carnage in the British Library which left dozens magically injured. He then walked out with several priceless books, including a copy of Shakespeare's First Folio.

Cuttlefish, the leader of London's Lyceum, first rose to notoriety over fifteen years ago, committing a number of magically-aided assaults and robberies against fellow sorcerers. Although he was never caught, he stopped being active many years ago.

But since the British Library attack, a number of recent magically-aided robberies have been linked to Cuttlefish, suggesting his so-called disappearance might have been more short-lived than we like to imagine.

The priceless artefacts stolen by Cuttlefish have not yet been recovered. Zopgraphos denies all knowledge of their whereabouts, and despite confessing to sorcery, maintains that he is not responsible for Cuttlefish's crimes.

Neither the SID nor the British Library were available to comment.

Dear Sir / Madam;

I would like to draw your attention to a few errata in Joost Meyer's recent article, "Cuttlefish Behind Bars".

To begin with, you claim that Cuttlefish is the leader of the Lyceum, which even a rudimentary internet search should reveal isn't true. Cuttlefish is well known to be a sworn enemy of the Lyceum, and has over his decades of activity stolen many books from them.

More worryingly, you use the term "muffin" to describe a small iced cake. Use of the term "muffin" to describe such a cake is American English, which there should be no valid reason for your publication to use; the British term is "cupcake". Furthermore, Cuttlefish certainly did not "joyfully" eat it during his robbery. It was frankly oversweet, and was, if truth be told, the only unpleasant note in an otherwise pleasant afternoon for him.

Finally, I should like to point out that Cuttlefish is not in fact behind bars as you state in the headline of the article. This cannot be true, as by your own admission, Zopgraphos is 24 years old, which would make him roughly nine years old at the time of Cuttlefish's first known crime. Furthermore, I myself am Cuttlefish, and despite the best efforts of the

Sorcerer Investigation Department (SID), remain free, and at liberty to export my unique brand of evil and charisma to the world. It is I who am responsible for the various crimes you list, and who intend to continue committing them for the foreseeable future.

If you would be good enough to amend the above points in your online article, and publish a retraction in tomorrow's print edition, I feel you will have done your readership a good service.

Yours faithfully,
Cuttlefish.

SIXTEEN

THE WHOLE TRUTH

In the olden days, when school broke up for Christmas, you didn't get a chance to talk to most of your classmates over the whole holiday. You had to stay at home, huddled by the fire, with nobody but your family for company.

Horrifying.

In the Age of Agora, I barely noticed when school broke up. Every day was packed with exactly the same running jokes, the same gossip, the same kaleidoscope of friend's faces, just now they had slightly different backgrounds. If I tried to escape, I'd end up missing everything. So I was trapped, squirming, at the centre of thousand invisible but deadly sticky threads connecting everyone I'd ever met. I could see why the Internet used to be called the World Wide Web.

Most of the Hector stuff was hidden from view. It was the kind of story that stayed under the surface, gliding between one inbox and another. But every now and then, it would surface spectacularly for us all to see.

Hazza posted a Demosophia article called *List of famous London stranglers* and added **Think they've left one out! @Hector S**

He'd got 31 kudos and counting for that one.

Even guys in the years above who I'd never talked to got in on the act. One of them posted a clip from a nature show called *Earth's Most Dangerous Places*. He'd written **Still safer than being in Year 8!**

45 kudos.

He didn't tag Hector in that one. By then, Hector had deleted his Agora account. Made sense, to be honest. He never used it for anything.

Sometimes, I wished I could do the same thing. I hated being the centre of attention. Knowing that half the school was thinking about me, talking about me, keeping their invisible eyes on me, even if they never mentioned me by name. I just wanted everyone to move on and forget the whole thing. But Agora had a way of keeping gossip alive indefinitely, like a patient on life support, ready to be resuscitated next term.

I'm only bringing this all up so that there's a chance you have some sympathy when you hear what happened next.

It happened because I was alone in Jess's room. Jess's mum had sprung in without knocking and said, "Cassie, if you wouldn't mind, I need to talk to Jess for a moment."

Jess's room had been completely designed by Jess's mum before she was born. The way Jess told the story, Jess's mum had raced home after hearing from the doctor that she was going to have a baby girl, and painted everything in sight a soft shade of lilac. (Well, not personally. Jess's dad had done the actual painting.) And Jess hadn't been allowed to change anything since, not even put posters up, in case they left a mark. The only picture in the room was of an adorable cat nestling with its adorable kitten, which Jess's mum had put up.

Jess's desk was always eerily neat because Jess's mum tidied it at least once a week. Only Jess's laptop and phone cluttered up its crisp surface. A few minutes after Jess had left, a message opened on the laptop screen. Her phone buzzed at the same time.

Tori: Jessjessjess!

The message hung there for a while, then caught fire. Its ashes blew away. Tori had turned on Agora Confidential, which deleted everything the other person said after you'd opened it. You only used Confidential for conversations so private that you didn't want to leave any trace behind.

I went to shut down the window, to stop any more of Tori's messages getting deleted. But as I got there, Tori wrote something else.

Tori: So...Jason.

I stared at the name so hard that I could pick out each pixel that made it. *Jason.*

Tori: you better be there Jess...this is important.

So what would you have done? Huh? Huh?

Yeah, that's what I thought. Now stop judging.

You: what's going on?

Tori: so glad I didn't ask him out

You mean, so glad he TURNED YOU DOWN! HA HA HAAAAA! I thought to myself. It wasn't the most gracious thought that had ever stumbled into my head.

Tori: he's different to what I thought he'd be like

You: how?

Tori: so stuck-up!

I was having so much fun that I'd forgotten what a truly terrible idea it was to keep talking to Tori. I decided to step things up.

You: you didn't ask him out then?

Tori: you know what happened...but i realised he was soooo different to what I thought

Changing the subject, eh? How interesting, I thought smugly.

Tori: and when you get up close his hair is kind of greasy lol

Tori: and he has no idea how to talk to girls, it's embarrassing

That was admittedly true.

You: so what did he say?

Tori: i don't know, why do you care so much?

You: just spill, missy

I was getting into character now. I was a natural at this. I was basically a professional spy.

Tori: he mentioned cass a couple of times

Tori: you might be right about that

You: about what?

Tori: you know...about him having a thing for cass

Tori: but why are you so sure about that? I just don't get it

This was getting awkward. I wondered if I really wanted to know any more about what Jess said to Tori when I wasn't around. But I had no choice now. I just kept typing myself deeper and deeper.

You: he keeps talking to her

You: when he thinks we're not there

You: haven't you noticed?

I didn't know I had it in me, to be honest. I could never have lied to Tori's face. Seriously lied, I mean.

Tori: then why hasn't he made a move?

Tori: you know what guys are like

Tori: they just ask out the first girl who's willing to talk to them for more than 5 secs

You: maybe Jason's different

Tori: it doesn't make any sense

You: what doesn't?

Tori: i don't want to sound mean or anything

Tori: but what would he see in cass?

Tori says: i mean, come oooooon

Tori: you still there?

You have logged out.

I was done listening to Tori. I ended up sitting on the toilet in the bathroom, door locked in case someone in Jess's family found me crying. Not crying exactly – the tears were angry tears, but they felt the same running down my face.

It wasn't as if I didn't know how Tori thought. I knew. I just hadn't realised how open she was about it to Jess. And how Jess listened to her, whatever else she'd said, listened to it all and didn't tell me a word. It had always been this way. They had this bond between them that I couldn't hope to break. They'd arrived from the same junior school, sharing the same memories, going to the same Hebrew classes. And now they were trading the same stories about me and Jason back and forth every evening.

I forced the tears to stop before my eyes puffed up, and waited for my cheeks to lose their blotchiness. I crept downstairs, keeping my breaths slow. I found Jess's family sitting on high stools around the kitchen counter, which was covered with newspapers, mostly open on pages about Cuttlefish. *CUTTLEFISH BEHIND BARS?* said the top one.

"I just don't get what this has to do with us," Jess was saying.

"Of course you don't. You don't remember." Jess's mum leaned heavily over the kitchen counter. "But it wasn't that long ago that we had to deal with Cuttlefish attacks happening on our doorstep, while the SID kept trying to tell us everything was OK. Whether or not the River People had a hand in it–" She turned, saw me for the first time, blinked. "Oh. Excuse me, Cassie. I'm sure you must hear about this stuff all the time." She looked at me wistfully. "Would you like something to drink?"

"That's OK, I'll get something myself." I wasn't actually thirsty, but if you didn't accept one of Jess's mum's offers, she'd keep asking you until you did, so I knew it was best just to take a glass of water early and get it over with.

"Nonsense!" she said. "Sit yourself down. Scott?"

Jess's brother looked through his hair at us in confusion, then rolled off his stool and stared up at one of the kitchen cupboards. By then, of course, I'd already sat down with my glass.

Jess's dad made one of his rare attempts to talk to me. "Good to see you, Cassie! Sorry to keep you so long. We were just having a family talk. Boring stuff. How's school? I'm hearing a lot about your new form teacher! Bit of a battleaxe, eh?"

"School's good, thanks," I said.

"Great!" he said, rubbing a hand over his pale stubble.

"And how have *you* been?" Jess's mum continued, trying to sound concerned. But there was something in her voice that was too pointed, too eager. Her eyes kept flicking to the plaster on my face. "We heard about what Hector did to you. It must have been quite traumatic."

"Kind of," I said, fiddling with my ring.

"He's quite clearly unstable. What more proof do we need?"

"It's not like that, exactly," I mumbled.

"Is there something else going on?" Jess's mum locked onto me with an expression that was somehow both compassionate and calculating.

"What do you mean? No. There's nothing going on."

"Really? That boy has obviously taken an unhealthy interest in you," Jess's mum replied.

And then she raised her eyebrow at me.

There it was, Jess's eyebrow, somehow transplanted onto Jess's mum's face, a neatly plucked monstrosity flying at me through space and time. She knew. She knew everything. She knew about Mum and Foni. She knew about Hector and me.

I'd tried to keep my secret sewn away deep inside me. But now it was lying on the kitchen counter, quivering squelchily in the midst of Jess's family. I was attacked by blind panic. If she knew, how many other people knew? Did Chloë's parents know? Did Tori's parents know? Was Jess's mum some kind of evil mind-reading sorcerer, revealing the latest sordid goings on between Mum and Foni at her book club each month?

Four silent faces stared at me. The halogen lights hovering above the kitchen counter flattened their faces into masks of concern.

If it hadn't been for what Tori had just said to me, maybe I would have taken a step back and realised it was impossible for her to know anything. All Jess's mum had been talking about was Hector's weird behaviour towards me in school. But I didn't realize this until too late.

"It's OK, Cassie. I know that boy's put you through a lot. But you can tell us the truth. The whole truth," Jess's mum cooed, eyebrow poised and ready to swoop.

I did. I told them about Mum's visits to the River People every week, all the times I'd been subjected to Hector. The afternoons spent trapped in that old house, full of rotting books. At some point along the story I started crying again. Jess's mum was there to catch the first tear with a napkin before it had fallen. I didn't go into exactly what I'd done just before Hector tried to strangle me, or any of the stuff I'd said, but it's not like any of that really mattered, and I couldn't remember my exact words anyway. *You make me sick.*

Besides, nobody but Hector would've flipped out just because of something that someone had said, so I don't see what difference it made. What mattered is how he'd gone completely psycho afterwards. And anyway, Hector heard that kind of stuff at school all the time. You should've heard the kind of things Baz said to his face, every day. They were much worse.

Nobody spoke for a while after I'd finished. Until Jess's mum said: "Your mother? And Persephone? Well, I... Goodness. Must have been quite a shock."

"You were very sweet, to tolerate Hector for so long," Jess's dad chipped in.

But I could tell in the way they talked, and in the way Jess couldn't look me in the eye, that they were shocked by me as much as by the River People.

Somehow, I'd ended up draped over Jess's mum's shoulder, clutching at her while the other three looked on uncomfortably. She gently pulled me away from her to look me in the eye.

"Don't worry," she said. "I don't know how, but I'll find a way to fix this. You won't have to worry about the River People anymore."

Jess's mum didn't have to do anything to help. I never went back to visit the River People again. For the rest of the Christmas break, Mum went off by herself instead. Her solo trips became more and more frequent. Each time she arrived back home, she would stand in the hall, calling up to me with the latest news from Omphalos.

First time: "Hector was asking after you today. He says he's still really sorry about what happened, and he hopes you'll come and see him soon. Look, they've given us Christmas presents to put under our tree!"

Fourth time: "Wouldn't it be great to clear the air a little? The longer you leave it, the harder it'll get to move on."

Last time: "Foni and I have talked things over, and…we've decided things aren't going to work out. So you don't have to worry about spending Christmas with the Skeuopoioses anymore."

Mum was standing in the doorway of my room. Her eyes were red. I didn't know why.

I'd never seen Mum cry before.

SEVENTEEN

MAGISTRA

No sunlight reached the librarian's desk. Only a low lamp illuminated her writing, its hushed warmth replicating the days when this room was lit only by candlelight. This was always the librarian's favourite time of day. The students had just been cleared out, leaving her alone for a few short minutes before she went home too. Just her, and myriad ancient books, packed like bricks from the floor all the way to the ceiling far above her head. There was no room even for windows down the sides of the long, thin room – the only natural light came through the magnificent Gothic windows that filled the walls on either end. The evening glow streaming through them couldn't make it all the way to her. It was only able to illuminate the statues keeping an eternal watch in the centre of each window: knights in armour, their swords impaling the ground at their feet.

The ceilings were so high that not even a stepladder would be able to reach the uppermost shelf – instead, a narrow walkway hugged the edge of the room, halfway up the wall. However, nobody except the Bodleian's librarians had been allowed to climb up to that walkway, or remove any books from these shelves, in living memory. The books' main purpose now was to act as a scenic backdrop for Oxford's students, as they bashed on their laptops at the reading tables.

The librarian preferred it that way. These weren't the kind of books many people would have any business reading.

The librarian's thoughts were interrupted by an apologetic cough at one end of the room. It was one of the Bodleian's directors, silhouetted under the window just like the stone knight. Like everyone in their profession, his years of faithful stewardship had made him look as frail and fussy as the books in his care. He dressed like someone twenty years older than he was, in a shapeless cardigan that hung off his small shoulders. His forehead was permanently grooved with worry lines. But who was the librarian to criticise? She herself had settled into middle-aged plumpness ten years sooner than she'd been planning.

"There you are! Glad I caught you." The director's footsteps were absorbed into the walls of books as he approached the librarian's desk. "I've been meaning to have a word."

The director spoke like every word he said was an apology for the fact that he was speaking at all. He finished every sentence with a grimace of regret. Another symptom of working in a library, sadly, where every act of speech was a *faux pas*.

"It's about this British Library incident," he continued. "I was talking to a security guard about it. Sounds like the SIDs are quite sure it's this Cuttlefish chap who's responsible. If so, I really think we ought to start taking better precautions."

"Don't you think that what we've done already is enough?"

Since the attack on the British Library, security measures around the Bodleian had gone into overdrive. They had installed metal detectors at every entrance. There was now nowhere a tourist could walk, free from the gaze of at least one surly security guard.

As if any of that was going to stop a man with Cuttlefish's special talents. But still, the librarian didn't feel too worried about the situation.

"Margaret, you know as well as I do that even with all the new security measures in place, we're nowhere near as secure as the British Library was to begin with. To do what he did, Cuttlefish must be an exceptionally dangerous sorcerer, and if, God forbid, he decides to show his face here…"

"Yes, yes. I see where you're coming from, believe me, I do. I've been having a lot of these conversations recently. The Board of Directors have been threatening to close this whole place down! In the middle of term time! Say the name Cuttlefish, and everyone seems to lose their head. Well, *I'm* not going to lose my head. We have a duty to stay open and carry on as normal."

The director bent over the librarian's desk and lowered his voice. Even in an empty library, it was hard to break the habit of silence. "I quite understand, but I did a little research about Cuttlefish recently. All the recent atrocities, as well as the ones from a while back. It seems like the only thing he ever steals are sorcery books, specifically…"

"Specifically Daedalus books. Yes, I remember. I was working here then, too. We were all terrified he was going to show up here sooner or later. But he never did!"

"He'd never attacked a target the size of the British Library before, either. It looks like he's more dangerous now than he was ten years ago." The director glanced nervously at the statues at either end of the long room, as if he were worried they might be eavesdropping. "And we both know there are several books in this room that he could very well be interested in. I've been getting it in the neck from the rest of the Board about this."

The librarian was starting to feel claustrophobic. She left her desk and crossed into the centre of the room, just to get a bit of breathing space. "Yes, of course, but that's no reason to worry. Cuttlefish has no idea about the books in this library. If he did, he would have tried to steal them years ago."

"Still, given the current climate, I really think we ought to consider moving them somewhere more secure."

Here we go again, the librarian thought to herself. She'd stuck her neck out over this issue before, and she was fully prepared to do it again. "The Board said the same thing ten years ago. Those books don't belong here, they're putting the students and faculty at risk, blah blah blah. But I'll tell you the same thing I keep telling them: these books have sat on these shelves for hundreds of years, they *belong* to this building, and they're part of its fabric and history. Taking them out of here, in response to a load of media hype about some petty criminal, would be... Well, it would be sacrilege."

The director circled on the spot, gazing up at the booklined walls with a distinctly sceptical expression. "These are very delicate times we live in. To be honest, we've been lucky to avoid the media scandal simply for having these books here. If, say, *The People's Voice* felt like running a scoop, heads would start rolling."

"That's because barely anyone outside these walls realises what's in here. And I think it's essential that we keep it this way, for everyone's safety."

The director sighed. "It's all very well for *you* to say this. If something were to happen, it would be my head on the block, not yours." The director bent over the librarian's computer monitor. His face looked pasty and ghoulish. "So how many of these...er, these *Daedalus* books do you think are in here?"

There were 13. "I couldn't say for sure, Alfred."

The director tapped something into the librarian's keyboard. "There are 13."

"Oh, really?"

The director strode across the room and gazed at a shelf just above head height. "And it looks like they've all been kept together." He gently prised one of the volumes away from its neighbours.

"Alfred, you shouldn't be doing that. You know how fragile the books in here are. We shouldn't take them off the shelves unless it's strictly necessary."

The director opened the cover. The book in his hands rasped resentfully. "Yes. There's the symbol. I saw it online. Hard to imagine why someone would go to such lengths over such a tiny little mark, isn't it?"

As if it had heard one insult too many, the book snapped shut over the director's hand. The director gasped and let go. But it didn't fall. It retained its vice-like grip at the end of his arm.

The librarian smiled. A thrill of excitement, of fear, of pride passed through her body. After years of waiting, of wondering...

Her time had come.

"I told you you shouldn't have done that," said the librarian.

"What? What do you mean?"

"You might have been able to fool everyone else, but you didn't fool me. Not for one second. I've been waiting for you to show your face here for a very long time. And believe me, I've been ready. *Impetum furem!*"

A book dislodged itself from a high shelf and flew, with the deadly precision of a bird of prey, straight into the director's stomach. Whatever bewildered question he'd been about to utter was blown out of his lungs. He staggered backwards, speechless.

Another book came away from its shelf and collided with the back of the director's head. More soon followed, divebombing the director from every side of the room. The director tried to raise his hands to ward off the blows, but with the heavy grimoire still weighing his arm down, it was impossible.

"You probably thought this would be an easy mark, didn't you, Cuttlefish?" said the librarian as books flew past her head. "You probably thought you'd find us running round like headless chickens, unable to stop you. But what you didn't realise was that the Lyceum have stood watch here for centuries, defending their collection from the likes of you. This place is protected by far more than a few cameras. *Evigilavero, antiquos custodes!*"

"*Velis, Magistra,*" replied two deep voices in unison.

The statues at each end of the library raised their marble swords. The creamy stone shattered, revealing metal blades underneath. The pair stepped off their plinths, sending tremors through the floor, and advanced towards the centre of the room, swords held high.

The director had discovered he could swing his trapped arm around like a kind of mallet to strike away the barrage of books. But his relief didn't last long when he saw what was approaching. "What are you doing?" he wailed.

"What's the matter, Cuttlefish? Not used to fighting people who can actually fight back? You're not a true sorcerer. Just a pathetic hustler who picks on the vulnerable. It was only a matter of time before the Lyceum cut you down to size. I'm glad I get to be the one to do it."

"This is a mistake! Whoever you are, please let me go."

"It's too late for that, Cuttlefish. You should have thought twice before trying to steal from the Lyceum."

The director stumbled out of the mound of books that was already half burying him, batting away further missiles as they plummeted from the shelves. He looked from one stone knight to the other as they continued their inexorable march towards him. Bent over from the book clamped around his hand, he made a dash for the door.

"*Appareat sigillum!*" said the librarian.

A wall of red flame erupted through the carpet at the director's feet, blocking his path. He barrelled into it, screamed in pain, and fell backwards. Bits of singed cardigan fluttered away from him, revealing blistering skin down his arms.

The flames continued their journey in a perfectly straight line across the room, before turning abruptly and streaking back across the room behind the director. The flames were low to the ground, but as the director turned and limped back the way he had come, they shot up once again in front of his path, making it quite clear that he would not be getting through.

The lines of red flame burnt back and forth through the carpet, until they had completed a perfect five-pointed star with the director at its centre. Any books lying in their way were quickly reduced to ash. A circle of red flame erupted through the carpet around the edge of the pentagram.

The statues came to a halt just outside the warding flames. The barrage of books died down. The director searched frantically for a break in the flames, nursing his many bruises and burns.

"Countless generations of Lyceum members have kept watch over this place before me," said the librarian. "That's a lot of powerful sorcerers with a lot of time on their hands. The enchantments they've woven into this room are never-ending. I suggest you don't test them any further."

"Margaret, please," wailed in the director. "Don't hurt me. Please!"

"Believe me, I wish I could just kill you and be done with it," said the librarian. "But I have some questions to ask you first. *Capere intrusore!*"

"*Protinus, Magistra,*" intoned the statues in perfect unison.

Two statues stepped unopposed through the barrier of fire and raised their swords to the director's neck. He was pinned between the two gleaming blades; one false move forwards or backwards would be his last. The third statue remained behind the director, just beyond the pentagram.

"Tell me, Cuttlefish, why are you trying to reassemble the Daedalus Set?"

"Margaret, I have no idea what you're talking about. Please believe me!"

"I know how much you pride yourself on your flawless performances, but if you keep this up you're going to put me in a very bad mood. You don't want to see what that looks like."

"I don't know anything about this Daedalus business. I got talking with a security guard downstairs, who thought the books should be taken out of here. He asked me to talk to you. That's all I know!"

"So you came up here just to warn me about Cuttlefish? Please. The Lyceum have been following your attacks very closely. We know how you work by now. For all your brilliant disguises, you're disappointingly predictable."

"I was only trying to help," sobbed the director.

"Cuttlefish, you're not the first to try and bring the Daedalus Set together. And you won't be the last. But you, and everyone else who attempts it, will fail as long as the Lyceum lasts. We won't let anyone make the same mistakes as Daedalus. You're going to give us every book that you've stolen."

"I can't! I can't!"

"You don't have a choice. One way or another, you'll hand them all over. The books you stole a decade ago. All the ones you've recently taken too. *Occidere eum!*"

"*Voluptatem nostrum, Magistra,*" chanted the two statues in the pentagram, swinging their swords together with a screech of steel.

The director's head rolled off his shoulders, his final helpless plea trapped forever on his lips. His body fell backwards, coming to rest at the feet of the third statue, who nodded solemnly and stabbed it for emphasis.

"*Opus vestrum,*" said the librarian.

"*Usque ad tempus, Magistra,*" replied the two statues, turning on their heels and making the long, gravid march towards their plinths on either side of the room. The director's blood gleamed on their swords.

The burning pentagram flickered and then died, leaving its ashen shape etched into the carpet. A few books which had been dangling half off their shelves tucked themselves firmly back into position.

The librarian contemplated the headless body on the floor. It was hard to believe that this was the man that had plagued the Lyceum for almost 20 years in his insane quest to bring the Daedalus Set back together. Now, at last, the plague was over. Once he'd handed over everything he'd stolen, almost the whole Daedalus Set would be safe in the Lyceum's hands. And hand them over he would, especially after a few days, weeks, months, whatever it took to break him.

That was the moment the librarian finally lost her head.

That wasn't quite right, actually. From her point of view, it was her entire body she lost, as she tumbled, suddenly weightless, to the floor. She came to rest with one eye pressed into the carpet, and the other fixed on a pair of stone feet walking away.

"Surprisum, surprisum, Margaretum," boomed the third statue somewhere far above her, as her world slipped from view.

EIGHTEEN

UNACCEPTABLE

Mum had had other boyfriends, if you want to call them that. When I was five, I'd come downstairs to find a man with curly hair sitting at our kitchen counter.

"This is Mark from work!" Mum had said brightly. "He's a new friend of mine."

Being five, I had no idea what Mark-from-work had done to deserve a special introduction, which none of Mum's actual friends had ever received, or why Mark-from-work was suddenly spending every weekend hanging out with us like he was my dad or something. Nor did I have any idea why Mark-from-work vanished one day, never to be mentioned by Mum again.

By the time Chris-the-musician turned up on the same chair at our kitchen counter, I'd wised up a little. I was nine. I looked him up and down coolly, said "Hi Chris," then turned on my heel and left. Chris-the-musician was far cooler and more handsome than Mark-from-work had been. He had designer stubble and wire-rimmed glasses, and he wrote music for adverts and TV shows, the kind of background jingles that are designed to be completely ignored. Every now and then, we'd be walking through a shopping centre or installing a computer program and he'd tilt his head and say "One of mine!" Where Mum had her boring study full of books and folders, Chris-the-musician had an entire room of his house filled with blinking electronics, cables, computer screens, and an electric guitar which he once sang me Happy Birthday on. When he was around, Mum would get ridiculously giggly and act more like a big sister than a mother. And Chris-the-musician would always treat us the same, call us both 'ladies' and write us both silly songs and buy us both gifts. All in all, I was very sorry to see him go. And when Mum told me the news, I was furious with her. It didn't seem fair that she should get the sole decision to cut him out of both of our lives.

Chris-the-musician had even spent one Christmas with us. That was a big deal. It had only ever been the two of us before that. Mum didn't have any family on her side. I hadn't been so keen on the idea, until I'd taken the wrapping off the flashiest all-in-one speakers in existence. I'd gasped, collected myself, then looked Chris in the eye and said "This one can stay," making them both literally blush.

The Christmas after that felt kind of lonely, with just the two of us again. But the Christmas after Mum and Foni broke up felt even lonelier. It was like Mum herself wasn't even there. Her eyes kept glazing over. During dinner, she stared at every forkful of food intently before she put it in her mouth, like it was hiding a dark secret.

The rest of the Christmas holiday had the same heavy atmosphere. When she wasn't at work, Mum spent most of her time in her study. Jess wasn't allowed to go to Camden Market anymore, just in case Cuttlefish leaped out of a phone box and killed her. And Chloë had never been allowed to go to Camden Market, so there wasn't a whole lot we could do. I spent most days one of their houses, just so I could escape from mine.

I hated seeing Mum like that. But I knew it was a phase we'd have to go through before things could go back to normal.

I wasn't upset because Foni was a woman. If Mark-from-work or Chris-the-musician had been women, it wouldn't have mattered to me. It would have just seemed like part of everyday life. And if Mum had announced to me that she'd started dating a woman – *literally any other woman in the world* – I'd have been surprised, but I would have got used to it.

But Foni? She was unacceptable.

By the time term started again, all my cuts had completely healed, and it looked like everyone had forgotten about it. Hector was back, a ghost flickering periodically in the corner of my eye.

Things might have stayed that way forever if it weren't for Parents' Evening cropping up a week later, and if Mum hadn't decided to actually show up for once. Normally, she promised she'd get home from work in time. Then she'd forget all about it, and write a grovelling card for me to take to my teacher the next day. But here she was, swooping around the cafeteria with a chirpy grin on her face, doing her best impression of a Normal Parent.

All the tables had been pushed up to form a ring around the edge of the room, and each had a teacher installed behind it, talking to a family unit. It was funny how different the pupils looked. Baz, for example. I didn't even recognise him for a moment, sat up straight with a parting in his hair, not saying a word while his two ferrety parents listened sadly to Ms Zima's damning pronouncements about their son.

Mum didn't bother waiting in line to talk to Ms Zima, or any of my teachers. Like some kind of awkwardness homing missile, she spotted Hector and Foni staring past each other in the middle of the room. They were easy to spot – the crowds of jostling families found a way to part around them, like there was an invisible force field in the way.

Foni looked completely different in a black suit. No shorts, or sandals, or weird baggy overalls in sight. If this was the side of her that people normally saw, she could easily get mistaken for a normal person. Her face cracked open into a wide grin as she saw us coming. Her back clicked as she stooped down to give me a hug. She didn't succeed, of course – I flinched backwards instinctively, and it turned into an affectionate pat on my arm.

"Cassandra! Long time no see!" said Foni. "How was Christmas?" She turned to Mum and gave her a double air kiss. "It's so nice to see some friendly faces here. I was beginning to wonder if I should have stayed at home."

"Don't be ridiculous!" said Mum, kissing her right back and giving her a tight squeeze. I looked away. I guess it had been one of those "let's stay friends" kind of breakups. Ugh.

Hector was right behind his mother, but didn't try to get too close to me. As soon as he saw me, he shuffled stealthily behind Foni. It didn't work, of course – he was too wide for that. I could still see him breathing damply into Foni's jacket.

There we stood, in delighted silence, forming a broken square with our bodies. Hector looked as sick as I felt. We'd entered the force field that surrounded the

River People, and now the other family clusters were giving us a wide berth, too, as they hurried from one table to the next.

"I expect Cassandra's been getting gushing reviews from all her teachers?" said Foni, at last, with a tortured wink at me. "Always the star pupil, eh, Cassandra?"

I nodded. "Hang on, I've just seen a friend!" I said, and fled for my life. Luckily, it was true: Jason was standing in a queue for one of the teachers. His mum had got into an excited conversation with Mr Kaplan in Arabic or something.

Jason looked a little bit surprised when he saw me heading his way. Which was fair enough: we almost never talked in school. Whenever he got too close, Jess and Tori's eyebrows would swoop in on him and peck him to death, leaving nothing but bleached bones behind, awkwardly grinning at us.

But it turned it was something else that had confused him. "Is your mum friends with Foni or something?" he asked.

"Oh? No. Not really. She knows all the other parents." (Not.)

We managed to exchange maybe another couple of sentences each before I spotted Jess and Tori in my peripheral vision, circling us like moray eels. Jason smiled sheepishly and said, "Better go to the next teacher."

Tori went straight in for the kill. "Look, Cass, between you and me, I wouldn't get involved with Jason. He's kind of a creep once you get to know him. Everyone knows it."

I didn't say anything. I just looked at her levelly. I could see the words she'd said the other night, scrolling over her face.

what would he see in cass?

The weird thing was, I used to be scared of her. Scared of Tori, just a little bit, for being so tall and well-conditioned. For her uncanny ability to crush boys with a single glance. For having the worldly wisdom of a seventeen-year-old.

But it had taken until now for me to see what I should have worked out ages ago. Tori was, despite everything she said, just another human being who didn't really know anything. She had no clue about relationships. And one thing she *definitely* didn't know about was me and Jason.

I'd had enough.

"We're not going out," I said.

Tori took a step back. "You know, that's so funny. Jason said the exact same thing. He said you weren't going out either."

"Why's that *funny*? Why would he say we're going out when we're clearly *not* going out in any way shape or form whatsoever?"

"OK, Cass, I hate to break it to you, but you two *are* going out. The entire school knows it. So there's no point in you two being in denial anymore. You may as well just accept it and move on."

Argh! She was still doing it. For a tiny second there, I was actually, like, *Maybe she's right. Maybe we are going out.* I had to actually shake myself to tell myself that she had no clue what she was talking about.

"This is stupid. Jason and I even talked about this. He said–"

"Oh my God, you *actually* talked about this?"

"There's a lot going on that you don't understand. OK?"

Tori smirked. "I'm sure there is." Then she flounced away.

I had about five seconds to myself before Jess tried to have a pop at me. Though it turned out I'd misjudged her. She wasn't here to talk about Jason. She was here for a Serious Talk.

"Cass," she whispered, like she was telling me she had six months to live, "I've never had a boyfriend."

I came very, very close to saying *Well, duh*... . If Jess had had a boyfriend, or even talked to a boy ever, the first thing she'd have done is come screaming about it to Tori and me.

"I don't know what's wrong with me. Am I physically repulsive, or something?"

"Jess. You're *way* prettier than me, it's not even *funny*. You even have boobs! What more do you want in life?"

"But you have Jason–"

So, remember when I said I'd misjudged her? Lies. I'd got it exactly right.

"OK, listen to me very carefully–"

"I know what you're going to say, you're going to be all like *I'm not going out with Jason, he just happens to be my new best friend who just happens to be a boy and why on earth would you think a crazy thought like that for*, and I don't care. It doesn't matter whether it's *official* or not. The point is that Jason's obviously into you more than anyone's been into anyone else in *history*. So you could go out with him if you wanted to and that's pretty much the same thing."

Foni's voice broke in on me, uninvited. "...as long as you're making sure to take some time for yourself, Helen. You'll burn out!"

I changed channels back to Jess, who was fractionally more interesting. "You know how jealous Tori is?" she was saying. "I didn't know Tori was *capable* of being jealous. I'd never have thought there'd be anything in the world for Tori to be jealous *of.* I mean, if I were that tall and ravishing…"

It was time to stop talking about Tori. "Is there anyone you even seriously want to go out with?" I said.

Jess thought for a bit. In the background, we heard Whittington School's Official Hottest Teacher, Mr Milliner, trying to console Baz's parents that their son had some redeeming features. Then Jess shook her head slowly. "I don't know…I think Hazza might like me. He's always staring at me in Maths."

"Yeah, he stares at everyone. You know why? Because he's a massive creep. If you so much as talk to Hazza, I will find you and mercy kill you. As a friend, I won't stand by and let that happen. I'd rather become cat ladies together."

"You're right. I don't know what came over me," said Jess, gripping my arm so tightly that her hand went white and my arm went whiter. "We'll be just fine. Just you and me, together, with cats. We don't need Tori's charisma or perfect skin. We'll be just fine."

I spotted Chloë in the distance and I ran at her like I was fleeing a nuclear explosion in an underground space mining facility.

"Are those two getting hormonally challenged again?" she said, flashing me her grandma-dimples.

And I suddenly remembered why I was still such close friends with Chloë, after all these years. She was the only sane person I'd ever met.

"Cassie!" Jess's mum said. "How are you holding up?" She looked at my face and neck with clucking concern. "Healed up OK, I see."

What was she talking about? I hadn't had any bruises for *ages*.

Jess's mum was at the top of her game: dark lipstick, sharp-angled glasses, clipboard, purple jacket to match Whittington's colours, firm handshake poised and ready to go. It's not like she needed to be there to talk to Jess's teachers – she was the head of the PTA, and had a direct line to the head's office. "I *must* talk to your mother before she slips away!" she continued. "In fact, is now a good time?"

Jess's mum took my forearm and guided me gently back into the jaws of Mum and Foni's awkward conversation.

"Helen!" said Jess's mum. "How *are* you? I'm so sorry I missed you on the way in. I was caught up in conversation, you know how it is!"

Mum turned around. "Hello! How are you, ah–"

So this was the mother of her daughter's best friend, the woman who treated me like a second daughter – they were basically inlaws – and Mum still couldn't remember her name. She didn't even have the energy to look embarrassed about it.

"Anne!" Jess's mum said. "It's Anne. I was wondering if I could have a quick word with you?"

"Of course," said Mum. "Foni, I'll just be a minute if that's OK–"

But Foni wasn't there. Foni had sidled away, one hand on Hector's back.

"How are you? Not too busy, I hope?" said Jess's mum with a sigh of relief.

"Busy? No, no," Mum said, staring anxiously at her phone.

"Would you mind taking a look at this?" Jess's mum held a piece of paper directly over Mum's phone screen. It said:

CONCERNS ABOUT THE RISK OF UPCOMING SCHOOL TRIPS

- *Proposed by: Anne Covley*
- *Seconded by: Jocelyn Fletcher*

Whittington parents would like to cancel school trips indefinitely. In light of recent terrorist attacks at both the British Library in London and the Bodleian Library in Oxford, we feel it's unacceptable to take pupils to tourist sites that might also be targeted, until such a time as the threat from Cuttlefish, the Lyceum, or other terrorist groups is reduced.

"I'd prefer it if you didn't call them terrorist attacks," said DCI Helen Drake, her words smoothly polished and neatly ordered. "There's no evidence of any ideological motivation behind the incidents."

"But you know what twisted views sorcerers hold. Wanting to bring back Ancient Greek law."

"It's only a minority of sorcerers who think that."

"Let's not split hairs. Whatever his motivation, Cuttlefish is a danger to our children. It's just not safe for them to be visiting central London right now."

"I quite understand, Alice," said DCI Helen Drake. "But I can assure you that this is possibly the safest time to be going on a school trip. Security has been tightened up at every tourist attraction in the UK. I know these seem like dangerous times, but we can't just barricade ourselves away until they pass."

Jess's mum's eyes lit up, as if the word 'barricade' had given her a new idea. "I'd have thought someone in your position would better understand the threat that sorcery poses our children."

"So would I." There was something else in DCI Helen Drake's voice now. It was a velvet curtain drawn in front of a brick wall. "And I think we should be grateful that Whittington is committed to providing a rich education to our children, and not trying to limit the good work they do."

Jess's mum smiled. "In that case, perhaps you'd consider supporting this motion?" She pulled another piece of paper off her clipboard and handed it to Mum.

CONCERNS ABOUT THE SPECIAL EDUCATIONAL NEEDS PROVISION AT WHITTINGTON SCHOOL

- *Proposed by: Anne Covley*
- *Seconded by: Jocelyn Fletcher*

Whittington parents are concerned that the provision for special educational needs is not high enough. Some pupils are struggling to adapt to a group learning environment, and falling behind as a result. This is having an unacceptable effect on the more high-achieving pupils, who aren't getting the attention they need.

If Whittington lacks the resources to provide this level of special educational care, we would like to suggest that certain pupils would do much better if they were directed to a specialist school.

Jess's mum waggled a pen enticingly at the bottom of the page, below a list of other parents' signatures.

"I'm sorry, Abby," said Mum firmly. "I can't possibly support this motion."

"Why not? All we're suggesting is that Whittington cater to its pupils' individual needs."

"By evicting Hector Skeuopoios."

Jess's mum breathed heavily at Mum. Mum breathed back. I decided it was time for me to leave before the breathing continued.

"I'm not trying to *evict* him!" Jess's mum snapped. "I'm trying to help him. He's one of several pupils who I think would benefit hugely from more individual attention, or if not–"

"Expulsion?"

"Every pupil at Whittington had a right to go to school without fear. Without this threat hanging over them."

"What exactly do you think Hector is capable of? He's a thirteen-year-old boy." Mum was all bricks now. "You think he's going to come into school one day and start shooting fireballs down the corridors?"

"You know, Helen, for a long time I wondered why you couldn't see things the way the rest of us could. But now I'm beginning to wonder whether I've seen the whole picture. That hug you gave Persephone seemed a little more than friendly."

"What on earth are you talking about?" Mum's wall was crumbling. Her face was pale, and pulled tight over her skull.

"I'm not judging you, Helen. You can date whoever you want, as far as I'm concerned. But I'm simply asking you to question your own judgement on this matter. Perhaps it's become clouded by…personal feelings."

For once, it looked like Mum didn't know how to reply. Her mouth opened and closed a few times, before she said, "I have no idea what you're trying to say."

I decided it was definitely time to leave. I made a stealthy step backwards. But I was too late. Mum's eyes flicked in my direction. I had my guilt written all over my face. She knew that I'd told Jess's mum everything.

Mum gave up trying to find a comeback. "Time to say hi to your teachers, right, Cass?" she said, with a horribly bright smile. "Well, it was lovely bumping into you, Ashley. Best of luck with the petitions."

"Thank you, Helen."

Jess's mum smiled, the corners of her mouth creasing tightly. She turned without a word to another set of parents (Hazza's parents, now that you ask) with a little scream of delight. Mum marched away, almost dragging me behind her. But Jess's mum wasn't quite finished with us. She called across the cafeteria, "Just so you know, I'll be telling the head what I and many other parents feel about the Skewpoises, irregardless. And I'm going to get something done about them before something terrible happens."

Before something terrible happens.

Sounds full of doom, doesn't it? To be honest, I'm not even sure that's what she said. Maybe she said something much less extreme – *this doesn't feel right* or *it's only a matter of time* – and my hindsight has exaggerated it into a full-blown apocalyptic prophecy. Because she was right.

Jess's mum was right about everything.

THE LYCEUM: A COCKROACH THAT CAN'T BE CRUSHED

Freya Hardlin

It sounds like something out of a far-fetched fantasy novel, doesn't it? A mysterious fanatical cult which is plotting the downfall of civilisation as we know it. But it's not. It's just the reality of 21st century Britain. A country infested by a dark and deadly force: the Lyceum.

Who are the Lyceum? A sorcerers' cabal? An organized crime syndicate? A terrorist network? They deserve all of these labels, and much worse. The Lyceum are at the centre of all the organised sorcery in Britain. Hoarding collections of sorcery books in dozens of secret locations. Distributing magical artefacts around the country. Corrupting our children with pro-sorcery propaganda. Sowing chaos and terror everywhere their influence lands.

This is hardly news. The UK has had a Lyceum problem for as long as it's existed. Even Samuel Pepys wrote about them in his diaries, comparing them to the plague-carrying rats that caused so much death and devastation in his time. So many times, we've tried to stamp them out or drive them away. But just like rats, all they ever do is scurry underground where we can't follow them, breed new converts to their twisted cause, then spring up again in ever greater numbers.

Today, we might look back at the Inquisition's sorcerer trials and burnings as barbaric. But at least they got the job done. Instead of the Inquisition, all we have nowadays is the Sorcery Investigation Department, a toothless department of the police force with no real way to tackle the Lyceum menace. Their so called "War on Sorcery" declared fifteen years ago was a national joke from the start.

For decades now, the Lyceum been a constantly bubbling cauldron of menace, blighting UK cities with daily magical violence. In fact, experts agree that the modern-day Lyceum are stronger at the present moment than they have been at any point in history. Why so? Well – though you can scarcely say it nowadays without being mobbed by the PC brigade – it's thanks to the arrival on our shores of huge numbers of immigrant populations, in particular London's Greek communities.

Why should this be such a hard thing to say? The Lyceum claim to have been founded by the Greek sorcerer Aristotle over 2000 years ago. Its adherents not only practise sorcery, but campaign through terror and propaganda for the legalization of all magic. They live by the barbaric traditions of Ancient Greece, a world where sorcery was freely and openly practiced. And given half the chance, they'd impose these traditions on the rest of us too.

I'm not saying that these ideas don't have a healthy following among native Brits too. They do. And they've been around for hundreds of years, long before the era of multiculturalism. I'm just saying it's little wonder that new recruits to this cabal are drawn especially from Greek communities. It's also little wonder that Greek communities have propped it up and provided it with protection from the SID ever since.

Of course, this isn't the attitude taken by Greek communities as a whole, which are for the most part moderate and have made good efforts to integrate with the rest of society. It's only one extreme element – hardline atheists – that allow pro-sorcery views to foment. But they can no longer turn a blind eye to the more radical voices in their society. Nor can the SID, who need to be able to investigate these communities properly, without fear of being branded a racist institution. How much longer can we afford to wait before the rot spreads?

274 Comments

pithAgora   *Less than 1 minute ago • Reply*

'barbaric traditions of ancient greece' are you joking? The greeks gave us democracy, liberalism, rule of law...you couldn't be writing this article if it weren't for their 'barbaric traditions'. Absolutely appalling journalism.

GorgiasGrrl   *1 minute ago • Reply*

Finally!!! Someone with common sense. I hope the
SID are reding this, and actually start taking the
problem seriosly.

Xena_Fun   *4 minutes ago • Reply*

anyone else think it's ironic that cuttlefish been doing
the job that the sid have been failing to do for years?
at least SOMEONES clearing our streets of lowlifes
and crimnals who have kept us living ni fear for years.

Sophie Cleese   *2 minutes ago • Reply*

@Xeno4n Yup. the fact that its taken another
sorcorer to do the job the SID cant says alot
about the so-called War on Sorcery doesnt it

Demo.Sneeze   *16 minutes ago • Reply*

the problem isn't greeks. It's atheists. Just look at the
evidence: - being an atheist is a choice, being Greek
isn't – it's impossible to be a sorcerer if you're
religious – most greeks are orthodox Christians. QED.

Pl8O   *22 minutes ago* • *Reply*

Exactly! @demo.sneeze Fact:... all sorcerers are
atheists... EVERY religion says sorcery is evil...
Natinal database of atheists = problem solved. If
they have nothing to hide they have nothing to
fear...

EpiK-Kurious   *27 minutes ago* • *Reply*

can someoen remind me y we stoped burning
w***hes at the stake? It worked dindt it?

Hippo Critical   *31 minutes ago* • *Reply*

[This comment has been moderated]

NINETEEN

SHOW'S OVER

Before I tell you how Hector got suspended, you have to understand a thing or two about football in Whittington School. If for some insane reason you wanted to play football during break, the only thing you were allowed to use were these yellow foam Balls of Horror that had been especially designed to absorb everything they touched – earth, wet leaves, dog poo – as they rolled across the ground. Every kick that you gave them, they'd get browner and soggier until they just glued themselves to the tarmac and refused to budge.

This meant that football worked differently in Whittington School than it did everywhere else. There were meant to be two teams, and two goals, and all the rest of it, but what actually happened is that all the players would take turns taking a running kick at the Ball of Horror, making it squelch morosely across the ground, until eventually it gave up the will to live and exploded, sending horrific quivering strips of moist brown sludge in every direction. Once that stuff touched you, it could only be washed out with holy water.

There were no winners.

Needless to say, none of my friends ever tried to play football. The only people who did were Baz, Schmaz, and O'Flaz, who lived for the sensation of the Ball of Horror smearing its juices all over them.

I suppose you need to know how to tell Baz's friends apart for this sorry saga to make sense. So here goes. Yaz was short for Yazid Alfour. He had long, greasy hair and thought he was cool. Hazza was short for Harry Fletcher. He had a long, greasy face and thought he was hot. Baz was short for Baskaran Nadkarni. He had a long, greasy everything and thought he was funny. And then there was Jason Kasikidis, of course. The only one out of all of them that was actually good at football, and the only one who treated the Ball of Horror with appropriate levels of disgust, shrivelling up his lips every time he had to take a shot.

Despite the game having no discernible rules, every now and then someone would take a penalty shot. And it would normally be Jason who took it, being the one with Actual Skills. That's how the nightmare began.

ACTIVITY CORNER!

Here's a scene depicting the intended trajectory of the Ball of Horror. Please add the actual trajectory of the Ball of Horror.

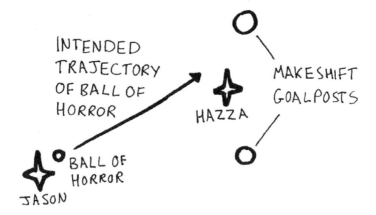

Full marks. Well done. Everyone should have seen it coming, especially as Hector's face was almost bigger than the goal anyway. But nobody did – especially not Hector, who just sat there not moving, his face wet and brown and bigger than ever before.

Jason was mortified. "I'm so sorry, man! Are you OK?"

A beat, then Baz, Yaz, and Hazza burst out laughing, making what Jason said sound like the setup to a particularly sarcastic joke. "Guys, shut up!" said Jason frantically, but nobody listened.

I was curled up on a bench with my friends at the time. I didn't see the moment of impact. By the time I'd looked over to see what was going on, the football players were leaning on each other to stop themselves falling over with laughter. Jason had taken a couple of steps closer to Hector, his hands held up in a sign of peace. But none of this was making any difference to Hector himself, who was staring down at the book he'd been reading. It had been just as unlucky as Hector. The open pages were flecked with mud. Hector's face quivered slightly, and a large brown chunk of mud slid off his forehead and landed with a squelch on the book.

Hector stood up, leaning forward on his hands. "I'm warning you," he mumbled.

Baz, Yaz, and Hazza stopped laughing abruptly. "*What?*" scoffed Baz.

"I said, I'm warning you," Hector mumbled, more quietly.

Baz's face lit up with glee, just like that time Hector peed himself. "Warning us about what? Wait, please don't…"

Baz's face fell sharply. His hands clamped themselves around his throat. His tongue fell out of his mouth, along with a strangled gasp.

I looked back at Hector. His eyes were narrowed at Baz. His mouth was twitching.

The same thing happened to Yaz and Hazza. Yaz leant over, his eyes popping, and choked out a yell. Hazza sank slowly to his knees, his upper half convulsing. "No! Get off me!" he shrieked, in a high-pitched voice.

My friends and I exchanged worried looks.

"He's doing it again!" said Jess, standing up.

Hector's deathly stare was filled with nameless pain as he watched Baz, Yaz, and Hazza becoming more choked, more frantic, their yelps and pleas piling on top of each other.

"We should get someone," said Tori.

But by the time we'd processed what was happening, it was over.

"Jesus, guys, can you give him a break for *one second*?" said Jason.

The three others dropped their performance and fell back into hysterical laughter.

Baz raised his hands for silence. Yaz and Hazza obediently stopped laughing. Then Baz said, "Seriously though, Hector. Please don't strangle me. I'm too young to die."

The three of them carried on laughing right where they'd left off. Hazza snuck a glance at me and nodded, like I should be joining in on this, like I was part of the joke.

Which of course I was.

Tori retched. "That was supposed to be *funny?* I can't believe how insensitive they're being."

"To who?" Chloë asked.

"To Cass, of course! Cass is still *traumatized* by what happened to her. Aren't you?"

Was I traumatized? I couldn't tell. I didn't know what being traumatized felt like.

"I suppose so," I said.

Jason walked over to Hector's picnic bench. "Look, just ignore them, Hector. They're jerks. All my friends are jerks, I know. But I really didn't mean to hit you, and I'm so sorry–"

That was when Hector started screaming.

I was prepared for it. The others weren't. The football players stopped laughing and gaped at the enormous noise coming out of that tiny mouth. Everyone who hadn't so far been paying attention flocked from all over the playground to see what was happening.

Hector climbed up onto the picnic table and launched a flying kick straight into the middle of Jason's chest. The two of them landed on top of each other. Hector punched Jason's head into the brick playground floor, then stood up, leaving Jason spread-eagled beneath him.

Baz, Yaz, and Hazza wiped their gleeful expressions off their faces as Hector approached them. But they were too late to run.

Hector charged at Baz, who was standing in the middle. He leaped up and wrapped his arms and legs tightly around Baz's torso, like some kind of demonic koala. The two of them keeled frantically from side to side like this, until Baz clawed him off and threw him to the ground. But Hector had grabbed hold of the front of his shirt, which ripped straight up the back and came away in Hector's hands.

It was like watching a cartoon when someone realises there's no ground beneath them, then starts to fall. Baz looked down at his bare torso, then up at the massive audience, then tried to snatch his ripped shirt back.

But Hector wasn't messing around. Not today. He dropped Baz's shirt and went straight for his nipples with truly deadly accuracy. His eyes lit up with fiery vengeance as he twisted remorselessly.

Yaz came up behind Hector and tried to pull him off by his armpits. But Hector held fast to Baz's nipples, making him scream out in fresh agony. Then Hector reached over his head, twisted his hands into Yaz's long hair, and wrenched them both to the ground.

Both Baz and Yaz began sobbing, for their own completely different reasons, leaving Hector stood up in the centre of the football pitch, looking like a tiny, poo-covered angel of death. Then – and I'm not sure what exactly was going on here, all I can tell you is what it looked like from the bench – he turned to Hazza, who'd just been standing there doing nothing at all, grabbed hold of his face and began to squeeze for all he was worth. It was like he was trying to crush his skull completely. Hazza grabbed Hector's face in retaliation. Both of them cried out, either in pain or war-rage. Hector only broke the deadlock picking up Hazza *by the head* and throwing him across the playground.

OK, maybe Hector didn't actually pick him up. But somehow, Hazza stumbled backwards, tripped over Baz, and landed – hard – on Yaz' stomach.

Needless to say, by now the entire population of the world had gathered in the playground to watch. But Hector didn't care about the attention. He was prepared to exact his sticky brown vengeance on every last one of us, if we gave him an excuse.

The teachers exchanged looks, none of them daring to approach Hector, who was still pawing at the ground and snorting. I could see a faint brown steam rising from his heaving body. In the end, nobody did anything: we just watched quietly as Hector the Relentless shrunk, slowly, back into Hector, That Guy Who Nobody Cared About. His shoulders slumped, his eyes rolled back to the ground, and he looked more miserable and terrified than he'd done ever before.

Only the head herself, Mrs Olufunwa, was brave enough to sail into the centre of the carnage, the Hand of

God held aloft to silence everyone in her path. She had a silk scarf draped regally across her plump body. "OK. Show's over. Please clear the area." The teachers snapped into life and swatted us all away from the battle arena, leaving behind Hector and his four innocent victims.

Over by the picnic bench, Jason sat up, dazed. Mr Milliner was standing between him and the crowds, warding us back with his arms and his smile, which remained debonair even in these dark times. I snuck round him and hurried over. "Are you OK?"

"Fine," Jason muttered, rubbing the back of his head. "How's Hector?"

"Hector? Fine, I think. It's the others you should be worried about."

"They deserve much worse," Jason said, taking in the scene of destruction. "Ever since what Hector did to you, they've not let a single day go by without reminding him. I'm not taking his side or anything, what he did was terrible, it's just…what's the point in pretending to strangle yourself every time he walks past? I don't get why they have to act like that."

As Jason talked, I helped him take a seat on the picnic bench. Then my attention was snatched away by Hector's pebbledashed book, still lying open.

It was a dictionary. Each page had two dense columns of text marching down them. I blinked a couple of times, thinking there must be something wrong with my sight. But no – it was the book's writing that was going funny, not me. The words in bold, the words being defined, were soft and rounded, like they'd been left out in the sun too long.

"It's Ancient Greek," said Jason, scanning the page.

"How do you know that?"

Jason looked at me quizzically. "Speaking Greek kind of helps."

I couldn't believe it, but the evidence was right there in front of me. How did Hector like to spend his breaks? By *reading* a *dictionary*. Not just any dictionary, but a dictionary of *Ancient Greek*. Just when you thought Hector couldn't get any more Hector, he found a way.

I glanced around the playground. The teachers were still forming a human shield around the scene of the carnage. Tori, Jess, and Chloë were still on the park bench, staring pointedly as far away from us as possible.

"Come on. Not even Hector reads dictionaries just for fun," I said, eyeing up his bag. Lo and behold, it contained another dark, heavy book. I pulled it out. It was even more exciting than a dictionary of Ancient Greek, if you can imagine such a thing. Solid blocks of Greek words filled every page.

"What does it say?" I asked.

"I can only speak actual Greek. I can't read this."

"What, and Hector can?"

Jason flicked through some of the pages, each filled with a dense block of the same squishy letters. "I suppose that's what the dictionary's for."

"This is *insane.* Why can't he just get a translation?"

I heard a shriek and looked up. Hector had spotted us. His jaw dangled in fear. His face was streaked with muddy tears. He scrambled to his feet. The head stopped him from coming any closer, and approached us instead. "Everything alright here?"

"Hector has sorcery books in his bag," I blurted out. "Look."

Mrs Olufunwa glanced over the open books on the picnic bench. Her lips quivered and smacked together.

"Well, we don't know *that,*" Jason clarified. "But I think these are written in Ancient Greek."

Jason was right. *He* didn't know they were sorcery books. But that's because *he* hadn't seen the giant underground library in Hector's house. I'd never bothered to open one of the books on its shelves. But it should have been obvious to me that you didn't build a library with a hidden door unless the books you were keeping inside were…

Grimoires.

"Why don't the two of you come with me?" she said at last.

The three of us packed Hector's books into his bag and took it inside. I tried not to notice Hector imploding with panic as we left.

Mr Kaplan put a comforting hand on Hector's shoulder then ran to catch up with us. "How have the two of you been?" he asked, with a wink. Great. Even the teachers were in on Tori and Jess's gossip.

We all piled into the head's office. Jason and I took the two chairs facing the head's desk, leaving Mr Kaplan to lean against the wall behind us. A couple of men who I didn't recognize, wearing black suits and black frowns, stood behind Mrs Olufunwa as she sat behind her desk. We placed the two books in front of her. Exhibit A. Exhibit B.

"Well," said Mrs Olufunwa. "Well, well, well."

She spoke with enough gravelly authority to mask the fact that she didn't know what to say. She wound her scarf over her shoulder and gazed imperiously around the room.

"I know that this reflects very badly on Hector," Mr Kaplan burst in, "especially in light of…everything. But I should say that he's been making a lot of progress recently, and we can't just throw that all away now. If we could consider showing him leniency, just this once–"

"Let's not get into this discussion immediately," said Mrs Olufunwa, holding up the Hand of God. I'd never have guessed she gave other teachers the Hand of God treatment too. "We need a clear picture of what happened first. Children, if you wouldn't mind going over what happened? And what you discovered?"

We said all we had to say. It didn't take long. While we were talking, one of the blacksuited men took notes on a laptop while Mr Kaplan glanced over the books hastily. Mrs Olufunwa nodded at us when we were finished. "Thank you. Is there anything you'd like to add?"

Jason and I looked at each other, wondering if this was a trick question, then shook our heads in unison.

"Good. In that case, could you find your way to your next classes? We'll work out what to do from here. Thank you very much."

Mr Kaplan ushered us out the door. A couple more suited men walked past us into the room. "When will Hector's mother get here?" I heard Mr Kaplan ask them as the door closed.

Jason stopped right outside the door. "We've made a huge mistake."

"Why would you think that?"

We headed down a corridor that led only to store cupboards and toilets. Jason paced out nervous circles around me. "Did you hear what Mr Kaplan said? They've called Hector's mum in."

"So?"

"The only reason they'd call his mum in is if they're thinking about suspending him. Or expelling him. And if those really were sorcery books…it could be even worse.

What do they do with underage sorcerers? Send them to juvenile prison?"

"If those are sorcery books, then isn't that what he deserves? This is what my mum spends her life trying to stop. There's a reason for that."

"But you know what he's like. He's not *dangerous*."

"He almost knocked you out just now!"

Jason made a few more circles around me as we batted the same old argument back and forth. The bell jolted us out of our endless loop.

"Let's just go to class and let the teachers deal with it," I said.

"You do that. I'm going to go back and ask them not to be harsh."

"Why would they even listen to you?"

"They probably won't. But maybe I'll feel a little bit less guilty." Jason marched back towards the head's office and I followed. He took a deep breath and knocked on the door.

There was no reply.

He tried again. Nothing.

He put his ear to the door. We couldn't hear any conversation coming from inside.

Very nervously, he turned the handle and pushed the door in.

Nobody had been left alive.

CUTTLEFISH
Trickster Of The Sea

Is there any animal more tricksy than the cuttlefish?

For starters, despite its name, it's definitely not a fish! Cuttlefish belong to the same family of animals as octopuses and squid: the **cephalopods**. Their small bodies are made up of a big, jelly-like head with ten **tentacles** around their mouths. Their unusually huge brains make them one of the **cleverest animals on Earth**.

And what do they use all their smarts for? Tricking other creatures of the sea, using a huge variety of **devilish tools**! They may look small and unimpressive, but in fact, they can **outsmart and kill** both predators and prey – even those many times their size and strength.

Cuttlefish can change colour, by revealing or hiding a huge variety of pigments arranged in layers under its skin. For this reason, it's often known as the **chameleon of the sea**, as it can blend in with its surroundings with ease.

In fact, its powers of disguise and deception are far better than a chameleon's. As well as having far more colours to choose from, it can change the texture of its skin, becoming lumpy or smooth, as well as arranging its tentacles to look like anything it wants. They can blend in with a smooth sandy floor or a lumpy coral reef in seconds, matching the **colour**, the **pattern**, and the **texture** of whatever surface they're on.

The cuttlefish doesn't just use its **masterful shape-shifting abilities** to blend in with its surroundings. More often than not, you'll see the cuttlefish flaunting all kinds of bright and bold colours, which flicker over its skin in **bewitching patterns**. Scientists don't yet understand why cuttlefish love to do this – perhaps they're talking in complex languages to other cuttlefish, or perhaps they're just showing off!

Sometimes, they suck lots of water into their bodies to inflate themselves, appearing much bigger than they are. They may also flash bright colours at their prey, to **hypnotise and terrify them** before gobbling them up. One of the favourite tricks of a male cuttlefish is to pretend to be a female, so that other male cuttlefish don't want to attack him!

The cuttlefish's awesome power of disguise isn't the only trick up its sleeve. Cuttlefish have suckers all the way along their tentacles, which grip tightly onto any creature it finds and never lets it go. Some species can produce a **lethal venom**, capable of killing much bigger creatures which try to eat it.

Finally, if a cuttlefish finds itself trapped in a corner by a stronger enemy, it has one last game to play: it produces a **cloud of ink** which blinds its foes, giving it time to disappear under cover of darkness.

Woe betide any sea creature who dares to cross the cuttlefish!

TWENTY

STAY ALIVE

It wasn't real.

It couldn't be real.

I told myself, over and over again, that I was seeing nothing but an illusion. But it didn't help. The illusion didn't budge.

Every surface in the head's office was streaked with soot. Books and ornaments lay piled against the walls, disfigured and mottled black. Chairs were bowled backwards into the walls. Slumped over the chairs…blackened human shapes. Charcoal statues without faces. Mrs Olufunwa, Mr Kaplan, the others who I didn't even know. I couldn't tell who was who. It didn't matter.

The only spaces in the office that had been left clean were a pair of pale rectangular patches on the head's desk. The spaces where the books had been lying.

The books themselves were gone.

That was the exact moment things got real. Before stumbling into a room of teacher corpses, this whole thing had been a bit hypothetical. Ooh, the River People are acting strangely. Ooh, Hector's bringing sorcery books into school. After stumbling into a room of teacher corpses: Ooh, everyone's been nyxed and we're next.

"This is magic, right? They're OK really, right?" Jason murmured.

"I don't know. I think so." If there was a way to tell real injuries apart from magical ones, Mum had never taught me it.

"We need to call the police," said Jason.

"The police? No, this is serious. I'm calling Mum." I took out my phone.

"Who could have done this?"

"Hector?" I suggested.

"No. No way."

"He's been reading sorcery books. Who knows what he might be able to do?"

"Nothing like this. Come on."

Don't get me wrong, I thought the idea was crazy too. Whatever weird stuff Hector was mixed up in, there was no way he could have done something like this. But it was the least crazy idea I could come up with. Who else could have done something like this? Except for…

"Cuttlefish," I said. "What if it's him?"

Another crazy idea. We both knew it. But we had nothing else.

A voice crackled from my phone. "Hey, kid. What's up?"

I switched to speakerphone. We did best to explain everything that had just happened, right up to walking in on a roomful of charred corpses.

"Have you called the police?" Mum asked.

"No."

"Don't bother. I'm dispatching a unit now. You're saying someone's nyxed a roomful of people just to steal a couple of books?"

"Yeah."

"Could this person know that you were in the room too?"

"I don't know. Yeah, I suppose so."

"Then you might be targets. You need to stay alive until I can reach you. Keep hidden. If it's too late for that, stay in a crowded place. If this sorcerer is trying to cover up their tracks, they won't want to cause a scene."

I was expecting Mum to be shocked, or at least a little bit scared. But if she was either of those things, she didn't show them over the phone. She seemed completely fine with the possibility of the two of us being nyxed.

"Keep me on the line and start moving," she finished.

I put the phone in my pocket.

We looked at each other.

"All right. Where are we going?" Jason asked.

I peered into the corridor, taking care not to nudge the door any further open. "Corridor is empty," I said. "What if we just went back to class? Pretend we didn't see anything?"

"The attacker will be looking for you there right now," barked the phone in my pocket. "Then he'll return to the office. You need to get out of the room, and move in the opposite direction from the class you're supposed to be in."

If I didn't know any better, I'd say Mum was sounding more and more excited. A little bit worried too, maybe, that her beloved only daughter was being hunted through her own school by a sorcerer. But mainly excited.

We glided down the hallway as quietly as possible, glancing down every forking corridor, through every open doorway. But nobody saw us. Nobody tried to stop us.

Classes had started, and outside the classrooms the school was silent.

We made it to the school library without being seen. It was a big, low-ceilinged room, empty except for a librarian, Stewart, morosely restocking books on the shelves. Deciding we had no better plans, we walked in as nonchalantly as possible.

"Our teacher sent us to work on a project alone," I told Stewart.

Stewart shot us a small-eyed stare, then nodded. We sat at a round table furthest from the door, on uncomfortably small plastic chairs. I grabbed a random book off the shelf and pretended to read the fascinating ocean facts it contained. Jason spread out some paper and made fake notes.

Our plan worked for all of seven minutes, until the intercom on the librarian's desk bleeped. "We seem to have two missing pupils on our hands," came the head's scratchy voice. "Cassandra Drake and Jason Kasikidis. Stewart, have you seen them?"

The librarian looked at us and licked his lips angrily.

"Wait! We can explain!" I stammered.

"You can explain yourself to the head," Stewart muttered, pushing down the intercom buzzer. "They're both with me in the library. I'll bring them over right away."

We knocked back our chairs, picked up our bags, and fled through the library.

"Stop!" Stewart said, giving exceptionally half-hearted chase. We darted underneath his outstretched arms, wove around tables and chairs, and escaped back into the corridor. I glanced over my shoulder to see the librarian scowling from the library door. Then, like some enchanted sentinel unable to overstep his bounds, he gave up and returned inside.

Jason glanced through a passing porthole and discovered an empty classroom on the other side. "In here!" he said.

We sat down at a desk in the middle of the room. After a moment's thought, I pulled us both onto the ground. "That was the head's voice on the line, wasn't it?" I hissed.

"Yep. And it must have been coming from the head's office," Jason whispered back.

"So either this is Cuttlefish or another sorcerer who can do mimesis."

"What's mimesis?"

"Never mind. Point is, Cuttlefish has got the whole school looking for us already. And he could be disguised as anyone. We have to stay completely hidden until Mum gets here."

The minutes passed like centuries. I stared at the floor and listened for footsteps in the corridor. The knot of terror in my heart got tighter and tighter.

"There's no other way to see in here, is there?" I murmured, a few centuries later.

"Just through the door," he replied.

I peered over the top of the desk to check. We were on the second floor, so it was impossible to see in through the windows. Someone hunting us would only be able to look for us through the porthole in the door.

I glanced through it, straight into a pair of bemused eyes.

"Damn it," I gasped as the door was flung open.

"Cass! I've just been looking for you," smiled Mr Milliner. "I don't suppose you've got Jason with you too?"

My spine twanged with fear. Jason and I looked at each other, silently weighing up how long we could stall by pretending not to be crouched behind the desk. Slowly, reluctantly, we stood up in surrender. I would have raised my hands if I weren't still clutching my rucksack to my chest.

"Head's office seems to think the two of you have gone AWOL! Don't worry, you're not in trouble. Why don't we head over now and sort this all out?"

I backed away nervously. "I'm sorry, Mr Milliner. We can't."

The maths teacher's eyes narrowed, though his grin stayed as roguish as ever. "Why not? Whatever's going on here, I just want to help you, okay?"

"Cuttlefish is in the school!" I garbled.

Mr Milliner's grin solidified, drained of all emotion, as if he had just been frozen in liquid nitrogen. "I'm… Sorry?"

"He's nyxed the head, and he's trying to find us next," added Jason.

"What? I just spoke to Mrs Olufunwa myself! She came into the staffroom," said Mr Milliner.

"It wasn't her. It was Cuttlefish!" I said.

The maths teacher nodded with steely sincerity. "I want you both to know that I'm taking this very seriously," he said at last. "How about we all go to the head's office and…"

"We can't go there! We can't go anywhere! Cuttlefish could be anyone. We just need to hide until Mum gets here."

"Until your mum gets here?" said Mr Milliner, frozen incredulity returning to his face. Before I could try to explain, the classroom door opened again.

"Miss Drake. Mr Kasikidis. We have been worried about you," said Ms Zima with her customary lack of worry, or any other emotion for that matter. "Why have you not been in class?"

"Ms Zima, these two are claiming that there's a sorcerer in the school," said Mr Milliner. "Cuttlefish, to be precise."

"Cuttlefish?" Ms Zima looked at us corrosively. "Children, the lunch break is over. It is time to put away your imaginations now."

"We're not making this up! We've seen it for ourselves," I said desperately.

"I have reason to believe this is a genuine threat," barked the phone in my pocket, making everybody jump.

"Cassandra, phones are not allowed in classrooms," said Ms Zima. Everyone ignored her.

"I'm DCI Helen Drake, with the SID," my phone continued. "Also Cass's mother. Cass has given me strong reason to believe that a sorcerer has attacked individuals in your school, and might be targeting Cass and Jason. Please stay together and stay where you are. I'll be able to explain the situation in full shortly."

"Cassandra, this had better not be some kind of joke," said Ms Zima.

"I'm sure we'll be able to figure this all out," said Mr Milliner.

The chemistry teacher held out her hand for the phone. I gave it to her.

"How far are you away?" Ms Zima asked Mum.

"Fifteen minutes."

Ms Zima shook her head sadly. "I'm afraid, in that case, you will be too late." She tossed the phone into the air and pulled two pins out of her bun. In the time it took for her hair to cascade around her shoulders, she had seized Mr Milliner by the back of the head and pushed the hairpin into his neck. He made an odd gurgling sound, the sound of liquid and air mixing in places in the human body they shouldn't be. The phone arced through the air and impaled itself on the second hairpin in Ms Zima's waiting hand. She withdrew the hairpins sharply, letting both the maths teacher and the phone fall lifelessly to the ground.

I was now at least 85% sure that this wasn't the real Ms Zima. Sadly, that nugget of information didn't help me figure out what to do next.

"Run!" screamed Jason, just milliseconds before I independently decided that running was a good idea.

I charged towards the door, still pointlessly clutching my rucksack to my chest like a newborn baby.

Jason threw a chair at Ms Zima's head and then followed suit.

Ms Zima blocked the chair with her briefcase, sending it spiralling into a window.

I reached the door first. A breeze kissed my hair, like someone was whispering in my ear. A hairpin vibrated in the door, glistening red. Moronically, I turned round to see where it had come from. As I did so, my rucksack jolted. A second hairpin stuck out from it, vibrating from the violent impact.

Ms Zima marched towards me, acidic amusement in her eyes. Inexplicably, she still had a razor-sharp hairpin in each hand.

Jason darted through the open door. I dropped my schoolbag and pelted after him. I didn't make mistake of looking round again.

We rounded a corner and burst into the first room we came to. It was a science lab, and this time it wasn't empty. Bored Year 11s, setting up equipment in groups all along the workbenches, turned with surprise towards the out-of-breath Year 8s stumbling towards the teacher's desk. And standing sternly at the front of the classroom –

I stopped short and stared in momentary panic. At the front of the classroom was Ms Zima, her eyes pale and unamused.

"Miss Drake. Mr Kasikidis. What brings you to my classroom?" she asked, in the exact same flat tone of voice as a few minutes earlier.

"We need to hide," I said. There was no chance of explaining ourselves more fully. "Just for one second. Please."

"What is the meaning of this? You are supposed to be in your own classes," she insisted.

Cupboards lined the walls of this room, both at ground level and just above head height. But none were large enough to crawl inside. All were probably packed with chemistry equipment anyway. We scrambled to the front of the room and ducked down behind Ms Zima's desk just as the door to the classroom gushed open again.

"Sorry to bother you, folks!"

It was Mr Kaplan's half-jokey voice. Mr Kaplan, who was nothing but a pile of ash in the head's office.

"I'm looking for a couple of runaway Year 8s. You haven't spotted them, have you?"

The chemistry teacher looked down at us with cold anger in her eyes. We shook our heads frantically, faces pleading. She looked up at the English teacher. Then back down at us.

"Alright, why don't you just come out?" called Mr Kaplan. "I know you're there. This is all getting a bit silly, don't you think?"

The class had fallen silent, except for a few suppressed coughs and mutterings.

"Whatever is going on here, let us all talk about it like adults," said Ms Zima.

Slowly, painfully, Jason and I got to our feet.

"That's not Mr Kaplan," I gabbled. "That's Cuttlefish. He nyxed Mr Kaplan."

Ms Zima looked at Mr Kaplan. Mr Kaplan shot her a *What's up with these crazy kids?* grin.

"Children, the lunch break is over. It is time to put away your imaginations now," said Ms Zima.

"Why don't we all go to the head's office and get to the bottom of this together?" suggested Mr Kaplan.

I got a plummeting sense of déjà vu as I stared into Ms Zima's nonplussed eyes. But I couldn't help trying to convince her one more time. "He nyxed the head," I said hopelessly. "And everyone else in her office. He's going to nyx us as soon as we're alone with him."

A flicker of fear entered Ms Zima's flinty eyes. "You are quite sure of this story?" she said.

"Yes. We're staying here until Mum arrives."

Mr Kaplan shook his head. "I really didn't want to cause a scene. But you've left me no choice."

Whistling a cheery tune, he thumped his briefcase onto a desk and opened it up.

My ears started ringing. We'd stalled as long as we could, but something told me we'd run out of delaying tactics.

I pulled Jason close. "We have to make a break for it down each side," I whispered in his ear. "He'll only have a chance to get one of us. Whatever happens, keep running. OK?"

He nodded.

Mr Kaplan took Hector's book out and opened it to the middle. Flames burst from the pages. He pursed his lips and blew through the flames. A jet of fire blasted across the room, engulfing Jason and Ms Zima together. Blinding heat filled the room.

The room echoed with screams. Twenty kids piled over chairs and under desks, towards the door. By the time I got there, I was at the back of the scrum.

The flames cleared. Ms Zima was nothing but a mound of charred limbs, smelling horribly like roast pork. But Jason was still standing there, looking even more confused than the rest of us to still be alive. All that had been burnt away was his jumper and shirt, which hung in shreds off his shoulders. Underneath, there was nothing but a thin layer of soot on his reddened skin, and a cross, glowing white hot, in the centre of his chest.

"Very good!" said Mr Kaplan, sounding more pleased than anyone else by this surprise. He dropped the burning book on a desk, his grin wider than ever.

The fire alarm started screaming.

Jason dived towards the door, but Mr Kaplan grabbed him by the chain that had just saved his life and yanked him backwards. Jason was caught by his neck, scrabbling for air, while the last of the Year 11s fled the room.

"Very sorry about this, Jason," Mr Kaplan said cheerily, trying to prise the chain of Jason's neck. "Nothing personal, you know."

Jason's eyes widened. Not because he was being throttled. Because he'd seen me.

The doorway was clear. I should have run for my life, just like we'd agreed. I shouldn't have tried to save him.

But here I was, turning to face Cuttlefish instead of fleeing from him, his burning book in my hands.

Mr Kaplan spotted me almost straight after Jason did. His grin didn't even think about leaving his face.

"Careful where you point that thing," he said. "The safety's off."

I blew.

The flames immediately went out.

It turned out you needed to be a sorcerer to do magic.

Don't worry, I had a Plan B. You didn't think I'd be daring to face down a deadly sorcerer without a Plan B, did you? Don't be ridiculous. I had a fantastic Plan B. An absolutely foolproof Plan B, almost as foolproof as my Plan A had been.

My Plan B was to throw the book at Cuttlefish's head and run away.

I know what you're thinking – *the throwing-objects-at-Cuttlefish's-head strategy never works! He always deflects the objects with his briefcase!*

But what you've forgotten is that this time, he wasn't holding his briefcase. He was holding Jason's chain. The book's corner caught him clean in the eye.

At the exact same time, Jason elbowed him in the stomach and pulled away. His chain snapped. Jason fell forward, already running.

See? A perfectly executed Plan B. Luck had nothing to do with it.

We darted into the hallway. Up ahead was a double door. Over the door was a fire exit sign. I'd never been so relieved to see one.

"Go that way. I'll stay inside," Jason shouted. "He can only follow one of us."

Jason peeled off before I could debate the idea with him. I flung myself through the double doors into cold sunlight.

But I wasn't done yet. Ahead of me was a desolate roofscape, a metal walkway picking carefully through brick vents, grey boxes, and other native rooftop flora before reaching the staircase down.

I didn't stop running when the metal walkway dinged with the arrival of two high heels. I didn't stop for the polite but firm cough that followed. Then a bullet burst through my arm.

I did stop for that. My muscle ignited with ragged agony. Pain's tendrils reached out and gripped my hand, my shoulder. I planted my other hand over the bleeding wound, not daring to look at it closely. My aching limbs slowed to a frantic walk, but I couldn't stop moving.

I dared a look behind me. Mrs Olufunwa was coming after me, her satchel over one shoulder, a gun in the other.

Jason's plan to split up had been perfect. Perfect up until the moment when Cuttlefish decided to follow me.

Look, I'm not saying I *wanted* Jason to get nobly nyxed by Cuttlefish, just to give me time to escape. But that had kind of been the subtext when he suggested the idea. His voice had taken on a gravelly, noble tone. He'd looked all geared up to retort, "No! It's better this way!" to my insistent pleas that we stick together, which admittedly hadn't existed. And now, he was fine, and I'd been shot in the arm by Britain's most famous sorcerer.

But I didn't have time to reflect on the chain of terrible decision-making that had led up to this moment. All I could do was dive over the walkway railing and onto the roof as another bullet pinged past my head. Keeping low, I darted between chimney stacks and electrical boxes, trying to keep something between me and Cuttlefish's gun.

I leaned against a large vent, gasping, and forced myself to peek at my arm.

It turned out I'd blown it totally out of proportion. The bullet had gone through the skin, sure, but only skimming the surface, leaving behind a raw pink patch. There was barely any blood. It was my school jumper that had taken most of the damage.

I'm not saying it didn't hurt. Because it hurt more than anything I'd ever felt. I'm just saying Jason, lightly braised from the waist up, was probably doing worse than me.

Mrs Olufunwa's coiffed hair glided like a shark's fin over the roof utilities. "Cassandra, where are you?" she trilled. "I just want a quick word."

Her statement was contradicted by the gun that she was still definitely waving in my direction. I crept away, keeping low, hoping for a chance to rejoin the walkway and get out of this place.

"Cass! This way!"

It was Jason! Somehow, he'd come back for me. Just like I'd come back for him in that classroom. He was crouched outside another doorway, his bag at his feet.

He smiled as I ran closer. Smiled, and raised his gun.

Pain flashed in my skull. Not actual pain, just a sort of brainshock at his fakeness. I should have felt it straight away. But I hadn't, and now I was going to be nyxed. There was nowhere left to hide.

I raised my palm to block him. As if that could ever protect me.

Jason's face and neck erupted with clenching muscles. He let out a guttural scream and fired two shots over my head, before dropping his gun. Then he collapsed stiffly.

I looked at my hand in wonder. What had I done?

"Great job staying alive, kid," said Mum, behind me, taser in hand. "I'll take it from here."

TWENTY-ONE

DCI HELEN DRAKE

The suspect thrashed on the ground as fifty thousand volts coursed through his body. All the magic in the world couldn't block a taser to the chest.

The inquisitor wasted no time. She kicked the suspect onto his stomach, dug one knee into the small of his back, and wrenched both of his arms up against his spine.

"Suspect is apprehended!" she yelled into her lapel mic. "I need backup. Rooftop." She twisted around to find her daughter still standing there. "Cass, get out of here. Now."

Her daughter didn't need to be told twice. She fled down the walkway, far out of harm's way.

The inquisitor paid for her words instantly. She was blown backwards by a pulse of clenching pain from the suspect's bag. Her muscles spasmed from the electrical discharge. The walkway gonged as she landed.

The inquisitor tried to shake off the pain, but she couldn't. Magical electricity was no less debilitating than the real thing.

Four police officers advanced on her position. They fanned out along the walkway, pointing their tasers uncertainly at both her and the suspect.

It didn't take the inquisitor long to realise why.

Crumpled under a fire exit door was...herself. Same blonde hair, same long green jacket. Same cool eyes, trembling slightly from the aftershock of the taser.

The inquisitor's doppelganger pointed at her. "The suspect is currently impersonating me, but don't be fooled," she yelled. "Apprehend him."

The four officers pointed their tasers from one version of the inquisitor to the other.

"This is the real DCI Helen Drake, as you can hear on comms," the inquisitor gasped into her mic.

The suspect's face fell. She turned and barged through the fire exit. A swarm of taser darts clattered against the door just behind her.

"Suspect has re-entered the building," the inquisitor barked into her mic as she gave chase. "All units, hold your positions."

She had scrambled several armed response units to secure the building's entrances. They looked almost identical to regular police officers. They wore black bulletproof flak jackets, bulging with their radios, personal cameras, and other equipment. Each jacket had a clear plastic chest pocket, containing either a religious symbol or a non-religious amulet of choice. Above that was their collar numbers: 374EK, 812EK, 719EK, 448EK. Unlike regular police officers, each member of this special force was carrying a gun.

Instead of drawing their guns, the officers behind her plugged fresh cartridges into their tasers as they moved towards the door.

The fire alarm hammered at her skull as she entered the school. The corridors were empty, evacuated many long minutes ago. No sign of the suspect anywhere.

Instinctively, she took a left-hand turn. "Stay in pairs," she called to the officers behind her. 812EK and 719EK went the other way.

The inquisitor glanced down a wide hallway lined with lockers. Another police officer, 666CF, was waiting by a classroom door, gun drawn.

"No lethal weapons!" the inquisitor shouted. "The risk of friendly fire is too high."

666CF turned and opened fire on them.

448EK cried out and collapsed against the lockers. 374EK dived behind the corner of the wall before she was hit too.

Instead of taking cover, the inquisitor returned fire with her taser. The suspect rolled out of the way and fled down the hall, still firing over his shoulder. Keeping her hand raised, the inquisitor gave chase, plugging her last taser cartridge into position.

"Stay in pairs at all times," she repeated into her mic as she ran. "Treat anyone alone as suspicious." She mentally cursed herself for failing to do this herself, just moments ago. For failing to spot the clammy ripple of illusion surrounding the suspect until it was too late.

666CF disappeared to the right.

Moments later, they reached the same turn.

The suspect was waiting for them just behind the bend. He shot 374EK through the head at point blank range, then swung his gun at the inquisitor.

At once, the inquisitor grabbed the suspect's wrist and twisted his gun out of his hand. The suspect swung a punch, his fist enclosed in a knuckle duster. The inquisitor stepped close, throwing the suspect off balance, and jabbed her elbow into his neck. Still holding onto his gun arm, she spun behind him and wrenched him into an armlock.

448EK darted into the fray and seized the suspect's other arm. Either the bullet-proof flak jacket, or the hamsa in its breast pocket, had saved him from a lethal bullet.

A tide of bats flew out of the suspect's bag and pelted the inquisitor, tangling themselves in her hair, pinballing under her jacket. She cried out and released the suspect. At once, he pivoted and slashed at 448EK's neck with a flick-knife.

The hamsa didn't save him this time. One hand over his spurting throat, he came to rest by 374EK.

The inquisitor wasted no time mourning her fallen comrades. Even before 666CF could pull the flick-knife out of his victim, the inquisitor twisted on one foot and kicked him in the stomach.

The suspect crumpled onto the ground. Fending off a cloud of bats, the inquisitor punted the suspect's bag as far as she could down the hallway. Without his books, he was nothing; she had worked out that much from her months of stalking him.

She aimed her taser at the helpless suspect's throat.

Then, pain. Juddering, clenching pain. The inquisitor screamed through clenched teeth as fifty thousand volts coursed through her body. She collapsed helplessly.

"Suspect is incapacitated," called 812EK behind her, triumphantly.

719EK knelt on her back and put handcuffs on her. "Enough with the bats," he said, swiping at them in frustration. "It's over, Cuttlefish."

Slowly, wearily, 666CF got to his feet. All his inconsistent weaponry had disappeared, leaving behind nothing but a regulation flak jacket and equipment. "Good work," he shouted to the others over the fire alarm. "I thought it was all over for me." He walked down the hallway and picked up his police bag before disappearing from view.

The inquisitor tried to open her mouth, but no words came out. Her body twitched from the aftershock of the electric current. Dead bats fell around her like autumn leaves. She lowered her head to the floor in despair.

By the time the inquisitor could speak again, the suspect had long gone. "I'm the real DCI Helen Drake," she croaked into her mic, "as you can hear on comms."

"That's what you said last time," 719EK jeered.

"Yes, and I was right."

The two officers whispered frantically to one another.

"So why were you alone? We were ordered to stay in pairs for this exact reason!" said 812EK.

The inquisitor didn't bother to explain what the suspect had done. "The threat's not over," she said. "Follow me."

719EK took her handcuffs off, shame written all over his face. The three of them left their fallen friends behind and made their way to the evacuation point. The playground.

The grating fire alarm was replaced by hushed hubbub as they stepped outside. They found themselves in a paved area full of picnic tables, lined by depressed shrubs. Beyond those was a rectangular sports pitch where pupils were arranged in shaky lines, each headed by a worried teacher.

The inquisitor scanned them all, her heart gripped by urgent fear. For whatever reason, the suspect was hell-bent on silencing her daughter. Something told the inquisitor he would not have given up yet.

A teacher caught her eye and jogged across the playground to her. "Can one of you explain what's going on?" he said, worry carved into his face. "We have a Year 11 class saying their teacher was...*burnt alive* by another teacher. The head and several members of staff haven't shown up. Some kids are missing too. We're praying they've run away. The police aren't telling us anything..."

"Mum?"

A dishevelled schoolgirl ran chaotically towards the inquisitor, eyes bright with happiness. Her pale skin glistened with sweat. Her schoolbag bashed against her back with every step. She raised her arms.

Relief gushed through the inquisitor's veins. She holstered her taser. "Darling! Are you OK?"

"I'm fine, Mum. Did you catch Cuttlefish?"

The inquisitor put a hand on her daughter's shoulder and gazed deep into her eyes. Just one look told her that everything was going to be fine. "Not yet. But we will."

In one fluid movement, the inquisitor drew her pepper spray and fired it at her daughter's face.

The girl screamed. Black smoke erupted from her eyes and mouth. Then it was coming from her collar and sleeves as well, her trousers and waistband. It billowed around her, engulfing them both.

The inquisitor didn't miss a beat. Maintaining her grip on the suspect's shoulder, she blindly jabbed through the smoke. Her fist collided with soft flesh. Moments later, a burst of clenching pain knocked her onto her back.

She recovered more quickly this time. She was already back on her feet, grabbing through the opaque air. Her fingers clenched onto fabric. An elbow rammed into her side. She threaded her own arm into it and pushed it up into an armlock position. Her eyes watered in the thick smoke, blinding her even more.

Someone else seized her upper arm and attempted to wrestle it behind her back. She twisted her arm anticlockwise, breaking out of their grip and seizing their arm in retaliation. She swept one foot into the back of their knees, forcing them to the ground.

The smoke began to clear. The inquisitor discovered herself holding a police officer in each hand. 812EK was pinned by an armlock; 719EK was kneeling. A few steps way was a cowering teacher.

There was nobody else.

"Did you see anyone running away?" she shouted to the teacher.

"N – no," he replied.

The inquisitor let go of the two officers. The smoke was thin enough now to make them both out clearly. She felt no trace of discomfort looking at them. There were no illusions here.

The suspect had vanished.

The inquisitor's rage was slightly softened by the sound of sirens beyond the playground walls.

Backup.

"Suspect must have gone back inside," she said, coughing violently. "Tell backup units to reinforce the perimeter. Everyone else, sweep the building. Suspect is blind and in a lot of pain. He won't be able to run far. But be cautious. He's still in possession of magical artefacts."

The inquisitor began the pursuit once again. There was no sign of the suspect inside the school. The fire alarm destroyed any chance of hearing fleeing steps. She sighed, and advanced down the hallway.

The inquisitor kicked open the first door she came to and scanned the room, her taser ready.

Empty.

Another officer did the same thing to the classroom across the hall.

They advanced down the room, sweeping each room they came to. Each was empty. Soon, they reached the front lobby, where four police officers blocked the entrance.

"Nobody's come this way," 335NH reported.

"Good. Hold your position. Don't let anyone in or out, no matter who they are or what they say." As she spoke, the inquisitor scanned 335NH, waiting for the skin-crawling sensation of illusion. But she felt nothing. Nothing at all.

She relayed the same message to the teams at each of the building's entryways. It was nothing they hadn't been told already, of course. Each team gave the same reply. No sign of the suspect. No sign at all.

"Any chance the suspect doubled back into the crowd outside?" 812EK said.

"Guess we can't rule that out," the inquisitor said. "We'll need to vet them all before they leave."

The inquisitor continued her search with increasing desperation. She swept room after empty room, until she came to the nurse's office. There, she found a boy hunched on the floor, face squeezed shut, hands over his ears, as if he was trying to squeeze himself out of existence.

"Hector?" she shouted over the fire alarm.

The boy didn't move. He hadn't seen or heard her.

812EK and 719EK stepped cautiously into the room behind her, tasers trained on the boy, looking to her for their next orders.

The inquisitor approached the boy and placed a friendly hand on his wrist. The boy flinched away and opened his eyes. They were red and puffy. He'd been crying for a long time.

But there was no tremor of uncanniness around the boy. The inquisitor knew without a doubt that he was who he appeared to be.

She motioned to the officers to lower their weapons. "Hector, what are you doing in here? Why didn't you evacuate when you heard the alarm?"

"Mr Kaplan told me to wait here until he got back. And he never did!" Hector said.

"What? And you didn't hear the fire alarm?"

"I heard it. But Mr Kaplan told me to wait until he got back. I didn't want to get in trouble."

The inquisitor took a few calming breaths. "OK. Well, I'm going to need to get you out of here. We have a sorcerer hiding somewhere in this building. Come with me."

The boy stood up quickly, and immediately clamped his hands over his ears again.

"Keep searching," she told the others. "I've got to get this guy out of here."

TWENTY-TWO

PUFF OF SMOKE

We ended up stuck in the playground for hours. I found myself thinking I should have just run clean out of there. But I'd wanted to make sure Jason was OK.

Which he was. So that was nice. A little burned, but only to the level you get from falling asleep while sunbathing. It looked painful, but still way better than what had happened to Ms Zima.

"What's happening in there?" Tori asked frantically. "The teachers don't know anything."

"Is that your mum?" added Chloë.

Jason and I looked at each other, then attempted to explain exactly what we'd been up to. As we spoke, a wider and wider circle of pupils turned to face us, wide-eyed. Even the teachers barged to the front to catch what we were saying.

Yaz started videoing himself like he was a reporter. Unfortunately, his attempts to be serious only made him sound like a football commentator. "This is Yazid Alfour, reporting live from Whittington School," he said breathlessly. "We've seen some truly incredible scenes today. Cuttlefish has literally fried a bunch of teachers and is now on the run from the police. I have with me a Year 8 pupil, Cassandra Drake, who can tell us more."

Yaz flipped his camera onto me just as I got to the bit where Mum tased Cuttlefish straight in the chest.

"No. Way," said Jess, eyes alight. "That is so cool."

Yaz crept around to take a panning shot of Jason's burnt torso, ending with a close-up shot of my bullet wound. Tori beat him away with a series of brutal glances.

Now that everyone was evacuated and together on the sports pitch, nobody seemed to be worried about what Cuttlefish could do to them. It was only Jason and I who were scared.

A few minutes later, Mum emerged, dumped Hector outside, and went back in. A police officer escorted him towards us.

"Hector!"

It was Foni. On the other side of the police officer barrier. She'd come around the back of the school to find us. But she wasn't being allowed any further.

Hector didn't seem remotely happy to see his mother. He shuffled towards the police barrier almost reluctantly, looking down. The officer with Hector held him back with a touch on the shoulder.

Foni got into a polite battle of words with the officers blocking his way. I'd never seen her look so emotional. Her eyes were red, like she'd been crying. I couldn't hear anything she was saying. But whatever it was, it didn't work. The line of officers didn't let her into the playground. She turned and shouted something at Hector.

But if Hector heard it, he didn't respond. The officer holding Hector guided him towards the rest of us. He didn't bother to come and join our line, where he belonged. He just stood on the sidelines, his face blotchy and drained, staring at nothing.

I spent the next half hour fending off questions about everything that had happened. In the background, more and more official-looking people showed up. A handful of journalists had joined Foni on the outside of the police barrier. Some were taking photos. There were more police officers too, whose only job seemed to be to hold the journalists back. People in regular business clothes marched back and forth, busily conferring with each other and taking notes. I guessed that they were SIDs like Mum. Several ambulances parked up and unleashed medical teams into the school. We just remained in our lines, the teachers and pupils equally scared and clueless about what we were supposed to be doing.

Finally, Mum came to find us, several police officers in tow. It was obvious from her grim expression that they hadn't found Cuttlefish inside.

"Listen up," she commanded. "I need to vet each of you. Then my colleagues will ask you a few questions, and you'll be free to go."

Mum set up a makeshift desk on a park bench. She made everyone in the school come to the desk one by one and recite their personal details to a police officer, a guy with a bulging forehead called Rich. Rich checked what everyone said against the school records, then got them to stare into an iris scanner. Meanwhile, Mum stared them very carefully in the face. Once they were cleared, they were escorted past the police barrier into a field, where some teachers were attempting to take everyone's minds off things with some group games.

Jason and I didn't join them. Mum didn't trust us to go out of her sight, so we waited behind the desk with her.

An SID marched up to us, tapping on a tablet. "We've made good progress tracking Cuttlefish's movements through the building," she told Mum. Then, to me, "Could you confirm that this is you?"

She held up the tablet, which held a grainy image of Jason leading me through the foyer earlier. We both nodded.

"Interesting. Very interesting," she said curtly. Then, to Mum, "They're showing suspicious behaviour in this footage. We think one of them may have been our suspect."

Jason and I stared at each other in consternation. The SID tapped at her screen as she explained it all to Mum.

"As you can see, ma'am, the two of them are holding hands here. And also here. Without any clear motive for doing so. And if we zoom in a little...see? Eye contact. During this sequence they hold each other's gaze for excessive lengths of time. A clear indication that one of them may have been charming the other. This all takes place three minutes before you got the call from them."

"Right," said Mum, looking at me sideways. "That does seem unusual."

"At this point, we lose them on CCTV, but they must have spent the next two or so minutes down an empty corridor, before returning...*here*. As you can see, still holding hands."

"Right. Right," said Mum. "But you're both saying this was definitely you?"

We nodded in unison.

"There you have it, Dayna," Mum said. "There must be an innocent explanation for this. Or maybe 'innocent' isn't the right word."

It was when Mum glanced at me again that I lost it. "It's not like that! OK? We'd just discovered all the teachers had been nyxed and we were desperately figuring out what to do."

Mum looked back at the footage of Jason and me frolicking around, hand in hand. "Right. You know, you don't have to keep this kind of stuff from *me*. I'm your mum!"

"I'm not keeping *anything* from you."

"Sure." Mum smiled fondly at both of us.

"With all due respect, ma'am, I've been trained to read body language," Dayna added. "If you take a look *here*, and *here*, you can clearly see a widening of Cass's eyes and opening of the mouth, which is a characteristic sign of being charmed."

"Have you been talking to Jess or Tori, or something?" I asked her.

"No, but thanks for the tipoff. I'll locate this Jess and Tori and corroborate your story with the two of them. Hopefully we'll get some clear answers soon." Dayna strode towards the remaining huddle of pupils, tapping her tablet.

Mum smiled benignly at Jason. "So you're…"

"A new friend," I explained.

"A new friend! Great. Great! Well, it's nice to meet you, Jason. I'm Cass's mum!"

"Um – hi."

"You're always welcome round to our house, if you want! No need to spend all your time together hiding down empty corridors. What's happened to you?"

"Burned. I was wearing a cross, which I guess is the only reason I wasn't nyxed."

Mum glanced over Jason's red skin with a decent attempt at sympathy. Then nodded at a couple of medics waiting by the ambulance. "Go and talk to those guys. Getting it treated will do a lot for the pain. Get some painkillers too."

"Painkillers? But the burn's magical. It's only in my head. Right?"

"Yep. But guess what? Pain is only *ever* in your head. Even pain caused by real injuries. So a dressing and painkillers should work just as well on magical burns as they would on real ones, for controlling the pain. Then with any luck you'll be back to normal by bedtime."

"Same for me?" I asked.

Mum looked at my arm and frowned, struggling to make out the slightly pinkened skin which the bullet had kissed. Then she nodded indulgently. "Sure! If you think it'll help."

I put my arm away in shame. To be honest, it wasn't even hurting anymore.

Two paramedics wheeled a patient on a gurney out of the school. "The police wouldn't let us out the front door," one of them complained. "Said we had to come see you instead."

"That's right," replied Mum. "I need to vet everyone who comes in or out of this building. Every single time. We're dealing with a mimetic here. He could be anyone."

"We have to get this person medical help!"

"They can wait until I've checked you are who you seem to be," said Mum.

They didn't challenge her again. They sullenly handed Mum their identity badges.

"OK. Now look me in the eye," Mum said.

Mum squinted into the face of one paramedic, then the other. "Nope. You're both clear," she said.

"What exactly are you looking for in their faces?" I asked.

"SID training," Mum said shortly. "You can pick up on mimesis quite easily, if you know what you're looking for." She looked at the blackened, barely recognisable face of the patient on the gurney. "Have we got an ID for this guy?"

"That's Mr Kaplan," I said.

Mum grabbed Mr Kaplan's unconscious head and turned it from side to side. She pulled open one of his eyelids. The two paramedics looked on in horror. "He's suffered a very serious attack, ma'am!" one of them said.

"We're all having a bad day," DCI Helen Drake snapped, letting Mr Kaplan's head loll to one side. "At least he won't have to remember it. You! Get back!"

Yaz had crept up to film Mr Kaplan. He scarpered immediately, saying into his phone, "Remarkable scenes here. This teacher looks like he's been burnt to a crisp. The word on the street is that this is all magic. But let me tell you, sorcery is just as realistic up close as people say…"

"Confiscate that phone," said Mum darkly.

A police officer blocked Yaz's path and held out his hand. Yaz handed his phone over without a fight.

Meanwhile, the paramedics wheeled Mr Kaplan away before Mum could inflict any more weirdness on him. Another gurney, laden with its own sinister sheeted mound, trundled towards us.

"How does your SID training thing work?" I asked.

"If someone were using mimesis to disguise themselves, I'd feel it," Mum explained. "I get a sense of wrongness about it."

Rich snorted conspicuously behind his desk.

"It's SID training which the regular police force sadly don't bother with," Mum said loudly. "And right now, it's the best hope we have, given we probably don't have Cuttlefish's iris scan in our database."

"I'll take this machine over your magical instincts any day. No offence," replied Rich.

DCI Helen Drake looked all geared up to deliver a stinging retort when two police officers stood to attention in front of her. "The building's interior has been completely cleared," one said. "No sign of the suspect."

"That's impossible," Mum said. "We know he went inside. We had at least three guys manning every exit point. More watching the streets around the building. He was completely blind and helpless. There's no way he could have got out without at least being spotted."

"We don't know for certain he went inside," the first officer pointed out. "He vanished in that smoke."

"I know what it looked like," Mum said tightly. "But he must be somewhere. I'm checking everyone who was outside. You need to go back and search again. Properly, this time. It doesn't matter how long it takes. We can't miss this opportunity. Damn it, I should have had eyes on everyone."

DCI Helen Drake cleared her throat disgustedly and returned to vetting the pupils in front of her. But everyone knew it was hopeless. Cuttlefish hadn't disguised himself as one of us.

Mum kept going, and going, and going. Even after every teacher and pupil had been checked, and the school had been triple searched, and everyone had gone home, Mum didn't stop. She lined up every SID and police officer still in the building and gave them the same treatment. She IDed everyone around the perimeter. Finally, she checked the crew working behind the desk with her.

"Helen, I've been sitting next to you the entire time!" Rich said. "When would I have had the chance to turn into Cuttlefish?"

"Just do it, and we can move on," she said. "I've got your entire squad to get through."

Finally, we were done. Mum's anger was written not just on her face, but in her hands, across the table, projected over every brick of the school behind her.

"Well, that just leaves me," she said. "Not that anybody but me would have noticed. Cass, ask me a question that only I can answer."

I racked my brain. "Er...why don't you believe in God?" Don't ask me why *that* was the first question that came into my head. There were six million more obvious things I could have asked.

Mum looked blank for a second. Fair enough, I was bringing up a two-minute conversation we'd had years ago. But then her face cleared and she said, "Because She doesn't exist. OK, everyone's been cleared."

"Everyone cleared, and no Cuttlefish," added Rich. "Looks like he really did vanish in a puff of smoke."

"No, he didn't. But somehow, he's got away." Mum's voice was as firm and level as always. Still, it was the angriest thing I'd ever heard her say.

CUTTLEFISH LEAVES ELEVEN FOR DEAD IN NORTH LONDON SCHOOL HORROR

Vinh Nguyen

- Cuttlefish rampages through school, targeting innocent children
- Botched SID operation leaves pupils and teachers trapped in school for hours
- SID 'no closer' to apprehending Cuttlefish

Cuttlefish's reign of terror escalated to a new level yesterday afternoon, as Whittington school in North London became the site of his latest atrocity. Pupils looked on in horror as Cuttlefish rampaged from room to room, chanting spells and "roasting" their teachers alive using magically induced flames. Seventeen people were nyxed in total. All are currently being monitored for signs of long-term damage.

"Explosion in one of the classrooms! ****'s going DOWN!" one of Whittington's pupils posted to Agora during the attack. "Evacuation, but teachers won't tell us what's up...they seem worried tho", another wrote a few minutes later.

The rampage ended in a shoot-out between Cuttlefish and several police officers, leaving dozens nyxed or magically wounded. "It was like nothing I'd ever seen," said one onlooker. "Cuttlefish was making weird prayers to Dionysus and Ares as he transformed into one person, then another."

The attack was followed by a police operation which seemed designed to increase the trauma even further. Officers deliberately prevented students and teachers from evacuating the site as they tried to flee from Cuttlefish. They were forcibly kept within the school grounds for many hours, with Cuttlefish presumed to be hiding inside the building.

Scotland Yard has issued the following statement: "We understand that decisions were made with the intention of apprehending Cuttlefish, which may not have placed civilian welfare at the top of its priority list. We are launching an internal investigation into why this was allowed to occur, and will be taking steps to review our policies and procedures."

However, Cuttlefish remains at large, and free to cause further devastation wherever he pleases. In targeting a school, he seems to be sending the chilling message that nobody, not even children, are safe.

553 Comments

Cesar Calamari   *1 hour ago • Reply*

This is just standard Peoples Voice scare tactics. Giving their readership want they want to hear, more unsubstantiated Cuttlefish stories. At least check your facts before you publish.

SepiaSue   *1 hour ago* • *Reply*

So @CesarCalamari you think we should be
protected from the truh? Classic.

Cesar Calamari   *1 hour ago* • *Reply*

No, I think TPV should check their definition of
'truth' before they publish stuff like this, this is
just as bad as Lyceum propogander. Open your
eyes @SepiaSue. We are being lied to.

SepiaSue   *1 hour ago* • *Reply*

Open my eyes??? Sounds like the kind of thing
Cuttelfish would say. Maybe you don't like
Peoples Voice truth because youre listening to the
Lyceum instead?

Cesar Calamari   *1 hour ago* • *Reply*

Just for the record @SepiaSue...accusing
someone else of being Cuttlefish is exactly the
kind of thing Cuttlefish deos, as you'd know if you
actually read up on the *facts* instead of
listening to this People's Voice bile...so if yu keep
vcalling me Cuttlefish what does that make you?

SepiaSue   *1 hour ago* • *Reply*

And trying to turn the argument back round on
itself is ALSO the kind of thing Cuttlefish does so
nice try @CesarCalamari or should I just tart
calling you CUTTLEFOSH – and even if your not

Cuttlefish your ejust as bad cos it's people like you that stop the SID from being able to do their JOBS properyl !!

Cesar Calamari *1 hour ago • Reply*

Literally starting to belive you might eb Cuttlefish. Nobody else is actually this stupide are they? Either I'm talking to the worlds greatest sorceerrer or the worlds' greatest cretin which isit

---

SepiaSue *1 hour ago • Reply*

OK I calling you out thisis a ***tROOLL ACCOUNT*** moderators sut it down pls

---

Cesar Calamari *1 hour ago • Reply*

Hhaa nice try...but I know you just made your accont to reply to me so if im a troll your a troll

---

SepiaSue *1 hour ago • Reply*

How did you know that??? U freaking CREEEPER and anyway you did the exact same thing in fact your LOGGING IN AND OUT every time you post another reply – don't deny it – you have to be because youre using the EXACT SAME COMPUTER I am so the game's up

---

Cesar Calamari *1 hour ago • Reply*

slow clap Wow, you finaly worked out that we mst be teh same person. Only took you a whole page of comments. I literally wrote everything you wrote and I'm still embarrassed to be in this conversation with you. Also, you've just as good as confessed that you're Cuttlefish. Nice going @SepiaSue

---

SepiaSue   *1 hour ago • Reply*

SHUT UP CUTLELFFISH IM NOT THE ONE WHO GOT INTO A FIHGT WIT THEMSLVES JUST FOR ATENTION AND ANYWAY NODBOSY IS LISTENIGN AND NOBODY CARRES SO JUST SHU TUP

Cesar Calamari   *1 hour ago • Reply*

[This comment has been moderated]

SepiaSue   *1 hour ago • Reply*

[This comment has been moderated]

Cesar Calamari   *1 hour ago • Reply*

[This comment has been moderated]

SepiaSue   *1 hour ago • Reply*

[This comment has been moderated]

Cesar Calamari   *1 hour ago • Reply*

[This comment has been moderated]

TWENTY-THREE

MY FAULT

It took a week for Whittington School to reopen. I don't know why they bothered – at least half the students didn't come back. Jess was nowhere to be seen. So, obviously, was Hector, not that anyone was looking for him.

We had a special assembly first thing in the morning. I was left sitting with Tori on one side of me and Chloë on the other. Mrs Olufunwa took to the stage and beamed us into silence with the Hand of God. Then she narrated the whole attack to us, in case anyone had somehow managed to forget. Which was strange, because she was one of the only people in the room who *had* forgotten. She'd been nyxed right at the beginning.

Then she summoned Ms Zima to her side. "Ms Zima will be on hand to speak to anyone who'd like to have a private chat about anything they experienced."

Ms Zima attempted a smile. "I'm a friendly face to talk to during these difficult times. I will make sure you have all the emotional support you need," she announced in a crisp monotone, her face devoid of all warmth.

"Some of you may also notice a few extra faces around school today," the head continued. "These are security guards, who are here to help us feel safe and secure as we go back to normal. If you see anything suspicious happening around the school, please don't hesitate to speak to one of them."

Mrs Olufunwa kept a white-knuckled grip on her podium as she talked long into the first period about how security measures around the school were going to work, and how she was going to personally ensure nothing like this happened again. The auditorium grew hot with a strange mixture of fear and boredom. Finally, she stepped away from the podium, before turning back to add:

"One final thing I should mention, to quash rumours before they arise. Hector Skeuopoios has been suspended from the school, as a result of an unconnected incident. Whittington doesn't permit bullying or physical violence of *any* kind, as you should all know by now. And last week's terrible events will not prevent us from upholding the school's principles as normal." Mrs Olufunwa nodded firmly to herself and strode off the stage.

The gossip about Hector's outburst against Baz, Yaz, Hazza, and Jason did the rounds along with the stories of what Cuttlefish had done. It didn't take long for the two events to become fused. By the end of the day, the rumours had become fact: Hector had been summoned to the head's office to be told he was getting suspended, then had some huge magical meltdown that took out half our teachers.

We did our best to go back to normal. The whole school did. We played our parts extra hard. The teachers were extra jolly as they tried to carry on with their lessons. Mr Milliner's roguish grin came with extra dollops of devil-may-care. Mr Kaplan stretched his rubbery face extra cartoonishly. Ms Zima had her hair in an extra tight bun.

But still, there was constant whispering in the corridors, knowing glances swapped between the teachers or the Year 8s. The less we heard about Hector, the more we had to guess. "Do you think he's coming back?" "No chance. He needs a special school." "You'd think, after what he did to Cass, they wouldn't be giving him any more second chances."

With Jess gone (apparently her mum had started forcibly homeschooling her), Jason ended up sitting next to me during English. "Hazza was put in a neck brace, you know," he said, showing me a picture on his phone. Hazza's greasy face was grinning atop a white cylinder.

"Looks like he recovered OK, then," I said. Weird how it took longer to recover from being incompetently bodyslammed by Hector than from being burnt to death by Cuttlefish.

"Yep. And he had it worst."

"How about you?"

Jason rubbed the back of his head. "I was fine. My burns disappeared by the evening, just like your mum said they would. Just had a tiny bit of concussion. But the others reckon that was Hector jumping on me."

That was another moment I'd forgotten: Hector punching Jason's head into the playground floor.

"I can't believe he did that to you. You did nothing wrong!"

"Didn't I?"

"I mean, you kicked that ball, but it was obviously an accident. Anyone else would have just laughed it off and forgotten about it."

"Would they? Even after everything else we'd done?"

"What do you mean?"

"You *know* what I mean. The others never give him a break. Sure, the football was an accident, but most of the time the way they treat him…it's all on purpose."

"That's just Baz and the others. They're idiots who think they're funny. They always have been. It's got nothing to do with you."

"Hasn't it?"

Jason was in a weird mood this morning. He had bags under his eyes. He looked like he'd aged five years in the last week. Up until now, he'd been mostly staring down at the books on his desk, but now he turned to me.

"Sure, I never join in with the others when they mess with Hector, but it's not like I ever try to stop them either. I'm just as bad. And now the whole school's been attacked, and Hector's been suspended, and it's completely my fault."

So *that's* why Jason looked so glum.

"Jason, it's not your fault at all! Hector didn't *have* to hurt you or anyone else. He *chose* to. Just the same as when he attacked *me* last term. He's also the one who got us nearly killed by Cuttlefish!"

"Was he?" Jason was apparently only capable of talking in enigmatic questions today. "Maybe if we'd never interfered, then none of this would have happened."

"Sure, maybe, but Hector is a sorcerer! We *know* that now."

"We don't know that. All we know is that he had some sorcery books."

"Give me one reason why someone might have a pile of sorcery books in their bag, other than because they're a sorcerer."

Before Jason could think of anything to say, Mr Kaplan cut off our conversation. "Sorry I'm late, everyone! There's no break for the wicked today."

We stumbled through an English lesson. Everyone did their best to pretend it was like any other lesson, politely ignoring Mr Kaplan when he broke off mid-speech to stare at his own hands in horror. None of us could really pay attention, though. At the end, Mr Kaplan asked us both to stay behind.

"I'm so sorry about what happened to the two of you last week," Mr Kaplan said, after the last of our class had funnelled out.

"It was nothing to do with you, sir!" I said.

"I know. But that criminal was wearing my face… That must have been a terrifying experience to live through. I can't help feeling like it was somehow my fault."

I'd seen Mr Kaplan performing every kind of emotion, but I'd never seen him do serious before. He rocked back slightly back on his desk chair, his hands clasped in front of him, his eyes roaming across his corny Shakespeare posters as if we weren't there. His face, which spent most of its life being squashed and mangled by its owner, was completely still. He looked like an Easter Island statue, his enormous cheekbones casting shadows over the rest of his face.

Jason and I pulled out chairs from the front desks and sat down.

"You had it worse. He nyxed you," I pointed out.

"Meaning I had the pleasure of waking up after it was all over, with no memory of Cuttlefish at all," he said.

"Doesn't getting nyxed give you brain damage?" I asked.

"Don't worry, there's not much left to save at this point," he said, tapping the side of his head jovially. But I could tell he was just trying to put on a brave face. There was something different about him – something haunted and afraid.

"I was hoping to peck your brains about something," Mr Kaplan continued. "I've heard so much about this Cuttlefish attack over the last few days, but barely anything about what happened between Hector and the other boys beforehand." Mr Kaplan smiled apologetically. "I understand I was there for the whole thing, but alas, I can't remember it now. Do you think you could fill me in?"

Jason and I recounted the epic tale of Hector the Relentless to Mr Kaplan. Jason was so unbelievably sympathetic to Hector that I wondered if he was still concussed. Mr Kaplan's face didn't move once while we were talking, not even when I told him about the sorcery books we'd found in his bag. And when we'd finished, he didn't say anything, just sat there in silence like he was waiting for us to carry on. Eventually, he said, stroking his neck agitatedly, "As I'm sure you know, I've been giving Hector some extra support this year, to help him keep on top of things. From what he's been telling me…"

"What kind of stuff has he been telling you?" I said.

Mr Kaplan kneaded his jaw, as if to check it was still there. "I don't want to get into anything specific. I'm sure Hector would want me to keep his confidence. But let's just say your name has come up. From the sound of it, you probably know Hector better than anyone else in your year."

"No, I don't," I said, glancing worriedly at Jason.

"You may know him better than you think. After all, he doesn't have many *close* confidantes, so–"

I twisted my ring back and forth, back and forth. "No. I don't. I really don't."

"OK, never mind, this is beside the point. All I mean to say is, you understand that Hector's got a lot to deal with, at school and at home, and whatever happened out there, you want what's best for him. Is that fair?"

Fair? Fair was a bit of a stretch. But I didn't have time to go into things properly just then.

"Yes, I suppose," I replied.

"How about you, Jason? I know it's hard to forgive what he did to you, but…"

"Absolutely," Jason said, with 1,000,000% more enthusiasm than I'd managed.

"Thank you both so much," Mr Kaplan slouched back in his chair. "It's so upsetting, having worked with him so much, having really made progress, for something like this to happen. For him to be suspended!"

"It wasn't his fault, sir," Jason said firmly. "It was Baz and the others. They spend their whole time getting at him every way they can. I don't even know why. He's never done anything to them."

"But still…he *did* have sorcery books. However much he's being bullied…why would he have sorcery books?" I added.

"That's just it. I'm not really worried about whose fault this is, or how this all started. I'm more worried about where this is going. Does that make sense?" Mr Kaplan pushed himself away from his desk, and got up to stand by the window, looking out into the flat white day. For a while, he said nothing at all. I started to wonder whether he'd forgotten what he was saying, or who he was. Then he began. "I learned recently that children who struggle to make friends, or get victimised in school are the ones most likely to develop an interest in sorcery.

Why did that interest me? Well, perhaps it's because I know just where Hector's coming from. My parents were both immigrants, you see. Turkish Cypriot. They spoke almost no English around the house. And neither did I, until I went to school, and discovered just what the other children thought of a kid who couldn't speak English properly." He laughed. "Let's just say they made it difficult for me to improve. Any time I opened my mouth, they'd laugh at me. Mock the way I spoke their language. It didn't take me long to discover that it was easier when I didn't speak at all."

Mr Kaplan's eyes were rippling. As he spoke, his voice became earthy with that accent of his, hidden just below the surface. "What I'm trying to get at here is…I understand the temptations of sorcery. When I was Hector's age…it seemed to offer me a way out of my life. A way to escape who I was. For a while, there were two paths I could have gone down, and…I was so young, and so unhappy, I could very easily have made a terrible mistake. Now, I was lucky enough to be saved. Someone came into my life who helped me find my voice. I just want to make sure Hector gets the same opportunity. Before it's too late."

"Why? What do you think he'll do, sir?" I asked.

"He won't do anything if he gets the support and compassion he needs from people around him, and if we're willing to give him a chance to redeem himself."

"You want us not to tell anyone about the sorcery books," I said wearily.

Mr Kaplan turned his hopeful eyes on mine. "I know it's a lot to ask, and it's not really fair on you. But something like this could destroy Hector's life. And if I get a chance, I think I can save it."

Jason nodded. "Sure. I get it."

I'd known what Mr Kaplan would say, because Mum had given me the exact same speech already. "Trust me, I'm taking what you saw very seriously," she'd said. "And I'm investigating this in every way I can. But if rumours get around the school that Hector had sorcery books, they could make this situation much, much worse. So please don't tell anyone. For my sake and Hector's."

I'd agreed, of course. But I hadn't been happy about it. I'd been chased by a sorcerer through my own school, and still the most important thing in her mind was for me to keep everything I knew about the River People a secret. Well, I'd had enough. If Mum refused to listen to me, maybe Mr Kaplan would.

"This isn't just Hector being weird," I said. "Something's not right about his mum. Or his house. It's full of creepy books and equipment."

"Equipment?" said Mr Kaplan. He twitched and looked around sharply. "What kind of equipment?"

"I don't know. Junk, probably," I said. "But I just get a bad feeling when I'm in there. And Mum told me I should pay more attention to my intuition."

Mr Kaplan nodded. "I understand. And don't think for a jiffy I'm not listening to you. I'm listening very closely indeed. I just think the best way to keep everyone safe and happy is to manage the situation without raising too much of an alarm. Does that make sense?"

It made more sense than what Mum had said. All she cared about was protecting the River People, no matter how dangerous they might be.

"Sure," I said.

Mr Kaplan's face stretched into rubbery joy again. "Thank you both. This means so much to me. And it will mean so much to Hector too. More than you can ever – ARGH!"

Mr Kaplan tipped backwards out of his chair. Jason and I jumped up and ran around his desk. He was curled up on the floor, twitching and jerking. It was almost like one of Hector's seizures, except Mr Kaplan's eyes were wide open and terrified.

The classroom door swung open. A woman in a flak jacket burst in, her eyes moving from Mr Kaplan to us. "What's going on here?" she barked.

"We don't know!" I said. "We were just talking."

"I'm fine! I'm fine," said Mr Kaplan from the floor. He'd stopped twitching. He smiled apologetically at Jason and me and dragged himself to his feet. "Very sorry you had to see that. Just a side effect of what he did to me. For a moment there, I thought my skin was burning up. I could see it blackening and cracking open... It was a little alarming."

The woman nodded. "Sorry to hear that. Sounds nasty."

Jason and I nodded in agreement.

"My doctor tells me these kinds of issues normally go away. Best thing to do is carry on as normal."

School wasn't the only place trying too hard to be normal. I found Mum waiting for me when I got home from school that day. She was lurking in the kitchen, armed with a steaming pot of tea, an epic chocolate cake from the shops, and a huge whacking great enormous smile all over her rosy little face.

"I thought we should do some celebrating today. I have some great news!" she said.

DANGER SIGNS

1. Tea
2. Cake
3. Smile
4. "I have some great news!"

Of the many terrible omens, 4 was by far the worst.

Just so you know why, let's revisit some cherished other times when Mum has said, "I have some great news!"

CHERISHED OTHER TIMES WHEN MUM HAS SAID, "I HAVE SOME GREAT NEWS!"

1. Mum: I have some great news! Your British Library Young Reader's pass doesn't expire until next month! So we can go after all!

Exactly.

I kept my rucksack on my back as I sat down, in case I needed to make a quick escape. There was a slice of cake already on a plate in front of me. Normally, the kitchen table was stacked high with old magazines. Today, it was empty. Sparkling clean. In fact, the whole kitchen was. All this time, I'd thought our kitchen was kind of shabby, when underneath there'd been a catalogue-perfect kitchen, all gleaming surfaces and glowing wooden doors, waiting to burst out.

I was scared.

To make things worse, it looked like Mum had taken her Concerned Face out of its box especially for the occasion. She sat down opposite me, and slid her own slice of cake within biting distance.

"Do you ever get lonely in this house, with just me and you?"

Of course. It was Foni. How could I have not realised? She'd been seeing her more and more. She was – they were – we were –

My horror must have been impossible to miss, because Mum just shook her head. "That's not what I meant. I'm not dating anyone."

Relief. Pure and golden.

"I just meant that recently, I've been so wrapped up in the Cuttlefish case that I've barely seen you. And the thing is, you haven't complained once. You've just got on with things. Well, that's not fair. Not fair at all. So, I've decided that it's time for things to change."

"Change? What do you mean? Everything's fine."

"I'm glad you think so. But I've decided that enough is enough. From now on I'm going to have a lot more free time."

"How come?"

"It's a funny story. Basically, the powers that be weren't too keen on how I tried to handle the situation at your school. Apparently, I should have been more focused on getting all the pupils to safety than capturing Cuttlefish. What nobody seems to understand–" the tea from the teapot missed my mug and splashed across the table " – is that when you have a mimetic like Cuttlefish on your hands, checking everyone personally is the only way you can be sure he's not hiding among you. But I won't bore you with the details, so to cut a long story short I've been given a free holiday!"

The cake tasted like ashes in my mouth. Sweet, chocolatey ashes.

"Don't give me that look, Cass. I'll go back once this has blown over. To be honest, I'd rather keep out of it as much as possible. They're also not happy that Cuttlefish appears to have targeted my own daughter's school. Apparently, this is evidence that I'm somehow implicated in the case more than I should be, or that my judgement is being clouded, or something. And who knows, there could even be some truth in that. The fact is that you were in real danger, Cass – you and the rest of Whittington – and I can't rule out the chance that it was somehow my fault."

Everyone seemed to think it was their own personal fault Cuttlefish had attacked the school. I didn't get it. Clearly, it was Cuttlefish's fault.

"Of course, whatever new team they're bringing in is going to take days or weeks getting up to speed, and who knows what atrocities Cuttlefish will commit in that time. But that's not something you or I will have to worry about for a while. Cuttlefish is someone else's problem now. You and I are going to kick back, relax, and have a sorcery-free couple of months. And to be perfectly honest I couldn't be happier." She picked up the teapot, plate, and mug (she'd never got round to pouring herself any) and slammed it all merrily into the dishwasher.

I grimly cut myself another slice of cake and chewed it slowly, staring Mum in the eye. She smiled back.

"I don't think it was a mistake," I said. "Trying to catch him in the school, I mean."

"Nor do I," said DCI Helen Drake, smiling relentlessly from the kitchen. "The mistake I made was giving in."

TWENTY-FOUR

ALL IN YOUR HEAD

Before there was sound, there was pain. Dull, throbbing, pain, coursing steadily through the prisoner's shoulders and thighs. Something was sticking up into his spine. If he squirmed, cool metal bit into his flesh, wrestling him down into wet rock.

Before there was light, there was sound. A steady, gloppy drip, somewhere behind the prisoner's head. It was laughing at him. It was in on the joke. If you could call the prisoner's torment a joke.

And before there were answers, there was light. The prisoner wrenched open his eyes, ignoring the stinging pain, and stared upwards, seeing nothing but faint shapes in a black abyss. He lifted his head as far as he could off his rock. Shafts of blue-tinged light rippled off the distant cave walls. Was it daylight, from some unseen fissure in the earth high above his head? It was impossible to tell.

The prisoner strained to look down at himself. Thick chain links laced across his naked body, smearing orange rust onto his skin. A filthy rag was the only thing protecting his dignity. As if dignity was a word that could be applied to any aspect of this situation. The prisoner dropped his heavy head back onto his rock pillow and closed his eyes.

Then, a voice in the darkness.

"I was dreadfully sorry to hear what happened to you yesterday."

The prisoner's eyes snapped open, and his head lolled towards the side the voice had come from. Whoever had spoken remained just out of sight.

"I was out of town. Visiting an old friend. Otherwise, I would have come here straight away, and we could have avoided all this unpleasantness."

The voice seemed coldly amused, with a faint sing-song accent that the prisoner couldn't recognize.

"Please…" the prisoner rasped. His dry throat had seized up.

A murmur of sympathy came from the prisoner's right. An arm, sleeved in blue velvet, appeared, holding a glass of water. The prisoner picked his head up and slurped greedily, not realizing how thirsty he was until cool water was running down his throat. Most of it splashed over his face and neck, but he didn't notice. He lowered his head with a gurgling sigh.

"Better?" the sing-song voice asked. "Good. Good! More?"

The prisoner nodded, and the process repeated. The prisoner drank most of the water this time, letting it fill his mouth before he swallowed it all in a dizzying gulp. The metal chains slid across his body, slackening enough for him to turn and look at his saviour for the first time.

A bottle-blue jacket, perfectly pressed, which shimmered in the cave's murky light. It would have been beautiful in any other situation. A white mask, frozen in riotous laughter, with high, arching eyeholes and jutting cheeks. No trace of a recognisable feature could be spotted behind this dazzling costume. He was nothing more than his mask. He was Mirth.

In Mirth's shadow stood Sorrow. Her mask's features were weighed down by the burdens of existence. Her eyelids and mouth drooped. She was dressed much more plainly, in loose black clothes that the prisoner couldn't make out in the gloom. On her shoulder was a huge eagle, dappled brown and black.

All three of them held the prisoner's gaze steadily.

The ensemble took considerably less time for the prisoner to see than it did to describe verbally. In fact, it was instantaneous.

The prisoner flinched. Sharp rock scraped along his back. The chain links tightened and held him down.

"No. No. No!" the prisoner gasped, turning his head away from the eagle.

"Ah. So you do remember, then," said Mirth. "Ariel wasn't sure whether you had lived through your experience yesterday. Which would have been a shame, as she would have been forced to repeat it."

Flashes of memory tormented the prisoner. That monstrous bird, its wings beating over him…

He squeezed his mind shut and tried to breathe.

"As I say, I am dreadfully sorry," he continued amicably. "Ariel was understandably upset with you, after everything you'd done. But she's calmed down now, and hopefully we can talk everything over without any more drama. Isn't that right, Ariel?"

Neither Sorrow nor the gargantuan eagle on her shoulder responded in any way.

"Let's begin with something easy," Mirth suggested. "Your name."

"Seraphim," the prisoner managed. "Pannayotis."

"It's lovely to meet you, Seraphim. For so long, I have wanted to meet the great Cuttlefish. The man behind the mask. I'm only sorry it had to be in such…unfortunate circumstances." Mirth glanced around the subterranean cavern.

"No. There's been a mistake. That's not me," said the prisoner. Every word he spoke had to be torn from deep inside him.

"You're not Cuttlefish?"

The prisoner stared into what he hoped was Mirth's eyes, and injected as much sincerity as he could into his shredded voice. "No. I've got nothing to do with him. This is a case of…" (he thrashed around to remember the right phrase) "…mistaken identity."

"There have been quite a lot of those recently, haven't there?" Mirth said. "And they always seem to end the same way. With an innocent sorcerer either up the river or in hiding. And a number of priceless artefacts missing. Grimoires which belong to the Daedalus Set. This concerns me very greatly, for I know what havoc those books can wreak if they are brought together. My duty is to prevent that from happening. You can call me Prince."

"You've got to listen to me, Prince. There's been a mistake. I shouldn't be here. I've done nothing wrong."

"Nothing wrong?" Mirth shot a look at Sorrow, at the eagle on her shoulder. "Are you sure that's a wise thing to keep saying?"

The prisoner caught the look, and a river of pain flowed through his intestines. He jolted, and the chains bore him into the cold rock once more.

"OK. OK. I made a mistake. Years ago. I admit that."

"You stole a number of Daedalus books from the Lyceum's own library. A library which had been maintained and guarded for over a thousand years. A library which had been entrusted to you, its chief librarian."

"It was a mistake. A big mistake. But I thought I was doing it for the good of the Lyceum!"

"So I hear. It was all a cunning trick on Cuttlefish's part, is that right? He convinced you to betray the Lyceum and hand its Daedalus books over to him."

"You don't understand what he's like," the prisoner rasped. "He convinced me that it was someone inside the Lyceum trying to assemble the Daedalus Set. He told me I had to help him hide those books. To *protect* them, you get it? To make sure they could never be brought together."

The eagle opened its wings and sprung off Sorrow's shoulder with an almighty screech. The prisoner recoiled, but the eagle didn't approach him. It soared into the open space above them, a mottled arrow becoming lost in the cavern's gloomy heights.

Mirth watched it make a few circles of the cave, his mask smiling in appreciation. "Of course," he continued. "You were only trying to stop Cuttlefish from getting his hands on the entire Daedalus Set, and trying to do the unthinkable with them. That's why, when the Lyceum found out what you'd done, you went into hiding for the next – what has it been now? – ten years."

"None of them understood! None of them! A few close friends thought I was just stupid. The rest thought I was Cuttlefish. What else could I do but hide?"

"What else indeed, Cuttlefish? Once in hiding, you wisely stopped trying to steal from us. You sat on top of your stolen hoard for years. But then your greed got the better of you, didn't it? You wanted to taste even greater magical power. So, a few months ago, you started stealing again. Giorgios Siskos. Keith Foley. Lukianos Zopgraphos. The SID may not have realized the connection between them, but the Lyceum do. They all had Daedalus books, didn't they? And then, you came after the Lyceum again. Trying to take even more Daedalus books in our care. You got lucky at the Bodleian. But without your books, you didn't have the strength to fight us. And here we are."

Mirth gestured at the vast cave they were standing in. At the chains criss-crossing the prisoner's body. At the rock to which he was bound.

"This place is Ariel's creation," Mirth said. "Breathtaking, isn't it? She did it all without the use of talismans or potions. And, thanks to you, without any Daedalus books. She's a very skilled conjurer. Perhaps the best conjurer I have the privilege of knowing."

Sorrow did not acknowledge this compliment in any way. But the conjured eagle did, swooping out of the darkness to land on Sorrow's shoulder once more. Sorrow recoiled a little from the impact, though her mournful mask gave nothing away. The eagle ruffled its feathers, gripped Sorrow with its talons, and stared levelly at the prisoner through its black eyes.

Mirth stroked the eagle's feathers. "So very beautiful, isn't she? Even though we all know she's not really there…it's impossible to not see her! To not appreciate her majesty! You, on the other hand, are nothing without a Daedalus book under your arm, are you? Just a two-bit con man. Alas, your dazzling stunts are behind you now. You will never hold a Daedalus book again, as you will not leave this cavern until you've told us where we can find your stolen books."

"Prince, I can't help you. I don't have them."

"So be it. I will just have to come back tomorrow and ask you the same question. After you have had time to heal."

Sorrow's eagle once again took flight, its wingspan casting a dark shadow over the prisoner. Its screech echoed around the cavern.

"No. Please, no. No. No!" screamed the prisoner.

The eagle swooped low and beat its wings over the prisoner's head. Dank wind cooled the sweat on the prisoner's face. The giant bird landed heavily on the prisoner's abdomen. Its talons gripped the prisoner's naked flesh.

"No! No! No!" continued the prisoner, thrashing uselessly.

"Are you hoping that it will at least be easier to bear this time? That you'll have got used to it? Well, think again," said Mirth. His singsong voice glided serenely over the turbulent depths of the prisoner's howls. "In fact, you will experience the pain even more forcefully, precisely *because* your body knows what's about to happen to it. It is primed. It is sensitized. The anticipation of what you are about to endure is so strong that you can already feel it! Isn't that right?"

Mirth was right. The eagle's talons were barely drawing blood, but with each dig and scratch, shockwaves of pain rolled over the helpless prisoner.

Mirth took his captive by the hand and gazed at him beseechingly. "Tell us the truth. You still have a chance."

"I don't know anything. I didn't do it. It's someone else you want. Please believe me."

Mirth sighed and let go of the prisoner's hand. "You were once a trusted friend of the Lyceum. I'm sorry things have come to this. But if you refuse to tell the truth – my duty is clear."

The eagle let out a chilling screech and slashed the prisoner's belly open. The prisoner screamed and flung his head backwards into the rock. The chains tightened.

Mirth grabbed the prisoner's hair and yanked his head up. "You will watch," he hissed into the prisoner's ear.

And the prisoner had no choice but to watch. He watched while the giant eagle ripped through his skin, peeled it open with its beak. He watched while the eagle's talons plunged deep inside him, closed around his intestines. He watched as the eagle beat its wings and rose up, pulling up the prisoner's guts like weeds from a flowerbed. He watched as his insides spilled over the edge of his rock bed and slopped around his body.

"Are you telling yourself that none of this is real? That it's all in your head?" said Mirth, into his ear. "You're right, of course. It is nothing but an illusion, what is happening to you. But that doesn't make it any less painful, does it?"

The eagle tore out bloody chunks of muscle with its talons and flung them into the air. Its wings beat harder and harder. Its screeches and the screeches of the prisoner were exactly the same. They echoed around the cavern, trapped and unheard by anyone on the surface.

Mirth was right. It was somehow worse than yesterday. Far worse. The horror of this time was amplified by every memory of that first time, as if the eagle were ripping through tender scar tissue left behind by yesterday's frenzy.

The eagle buried its head deep inside the shredded hole it had made in the prisoner's belly. The prisoner could feel it pecking, nosing up underneath his ribcage.

Then its beak clamped shut, and with a powerful beat of its wings, it launched itself with a spray of viscera high into the air. In its beak, it held the prisoner's liver, a sagging brown sack. A long, stringy intestine led from the liver back into the prisoner's guts, like a newborn baby's umbilical cord.

The eagle flung its head from side to side, shaking arteries off the liver, while its talons ripped through the tissues still connecting it to the prisoner. The eagle's head, breast, and talons were a dark glistening red. It soared upwards, the liver still clutched in its beak, and dissolved into the darkness.

"Don't worry," Mirth said soothingly, letting go at last of the prisoner's hair. "None of that really happened. In time, your mind will be able to unweave the illusion and return you to reality. This time tomorrow, you will be completely healed. Only your memories will remain."

The prisoner's consciousness swam in a sea of anguish. His body was nothing to him now but a prison of torment, torn apart, disembowelled.

"If you're hoping you'll die soon, think again. You will not be allowed to forget what happened here. If you do…it will all have been for nothing."

"Please…" the prisoner whispered, every word a new hell. "Let me go."

"Oh, I would like to let you go. It upsets me, having to watch this. But the gods do not tolerate liars and thieves. Neither does the Lyceum."

Seeing the faintest chance of salvation, the prisoner took a deep and agonising breath. Air rushed around his open abdomen and ribcage in ways that should not have been possible. "I…can help you. Stop…the real Cuttlefish. That's all I ever…wanted."

"Don't worry, Seraphim. We have already taken our own measures against you. Thanks to your hard work, we have precious few Daedalus books left in our care. We knew it was only a matter of time before you tricked us out of those, too. So Ariel here has taken the remaining ones out of our own libraries and hidden them somewhere even I don't know about, to ensure that no matter what, you never get your hands on them."

It was now, for the first time, that Sorrow spoke.

"What?"

Mirth left the prisoner to his endless torments and turned to Sorrow. "I was only explaining to Cuttlefish that he will never be able to complete the Daedalus Set, as you yourself have taken our grimoires to safety."

"What? No, I haven't."

"You did it this morning! I *watched* you!"

A pale and bloated realization surfaced in the prisoner's mind. It tasted of bitter vindication. "He's got them," he gasped. "You were wrong about me...and about him...and now he's got everything. He's going to...finish what he...started. You can't...stop him."

"Shut up," commanded Mirth, his moulded grin savage and unyielding. Grabbing Sorrow by the shoulder, he manoeuvred them both to a distant corner of the cave. Hissed discussion echoed distantly over the sound of dripping water. The prisoner floated on the edge of both death and insanity, with only his neverending pain anchoring him in consciousness.

Eventually, Mirth and Sorrow returned to his side.

"Mark my words, we will find Cuttlefish and we will take back everything he has stolen from the Lyceum. As for you...We will grant you peace."

Smiling, Mirth turned on his heel. Sorrow followed suit, albeit without the smile.

The eagle descended one last time. Its bloody talons wrapped mercifully around the prisoner's neck and carried him to a place without pain.

TWENTY-FIVE

BETTER SAFE THAN SORRY

Jess's mum called a PTA meeting.

It wasn't an official PTA meeting. Jess's mum was the chairman of the PTA, so she could have called an official PTA meeting if she'd wanted to.

But this one wasn't.

"I think it's important that we get everything out in the open," she said. "It's our own fault we're having these troubles – because we're not communicating with each other."

She didn't announce the meeting in school or anything. But everyone quickly knew about it.

"Of course, it's important that the River People don't hear about this," she said. "It wouldn't be fair to accuse them of anything prematurely. Not before we've gathered all the evidence."

Jess's mum was standing in the centre of her living room as she was saying all this. Packed in around the edge were a pretty hefty number of parents. Chloë's mum and stepdad were there with her, as well as her younger brother. Tori had even managed to drag her mum away from whatever she spent her life doing, although her dad and older sisters were nowhere to be seen. Jason and his family hadn't turned up.

"Scott, could you go and get the rest of the biscuits?" she said. "They're on the kitchen island."

Jess's mum had put two plates of biscuits on the coffee table. But they'd already been eaten, mainly by me. Hey, I was in prime position next to the table. It couldn't be helped.

Jess's older brother was slouching in the doorway. He pushed his way past a couple of people standing in the hallway, and came back armed with two packets of Party Rings. Unable to come any further into the room, he lobbed them at the coffee table. They landed with a little red spray in the pot pourri.

Jess's mum had also offered everyone tea when they'd arrived, but luckily no-one had said yes, because that would've been a nightmarish boiling operation. Instead, everyone was perched like mermaids at rush hour all over Jess's sofa set, leaning forward with their hands on their knees.

Jess's mum stood on the table, batting the overhead lamp out of the way. It swung about, making shadows spin in circles around everyone's tense faces. It was already dark outside, so the curtains were drawn. It felt like we were planning a battle from an underground bunker, but instead of miniature armies we had Jammy Dodgers.

"We all know why we're here," Jess's mum began. "For many of us, the threat of sorcerers was something far away, something we didn't need to worry about. But now, our own children have become victims. It's a miracle that no pupils were hurt. We need to come together, as a community, to make sure nothing like this can ever happen again."

Heads bobbed on every side of the room. The only person who didn't react was Mum, who had taken a seat by herself on a wooden chair opposite mine. She watched Jess's mum unmovingly, with her arms crossed.

"When an incident like this happens in our midst, we have a duty to ask ourselves why. Why us? Why now? Which brings us to the question of Persephone Skeuoeupoiois–"

"Skeuopoios," Mum said pleasantly.

"What?"

"That's how it's pronounced. Ski – you – oh – poy - os."

Jess's mum smiled indulgently. "Greek names are impossible to pronounce. Let's just call her Foni. Ten years ago, Foni's husband Melanthios was prosecuted for numerous counts of sorcery, theft, and possession of magical materials. He was the man the papers called Cuttlefish. Shortly afterwards, Foni was also imprisoned for eight years. She's only just been released."

Jess's mum spun around a few times while she waited for these words to sink in. She was in socks and the coffee table was well polished, so the effect went on for longer than anyone needed.

But my mind continued spinning long after Jess's mum had stopped. Hector's dad was Cuttlefish. Foni had been imprisoned too. The SID had known this all along. *Mum* had known this all along, and she'd never told me. Judging by everyone's calm expressions, I was the only person who *hadn't* known all along.

"Did you know?" I hissed at Jess, who was squatting on the floor next to me.

Jess nodded, bewildered. "Didn't *you* know? That's why they've only just moved back."

Of course. Hector had told me as much. How they'd always lived in Omphalos. How they'd had to move away for a while. And how they'd only come back years later. In all the time I'd spent down there, I hadn't bothered to ask why. And now I knew.

These bombshells threw up more questions than answers, though. Hector's dad was dead. Wasn't he? How could he be Cuttlefish? And if he and Foni had been in prison, then why had Mum told me, again and again, that the River People were innocent?

"Like everyone in this neighbourhood, I was surprised when Foni decided to return to her old house. I'd have thought she'd want a fresh start, away from everything she and her husband had done. But I was perfectly prepared to look past it, and turn over a new leaf. However, since coming back, Foni hasn't made the slightest effort to integrate herself into our community."

Mum winced loudly. A couple of other parents shifted slightly on the sofa.

"For example, where were they at the Whittington carol singing?" Jess's mum continued. "Nowhere to be found. They may be atheists, but my own family is Jewish and we wouldn't *dream* of missing carol singing. It's an important community event!"

"When was carol singing?" asked Mum blandly.

"A week into the Christmas holidays," shot back Jess's mum. "It would be lovely to see you there one day. It's always such a nice evening. But we're here to address one simple question. Whether the River People–"

"If I may interrupt?"

Jess's mum's face twisted in frustration for a split second, before relaxing into a smile. "Please, go ahead, Helen."

"I'd prefer it if you didn't use the term 'river people'. SIDs and sorcerers may describe getting sent to prison as being sent 'up the river', but that doesn't mean we need to remind everyone of Foni's jail term every time we talk about her. And Hector has never been in jail. Can't we just call them both by their names?"

"Of course, Helen, my mistake," Jess's mum said, getting thrown quite literally off balance. She was teetering on the edge of the coffee table, Party Ring crumbs getting embedded in her socks. "I can't help it if I find 'River People' a bit easier to pronounce than the name *Skueepiois*, but if it means so much to you I'll do my best. What I called this meeting to discuss is the connection between *that family* and Cuttlefish's current crime spree. We all believed that Cuttlefish was killed ten years ago while resisting arrest. But all of a sudden, he's come back to life, the moment the Skiopioses returned to their old house."

"Sorry, Anne. A couple of minor clarifications?"

"Of course, just let me finish–"

"I'm afraid I can't do that, Anne." For a second, I couldn't work out whose voice that was, then I realised it was Mum's. She sounded different from usual – colder, deeper. That's right: Detective Chief Inquisitor Helen Drake had been roused from slumber.

DCI Helen Drake uncoiled herself from her seat and loomed over Jess's mum, eyes glittering. "Firstly, Melanthios Skeuopoios was not killed while resisting arrest. Yes, he was killed by police *during* his arrest, but the inquiry conclusively ruled that the killing was unjustified, as Melanthios showed no signs of resistance. Secondly, Melanthios was never formally charged with Cuttlefish's crimes. In fact, the case against him was posthumously dropped, and the identity of Cuttlefish remains unknown."

"Thank you, Helen," smiled Jess's mum, "but there's no time to get bogged down in quibbling details. Everyone knows that Melanthios was Cuttlefish. Why else, the moment Melanthios was dead, did Cuttlefish disappear?"

"Until last year," DCI Helen Drake pointed out.

"My point exactly," returned Jess's mum. "There's one obvious solution to this mystery, which the SID seem determined to ignore. Melanthios Skyapious *didn't die*. He faked his own death to evade arrest, and he's been lying low ever since, waiting for his wife to return to him so that they can continue where they left off!"

Jess's mum gazed proudly at all of our speechless faces. "You really think a sorcerer as powerful as Cuttlefish would have let himself be killed so easily? Or is it more likely that he pulled the wool over the world's eyes so he could escape justice?"

"There's another, arguably more obvious solution to this mystery," Mum said. "And that is that Cuttlefish is someone totally different, and the Skeuopoios family are innocent victims of police brutality."

"You surely can't believe that after the attack on our children's school!" fired back Jess's mum. "Not after all our children's *lives* were at stake…"

Jess's mum's face crumpled up suddenly. The light from the overhead lamp made it look like she had big gashes running all the way through her head. She stepped quickly out of the light and into the shoulder of Jess's dad. Jess's dad took her glasses off before they got crushed, then awkwardly rubbed her back. Everyone listened to her muffled sobbing for a while, not sure whether this was part of the speech.

"Speaking as a mother, I'm just as mortified as all of you that something like this could happen. I was as shocked as all of you. But speaking as an inquisitor, let me assure you that I'm doing everything I can to bring Cuttlefish to justice–"

"Rubbish!" Jess's mum shouted. She'd turned back to face Mum. Her cheeks had gone blotchy, and her mouth was quivering. "You've just stood by and watched. You don't seem to think there's a threat at all. Your own daughter has been put in danger more times than anyone else," (aw shucks, now *that* was more like the recognition I deserved, although I sure didn't want it anymore) "and you've ignored her completely! Either you're insane, or you're in denial."

The living room was supposed to be a sanctuary from the unknown terrors of the night outside. But now it was a duelling ground with no escape. My mum and my best friend's mum stared icily at one another across the packed room. It was – and I'm saying this as a person who'd had Hector Skeuopoios in her life for a good six months – the most awkward situation I'd ever been in. There weren't even any Party Rings left to ease my pain.

It quickly turned out that this moment was only the second most awkward moment in my entire life. The most awkward moment came seconds later, when Jess's mum looked at me as I tried to hide below the coffee table.

"Cassie. Perhaps you'd like to tell us what you've been through."

No thank you, Anne. No, I wouldn't like.

It was like watching a particularly violent and hatred-fuelled ping pong match, only now the ping pong ball had gone hurtling into the spectator stand and taken my head clean off. Everyone stared at me while I tried to communicate my extreme unhappiness about everything to Jess's mum using the power of my eyes alone.

"Well. If Cassie doesn't want to share – perfectly understandable, the poor thing – then perhaps I should. She was physically assaulted by Hector. Isn't that right?"

I weighed up whether I could set the curtains on fire, creating a distraction long enough for me to dive into the pot pourri and swim to safety. In the end, I realized I had no choice but to say something.

"That was different," I squeaked.

"Don't be ridiculous, Cassie. That's probably what your mother told you, isn't it? That it was just something to be ignored. But that's what's got us into this situation – ignoring what's in plain sight. We ignored Hector's erratic and violent behaviour, and now he's been suspended after assaulting four pupils. We ignored his family's criminal history, and now our children have been put in the firing line. So, Cassie, don't be afraid to tell us what really happened."

I went looking for Jess, my Partner in Awkwardness, but she wasn't home. She was staring at the ceiling, pretending she hadn't heard anything.

"You see?" Jess's mum said, pointing at me tenderly. "She's reluctant to admit it, because she's been told to ignore what should be obvious to everyone here! We can't keep ignoring this. But I don't think we should bother taking this to the SIDs either." She looked a little less sure of herself now, but she carried on. "I don't think the SIDs are equipped to deal with the current situation. They're simply too weak. So what I propose we do is take what we know straight to the newspapers. They'll expose the River People for who they are in no time. If Melanthios is still alive, as I believe, they'll sniff him out. If that doesn't provoke a full-scale police investigation, at the very least it should drive them away from our neighbourhood, and we'll be able to sleep a little better at night."

"Anne, I think I'm beginning to understand you," Mum said brightly. "What you're saying is, if you went to the local police station, they'd soon tell you what I'm telling you now. That they can't do anything about the Skeuopoios family, because they'd have no *evidence* to convict them with. Equally, they might take Hector's *physical assault"* (Mum made sure to look right at me) "as a sign that the boy needs support, not that he comes from a family of criminal masterminds. But what you're is saying is that, in dangerous times like this, we simply don't have time to worry about the *evidence*. We have to act now, to protect our families, before it's too late. Better safe than sorry."

I'd have known that tone anywhere. It was the one Mum used on me whenever I talked back too much. Whenever she thought I was being stupid beyond belief.

Jess's mum froze, tugging her Star of David necklace as she tried to work out what was going on. Eventually, she replied, "Well... *exactly!"*

A few of the family units nodded and looked approvingly at each other. A few more frowned as they tried to pick apart what exactly Mum had said.

"I think taking our story to the media would work brilliantly," Mum carried on. "That's what terrifies me about it. Because however sure you are that Melanthios is somehow still alive and committing Cuttlefish's crimes, I'm sure you can agree that you *might* be wrong. There's still a chance that the Skeuopoios family have absolutely nothing to do with any of this. Right?"

Jess's mum nodded grudgingly. "But the fact is–"

Mum held up her hand. It wasn't a bad impression of Mrs Olufunwa's Hand of God – it worked just as well to kill off the murmurs that had started to spring up out of the corners.

"Let's imagine that they're completely innocent. Will the media notice this inconvenient fact? Will they care? Of course not. They'll wait for a dry patch, when Cuttlefish hasn't been up to anything for a while, then they'll burn Persephone Skeuopoios at the stake. A Greek atheist – nobody burns more brightly than that once you set a bit of kindling around them. Even if no police investigation is ever launched, her life and Hector's will be reduced to ash in no time. You don't believe me? Just look at Hector. He's suffered the consequences of these vicious stories ever since he set foot in Whittington School. He's been bullied remorselessly. True, this probably doesn't apply *directly* to most of you," (and now she was looking straight at me, and it wasn't DCI Helen Drake anymore, but plain old Mum, closer and more real than I could bear) "but the boy's life has been made into a living hell, thanks to the rumours around his family. We should think long and hard before we do anything to hurt them further."

Just before the point when I think I would have started to melt in agony, Mum sat suddenly down, leaving behind a space that nobody dared to fill any more.

Finally, Jess's mum spoke. The slight tremor in her voice had gone. She was completely calm.

"Helen, I agree with you completely. I'm as sorry as you are that a child like Hector has been caught up in this – whatever his parents are up to is not *his* fault, and what Hector needs is the individual care and support that a special education school is able to give him. But this doesn't change the *very real* possibility that Melanthios is alive, and behind all of this. We can't let any *personal feelings* cloud our judgement."

There was another murmur wave.

"What are you trying to say?" Mum said. "Just because I'm one of the few people in this room to have actually spoken to Foni–"

"Come on, Helen, you can be honest with us. You're closer to Foni than you're letting on, aren't you? How can you trust yourself to be objective when it comes to your *girlfriend?*"

Mum's mouth opened, but no sounds came out. She just stood there, agape.

"When I found out, I was a little confused," said Jess's mum sweetly. "I think we all were. A pair of widows, suddenly wanting to shack up together? An inquisitor and a convicted felon? But now it all makes sense to me. You're as much a victim of Cuttlefish as our children's teachers. Don't you see?"

Mum said nothing.

"Cuttlefish is committing crimes all over this city, while his own wife has charmed a senior investigator of his crimes into falling in love with her. The two of them must laugh to each other every day."

"You have no idea what you're talking about," said Mum.

"Yes I do, Helen. Cassie confided everything in me, because she couldn't speak openly to you anymore. She's known the truth all along. She's tried to warn you. But you refused to listen to her. You insisted that she visit the River People over and over again, while you carried on your little affair with Foni."

"That's not true," Mum insisted. "That's not true."

"Isn't it? I think we should let Cassie speak for herself."

Again, every pair of eyes in the room flicked to me, dozens of lasers burning through my skin.

"I know it's hard, Cassie," Jess's mum murmured to me. "I know these last few months have been difficult for you. More difficult than anyone in this room could imagine. But tell everyone what you told me, and we can finally start to make things right."

I tried to swallow, but my mouth felt like I'd just been eating pot pourri rather than Party Rings. Even my eyes had dried up and shrivelled away. I could feel them scraping in their sockets as they turned to look at Mum.

Mum was staring at me with glassy calm. Whatever emotional ride Jess's mum had just taken her on, she'd jumped firmly off, and she was back on solid ground. But she was still staring at me.

"I..." I started. I didn't know. How could I? Everything Jess's mum had said was crazy, but so were all the facts. And at least Jess's mum was trying to explain the facts. Mum just didn't seem to care about the facts any more. She never had. She'd known the truth about Foni from the start, but instead of staying away, she'd *dated* her, dated that old sunken-eyed hag.

But...

It was Mum. I stretched my mind as far as it could go, and still I couldn't make it believe that Mum could be wrong about this. Mum was never wrong. Not when it mattered.

"Fine," Mum announced. "I didn't want to say this, but it looks like I have no choice. When Foni was released from prison, I had my misgivings too. Just like you, I suspected there was more to her than met the eye. That's what brought me to Omphalos. I only took Cass to make it look more like a social call. Yes, there was a misunderstanding a while back when Foni revealed she was developing certain feelings for me, but we were never dating. After spending plenty of time with her, I've come to the conclusion that there's not a trace of magical activity taking place inside the house. As I'm sure Cass has seen too."

The room pressed in on me again.

I tugged on my snake ring. "It's true," I told Jess's mum. "What I told you last time was a mistake. I'm sorry." My face heated as this flaming lie burst out of it.

"*What?*"

"I…got it all wrong."

"But – you said…" Jess's mum spluttered. "Can't you see? This is all part of it. Foni is a dangerous woman! Just as dangerous as Cuttlefish himself!"

A couple of parents in the shady corner next to the TV coughed and looked at each other. The background whispering was getting hard to ignore.

"The most dangerous thing about my friend Persephone is her taste in home decoration," Mum concluded firmly.

"*Your friend Persephone,*" Jess's mum screamed, "*is a WITCH!*"

EXPOSÉ

NO JUSTICE FOR SKEUOPOIOS FAMILY

IT SOUNDS LIKE SOMETHING OUT OF A DYSTOPIAN HORROR FILM. THE POLICE KICKING DOWN YOUR DOOR AND KILLING YOUR FAMILY WHILE YOU SLEEP. BUT IT'S NOT. IT'S JUST THE REALITY OF 21ST CENTURY BRITAIN. A COUNTRY SO CORRUPTED BY FEAR THAT IT HAS BECOME THE GREATEST DANGER OF ALL.

THE METROPOLITAN POLICE HAVE FINALLY RELEASED THE RESULTS OF THEIR INQUIRY INTO THE SKEUOPOIOS TRAGEDY. AND IT HAS TWO THINGS TO SAY FOR ITSELF:

1. MELANTHIOS SKEUOPOIOS WAS COMPLYING FULLY WITH POLICE AT THE TIME HE WAS SHOT DEAD. HE WAS

NOT ATTEMPTING SORCERY. HE WAS
NOT ATTEMPTING TO RUN AWAY. HE
WAS NOT ATTEMPTING TO HARM
ANYONE.

2. GIVEN THE INFORMATION THEY HAD
AT THE TIME, THE POLICE COULD NOT
HAVE BEEN EXPECTED TO ACT
DIFFERENTLY. THERE WILL BE NO
MEASURES TAKEN AGAINST THE
OFFICERS INVOLVED.

HUH? SURELY WE MUST BE MISSING
SOMETHING? BUT NO. OUR REPORTERS HAVE
SCOURED THE REPORT AGAIN AND AGAIN AND
KEEP FINDING THE SAME TWO MESSAGES.
THE POLICE HAVE BROKEN INTO A FAMILY
HOME AND TAKEN INNOCENT LIVES, BUT AS
FAR AS THEY'RE CONCERNED THEY'VE DONE
NOTHING WRONG.

DON'T FORGET, THE CHARGES AGAINST
MELANTHIOS SKEUOPOIOS WERE DROPPED
MONTHS AGO. ONLY SIX WEEKS AFTER HIS

SHOOTING, IN FACT. WHATEVER REASONS THE SID HAD FOR DIRECTING POLICE TO ARREST HIM SEEMED TO MYSTERIOUSLY VANISH THE MOMENT THEY INVESTIGATED FURTHER.

AND NOW, WE HAVE PROOF THAT SKEUOPOIOS WASN'T EVEN RESISTING ARREST. AS FAR AS THE LAW IS CONCERNED, HE WAS INNOCENT ON EVERY COUNT.

BUT AN OFFICIAL DECLARATION OF INNOCENCE WON'T MEAN MUCH TO SKEUOPOIOS'S WIDOW, PERSEPHONE. OR HIS SURVIVING THREE-YEAR-OLD CHILD. THEIR FAMILY, DESTROYED IN THE NAME OF JUSTICE. AND NOW, THEY'RE BEING TOLD THEY CAN'T EXPECT ANY JUSTICE THEMSELVES.

OF COURSE, PLENTY OF YOU OUT THERE STILL BELIEVE SKEUOPOIOS WAS CUTTLEFISH. THE BEST EVIDENCE YOU HAVE

OF THAT? THE FACT THAT CUTTLEFISH HAS
GONE MYSTERIOUSLY QUIET SINCE THE
SHOOTING.

BUT TO THOSE OF YOU THAT STILL THINK
CUTTLEFISH IS THE BOGEYMAN: WAKE UP.
OUR POLICE FORCE HAS BECOME SO
OBSESSED WITH FINDING AND DESTROYING
THE BOGEYMAN THAT IT HAS BECOME THE
BOGEYMAN.

BE CAREFUL WHO YOU PRAY TO. YOU MIGHT
BE NEXT.

TWENTY-SIX

PUNISHED ENOUGH

In the end, they put it to a vote.

"Democracy!" Jess's mum screamed.

It wasn't really a vote, more a shouting contest between the parents who thought we should report them and the ones who thought we shouldn't. Tori's mum, who hadn't really had a clue about any of this before the meeting, had been won over by Mum's speech at the end. And it turned out she was a trained soprano, so Mum's side had an easy victory. We left Jess's mum wretchedly chewing on a final Jammy Dodger that she'd found under a sofa. She had one arm around Jess.

I tried to catch Jess's eye again on the way out, but she wouldn't look my way.

As we walked home, I was half worried about what Jess was going to say next time I saw her, and half wondering why the only true thing Mum had said about Foni was on her dangerous taste in home decoration. There was a tiny chance she hadn't lied, and she was just being thick, but mainly I was guessing she'd lied. Her lies were so thick and entangled that I didn't know where to start unpicking.

I started with "So you knew she was a sorcerer? All this time?" Maybe it wasn't the most important question right now, but I had to start somewhere. We were already out of sight of Jess's house. We'd walked in silence a long way.

"Who said anything about Foni being a sorcerer?"

"She's been in prison for years!"

"Not for sorcery."

"For what, then?"

Mum sighed, as if I were a pesky child asking just another pointless question. "What does it matter now? It's all in the past. Foni's served her time and deserves to move on."

"What was it?"

Mum rolled her eyes. "Fine. Attempted murder."

"*What?*" I stopped dead. She had to be joking. But she clearly wasn't in a joking mood. "Foni's a *murderer?* You knew, and you never told me about it? You made me go down there! Anything could have happened!"

"I said *attempted* murder," Mum said crabbily, as if *I* were the one being irrational. "And it wasn't what it sounds like. Foni was never going to hurt anyone."

"What the hell was it, then?" I yelled, my voice echoing down the dark street.

"Do we have to have this conversation here?"

"Yes." I folded my arms.

Mum sighed and stopped walking. "Ten years ago, the SID was convinced that Melanthios Skeuopoios was Cuttlefish. The police conducted a dawn raid on his house. They found him awake, and holding what they believed was a magical weapon. They ordered him to drop it. He didn't comply. So they shot him. Then they discovered that he hadn't been holding a magical weapon at all. He had been holding Hector's baby sister."

Mum broke off. Thick fog had turned the streetlamp into a bright yellow halo around her head. I couldn't see her face. I wondered if I should say something. But it didn't matter. I had nothing to say.

"After that, they were desperate to prove him guilty, of course, to justify what they'd done. They stripped his house bare, looking for his supposed collection of stolen sorcery books. But they failed. They were forced to admit they'd made a terrible mistake. Then, two years later, Foni was arrested in the house of the police officer who'd pulled the trigger on her husband and daughter. She was carrying a gun. For that, she got a sixteen-year sentence. She served eight before being released last May."

Mum stood in her yellow spotlight, arms crossed tightly. Without noticing it, I was in the same pose, a few metres behind her, in the darkness.

"The police would never do that," I whispered. "They wouldn't shoot someone in their own home without even giving them a chance."

"I don't want to believe it, either," said Mum. "But it happened. It happens all the time."

It's so hard for me to admit what I felt at that moment. It wasn't pity for Foni, or Hector. Nor for his father or sister. It was nothing but disbelief and anger. Disbelief because I couldn't imagine the police making a mistake as colossal as that. Not even when Mum told me. And anger that Hector had never told me any of this, not in all the time I'd spent trapped in his house.

Not that I'd ever asked.

And it's even harder for me to admit what I said next.

"That's...horrifying. I had no idea. But...none of that makes him innocent. None of that proves he's not

Cuttlefish. Did the SIDs find that secret room in the basement when they searched?"

"No. They didn't. But you've seen it. It's empty."

"Still pretty suspicious, don't you think? What would they need a huge secret room in their basement for?"

"That room was there before the Skeuopoioses arrived. Why should it have anything to do with them at all?"

"How should I know? That's your job! Don't you think it's even a *tiny* bit suspicious?"

"I think it would look *very* suspicious, to anyone who was at that meeting. Which is why I'd appreciate it if you didn't tell anyone at school."

"Why do you keep wanting to cover up for them? You were never spying on her. You *were* dating. You lied to everyone, and you made me lie too. I should have told everyone the truth."

Mum shot me a glance I'd never seen before. It was almost disdainful. "Of course I lied, Cass. None of the people in that room would be able to understand the truth. It was eight years ago that Foni was sent up the river, and now this neighbourhood call them both the River People. It's not enough for everyone that Foni's life was destroyed once already. They'll do anything they can to make sure she never gets a chance to rebuild it."

"But how do you *know?* How can you be so sure she's innocent?"

Mum stepped out of the streetlight's yellow glow. Her face plunged into shadow. "Cass, remember me telling you about my SID training? Which allows me to sense sorcery when it happens?"

"Yes."

"Well, I wasn't exactly telling the truth. I don't get that ability from SID training. It just comes naturally to me. I'd know right away if Foni were using sorcery. But I'll never be able to explain that to them."

"Why not?"

"Because… Because there are two types of people in the world. The ones who'd laugh at me for thinking I had some kind of special ability, and the ones who'd be afraid of me. Some extremists would say an SID like me shouldn't have these kind of talents. They might even start to think *I* should be locked up. When in reality, my nose for sorcery is exactly what make me so good at my job."

"So…it's something you were born with?"

"Not exactly. Sorcery is a just a skill like any other. Like music, for example. Sure, some people are naturally more musical than others. But it still takes hours of practice to become a good musician."

"I think I have it too. I felt something wrong whenever I saw Cuttlefish. A ringing in my ears."

Mum smiled sadly. "You're your mother's daughter."

"So it *does* run in families?"

Mum shrugged. "Any skill runs in families, at least a little. I have it. You have it. Your dad had it too, for what it's worth. That's what made him so good at what he did."

I jumped a little, like I did every time Mum mentioned Dad. It was always so rare and unexpected.

"But these are dangerous words, Cass. Ever wondered why Jess's mum has it in for Hector as well as Foni? It's because she thinks Hector is doomed to end up like his sorcerer parents. That's why she's been trying to get him kicked out the school all year, even though he's never done anything wrong. It's down to us, Cass, to stand up for him. Stand up for both of them."

"It's down to us to *lie* for them?"

"I'm glad you're finally getting it. Now can we get home? I'm freezing." Mum turned and trudged away from me.

We'd almost managed to reconcile our differences over Hector. Almost. But my anger was flaring up again.

"Do you know who you sound like?" I called after her. "Cuttlefish. He tried to cover up what Hector had done, by nyxing us. But it already *is* too late for Hector. He was reading sorcery books in school. He deserved to be suspended."

"Oh really? And do you think he deserved to be practically orphaned at the age of two? To lose his father and sister, then his mother, one after the other? Do you think he deserved to grow up never truly understanding why his family had been killed by the people who were supposed to be protecting them from harm? And do you think, now that he finally has his chance at a normal childhood, he deserves to be shunned by everyone for a crime that he doesn't remember and that he didn't commit?"

Mum's words became louder and louder as she marched on through the fog. I caught up with her. "You know I'm right, don't you? You *know* he had sorcery books. And you're covering up for him, just like he wants. You're ignoring all the evidence that's staring you in the face!"

We turned into our road. A low brick wall hugged the corner of the pavement. Mum sat down on it and pulled her jacket tight around her. "Sit down," she said.

I did.

"Ten years ago," Mum said, staring at the ground, "I was on the team trying to capture Cuttlefish. It was me who first named Melanthios as a suspect, and me who wouldn't rest until I'd collected enough evidence to justify that dawn raid. Even after he and his daughter were killed, I *knew* we'd found the right person. As I tried to find the one clinching piece of evidence that would prove it, I became angrier and angrier at the way he'd managed to orchestrate everything so perfectly, even from beyond the grave. There were no books, no eyewitnesses, no forensic evidence, nothing at all that linked him to any of Cuttlefish's crimes. But still, we all knew we'd got the right guy. After all, Cuttlefish was never heard from again. What did it really matter if we couldn't prove Melanthios's guilt? We'd still punished him, and ended his dangerous crime spree."

Mum blew out heavily. Her misty breath curled into the fog surrounding us. "But now, Cuttlefish is back. And nothing is certain. Perhaps Melanthios had nothing to do with Cuttlefish after all. There's only one thing I'm certain of. That family has been punished enough."

TWENTY-SEVEN

DON'T CAUSE A SCENE

"Are you sure you don't want an oyster? I've ordered far too many. I'll never be able to finish them."

"I didn't come here for oysters. I came here to put an end to this insanity."

"We used to be friends. We used to share oyster platters all the time."

"Neither of those statements are true, Cuttlefish."

"Still. I got hungry. I'm sure you must be too. Go on, help yourself."

"I don't intend on dragging this meeting out a second longer than necessary."

"I wish I could say the same."

There followed an ominous silence. The airy cacophony of St Pancras International Station could not penetrate the sombre atmosphere around this particular table of this particular champagne and oyster bar. The Bard and the Philosopher stared unflinchingly at one another. The dog at the Philosopher's feet muttered and scratched her jaw. The silence was only broken by a large, buttery slurp as the Bard attempted to eat an oyster off its shell without breaking eye contact, and failed at both objectives.

"I thought we agreed on keeping this meeting low profile," said the Philosopher. "Using disguises."

"I *am* in disguise! Or are you so culturally oblivious that you don't know who I am?"

"Coming to this meeting dressed as Shakespeare does not qualify as being in disguise."

Indeed, the Bard had spared no detail in preparing his costume. His face was powdered white, and rose to a round, bald head. The hair on the side of his head had been left to grow long, and was swept back behind his ears. He was wearing a black tunic, what looked like black tights, and an enormous ruff that made his head look like it was operating a flying saucer.

"That's where you're wrong, my old friend. After all, who would dream of suspecting innocent little Shakespeare?" The Bard fluttered his eyelashes in a terrible impersonation of innocence. "You, on the other hand, have strolled in dressed as the father of sorcery himself! Are you insane?"

"I'm not *dressed* like Aristotle, I'm merely adopting his persona, which nobody beyond a few fusty historians would recognize," hissed the Philosopher. He was right; his tousled brown hair and beard was not enough to turn any heads in his direction, especially given the grey suit he was wearing. "*Your* face, on the other hand, is shown to every schoolchild in Britain. Given that every SID in this city is actively hunting you down, you could at least have tried to blend in."

"They'll be expecting me to blend in right now," the Bard replied. "Only a madman would stroll into St Pancras International Station dressed as Shakespeare while he's the target of a citywide manhunt." He turned to a couple of ogling tourists who'd silently stopped near their table. "Yes, I know. It's me. Go ahead and have a good long stare." He turned back to the Philosopher. "Can't get a moment's peace nowadays. This twenty-four seven celebrity culture is wearing me down."

The Philosopher glanced around the oyster bar. It was positioned at the back of the station's main concourse. Groups of travellers pushed suitcase-laden trolleys towards the waiting trains, chatting idly in various European languages. They probably had nothing more pressing to worry about than what to have for dinner. Most probably didn't even have that to worry about; they probably had a loved one waiting in their various European homes with dinner ready for them.

The Philosopher leaned across the table and spoke in a static hiss. "You've wasted enough of my time already. Who are you? And why are you intent on assembling the Daedalus Set?"

"I'm nobody. And I'm finishing what Daedalus started. I'm going to build the God Machine."

The Philosopher's blood curdled. He'd guessed this was the case. But it still chilled his soul to hear the words said out loud.

"As I should hardly need to say out loud, the God Machine is just a myth. Daedalus was a far cleverer man than you, and he failed to build it. He lost his sanity, and then his life, in the attempt. So will you, if you carry on down this road."

"Ha!" retorted the Bard. "That's rich. Almost as rich as the butter sauce on these oysters. You just want the power of the Daedalus Set for yourself."

"Believe me, nobody in the Lyceum is stupid enough to follow in Daedalus's footsteps. We're only taking the books back so we can keep sorcerers safe from their power."

The Bard picked up an oyster and slurped it out of its shell. "I'm sure you'd like me to hand everything over to you. Ah, if only things were that simple." A trickle of melted butter ran down his chin and soaked into his ruff. The Bard looked down and tutted in annoyance, swivelling the ruff round until the stain was at the back of his neck. "I just can't get the hang of this."

"What exactly is stopping you?"

The Bard simply shook his head sadly. "The issues at stake are more than you or even I can comprehend, my naïve young friend."

"Try me."

"Ah, if only I could, as you so naïvely put it, try you. Wouldn't that be simple?"

"Yes. It would."

"I'm at the end of a road that I've been travelling down for years. I am too far over the horizon now. Too far to simply turn around and return at your call."

"So. The rumours are true. You're mad, aren't you? Those books have already destroyed your mind."

"Luddites have been calling sorcerers mad for millennia, Prince!"

"And sorcery has driven those who wield it recklessly mad for just as long. Just ask Daedalus."

"I already have. Daedalus was blessed with a divine insight that you will never experience."

"In my experience, madness and divine insight are much the same thing."

"I couldn't agree more." The Bard placed his chin in one elegantly cuffed hand, no doubt deciding on what vague and illogical statement to say next, but got distracted by a waitress passing with a bottle of champagne. He snatched it from the waitress's hand and pulled the cork out with an ostentatious pop that made everyone in the restaurant turn to look. He poured out two flutes. The waitress observed this, with a face as beautiful and expressionless as the moon, before retreating to the bar for another bottle.

A guard standing in the station entrance strolled over and studied the scene hard for a few moments.

"Is this really a time for champagne?" said the Philosopher dourly.

"It's sparkling wine, actually," corrected the Bard, reading the label. "Even this place isn't serving the authentic stuff anymore. Typical."

"Does it make a difference?"

"Authenticity makes *all* the difference! It's what sets reality apart from fantasy. Too many people spend their lives trying to be someone they're not, presenting a mask to the outside world. But I am different. I am nothing *but* the mask. That's what makes me the only truly authentic person in this play-acted world!"

A passing family overheard the Bard's booming speech and stopped to listen. He raised his champagne flute to them and then downed the entire thing in one. He nudged the second glass of champagne across the table.

"I don't drink."

"Neither do I. If we're going to negotiate our terms like adults, clouded minds are the last thing we need." The Bard emptied the second glass disgustedly onto the watching family. The waitress hurried over, her eyes straining with apology. The bartender looked at them sternly from behind the bar, clenching his thick sideburns.

The Bard clearly thought he was here to play. Never mind. The Philosopher was about to bring playtime to an end.

"There is no negotiation to be had, Cuttlefish. The simple fact is – we know who you are. Melanthios Skeuopoios."

The Bard stared blankly through the Philosopher. "Sorry. Name's not ringing a bell."

"We knew you would play dumb with us. So to speed up the conversation, we took the liberty of acquiring these." The Philosopher placed a tablet on the table in front of the Bard and flicked through a series of photographs on its screen. A worn-down neoclassical house. A woman in a shapeless cardigan, coming out of the Highgate tube stop. A boy in a purple jumper, a heavy schoolbag hanging off his back. In each photo, the subject was unawares, caught in a blur, at an odd angle. But anyone who knew these people would be able to recognise them at once.

From his nonplussed expression, the Bard seemed to have no idea who these people were.

Resolutely, the Philosopher continued explaining.

"You did well, hiding from both the Lyceum and the SID for so long," he said. "But you made a mistake, striking out at your own son's school. I'm sure you had a good reason, but it didn't take long for us to put the rest of the pieces together."

The Bard gave no indication that he was listening.

"Can't you see we're on the same side, Melanthios? You should be fighting these Luddite pigs alongside us, not hurting us for the sake of your doomed project. But you've pushed us too far, and we have no choice but to retaliate. We may not know where you're hiding, but we know where to find your wife and son."

The Philosopher looked the Bard squarely in the eye to show how serious he was. The Bard did not return the favour. He had become distracted by the moonfaced waitress, who was bending over a suited couple sipping champagne. "I'm afraid lunch is now over," she was explaining. "Would you like your bill?"

"Melanthios, do you understand what I'm saying to you?" the Philosopher snapped. "The Lyceum do not make idle threats. We will retaliate against Persephone and Hector unless you start co-operating."

"Do what you must. I have no intention of co-operating with you."

"Then for the love of the gods, why did you want to meet me?"

"Only to get to know you a bit more personally, while sampling the oysters which I've been told are excellent here. So far, the plan's been a total disaster on both fronts. I'm still sensing a great deal of friction in our relationship, and these oysters have been salted beyond all reason. I'm not sure I'm even going to be able to finish them." The Bard ate another oyster noisily, uncrossing and recrossing his legs. "I think I know why Shakespeare wrote all those tragedies now. It was the constant crotch chafing. It's enough to push anyone over the edge."

"The Lyceum will take whatever action is necessary to reacquire the Daedalus Set," the Philosopher hissed, his rage building. "Do you understand?"

Sadly, the Bard had become distracted again, this time by a young child in pigtails shyly approaching their table.

"Please?" she asked abruptly, holding up a copy of *The Complete Works of Shakespeare.* Her attractive European family were huddled a few steps away, nodding her on.

The Bard's face softened. "Well, I suppose it's no bother." He removed a peacock-feather quill from behind his ear and signed the front page with a flourish. He looked up with a smile, to find the girl's parents holding a camera hopefully. He gave the book back to the child and smiled for the photograph. "Make sure to follow me on Agora! @ChampagneShakespeare," the Bard told the girl's parents.

The girl's mother nodded rapturously and thumped her own edition of *The Complete Works of Shakespeare* on the table, with a rattle of empty oyster shells. "There was a gift shop downstairs. We bought them especially."

The waitress stuck her expressionless face in the tourists' path. "I'm sorry, Ma'am," she explained. "These men are trying to have a private conversation."

"Don't be ridiculous!" the Bard shouted, loud enough for the entire station, if not the entire world, to hear. "We don't mind the company. Do we, Aristotle?"

An orderly queue of tourists brandishing cameras started to form.

The Philosopher leant across the table, pushing the champagne bottle out of the way. "I don't know what kind of game you're playing, but I assure you–"

"For your family, are they?" the Bard was saying to a stack of identical books that had just been parked in front of him. In the distance, two guards were communicating tersely and watching them, their arms folded across their chests.

"Don't cause a scene, Melanthios," said the Philosopher. "This is an issue between you and the Lyceum."

It was the wrong thing to say. The Bard threw back his head and shouted, "Oh, so I'm causing a *scene* now, am I? And what would an uncultured man like you know about *scenes*, anyway?" His words clanged around the station, louder and clearer than any of the tannoy announcements. He slipped his cloth bag off his shoulder and emptied a heavy book onto the table. An icy heat gripped the Philosopher's brain as he recognized it.

Shakespeare's First Folio. One of only 200 or so in existence. No doubt this was the one that had famously been stolen from the British Library just months ago.

"I don't know why we bothered trying to reason with you. I really don't." The Philosopher stood up, discovering he was hemmed in by the tides of tourists now watching their conversation with fascination. His dog paced in circles around his feet, bewildered by all the humans.

"Ladies and gentlemen!" the Bard boomed, projecting his voice across the concourse and drawing yet more audience members to see what the fuss was about. "I apologize for the delay, but the show is finally about to begin!" The Bard flipped open the huge book on the table, sending both champagne flutes careening to the floor. The bartender and waitress looked tensely at one another but did nothing. "Today's work: Julius Caesar. A tale of loyalty and betrayal like no other! My friend here is just about to play the part of Brutus–"

"Fine," said the Philosopher, his voice contorted with the effort of being heard over the thronging crowd. "If you refuse to end this performance, we'll have no choice but to end it for you." The Philosopher pulled a gun from his inside pocket and pointed it, with uncanny accuracy, directly at the Bard's appendix.

The Bard looked more indignant than alarmed. "How uncouth. Who'd shoot the great Shakespeare?"

"The great Shakespeare is dead."

"The very idea! Shakespeare is immorta–"

The Bard was interrupted by the Philosopher firing his gun, with uncanny accuracy, directly into the Bard's appendix. The Bard tumbled backwards with a faint cry of "Uncalled for!", two shapely legs flying in the air. The noise lashed out at the crowd, echoing gruesomely around the hall. The bartender dived behind the bar, where the waitress had long ago taken up hiding.

Several guards converged on the crowd but found themselves unable to see what was happening at its centre. The audience was too thick to let them through. They had been promised a show, and a show is what they believed they were watching. They didn't for a moment believe that they were witnessing two of the country's most dangerous sorcerers come to loggerheads.

His breathing coming in uneven judders, the Bard pushed himself onto an elbow. "You cream-faced loon!" he cried, pointing his cuffed hand at the Philosopher. "You bolting-hutch of beastliness! You elvish-marked, abortive, rooting hog!"

The Bard's head lolled back into the lap of a Belgian woman. "I better brook the loss of brittle life than those proud titles thou hast won of me. They wound my thoughts worse than sword my flesh!" His head fell to one side. His dying eyes tried vaguely to focus on the Belgian woman's. "O, I could prophesy, but that the earthy and cold hand of death lies on my tongue!"

"Shut up, Melanthios," said the Philosopher. "Nobody's impressed by this little show."

Judging by the expressions in the crowd, the Philosopher was staggeringly wrong. All were leaning forward with swelling eyes, trying to get a glimpse of the dying man. With a stately slowness, the Bard raised one finger to his tongue and dampened it a little, before using it to turn the page of the heavy book that had somehow landed on his lap.

"Mount, mount, my soul! Thy seat is up on high, whilst my gross flesh sinks downward, here to die. I kiss'd thee ere I kill'd thee. No way but this: killing myself, to die upon a kiss," the Bard whispered, his voice coming in fragile gasps. With the last of his strength, he lifted his head upwards. The Belgian woman instinctively lowered her head, and their lips met. For a moment, both were suspended in eerie silence. Then, with an audible sucking noise that nobody failed to hear, the Bard released his hold on the Belgian woman's lips, his powdered face alight.

"It can't be…" he said, amazed. "Somehow, I've been saved! My life is spared! How could such a miracle have occurred?"

He looked at the Belgian woman, then down at himself, then back at the Belgian woman. "Perhaps…although it seems so improbable…but yes, it's the only way…"

In one swift movement, the Bard let go of the Belgian woman and sprung onto his feet, smoothing back his hair and reaching adoringly towards the domed glass ceiling.

"It's true love's first kiss! It's the only thing which could have carried me back from death's door! I feel great! Even my indigestion from those vile oysters has gone!" He dived down and picked up his book from the floor. "But soft! What light through yon window breaks–"

This time, the gunshot sent the Bard flying sideways, windmilling his hands and feet across the floor. Collectively, the crowd stared down at his heaving body, then followed the sound back to its source. It was the bartender, a rifle tucked under his arm and a fearful mask covering his face. He didn't so much as flinch when he felt the attention turn to him.

"I've had to put up with this all afternoon," was all he said by way of explanation. "If I hear one more word out of his smug mouth, I swear to the gods–"

"*Et tu, Brute?*" the Bard gasped, gazing up at his second murderer, while one hand scrabbled discreetly across the ground for the Folio.

"How the hell is he still talking?" muttered the bartender incredulously.

The Philosopher stared at the squirming Bard. "Of course. That book. He's drawing power from it."

"What, the Shakespeare book?"

"Yes. Get it away from him. Now!"

The Bard pulled the heavy book towards him, just as the waitress sprung up from behind a display rack, her blank face now concealed behind a mask of anguish. She fired two shots from snub-nosed pistols in each hand, sending the Bard slumping firmly to the ground.

"That book can't protect you forever," said the Philosopher. "One way or the other, you're going to die."

It was clear from the expression on the Bard's face that he had no intention of dying, and that he was instead trying to think of a comeback. However, he never got the chance to voice it. The Philosopher kicked aside the table, sending oyster shells skidding across the floor, and advanced on where the Bard lay. He bent down and tried to wrestle the grimoire away from the bullet-ridden Bard. But he had no luck: the Bard was clinging onto his Compleat Works as if his life depended on it. Which, the Philosopher now realized, it most certainly did.

The Philosopher gave up trying to prise the book away, and stood up over the helpless Bard. He span the cylinder of his revolver and fired straight into the Bard's chest. Fired again. Opened the cylinder, pressed six bullets into each compartment, closed it, cocked the gun, and fired six more times. The Bard's body jerked violently under each impact.

"Before you succumb to your inevitable death," said the Philosopher, "know this: your wife and child won't see the light of day until you've told us where the Daedalus Set is. Every waking second will be a fresh torment."

Alas, the Bard was too wrapped up in the sound of his own declamation to notice what the Philosopher was saying. "Tongue, lose thy light! Moon, take thy flight! Now die, die, die, die, die." With each 'die', his voice grew fainter and fainter, until the last one was just a wisp of air forced out of his mouth. With a final kick of his white legs, the Bard lay still.

It was now that two guards finally pushed to the front of the audience and took in the spectacle for the first time. The Philosopher and two masked figures loomed over the dead playwright, their guns lowered but primed for action.

"We have a situation," one of the guards barked rapidly into his mic. The exact details of the situation, he never got a chance to specify. The waitress raised her guns and shot both guards simultaneously. The crowd drew back, wondering for the first time what kind of show they were watching.

"We need to grab him and get out of here," said the waitress, her urgent voice jarring with her grotesquely sad expression.

"Agreed," said the bartender, swivelling to blast another guard away with his rifle.

"Sure he's dead?" asked the waitress.

"A magical ward is only so powerful. Even an enchanted Folio can't have held out against what I just did," the Philosopher replied.

The bartender gave the Bard an experimental kick in the side.

The Bard didn't flinch. He just lay stretched out on the tiled floor with a beatific smile on his face.

The Belgian woman was quick to reclaim her job as the Bard's final resting place. "Qu'est-ce que vous avez fait?" she wailed, cradling the Bard's head against her bosom. "You murder! Murder Shakespeare!"

"This is ridiculous. Shakespeare's dead," said the Philosopher.

The Belgian woman raised her brimming eyes to confront him. "Yes. I can see that." Dropping the Bard's body, she charged at the Philosopher, yelling at him in French. Stunned, he did nothing at first to protect himself from her volley of slaps and jabs. For a moment, it looked like the Belgian woman had a serious chance of taking him down. Then there was another gunshot, and her body folded lifelessly and cracked against the ground.

"I had to do *something*," the Philosopher threw out angrily to the Belgian woman's enormous family.

The audience blinked as if waking from a dream and gazed with fresh eyes at the bodies lying across the restaurant. Horror rippled through the crowd, starting with the Belgian woman's group and spreading through each face in turn until a sea of rage surrounded the masked sorcerers, pinning them against the bar.

The bartender jumped onto the counter, his rifle swinging from his shoulder. "You see that woman? She made the mistake of upsetting a member of the Lyceum. I trust nobody else is planning on making the same mistake." To illustrate his point, he turned and fired at a pair of guards who had crept around the back of the restaurant area. They tumbled backwards and came to rest neatly on either side of a restaurant booth.

But this still wasn't enough. The swelling tide of anger around them had swept away any sense of fear.

What had started out as a battle of three against one had become one hundred against three. Further back, guards were circling the area, helping the more sensible travellers to flee the station.

"Time to go," said the Philosopher. "Get Cuttlefish, get the book and get out of here."

The masked waitress glanced down. "He's gone."

"What?"

The waitress nodded at the spot where the Bard had fallen. There was nothing there now but a lacy handkerchief. Gone too was his folio.

"It's impossible."

"It's happened, Prince."

A flash of green in the Philosopher's peripheral vision made him turn just in time to see a half-full bottle of champagne hurtling towards him, thrown by someone within the bloodthirsty mob whose identity he would never know.

The Philosopher had been the victim of countless magical attacks in his time. He'd been shot, stabbed, burnt, frozen, and electrocuted on more than one occasion. However, each of these occasions he'd prevailed by reminding himself that the pain he was feeling wasn't real, that the untold horrors being done to his body were only illusions.

The champagne bottle, however, was as real as could be. It struck him between the eyes, pitching him into unconsciousness.

Well, technically it was sparkling wine. A fact which turned out to make no difference at all.

TWENTY-EIGHT

LOOKING OUT FOR YOU

That family has been punished enough. I didn't understand what Mum was trying to tell me that day. It just seemed to me that she was so focussed on what had happened to them in the past that she couldn't see what they were doing in the present. All I could think about was how many times Mum had lied. I sat on my bed that evening thinking of all the times Mum could have told me the truth about everything; how instead she'd lied and lied and lied to me and everyone else. How she no longer even cared about finding out the truth. And how, whenever I stumbled on some piece of the story, her only response was to tell me I had to lie and cover it all up alongside her.

So when I got the chance to find the truth for myself, I took it. It made total sense at the time. It was only later, after the damage had been done, that I understood what Mum had been saying. And why she'd had to lie for so long.

It all ended on a damp Thursday. There was nothing special to mark it out. It was near the end of term. Almost all the pupils were back at school. All except Hector, of course, who was still suspended.

Even Jess finally came back. Tori and Chloë went in for a hug when we saw her. "Enjoy your holiday?" Tori said to her with an oh-so-subtle eyebrow raise.

I hung back, not sure whether I belonged in the group hug moment. I was still furious with Tori. I'd last seen Jess during our mothers' epic showdown in front of everyone.

But now, Jess looked at me and said, "Look, um, Mum says she's sorry about everything. And I'm sorry too."

"What are you sorry for?"

"I'm not really sure. I just felt like that meeting went a bit weird and you might be angry."

"I'm not angry with *you*, Jess. Are you angry with me?"

"Why would I be angry with you?"

Jess smiled in relief. And everything went back to normal.

For precisely seven hours, until Jason found us at the end of the day.

He was out of breath. Sweating slightly, too. "Can I talk to you for a second, Cass?" he panted.

Seriously, the guy never seemed to learn. Tori, Jess, and Chloë were literally right there. In one perfectly coordinated movement, they drew back to a respectful distance, from where they still had a perfect view of the evening's entertainment.

"It's about Hector," Jason said. "They're going to do something really stupid. The guys, I mean. They're going to go to his house. We need to stop them."

"What?"

Tori and Jess looked, if anything, even more excited by this news than by whatever else they'd been imagining Jason would say.

"Ever since that meeting at Jess's house, they've become more and more sure that Hector is some crazy sorcerer who's trying to kill us all. And now they think his dad is Cuttlefish, too. They're going to his house before his mum gets home, so they can find evidence to prove it. You need to show me where it is, so that I can stop them before they do something stupid."

"How are you going to stop them?" I asked.

"I have no idea. They're all ignoring me on Agora. I'm just following along in the group chat. I have to try and talk to them in person."

"That sounds dangerous. I'm not sure we should get involved."

I was terrified. Not terrified of Hector. Not terrified of what Baz and his idiot friends might do. I was only terrified that, if I set foot in Omphalos, the others would somehow figure out how many times I'd been there before. They'd see the connection I had to the house, the connection between Hector and me. The rot deep beneath the house would somehow reach up and infest me. And they would leave me for dead. Sounds stupid, I know. Sounds crazy. But that was the only thought in my mind.

"It's okay. We'll come too," said Tori.

"They won't be able to do anything that bad in front of us," agreed Jess.

"And nor will Hector," said Tori.

So there it was. I had no choice. I never had a choice. Omphalos had caught me in its web a long time ago, and however hard I fought to escape, it managed to pull me back again.

"I don't like this," said Chloë. "Those guys *really* hate Hector. They might do something awful. I think we should tell someone."

Jason nodded reluctantly. "Okay. You do that, and hopefully the rest of us can sort this out before anything happens."

Spoiler alert: we didn't.

Chloë disappeared back into the school. I led the others through the thinning purple crowds, until it was just the four of us stalking through silent streets under a darkening sky. Jason kept his eyes glued to his phone.

"Yaz has just arrived," he muttered. "The other two were waiting for him. But they're going to head in now. Cass, how far are we?"

"We're already here," I said, pointing as we rounded a corner. There it was. The mini roundabout. The tall, dark hedge. The top floor of Omphalos rearing over the top, its windows dead and empty.

We saw them when we got to the front gate. Baz, Yaz, and Hazza were crowded onto the front porch, their backs to us. The front door was open. Who could have guessed it – the front door had been perfectly functional all this time. It was just the River People who chose to scuttle round to the back of their own house to get in and out.

We drew up the garden path behind them.

"...just wanted to come and hang out for a bit, Hector," Yaz was saying.

"We miss you so much at school," added Hazza. "We wanted to see how you were doing."

Hector mumbled something indistinct. Whatever it was, it made the others snigger.

"Do you kiss your mother with that mouth?" asked Hazza, with a drawly accent.

"Watch out, the party's getting bigger," said Yaz, noticing us for the first time.

The guys on the porch drew back to reveal Hector standing in the doorway. For someone who'd basically had a free holiday for the last few weeks, he didn't look too happy. His face was puffy. His T-shirt was stained and slightly too small for him, revealing a little roll of fat hanging out of his pyjama bottoms. He looked like he hadn't washed, or slept, or even eaten for days. Most people who got suspended would at least make the most of it.

"Jason, why have you brought all these girls?" asked Baz. "We were hoping to have more of a lads' night in."

"Yeah. Maybe order a pizza. Play a few video games. All good with you, Hector?" said Yaz. The other two snorted again.

"Well, we want to join too," said Jason. "Right?"

Tori, Jess, and I looked at each other. "Right," I said. I had no idea what I was supposed to be playing along with, who was insulting who, anymore. But I figured if I had no clue what was going on, chances are nobody else did either.

Baz smiled nastily. "Okay then, ladies. Let me explain what's going on. Hector here thinks he's a big scary witch. He doesn't have any friends, so he scurries home every day after school and spends all night trying to cast hexes on the rest of us. And we're going to prove it. Either you can stay and help us, or you can get out of here. It's up to you."

"You're not going to be able to prove anything, Baz," said Jason. You're just going to be breaking the law, if you go in there without permission."

"Breaking the law? *Breaking the law?* This guy is plotting to kill us all. I don't give a damn about breaking into his house. He's going to get what's coming for him."

"Look," said Yaz in a reasonable tone of voice, "all we want to do is look around. If we don't find anything suspicious, we'll leave."

"And if you're not a sorcerer, then we're not going to find anything suspicious, are we? So no harm done," Hazza chipped in.

"I don't want you to touch my things," said Hector.

"Yeah? We don't want to touch them either. But we promise we'll be really quick," said Baz.

"This isn't right, guys," said Jason. "Imagine if someone did this to you."

"Shut up, Jason. We're not the ones going around casting curses on people behind their backs," said Baz.

"Help me out here, guys," said Jason, looking from me to the other girls. "Please!"

We looked at each other silently. Tori appointed herself to speak for us.

"To be honest, I don't see what the big deal is," she said. "Yaz has a point, Hector. If you're not doing anything weird in there, why can't you just let us see for ourselves? Then this whole problem will go away."

"Thank you!" said Baz, pointing at Tori like a game show announcer.

Jess shrugged. "It can't do any harm," she said.

"You girls want to help us search?" said Yaz. "We can take one room each. It'll only take a few minutes."

"Guys, this is crazy! You can't do this!" yelled Jason. "Cass, you don't agree with this, right?"

"Me?" I asked, as if this question were a total surprise to me. It bought me a precious extra second to figure out what to say next. But at the end of it, I still had no clue.

I knew Jason was right. I knew that what the others were trying to do was wrong. So wrong. But I also knew something that the others didn't. I knew that Omphalos was sitting on more secrets than they could possibly imagine.

Instead of answering Jason, I walked up to Hector. "OK," I said. "I'll try and get everyone to walk away, but only if you can answer one simple question. Deal?"

Hector said nothing. I took that as a yes.

"All I want to know is, what's that room in the basement for?"

Hector liquefied before my very eyes. Where there was once a boy in pyjamas, there was now an undercooked jelly in the exact shape of a boy in pyjamas. "No," the jelly whispered. "Please."

"Seems like a reasonable enough question," Yaz said. "What's in the basement?"

"Nothing," Hector breathed, staring deep into the porch paving.

I wanted to help him. Really, I did. I wanted this all to be some kind of mistake. But I couldn't just deny what I'd seen. I couldn't pretend it was normal to have a huge secret library in your house. Not after everything that had happened. Not after all the damage that had already been done.

"If I didn't know any better, I'd say you were lying to us, Hector," said Hazza. "You wouldn't do a thing like that, would you? Not to your best friends?"

"Or at least the closest thing you have," Yaz sniggered.

"Please, Cass. It's nothing," pleaded Hector, raising his hands to me in prayer.

"Whoa!" said Baz, stepping in between the two of us. "Don't you dare lay a finger on Cass." To me, he added:

"Don't worry, Cass. If he goes psycho on you again, we'll protect you."

"You got that right," said Yaz, towering over Hector.

"Calm down, guys," said Jason. "Nobody is going to get hurt."

"What the *hell* are you talking about?" said Baz, rounding on Jason. "This goddamned witch scratched my face open. He smashed your head into a pavement. He tried to *strangle a girl to death*. Why do you keep standing up for him? You know what, I'm done with this stupid conversation. Me and anyone else who wants to join are going inside that house to find out the truth." Baz stared at Hector. "And we're going to start in the basement. Now let me in."

"No," Hector replied.

Baz looked from Yaz to Hazza. Then back at Hector. "Well, we tried to give you a choice."

Baz grabbed Hector's pyjama top and twisted. Held him in position so he could punch him straight between the eyes, again and again.

Jason grabbed Baz by the shoulders and pulled him back. Baz dropped Hector and wheeled round to elbow Jason in the face, before kicking him halfway across the front garden. Jason staggered to his feet and raised his arms just in time to protect himself from the worst of Baz's mad punches. "*Get – out – of – my – way!*" Baz roared between jabs.

Yaz and Hazza didn't give Hector a chance to run. They pounced on him like rabid dogs. He was knocked to the floor in an instant, buried beneath a wave of kicking and stamping. He didn't try to defend himself. There was nothing he could do.

Baz left Jason with one final knee to the stomach before returning to Hector. Tori, Jess, and I pulled him to his feet as fast as he was able.

"Get...him...out of there," Jason gasped, as soon as he was able to speak again. His forehead and nose were bleeding. "They won't...want...to hurt you. Just...get... between them. Get him...out."

The three of us looked through the open doorway. Baz took a run-up and kicked Hector square between the legs. Hector's body shuddered and curled up like an insect.

My blood ran cold. What was I supposed to do?

The others agreed with me. "No way am I going in there," said Tori with finality. "We need to get you some first aid or something."

"I'm fine," growled Jason. His breathing had just about returned to normal. "But they're going to...kill him. Please. Cass."

Jason was right. Reluctantly, I went inside. The others followed me, a couple of steps behind. "Okay, that's enough!" I said, as commandingly as I could.

To my surprise, they actually listened. All three of them stepped away from Hector's limp body. Baz paused briefly to admire his handiwork, then gave Hector one final kick to the stomach, like an artist adding one final brushstroke to complete a masterpiece.

"Right away, madam," said Yaz, with a small bow. "I think we paid him back in full, don't you?"

That's when I realised. They thought I was on their side. They thought I was part of their club of Hector's victims. They had beaten Hector up to avenge me, as well as them.

I considered throwing up. But this situation was already enough of a mess.

"Right, let's go to the basement," said Hazza. "Do you want to lead the way?"

"No," I whispered, looking at Hector. He wasn't moving.

"All right then," said Baz. "This way!"

Baz headed down the hallway. He pulled the basement door handle down.

That's when Hector started to scream.

I still don't know how such a big sound could fit out of such a small mouth. It was the kind of noise that came out of a plane engine. It tore the air apart. It came from every corner of the room at once. It spared nothing.

Hector arched his back as he screamed. His limp body rose slightly off the floor. His arms twisted and knotted around themselves. His eyes snapped open, and locked onto Baz.

The basement door swung open.

That's when Baz started to scream too.

Whenever I remember what happens next – and believe me, I remember it whether I want to or not – it's always happening as if for the first time. It's a scene that refuses to be left behind in the past, but clings onto the present, forcing me to drag it behind me wherever I go.

It starts with that scream. Hector screams, and the basement door swings open, and the darkness on the other side reaches through and takes hold of Baz. He stumbles backwards into the wall as insects swarm across the floor and up his legs. He's screaming, but you're not listening. You can do nothing but watch as they scale his body, over and under his clothes. Baz scratches and slaps at his face, but there's nothing he can do. They burrow into his ears, squeeze around the back of his eyes, and all of a sudden his screaming stops and he falls to the floor.

The others turn and flail desperately away from the basement door. But the swarm doesn't stop. Scorpions with stingers curling above their heads. Millipedes gliding over the carpet like miniature trains. Furry spiders, their bodies lifted above the black sea of bugs around them. It reaches Jess and Hazza first. Jess tries to stamp them off as she runs, but they're coming too fast. They cling onto her shoes, and then her legs, and then all over her body, unmoved by her frantic twitching and slapping. She shrieks, but the sound is eaten alive by Hector's scream.

Hazza staggers into the wall as insects crawl up his legs. The wall caves inwards, the wallpaper blackening and peeling off, the board underneath dissolving into rot. A cloud of white spores billows up from the rotting cavity. Hazza tries to push himself away, but both his hands are trapped. The mould consuming the wall spreads its black tentacles across his body. His skin splits open, and cotton-wool fungus springs up in the open wounds. Next come clumps of toadstools, nosing out through the cracks in his flesh, through the thin skin of his neck, out of his eyes. One by one, his teeth fall out of his blackening gums like rotten fruit from a tree, and slimy grey mushrooms unfurl in their place.

Tori is the first to reach the front door. She takes hold of the handle and twists. Hector looks at her. The handle breaks off wetly in her hand, slithers out of her grip and coils around her arm. She claws the worm off her skin, but only manages to rip it in half. Its nose continues to slither blindly up her body, while its tail comes to life in her other hand. They multiply under her clothes, bursting out of her collar. She opens her mouth to cry out, and a dozen white worms slither down her throat. Heaving and shaking and gasping for air, she sinks to the ground. The worms eat her from the inside out.

Yaz stops short of the front door and looks for another way out. His eyes light on Hector, who has risen to his feet, both rigid and bent like a puppet dangling from a single string. He raises his hands, and the insects swarm down the corridor towards him. The others kick them off as they try to run.

"What the hell are you doing?" Yaz shouts at Hector.

But Hector doesn't answer him. Hector does nothing but scream endlessly and stare straight into Yaz's eyes.

Yaz swings a punch at Hector's face. Hector's head snaps back. The house shudders in pain. And the knuckles of Yaz's hand turns black. Rot creeps up his arm. Black boils appear on his flesh, burst open with a spray of pus.

Yaz tries to kick Hector in the stomach. But as his foot connects, his knee rips apart and the lower half of his leg slides out of his trousers. Yaz topples over at Hector's feet. Maggots squirm and rise in the open sores covering his skin. His body melts away.

It's not real. It's not real, you tell yourself over and over again. But it doesn't help.

Jason grabs you by the arm and pulls you into the living room. For a moment, the room looks like it should. A dining table piled high with books and magazines. Ugly rose wallpaper. A pair of big, threadbare sofas staring at each other over a coffee table. But in the next moment, the roses on the wall are turning black, their petals drifting to the floor. Patches of mould are rippling across the walls. Spiders and beetles and millipedes are crawling out of the gaps between the sofa cushions.

You jump onto the coffee table. Jason jumps up behind you, but catches his shin. He doubles forward. His hand lands straight into a vase of roses in the middle of the table. He gasps in pain and pulls his hand out. His arms are carved with red gashes, and leeches are feeding on his open wounds. With a strangled moan, Jason lifts up his shirt to find more leeches on his stomach.

They're everywhere.

Hector swallows his scream. His body goes limp for a moment, then thrashes around wildly on top of his insects. All around me, the rot darkens, the insects scurry closer.

But they don't touch me.

And then Hector's thrashing is slowing down. The insects grind to a halt. A few of them die. The rot stops spreading. The only sounds left are the low panicked whimpers coming from the survivors. Jess, Jason, and me.

I didn't realize what had happened to him straight away. Hector, I mean. It was only as I looked down at him, curled up in the hallway, his eyes vacant, that I remembered. He'd had another tonic-clonic seizure.

He was slowly coming round again. He blinked and licked his lips. All around him were dead insects, lying curled on their backs just like him. He recoiled in horror and staggered woozily to his feet.

"What happened?" he said, looking from Jess, to Jason, to me.

Jess and Jason said nothing. They'd been spared, somehow, from death. But they were still covered head to toe in bugs. Their faces were masks of fear and disgust.

I'd rather not tell you exactly what came out of my mouth next. Most of it wasn't words at all. And the bits that were words weren't very nice. "You *freak*!" for example. "What's *wrong* with you? Don't you get what you've just done? No, you're too stupid to get it. You're too stupid to *live.*"

I stepped very carefully off the coffee table. The insects didn't move. I wasn't sure if they were alive or dead, but whatever they were, they didn't seem interested in attacking me. "You know, we defended you. To the whole neighbourhood. I actually stood up and *defended* you." OK, maybe not quite true. Mum had done most of the standing up and defending. But I'd been there for moral support.

It didn't make a difference what I said anymore. Hector was silent.

"But you're even worse than they said. I should have told everyone what you're really like."

But it was useless. Hector wasn't listening. "What happened?" he repeated, gormlessly. He touched his bleeding forehead and looked with surprise at his red fingers.

The front door burst open. Mr Kaplan stood in the doorway, all ten feet of him. He had a satchel strapped to his gangly body and a clown-like grin strapped to his face.

Our English teacher surveyed the scene in under a second. Hazza's fungus infested body, fused into the rotten wall. The dead insects hanging out of Baz's bleeding ears and eye sockets. The worms lying thick over Tori's remains. The maggots squirming in Yaz's flesh. His grin recalibrated almost imperceptibly into a grimace of horror. His hands flexed and crawled all over his chest like they had minds of their own.

"Are any of you wearing an amulet?" Mr Kaplan said sharply to the three survivors. "Religious symbols. Anything like that."

Jess and Jason nodded as minimally as they could.

"You need to get them off as fast as you can."

"Why?" asked Jason.

"So that I can fix this."

The two of them hesitated, both too afraid to move.

"Quickly!" he said. "You don't have much time."

Shivering, Jess undid the top button of her school shirt and pulled out her Star of David. Its chain brushed against a spider sitting on her collarbone, which scuttled out of its way. Jess shrieked, but managed to unclip the necklace. Jason did the same with his cross.

"Drop them to the ground," said Mr Kaplan.

They did.

The creepy crawlies covering their bodies burst into life instantly. The spider on Jess's collarbone sunk its mandibles deep into her neck. Jess shrieked and slapped at every inch of her body. Her bites swelled red and leaked pus. It didn't take long for her to give up the fight and sink to the floor, her body spasming and jerking and finally lying still.

The leeches covering Jason's body ballooned. Their glistening black bodies became purple. Some of them burst, spewing Jason's blood across the coffee table. His face turned white and he collapsed.

"There we are! Fixed," said Mr Kaplan brightly. Then he looked at me. "All except you. I wonder what your secret is?"

"Don't hurt her!" Hector pleaded. "She was just trying to look out for me."

"Look out for you?" Mr Kaplan buried his head in his hands and laughed. His shoulders shook so hard they seemed to collapse in on themselves. He kneaded his eye sockets and temples, harder and harder, until his skin rubbed clean away from his face. The man who stopped laughing and drew himself upright wasn't Mr Kaplan anymore. It was Melanthios Skeuopoios. The man who'd been shot down in his house. This house. I recognized him from articles I'd looked up after Mum had told me what happened.

Melanthios was solidly built, thick arms and a thick neck. His eyes were set deep into his big head. His hair was somehow short and scruffy at the same time.

He briefly locked eyes with me. A sharp whistle jabbed in my ears, making me flinch away. Then he turned back to Hector.

"Hector, Cass isn't looking out for you," said Melanthios. "*I'm* looking out for you. Just like I did at school. We can't leave any witnesses behind."

"She knows everything already," begged Hector. "Please don't hurt her."

"Fine," said Melanthios softly. I let my muscles detense slightly. "I'll find another way to deal with her, if that's what you want."

"I don't want you to deal with *anything*. I want everything to go back to the way it was. I wish you'd never taught me sorcery."

"But look at what you're capable of! You've finally stood up to the bullies. On your own. Just like I promised you would one day. You have such a gift. You can't throw it away just because you haven't learned to use it yet!"

"It's not a gift. It's horrible. I hate it!"

"Lots of sorcerers would kill to have your talents. They *have* killed. And you still have so much further to go."

"My mother was right. It's evil and wrong."

"Your mother married the great Cuttlefish for a reason. And you're his son. You were born to be a sorcerer."

A door somewhere in the back of the house slammed.

"Sing of the devil!" said Melanthios, looking at his watch.

"Hector!" called Foni cheerily from the kitchen. "I picked up a few things from the shops on the way home. What sort of dinner are you in the mood f–"

Foni's voice got closer and closer, until it abruptly stopped.

She was standing in her living room, wearing a grey suit. A plastic bag dangled off the end of her arm, rustling half-heartedly. She looked around the room. She looked at the dead insect bodies littering the floor, at the smashed vase, at Jason's shrivelled body. She followed the trail of decay into the hallway. She looked at the other bodies. She looked at her son. She looked at Melanthios. She looked at me.

"Honey, I'm home!" said Melanthios.

TWENTY-NINE

FACELESS MONSTER

A bird whistled cheerily somewhere deep within Highgate Cemetery. It had a good reason to be cheery; it wasn't one of the unfortunate souls currently standing inside the old, gloomy house that stood on its border.

Of the unfortunate souls inside Omphalos, most were, for the time being anyway, dead. Left alive were a schoolboy with troubled eyes, a terrified schoolgirl, an identity thief, and a tired grey woman wearing a tired grey suit. They watched each other with varying degrees of fear, hatred, and amusement. Strewn at their feet were the corpses of six schoolchildren, in various stages of decomposition.

The identity thief strode towards the tired grey woman, nudging aside one of the corpses with his foot. "Are you impressed by our son's handiwork?" he said. "One day, he might even be able to surpass me!"

The mother ignored the words of the identity thief. "Who are you?" she said emotionlessly.

"Me? I'm nobody. Nobody at all. Nobody compared to the great Cuttlefish. I have to tell you, and I'm sure you get this a lot, but still…I'm a *huge* fan of his. Absolutely *huge*. A lot of sorcerers thought he was gone for good. But now he's more famous than ever! A name like Cuttlefish…it can never truly die, you know? It's…inspirational. No, really. I mean it. Inspirational."

The mother's grey expression didn't change.

"Inspirational," the identity thief said again, as if that might be the adjective that clinched it. It wasn't.

"All I've wanted for the last ten years is to leave Cuttlefish dead and buried, where he belongs," said the mother. "But you resurrected him, just when the world was beginning to forget. Why?"

"What are you saying? That I'm some kind of…*identity thief?*" laughed the identity thief. "I grew up reading about Cuttlefish's ingenious crimes. He was a hero to me! While I was growing up, I didn't know who I was, who I was supposed to be. He gave me a voice. An identity! All I dreamt was that one day, I might be as famous as the man with a thousand faces. I never could have guessed that one day, I would *be* the man with a thousand faces!"

"You had no right."

"No, *you* have no right to forget him! He'd pieced together most of the Daedalus Set. He was about to build the God Machine. Then he was murdered by the police in cold blood, along with his daughter. *Your* daughter!"

"My life was destroyed by an insane quest to build the God Machine. Everyone I love has paid the price. My son grew up as on orphan while I rotted in prison. All for the sake of a stupid myth."

The identity thief shook his head gleefully. "The God Machine isn't a myth. Melanthios was close, I'm sure of it. But don't worry. I'm going to succeed where he failed."

"You're only going to ruin your life too."

"I'm already closer than he ever was. I've found almost every book in the Daedalus Set."

"I suppose you've come here for the ones in this house."

The identity thief shook his head. "I already have them all! Hector has given them to me. One by one. In exchange for my tuition."

The mother stared at his quivering son. "Is this true?"

The schoolboy looked down and said nothing.

"Whoever this man is, he's manipulated you. All he wanted was those books. That's the only reason he's wormed his way into your life."

"I'll be gone before long, if you'll agree to help me. I'll even protect you from the Lyceum."

"The Lyceum?"

The father unbuttoned his shirt to reveal a bottle-blue jacket underneath. He removed a theatre mask from its pocket and placed it over his face. "Somehow, they've got it into their heads that your husband is still alive," he said, his voice lilting and nasal. "To make things worse, they know where you live. And they're threatening to take you and Hector hostage to get to him. But don't worry. I can protect you. I'll blow them off the scent. All I want in exchange is the equipment your husband was working on."

"Equipment?"

With an elegant gesture, the masked man brushed a piece of dust of his shoulder. "Cass told me there was equipment in this house. Something your husband made. Give it to me and I'll wash out of your hair forever."

The mother shot a confused look at the schoolgirl. *Equipment?*

Of course. That conversation in the classroom. With her English teacher.

"I didn't mean...anything like this," the schoolgirl butted in nervously. "I just meant...antique letter openers. And stuff. Nothing like a...*God Machine*?"

Suddenly, everything made sense. Well, not *sense* sense. But she was drifting in the right direction.

When the teacher had burst in, the schoolgirl had felt nothing strange. No ringing in her ears. As soon as he'd transformed into the father, that tinny jolt of uncanniness had begun. She could still feel it now. That meant only one thing.

"You're Mr Kaplan," she said.

The identity thief narrowed his eyes at the schoolgirl. But try as he might, he couldn't stay angry. He pulled off his mask to reveal a wide, elastic grin. The English teacher's grin.

"Full marks! Top of the class as usual, Cass. Why am I not surprised?"

The ringing in the schoolgirl's ears stopped. She was looking at the identity thief's true face.

"Benediktos Kaplan," the mother murmured. "Of course. Those remedial classes with Hector. I had so much faith in you. I really thought you wanted to turn his life around."

"Oh, I have! I showed him how to defend himself against the bullies and the gossips." The identity thief gestured around the room. "And look how you've triumphed, Hector! Look how much stronger you are than all of them put together, when you put your mind to it. They tried to stamp you out, and you rose up and bit them back."

"He shouldn't *need* to defend himself!" the mother insisted, her voice wheezing. "He should have the right to fit in and lead a normal life, just like everyone else!"

"You're right. He shouldn't. But that's not the world he lives in, Foni. He lives in a world where his own national identity has been stolen from him, where being Greek is a crime by itself. Hiding away and denying who he is won't save him. The rot is too deep for that. Sooner or later, it's going to burst out. When it does, we need to be ready to fight. You were too weak to teach him how, so I did."

"The playground bullying and the school gossip goes away."

"Not true! The playground bullies grow up and become police officers with the right to *kill* us if we dare stand up to them! And the school gossips become journalists who tell the world that *witches* are the ones to blame for everybody's problems! We run and we hide from this faceless monster that wants to destroy us. But we shouldn't live in fear of these people! They should be the ones who fear *us!*"

"I used to think like you, Benediktos. When my husband and daughter were killed, I tracked down the police officer responsible. I wanted to execute him for what he'd done to us. But when I saw the fear in his eyes, I couldn't do it. He wasn't a faceless monster. He was a human who'd made a terrible mistake."

The teacher guffawed. "How beautiful! Did he think the same thing about your husband as he opened fire? Did his buddies show you the same compassion as they carted you off to prison?" The teacher turned to his young protégé. "I see now why you hate yourself so much. You lost the wrong parent. Cuttlefish would never–"

A howl of pain ended the teacher's speech. A javelin knocked him backwards and pinned him against the wall, vibrating from the impact. The mother was vibrating too, her throwing arm stretched in front of her. But it was the mother, not the teacher, who was howling in pain. The teacher was only looking down at the weapon impaling his stomach with mild approval.

"Now, this is more like it," he said. "See, Hector? This is how you stand up for yourself. Even your mother knows how it's done, deep down."

"You know *nothing* about me. Or my family," the mother hissed, rage spilling down her cheeks. "You're right about only one thing. Hector *did* lose the wrong parent. Melanthios was innocent. *I* was Cuttlefish. I should have died in his place."

The teacher's eyes glazed over. His face went starry and slack. For a moment, it looked like the javelin was finally doing the job it was supposed to, and killing him. But no; now the rubbery face was stretching into wide, gaping delight. "*You?* That's…that's…*brilliant!* That's *perfect!* That's the best Cuttlefish play I've ever–"

The second javelin went in just under the teacher's collarbone, knocking the end of the sentence clean out of his lungs.

"Fair…enough," he gasped, with great pain and difficulty. "Probably…deserved that one. But you'll… have to do better. Came…prepared."

The teacher pulled both javelins out of him, one after the other. Then he removed two heavy books from somewhere inside his jacket. Each had a hole through its centre, where it had caught a javelin. He clapped the books together and pulled a long wooden pole out from between them. The books widened and flattened into the head of a battleaxe.

Advancing gleefully on the mother, the teacher swung his weapon in blindingly fast figure of eight patterns that achieved nothing except for cutting the coffee table in half. With each swing, his quarry seemed just out of reach, until suddenly, the battleaxe was arrested on its way into a final, killer blow.

The mother had blocked the axe with a simple bronze sword, held above her head. Grimacing, she sent her assailant staggering backwards.

"I can't tell you what an honour it is to duel the great Cuttlefish," said the teacher, arcing the battleaxe towards the mother's head. It was alive with sinister runes. They were so numerous and so glowing that his enemy's sword looked frankly shabby next to it.

The mother met the attack and beat it away. "You still think this is some game?" she cried. "One day, you're going to realize it's not." Sword met axe again and again, tirelessly clanking and shrieking off each other. The children were forced to leap out of the way as the two adults barrelled around one another, dodging and blocking with wildly differing levels of enthusiasm. The mother's face was set in grim determination, while the teacher's was alive with happiness.

As the parries and ripostes mounted on one another, the bronze sword lengthened; the axe thinned and split into multiple teeth down the weapon's long stem. The fight didn't slow down for a moment. One of the axe's jagged teeth caught the bronze sword and twisted it out of the mother's grasp. Triumphantly, the teacher brought down his weapon on his helpless victim's neck.

With a screech of yellow sparks, the battleaxe bounced out of the teacher's hands. Heavy bronze armour now coated the weaponless warrior head to foot. Her piercing eyes gazed out of a gleaming bronze visor. She pulled two curved daggers from her waist and kicked her attacker square in the chest.

"You're the only faceless monster," snarled the warrior, her daggers clenched in front of her. "You treat other people's pain like it's some work of fiction for your entertainment."

"At least I'm not in love with a monster," came the sardonic reply. In the place of the teacher, there was now a blonde SID officer wearing a long green coat. "At least I'm not the stooge for an inquisitor who wants our people wiped off the face of the earth!"

The warrior lunged at the SID. Her dagger sunk deep into another grimoire which the SID had produced in the nick of time. The warrior wrenched the book out of the SID's hands and tossed it away. The SID only smiled and opened her green jacket to reveal it was lined with ancient tomes.

"You'll have to try harder than that, Cuttlefish!" she declared.

The SID drew a can of pepper spray from her holster and fired at the warrior. Blue fire streamed from the nozzle. The warrior turned her back into the blast, letting it wash over the plate armour.

The SID dropped the pepper spray in favour of a handgun. Bullets ricocheted off the warrior's bronze chestplate and helmet. The warrior retaliated with a toss of a discus. The SID dodged the attack, fired a few more useless shots, then flung the gun at the warrior's head for good measure. She wasn't unarmed for long. Already, she had a military shotgun in her other hand. She fired. A ball of green flame engulfed the warrior, knocking her over a sofa.

The warrior rolled quickly into a low crouch. The SID, seeing her chance, drew an automatic rifle from her jacket and climbed onto the other sofa to take aim.

Before she had a chance to fire, the warrior sprung. Her bronze armour fused and swelled outwards, taking the lumpy form of the rapidly expanding muscles underneath. The tall crest of hair on her helmet proliferated down her head and neck, becoming a thick mane. Long claws erupted from her hands, which grew into thick, furry paws.

Of course, the elegant details of this transformation went by too quickly to be appreciated by the terrified schoolchildren. All they saw was a woman in full battle armour leaping up, and a golden lion barrelling into its prey. Prey which, it soon transpired, had become predator itself: the lion landed on top of a silver-furred bear, who rolled and kicked it straight off again.

The two beasts circled each other warily. The lion pounced, slashing at the bear's chest with its claws. Two books fell out of the bear's fur. The bear roared, revealing three rows of pointed teeth, which it used to seize the lion's paw. In the brief time it took for the lion to wrench itself free, a pair of enormous furry wings unfurled from the bear's back and beat powerfully. A vortex of air rushed through the room, spraying dead insects over the furniture and knocking the lion against the kitchen door.

The golden-fleeced lion opened its mouth and let out a blast of liquid fire. The jet of fire was followed by a volley of venomous spikes from the lion's tail, which had been replaced, on closer inspection, by a snake's rearing head.

Its fur singed, the wingèd bear roared and jumped on the lion, closing what very much looked like a crocodile's jaw over the lion's head. The lion retaliated by multiplying its legs and arching a long black tail over both of their bodies. A stinger, hanging like a plump fruit at its end, came down on the bear's back and dug deep into its flesh. The bear howled, released the lion's head, and smashed at the scorpion's carapace with its claws. The stinger withdrew, carrying an impaled grimoire with it.

The schoolgirl, meanwhile, had failed to contribute to the battle unfurling around her in any meaningful way. There may have been many reasons for this. She may have been respecting the age-old sorcerer's code, maintaining a principled neutrality during the duel. She may have felt she had no relevant skills to contribute. She may have been unsure whose side she was on – the teacher's or the mother's – and even if she did know, she may have been struggling to work out who was whom. Finally, she may have been gripped by an all-consuming fear that locked her mind against any conscious thoughts and replaced them with primordial survival instincts: don't move, don't breathe, don't blink.

Locked into an embrace, the duellists melted and reformed in ever-new, hideous shapes too rapidly for the eye to keep up. One of the two creatures finally launched itself away from the melée. It now seemed to be half minotaur and half manticore, which, given that a minotaur was half-man and half-bull, and a manticore was half-lion, half-scorpion, and half-bat, was a combination that no healthy imagination could have devised. A steady stream of purplish liquid flowed from its side as it lumbered away. Parts of its body were still shifting, tentative new appendages emerging to help support the dying beast's journey, but they couldn't help staunch the flow.

The victor reared up, its body scaled and black. It contracted into a roughly human shape, with a green-eyed face emerging from the black scales covering its head. It loomed over its bleeding, shuffling conquest and pulled book after magical book away, until it could find no more.

"Looks like the show's over," squealed the bleeding creature. "But may I just say one thing–"

The black-scaled fighter drove an ebony sword deep into its foe's chest.

The creature screeched and thrashed in pain. But it had no more places to run, no more mutations to adopt, no more tricks up its sleeve. It coalesced into the familiar form of the English teacher and lay still. Silenced at last.

Sharp red beams of light sliced through the living room from five directions at once, pinning the black-scaled beast at its centre. It glanced down at the beads of light flickering on its chest. The scales fell from its eyes, leaving the numbly desolate mother standing in its place. She tried to lower her hands, but she was too late. Ten years too late.

It sounded like one shot, echoing back and forth around the house. In reality, it was five separate shots, each finding their target at the same time. The living room windows exploded inwards. The mother's body span violently and collapsed.

"Police! Don't move!" crackled an amplified voice from the garden. The laser beams were replaced with five blinding white torch beams, lighting up two terrified schoolchildren standing on either side of the mother's body.

The schoolgirl froze before her brain had even registered the command. But the schoolboy ignored it and sank to his knees. He rolled his mother over. "Μητέρα!" he said.

His mother didn't respond.

"I said don't move!" The voice grew louder, the lights brighter. Five figures dressed entirely in black stepped up to the broken windows.

The schoolboy stood up. "Είναι δικό μου λάθος," he said. "Λάθος μου!"

"This is your last warning," shouted another voice.

"Λάθος μου!" the schoolboy said again, his body arching upright and his hands twisting. "Λάθος μου! Λάθος μου! Λάθος... Λάθος... Λάθ... Λάθ..."

The schoolboy's body jerked violently as it was hit by bullets from five directions at once.

"The threat has been neutralized," one of the police officers said with satisfaction.

It was standard police procedure to fire on anyone who presented a lethal risk to a police officer or civilian, and who failed to follow police commands. Any objective witness would agree that the schoolboy had failed on both these counts. Any objective witness would have heard him screaming spells, moving strangely, and repeatedly refusing to do as the police said, moments before he was shot.

True, if the objective witness had spoken Greek, they'd have pointed out that the boy's last words were *My fault!,* which once translated did not sound much like spells. And if the objective witness had been a psychiatrist, they might have recognised the onset of a tonic-clonic seizure in the schoolboy, which made it impossible for him to follow police commands.

Unfortunately, there were no objective witnesses to be found in that gloomy house. There were only five armed police officers, seven innocent victims, two neutralised threats, and one survivor to tell the tale.

THIRTY

NO ESCAPE

"Don't move, madam," barked one of the police officers.

It's not like I had plans to.

I didn't move. I didn't breathe. I didn't blink. I swallowed back the uncanny chill creeping over my scalp.

Two police officers kept their guns trained on me, while the other three came in through the front and back door. They traipsed through the filth and bodies until they were by my side.

They were both dressed like the team that had been in Whittington after the attack. Light glinted off their dark visors.

"We need to place you in handcuffs, madam," one of them said apologetically. "You're not under arrest. But we're not taking any chances."

My arms were guided behind my back. Steel gripped me by the wrists. I barely noticed. All I could see was Foni and Hector falling to the ground, one after the other. Gunshots echoed round and round my mind.

One officer sidled up to Foni with his gun stuck in her face, as if she might leap up and wrench it out of his hands. Then he dropped to one knee and felt for a pulse. "Definitely a goner," he said proudly.

He did the same thing to Hector.

I shut my eyes, but there was no escape.

Something pressed against my shins. It was a sleek, trembling bloodhound. Its nose – more like the entire front half of its long face – quivered with excitement. It sniffed me cautiously, then barked in satisfaction and retreated behind the nearest police officer, the one in charge.

"She's safe," the leader called to the others. Then he stopped in front of me. "We still can't release you until we've asked a few questions."

I nodded vaguely. I barely heard the questions. The obvious stuff: my name, my age. I was staring at Hector, curled up on the ground. Not at Hector, more through him.

Another police officer had been shining his torch into the face of each body in turn. "Looks like seven magical homicides total."

"Did you see what happened to these people, Miss Drake?" asked the leader.

I nodded.

"Nyxed?"

I nodded.

"Well, don't worry. They're all going to be OK. You know that, don't you?"

I nodded.

He said nothing about Hector. Or Foni.

He took his bloodhound and picked his way around my decomposing friends. The bloodhound sniffed each body in turn, giving Tori's face a lick. I wished I had the innocent, magic-free mind of a dog just then. I wouldn't have to deal with the stench of rot. Or the uneasy ringing in my ear.

"Bingo!" said another officer triumphantly, picking up one of the many books that had been tossed aside during the battle. She let it dangle from her hands by the front cover, showing us all the little torch symbol on its front page.

"Caught red-handed. Finally. We've waited a long time for this," said the leader.

"We got about a dozen right here," the first officer said, sweeping her light around the living room. "I bet the others aren't too far away."

The other officer turned to me. "Any idea where Melanthios Skeuopoios is?"

"Dead," I whispered. Along with everybody else.

"That's what we were all led to believe. But now we suspect otherwise. Sure none of these folks claimed to be him?"

"Yes."

The first officer shone a light in Foni's face. "That's Persephone," she said. "The wife."

"A whole family of witches," the leader said. "Can't say I'm surprised."

"Who's this?" the first officer asked, directing her light at Mr Kaplan, still pinned by a black sword to the ground.

"He's Cuttlefish. He's the one you need to arrest."

The leader looked at me blankly. Admittedly, he'd been looking at me blankly the whole time, because he was wearing a visor. But he was looking at me especially blankly just then.

"Doesn't look like Melanthios," one of them muttered to the other.

"He's a powerful identity thief. Might be able to retain a persona after being nyxed," the other replied.

"It's not Melanthios. But it is Cuttlefish," I insisted. I had no idea who my English teacher really was, or what he was trying to do, but I knew that he was responsible for Foni and Hector being killed. I wasn't going to let him get away with it.

"He was the one who brought all those books in here," I continued. "They weren't here to begin with."

The police officers conferred quietly for a few moments. Heavy bumps and sliding noises emanated from upstairs.

"Miss Drake, are you aware that it's an offence to mislead an officer of the law?" the leader said.

I nodded.

More conferring.

Two more officers clattered into the room. "Swept the whole house," one said. "Nobody else home. No obvious hidey holes for Melanthios."

"We also found an office," the other said. "No obvious grimoires lying around."

"No surprises there," the leader replied. "He won't have left thousands of pounds' worth of stolen property lying on a desk. Miss Drake, do you have any idea where someone could hide a large number of books in this house?"

I had to admit, I had at least one idea on that point. Namely, the huge secret library in the basement. But from what Mr Kaplan had said earlier, all the books in there had been taken by him. The police weren't going to find what they were looking for down there.

So I lied. It wasn't a big lie, not a lie that would ever make a difference. I just felt I owed it to Foni and Hector to stand up for them, to try and clear their names. I'd never managed it while they were alive, but they didn't deserve to go down in legend as a couple of crazy sorcerers.

"No idea," I said, fiddling with my ring.

"All right," said another officer. "Guess it's time to strip this house top to bottom."

"There's nothing here," I blurted out.

"Really?" said the leader. "You seem very sure on this point."

"I'm telling you, that guy confessed to everything," I said, waving at Mr Kaplan with my handcuffed arms. "Foni and Hector are totally innocent."

The police officers stared at each other again. I had no idea what was going through their minds. Fear that they'd just executed two innocent people, I hope. Because that's what they'd done. I had no idea what the whole truth was, but I knew that Foni and Hector had been punished enough before this night. They hadn't deserved to die.

"Perhaps it's worth trying…you know, another approach here?" suggested one of the officers to the leader.

"Very well," said the leader. He tossed his gun over his shoulder and pulled the visor off his head, revealing a madly grinning face with dark eyes staring straight at me.

I darted back in fright. It wasn't his face at all, just another mask. The happy mask, straight out of the classic theatre symbol. A woman, wearing the sad mask to go with it, strolled up and stood next to him, copying his crossed-armed pose. She was wearing a velvet jacket which shimmered murkily in the torchlight. So was Happy, in fact. Their black uniforms had vanished.

"I should explain," said Happy, still grinning at me. His eye and mouth holes were totally black – I couldn't see any of his face through them. "I'm afraid we are not police officers. We are Lyceum sorcerers. Don't be fooled by our lack of weapons; if you try to run, we will catch you and we will nyx you. If, however, you co-operate with us, we...well, I won't lie to you, child, we will still nyx you eventually. But we will make it considerably less painful. Now, would you like to reconsider what you've told us about Cuttlefish? Or our stolen books?"

I glanced behind me. Three more masked figures stood there. Their dress sense varied wildly – they weren't all wearing velvet jackets, but they did all have masks. Each of them a different frozen expression. Scared. Angry. Shocked.

Don't ask me what their plan was. All I knew for sure is that they seemed to hate Cuttlefish as much as I did. So it was even more important for them to know the truth.

"He's the one you want," I said frantically, gesturing at Mr Kaplan.

"Let's just take 'em all with us," suggested Angry. "They can tell us themselves who's who."

"Won't bring us any closer to Melanthios," Scared said.

"He'll give himself up if we've got his kid," pointed out Angry, rolling Hector over with her foot.

My eyes filled with tears, the tears that had been too numb to come when I thought they'd really been shot.

Foni and Hector weren't dead. Their deaths had been magical, just like everyone else's. Sure, they were about to be kidnapped and tortured until a long-dead man gave them all the books Mr Kaplan had hidden away somewhere. But at least there was hope that something or someone would come along and save this situation. Possibly even...

Possibly even me. The shock clearing from my mind had left behind a vague sense of…well, maybe optimism was a bit strong. Resignation, let's say. I had no real chance of escaping, especially given my handcuffs had annoyingly *not* vanished along with the rest of the police equipment. But I had to at least try and make this situation right. I glanced furtively around the room. The sorcerers were in between me and the front door, but I had a clear line to the kitchen. I just needed to find a moment when they were distracted, such as…

NOW!

I ran through the kitchen door. Angry noticed first, grunted with surprise and came after me. I jumped backwards into the back door, catching the handle with my cuffed hands.

A shot rang out behind me. The doorframe exploded into splinters as I barrelled outside.

I darted around the side of the house, to where I could see a precious sliver of street through the hedge…

Shock had come out the front door and was already charging towards me.

"HELP!" I screamed, over and over again, in the general direction of the street.

Shock raised some huge device to her shoulder. If I didn't know any better, I'd have said it was a crossbow.

I turned and fled, back around the side of the house.

A barely audible snap behind me. A crossbow bolt ruffled the hair just by my neck. My ears sang.

But I didn't stop moving.

Angry appeared from the back of the house. He'd traded his gun for a crossbow too. It was pointing at me.

I turned and dashed towards the garden fence. It was too dark to see the railings, so I had only a vague memory to guide me…

There! A missing railing. I turned sideways and squeezed through the gap, just as another bolt sang through the darkness somewhere too close to dwell on.

Thank God for Hector's bizarre rambling. Thank God he'd told me about the place where his garden connected to Highgate Cemetery. And thank God this place was – what's the word he'd used again?

Consecrated. Protected from magic of all kinds.

Another crossbow shot behind me. The bolt glanced off a nearby railing. I jumped into the cemetery, collided almost immediately with a knee-high gravestone and tumbled onto my face.

My hands still stuck behind my back, I fish-flopped back to upright.

Maybe Hector had been wrong about the consecrated ground thing. My handcuffs were still trapping my arms behind my back.

Or maybe these were real handcuffs. Maybe those were real weapons.

I didn't want to think about it. I just wanted to escape.

Shock had reached the gap first, but couldn't fit through. "Ariel! Lucky! Over here!" she called.

I didn't waste a moment more. It was pitch black. Dense trees covered even the soft green glow of London's night sky. I wouldn't be able to run. I stared at the ground in front of me, willing my eyes to adjust as fast as humanly possible, and stepped delicately through the undergrowth. Behind me, one Lyceum member and then the next squeezed themselves through the railings, their feet in the wet leaves impossible to miss.

And that, basically, was how I found myself being chased through a cemetery by four ruthless sorcerers. Looking back on it, it might all sound like a big zany adventure to you, but just so we're clear, it didn't feel like that at the time. Sure, they couldn't do magic in here, according to Hector anyway. But I was still one teenager and they were four fully grown adults, making it an uneven fight even if you ignored the fact I was in handcuffs.

"Spread out," one of them commanded. "She can't be far."

A few shrubs rustled in unison behind me. I tilted my head, and a sliver of phonelight caught my peripheral vision. I kept moving, nearly headbutting a tree before stumbling down onto a path.

"Quiet!" a voice said. The approaching rustling stopped. "I heard something."

I stopped moving. All I could hear was my heart beating.

"Think it was that way," said the same voice.

I had no idea if they were coming in my direction or not. I just kept moving. I hurdled awkwardly over several rows of gravestones that were packed tightly together, before joining a path which wound steeply up between boulders. I stopped at the top and dared to look around a little. No sign of the lights.

This might be the best chance I'd get to call for help.

I was just able to tug my phone out of my pocket with my handcuffed hands. I turned the screen on behind my back, then twisted round to peer at it…

"Over there!" a voice called.

I looked up. A pinprick of white had appeared out of the darkness, flickering in and out of view as it picked its way through the trees to me.

Either I could keep trying to call, providing a handy beacon for everyone to find me. Or I could give up and start moving again.

I was already this far into the call. I decided to dial 999, and hope I'd connect before they reached me. Turned out it was pretty difficult to hold a phone with one handcuffed hand and use it with the other, especially when you could barely see what you were doing.

I looked up. The white phone light was dancing ever closer. Close enough that I could hear the swish of grass against legs.

I stuffed my phone back into my pocket, already moving again. There was no path here, just brambles that tore through my trousers but let me pass. I thought I could hear angry muttering as the brambles worked their violence on the sorcerers' velvet clothes. Oh, well. Even if I got caught, at least I'd have ruined all their suits.

I must have been in one of the more forgotten corners of the cemetery now. Fragments of gravestone were all that remained, impossible to tell from the rubble littering the earth.

A row of mausoleums loomed up in front of me. I slipped between two of them. It felt safer off the path. Harder to move, but harder to be seen. Another row of mausoleums up ahead. And then...

Nothingness. Void. I was weightless, my stomach lurching.

Impact. Earth punched me almost senseless.

It took me a while to realize what had happened. I'd walked straight off a wall. The land rose and fell so sharply in Highgate Cemetery that you could often stumble across escarpments and miniature cliffs.

Or, in my case, over them.

But I'd been lucky. A metre to the left, and I'd have landed face first on another mausoleum. And as I plummeted, I'd instinctively reached out to catch my fall.

I hauled myself up to kneeling position and looked at my hands in wonder. My palms were covered in scratches, but the cuffs around each wrist were no longer attached to each other.

This consecrated ground was doing its job. The sorcery was unravelling.

I was free.

"That way," someone said.

Time to go.

I stood up. Pretty quickly, I was on a wide gravel path. Must have been one of the major roads through the cemetery. I couldn't figure out which one. But I reckoned it had to lead to an entrance sooner or later. I broke into a silent run, bouncing cat-like on each foot.

Muttering. Two pinpricks of white light on the road ahead of me. Looks like they'd found a better way down the escarpment. I turned and tiptoed back the way I'd come.

I reached a crossroads. A tall signpost helpfully pointed the way to every famous dead person you could ever want to meet.

I knew where I was. I took the path towards the exit. Familiar gravestones loomed out of the darkness on either side of me.

And there it was – the entrance booth. Behind it, the towering, ornate entrance gates.

Locked.

A tiny sob welled up inside me. It didn't seem fair. I'd tried so hard. I'd defeated so many odds. I'd come so far. And here I was, trapped by a mindnumbingly obvious flaw in my plan.

There was no escape.

I turned around. Two white lights advanced towards me. Two pairs of boots marched rhythmically down the gravel road.

I darted off the path, following the border fence. The only plan I had left at this point was to keep moving around until I found a section of fence low enough for a wounded and possibly concussed child to get over. But instead, I stumbled straight over a root and fell onto my face for, that's right kids, the third time that evening.

Scared loomed over me, his eyes and mouth nothing but black pits, and offered me a gentlemanly hand up. I didn't take it. I instead got to my feet and broke into our heroic sprint through the underbrush. Unfortunately, Scared had already grabbed hold of my collar, so I didn't go anywhere. He then put one arm around my waist and hoisted me onto his shoulder. I screamed for help. He clamped a gloved hand over my mouth and carried me back to the main road, holding me at arm's length, because needless to say I was trying to kick him in the face.

Happy was waiting for me on the road, his arms crossed like a disappointed teacher.

"Well played, child," said Happy. He actually sounded totally sincere about it. "You will be rewarded with a swift death."

"You think we should just nyx her once we're out of here?" Scared said conversationally, wrenching both my arms into a firm lock.

"I think she knows more than she's letting on," said Happy. "I say we keep her alive to see if we can extract more information first."

We traipsed back through the cemetery, in the vague direction of Omphalos. After a satisfying amount of difficulty and stubbed toes, the pair of sorcerers managed to find the gap in the railings that we'd come through. (I sure didn't help them.)

As soon as we were back in the garden, Happy turned to me. "Let's not take any more chances with you." He ripped off the rusting remains of my handcuffs. Then he took out a long, thick-linked chain, wrapped it around both my arms, and attached one end to Scared's wrist. "Sorry, Frank," he said, locking us both together with a humongous padlock.

We heard the high-pitched whining as soon as we entered the house. "Laelaps!" called Happy, following the sound into the study. Scared and I followed suit.

A middle-aged woman – the one who'd not been able to fit through the railings – lay spreadeagled across Foni's desk. Her neck had been split open. Next to her head was Foni's antique letter opener, slick with fresh blood.

"Someone else is here," said Scared.

"I *knew* you were keeping something from us," said Happy, rounding on me with a pistol drawn. "Who else is in this house?"

"Nobody!" I cried.

"Nobody? Where have I heard that before? Ah, yes. Think you're being clever, do you? Are *you* Cuttlefish? I swear to the gods, if you're trying to take us all in with an innocent little girl act, I will make you pay for it."

"Prince, she can't be Cuttlefish. Cuttlefish is dead next door. And she can't have been the one to do this. We've just been chasing her around outside."

"Where are the others?"

On cue, Angry and Sad walked into the room. Saw the dead sorcerer. Saw Happy pointing a gun at Scared and me, his dog whimpering at his feet.

"Lucky! Check the living room," said Happy. "Are the bodies still there?"

Angry ducked out and reappeared a moment later. "One of them is gone."

"Which one?"

Angry pointed at me. "The one she called Cuttlefish."

THIRTY-ONE

NOBODY

The study was normally a warm and inviting room. Its antique and unkempt furniture, hemmed in on all sides by towers of old books, gave it a well-used feel. However, this was not one of its better days. A dead sorcerer was flat on her back across the desk, whose green leather surface was struggling to absorb all the blood coming from her neck. Around her were her four Lyceum conspirators, exchanging glances. It was impossible to guess what any of them was thinking, as they wore Greek theatre masks twisted into grotesquely exaggerated expressions. Shackled to one of them was a schoolgirl with mud down her purple jumper and tears in her trousers.

"Whoever this fellow is," stated Mirth, "it seems pretty likely that he's the one behind this. Whether or not he's actually Cuttlefish. Agreed?"

The other sorcerers nodded.

"So, child, tell us again who you think he is." Mirth kept his pistol trained on the girl as he spoke.

"Er, well, he's my English teacher?"

The four sorcerers looked at one another quizzically.

"That is not relevant information," stated Mirth. "What else do you know about him?"

The girl instinctively tried to put her hands up every time the pistol was retrained on her, before remembering that she was still handcuffed. "Well, just before, he said he'd been the one stealing all the books. He said he was trying to build the God Machine with them."

All four sorcerers stared sorrowfully into the distance. Especially Sorrow.

Finally, Rage said, "So it's him. He's the one we want."

"Cuttlefish?" said Terror.

"Doesn't matter what we call him. He's the one that's stolen from us. We need to find him and eliminate him," said Sorrow.

"Then who on earth was Melanthios Skeuopoios?" snapped Mirth. "And what are we all doing in his widow's house?" His bloodhound yapped and snarled at his feet.

"Just another one of his targets, maybe," said Terror. "Point is, he's got away."

"We've all been taken in by him. Again," snarled Rage. "This kid was telling us the truth from the beginning, and instead of listening to her, we've fallen into his trap."

"Or maybe she's an accomplice of his. Maybe she led us away from the house on purpose, giving him a chance to strike," said Rage.

"The kid looks ten years old, Lucky," Terror pointed out. "She's not some master villain. Unless it's a persona."

"We've just been playing hide and seek on consecrated ground," Mirth said. "She wouldn't have been able to keep up a persona in there. In fact, she's the only person here I trust. Not *now*, Laelaps!"

Mirth batted his bloodhound on the nose. She flinched but continued to growl steadily at Mirth with her ears pulled back.

"What's that supposed to mean?" said Terror.

"I mean, if Cuttlefish is hiding, he's probably hiding in plain sight. Like he always does."

"You – you think he's one of us?" stammered Terror.

"Impossible," scoffed Mirth. "He would have to have killed one of us to replace them, while they were alone. But we've been together the entire time."

"Not when we had to go running after her," said Sorrow bitterly. "We split up."

"We shouldn't have done that," said Terror, fear creeping into his voice.

"Obviously, we shouldn't have done that," snapped Rage. "But we did, and now one of us might not be us."

"This is ridiculous," laughed Mirth over the wracking noise of barking. "If one of us were an identity thief, Laelaps would have sniffed him out instantly. And you haven't, have you, Laelaps?"

Mirth reached out to touch his dog on the head. She ducked away and bit him sharply on the hand. A shot reverberated around the study. Mirth cried out and folded backwards. His bloodhound danced away in fright. Terror and Rage both span around and pointed guns at Sorrow.

"We've been stupid," said Sorrow, lowering the revolver she'd just fired. "Laelaps has been telling us the moment she got free. We just weren't paying attention."

Rage lowered his gun. "You're right," he said furiously. "Cuttlefish must have ambushed Prince before he went looking for the kid."

"What, and taken his persona then?" asked Sorrow.

"Yeah."

"Impossible. He was on consecrated ground up until recently. He couldn't have had a persona there."

"You think we made a mistake?" said Terror. "But Prince is Laelaps's master. There's no way she'd act like that towards him."

"Unless she'd just been spooked by seeing Cuttlefish kill Hypatia," said Sorrow, nodding at the body on the desk while keeping his gun trained on Terror.

"Okay," said Terror. "Maybe Cuttlefish is still one of us. But there's still a way it could be Prince."

Rage also kept his gun pointing at Terror. "Go on."

"We're all wearing our masks. Maybe Cuttlefish didn't need a proper persona this time. Maybe he just stole Prince's mask."

Rage gestured at the fallen Mirth with his gun. "Take it off, then."

Trembling, Terror knelt by Mirth and removed his mask. Behind it was a Korean man's face, wearing an oddly haughty expression even in death.

"That's him," said Rage. "That's Prince."

The bloodhound emerged from under the desk and pawed at Mirth's face, whimpering.

"Looks like Laelaps has forgiven Prince now, anyway," said Rage incredulously.

"So if it's not Prince," said Sorrow, "then which one of us is it?"

"Only other possibility is you, Ariel," said Rage.

"What? How?" cried Sorrow.

"You were the last to come back from the cemetery. Prince, Frankos, and the girl all came back together. No opportunity for one of them to be ambushed. I came back a little later, and you were right behind me. If I'd been ambushed, you'd have walked into it. But you were last. Now, if I were him, I'd wait for the last one of us to come back so I could pick him off without the others noticing."

"Yeah, maybe," said Sorrow, trying to sound confident. "But you said it yourself. There's still a chance it could be you."

"Why don't we let Laelaps decide?" said Terror.

Terror glanced nervously at the bloodhound, who was now licking her dead master's face mournfully. "We can't trust Laelaps. She's clearly been spooked."

Rage knelt by the bloodhound and scratched her rear. The bloodhound tilted her head affectionately and gave his hand a lick. "She seems fine with me," he said. "Your turn."

Sorrow put hand on the bloodhound's head. The bloodhound immediately darted away and reared around to face her, her ears and lips pulled back.

Another deafening shot rang around the room. Sorrow's head exploded. Red mist shot out of her mask's eyeholes. Terror turned his gun to Rage.

"Sorry, Lucky," he stammered. "I don't want to kill you. But I don't want to give you a chance to kill me. You were alone as well. You could be him."

Rage reflexively pointed his gun back at Terror. "You don't want to trust me? Fine. I've got no reason to trust you either."

"Be reasonable, Lucky. The two of us have got to get all these bodies out of here somehow. These two, and the two next door. We can't afford for another one of us to get nyxed. But you know you can trust me. I was with Prince and the girl the entire time. I've been handcuffed to the girl since we left the cemetery! I can't be Cuttlefish."

At that moment, the bloodhound advanced on Terror, a low growl caught in the back of her throat.

"Laelaps still seems to like me more than you," observed Rage.

"Whatever. I'm not much of a dog person."

The bloodhound arched up in front of Terror, teeth bared to the gums. Terror flinched back.

"Really? But Laelaps's nose never lies."

The bloodhound padded closer, cocked her head and looked the schoolgirl straight in the eye. The schoolgirl couldn't help but stare back. It was an uncanny expression in the bloodhound's face. A knowing expression. One of the bloodhound's eyes closed, very slowly and deliberately, before opening again.

But now, the bloodhound was focusing all her attention back on Terror.

The girl knew what she had to do.

She cleared her throat. "Um, actually…"

Rage's eyes darted towards her. "What?"

"This guy is lying. I wasn't handcuffed to him the whole time. I was handcuffed to the other guy."

"To Prince?"

The girl touched a silver ring on her finger, and took a deep breath. "Yes. We came back alone."

"What?" shrieked Terror, aghast. "That's not true! That's not true! I've been with you the whole time!"

"She's the only one we can trust," said Rage. "You said it yourself."

Terror turned to the girl. "Why would you say that?" Then he looked at the dog. His eyes slowly widened. "No," he whispered. "Wait…"

Terror lowered his gun to point at the bloodhound. But he was gone before he'd had a chance to fire. He collapsed into a stack of books, bringing the girl down with him.

"How the hell am I supposed to get out of here now?" Rage muttered to himself. "And how the hell did we let this happen in the first place? We must have made a mistake somewhere... Hang on a minute."

Rage stormed over to the girl and aimed his gun between her eyes. Handcuffed to a dead man, there was nowhere she could go.

"Prince said the same thing as Ariel before he died. You *were* handcuffed to Frankos from the start. Which means you lied. And before you die, you're going to tell me why. You can't be Cuttlefish. Which means you lied before as well, and nobody is behind this. Nobody is Cuttlefish."

"I've been telling you that from the start, Lucky," growled a husky female voice.

A dark shape had reared up behind Rage. It was the bloodhound, tottering around on her hind legs. Strapped across her chest was a microgun, a weapon so huge that both her front paws could barely reach around its long, sleek barrel.

Rage had only turned halfway round, and his mouth had only dropped halfway to the floor, when the bloodhound fired. The end of her microgun blazed with light. A roar like fireworks filled the study. Rage's corpse – for it was already a corpse – was picked up and slammed against the bookcase, pinned there by the sheer force of bullets slamming into it. By the time the bloodhound had finished shooting, Rage's body was barely fit to be called a body anymore. It peeled off the books and spread across the floor.

The bloodhound lowered the minigun. It retracted and folded into itself, until it was nothing but a leatherbound book.

"That was a close call," she said.

THIRTY-TWO

THE GOD MACHINE

There are a few sights in this world more tragic than the sight of a dog trying to clap. But it was probably the perfect conclusion to the day I'd had. Laelaps was rearing up and trying to bring her paws together, but they didn't bend the right way. And even if they could, they wouldn't have made the right sound, because paws are designed to be as quiet as possible. Still, I appreciated the effort.

"Wow!" said Laelaps. "Just… Wow! That was incredible performance, from start to finish. The way you managed to draw everyone out of the house – that was *perfect*. I'd never have thought of that myself. But it was a lifesaver. And the way you delivered that lie at the end! How did you keep such a straight face? And did you see that guy's expression? When he worked out what was going on, just before he got shot in the face? Absolutely hilarious! I wish I could have videoed that. All in all, that was an incredible turnaround. I really wasn't sure we could pull that one off."

It was like the dog actually thought I was on her side. After everything she'd done.

"You know, I've spent a long time wondering exactly how you and Jason got away from me at school," the dog continued. "But now, I can see how you did it. You're craftier than you look, aren't you? Of course, I've completely forgotten everything that happened that day. Had to blow myself up to avoid being caught by the SIDs. I've got no idea what you did to outwit me. But from the looks of things, you deserved your victory."

I said nothing.

"Why are you looking at me like that?" said Laelaps, scowling as much as it was possible for a bloodhound to scowl. Mr Kaplan had dropped the stupid gun, but not the stupid dog impression. "I just saved your life from a band of feckless sorcerers. The least you could do is show a little gratitude."

"Is this what you wanted?" I said. My whole body was trembling.

"What I wanted?" Laelaps scratched her chin and glanced around at the corpses littering the house. Then she shrugged. "Not really. But I try not to become too attached to my wants. I let my *kismet* guide me. And look how it's worked out! Everyone has got what they deserved."

"Then why did you make all this happen?"

The dog tilted her head quizzically. "Make what happen?"

"All of this!" I shook my handcuffed body at the pile of corpses in the room. I hoped he'd take that to include the corpses in every other room too.

"Cass, I didn't make *any* of this happen! I'm only here to try and fix things as best I can."

Mr Kaplan, whoever he was underneath his teacher performance, had stopped seeming human to me, just some kind of faceless monster that I could never understand. He wore emotions like he wore personas: chosen to win people over as easily as possible. But behind that, he was nobody.

"Liar! Everyone thinks Foni is a criminal, thanks to you. You're the reason Hector got beaten up today. You're the reason my friends got nyxed. And if that weren't bad enough, you're the reason the Lyceum are trying to torture Foni and Hector."

You've never seen a dog looking more affronted. "Is that really what you think? *You're* the one who's made everyone suspicious of Foni and Hector – spreading rumours about them at every turn. *You're* the one who egged on these bullies, until they decided to come here. *You're* the one that makes Hector lose control and hurt people. Most of the time, that kid can't hurt a flea. But you've mastered the art of making him snap, haven't you?"

For a second, I almost thought he had a point. It was amazing how he could persuade you that almost anything was true.

"I didn't bring the Lyceum here. *You* did! If you hadn't gone snooping on Hector in school, shouting your mouth off about those sorcery books he had, I would never have been forced to cover up for him, and the Lyceum would never have discovered the Skeoupoioses. They told me so themselves. All I do – all I *ever* try to do – is stand by Hector's side. Protect him from the bullies. Protect him from the Lyceum. If you weren't in his life, I wouldn't have to worry."

"And if you hadn't decided to become Cuttlefish, none of us would have had to worry either," I shot back. "You're a mimetic. You could have been anyone. You could have stolen those books any way you wanted. But you chose to be Cuttlefish, and now you've destroyed Foni and Hector's lives."

Laelaps trotted around the back of Foni's desk. Then a girl stood up behind it. A girl whose pale face was flecked with earth.

It was me.

"Who would you be if you weren't Cassandra Drake, huh?" said the new me. As she talked, she rummaged through Foni's desk, and sifted through the piles of books and notes by its side. Still obsessed with finding what she came here for, I guessed. Even after everything that had happened. "What would be left if you stripped away your name, your skills, your family, your friends, your role? Nothing, that's what. Our identity is the most important thing we have. It's the one thing that truly belongs to us. It's the one part of us that will outlive us after we die. You really don't feel that's important? Fine. But all I've ever wanted is an identity I can be proud of. Cuttlefish's identity was there for the taking. So I took it."

The other Cass's voice was way more high-pitched and childlike than mine. Or maybe it wasn't. Maybe Cuttlefish knew what my voice sounded like better than I did.

"Well, it didn't work. You didn't get what you wanted." I stared myself in the eye, refusing to show myself how freaked out I was.

The other me shrugged. "Maybe not this time. But there's more than one way to skin a rat. After I nyx you, nobody but me is going to have any idea what happened tonight. So I'll just be able to come back another day and try again. One way or the other, Persephone will give up her secrets to me."

"What about them?" I nodded at the dead sorcerers around us, one of whom was still handcuffed to me.

"I suppose they'll come back too, won't they? Or maybe they'll wake up before Foni and do something straight away. These things are hard to predict."

My mind churned. I could see it now. The horrifying mess we were in was just the beginning. Far worse was going to come. Either the sorcerers would wake up first, and abduct and torture Foni and Hector just like they promised. Or if not, someone else in the Lyceum would. And even if they managed to avoid that… What would my friends say, when they woke up and found out they'd been nyxed in the Skeuopoios house? What would the rest of the school say? What would they do?

And watching it all would be Mr Kaplan, my innocent English teacher. The worse this mess got, the happier he would be. The more chances he would have to get what he wanted. The God Machine.

I was the only person in the world who knew the truth. But I was going to wake up tomorrow knowing none of this. Thinking that I'd been just another innocent victim of Foni or Hector. And whatever I said to incriminate them, I'd play right into Mr Kaplan's hands.

My chest felt empty. I've been given so many chances to stop this. I'd thrown them all away. And now, the only role I had left to play was to become another one of Mr Kaplan's human weapons, used unwittingly against Foni and Hector. Unless, by some miracle, someone stopped him tonight.

The other me had started sifting through Foni's filing cabinet.

"You think the God Machine could fit in there?" I asked, trying to keep the incredulity in my voice to a bare minimum.

My mirror image shrugged. "Nobody knows what the God Machine is. It could be any size. So I may as well start…"

She trailed off and stared at me, her eyes suddenly alight. The roiling dust in the air seemed to slow, sparkling under the study lights. "What equipment *did* you see in this house?"

I began to worry whether I'd made the worst mistake of my life. I told myself that no matter what, the situation couldn't possibly get worse than it already was. Then I remembered how many times I'd already thought that this evening and been proved wrong.

"I told you already," I said, looking away. "Nothing at all. Just, like, the letter opener. Other old stuff."

My doppelgänger flashed me a childish and wonky grin. Is that really what I looked like when I was happy?

"You're lying, aren't you?" she said. "I have to say, I was impressed by your baldheaded lie to that Lyceum sorcerer earlier. But it won't wash with me. I always know when someone's lying."

"I'm not lying," I pleaded. "Hector's not shown me anything. I'd never even heard of the God Machine until tonight."

"I'd always suspected it, you know," she said. Her voice climbed higher and higher with excitement. "For Cuttlefish to work on the project for so many years, and leave nothing behind… Everyone assumed he'd taken his progress to the grave. But if it was Persephone all along – she could have kept working at it. Maybe she's still working on it now!"

I said nothing. I knew better than to deliberately fuel this train of thought. It didn't take the other Cass long to notice. She squatted in front of me and looked me straight in the eye.

"You're being awfully quiet," she said. "What are you thinking?"

"Nothing," I said as firmly as I could. "Foni's never talked about anything like this to me."

"I'm sure she hasn't!" she said. "But Hector has. Hasn't he?"

I avoided Cass's gaze. I pressed my thumb into the emerald snake eye on my ring. "I don't know what you're talking about," I murmured.

Cass started pacing around the study again, absentmindedly avoiding the bullet ridden bodies of the Lyceum as she did so. "It doesn't make sense," she said, more to herself than me. "But if it were anywhere, it would be here...you know, Hector confided in me that he'd shown you many things he shouldn't have. Many secrets of Omphalos, that his mother wanted to stay secret. He told me that he'd wanted to prove his friendship to you. Do you know what I'm talking about?"

I did. Of course I did. But I didn't dare say anything out loud, in case I gave the game away.

Cass stared at my expression intently. "He showed it to you, didn't he? He actually showed it to you. You can't imagine how many sorcerers would have killed to be in your boots!" She tilted his head at the bodies scattered across the study and smiled. "Or maybe you can."

"Hector didn't show me anything," I insisted. "Hector doesn't like me."

The other me smiled cynically. "Now, Cass. You *know* that's not true. I *know* you know that's not true. Cass, Hector is *obsessed* with you. He likes you more than anyone else in school. He might even like you more than his own mother. I've tried to point out to him so many times what a colossal mistake he's made in trusting you but… He just wouldn't listen. He really thought you were his friend."

"I'm more of a friend to him then you are," I retorted.

"Is that what you think?" There was something new and horrible in my own voice, as it came out of that other mouth. Something dark, and sickly sweet. "While you and your friends have been doing everything you can to make Hector's life hell, I've been by his side, reassuring him that things will get better. I've been showing him how to work magic, so that he can rise up one day and outshine you all. Meanwhile, what have you done? Lied to him. Manipulated him. Humiliated him in front of the whole school. That time he wet himself after you refused to admit you'd talked to him? He may have forgiven you for that, but I haven't. That time you got him in trouble for those books he was trying to give me? He might have been arrested if I hadn't covered up for him. You remember all of this, right? You've crushed him over and over again, in every way you could possibly dream up. Why, Cass? What's he ever done to you, other than try to be a friend to you?"

It wasn't my voice anymore. It was Hector's.

And there he was, standing in front of me. His right eye was swollen shut. Blood oozed from his forehead.

"But despite all the ways you showed your contempt for him, he couldn't tear his mind away from you," Hector said, his voice small and pathetic. "Every session we had together, he'd say, "Do you think she likes me?" or "Do you think she really means what she said this time?" And sometimes, all I wanted to do is shake him and say, "No! Cass hates you, and all she does is hurt you, like everyone else in this school, and the sooner you cut her out of your life the happier you'll be!"

Hector stared directly into my eyes. My ears rang with uncanniness. "I never said that, of course. I just suggested, as kindly as I could, that he'd be better off staying away from you. But he couldn't do it. He thought your mothers were going to get married, that soon the two of you would be brother and sister. He was *so* happy about that. He really thought it would make his life perfect. But you put an end to that, didn't you? You made it your mission to drive your parents apart. And you succeeded. You'd make an incredible sorcerer, you know, if you put your mind to it. Deceit is second nature to you."

"You know nothing about me," I said, my voice cracking.

"At first, I thought you must be doing it all unintentionally," Hector said, wiping a stream of blood away from his good eye. "All the pain you inflicted on him day after day. I just thought you were too young and naïve to see the effect you were having on him. But you knew all along, didn't you? You knew, and you just didn't care. You'd sooner shoot Hector down over and over again than let him so much as look at you." Hector's voice wobbled, and his eyes overflowed with tears.

"I know what you're trying to do, and it won't work," I said, my voice crumbling away underneath me like sand.

Hector's tears had already dried on his cheeks. "Oh, you think this is sorcery? Sorcery is an illusion. This is just the truth. The truth is, Cass, it would have been so easy for you to make Hector feel happy once in a while, but you were too wrapped up in your pathetic, selfish concerns to bother."

Hard to believe I'd once been afraid of Hector's insects. Or the sorcerers' guns. Just then, I'd have done anything to end this pain. End it, and wake up the next day remembering nothing. Able to go to school and hang out with Tori and Jess and Chloë, as usual, not knowing the truth about Mr Kaplan. Not knowing the truth about myself.

Hector's voice became tender. "It's a pity I have to kill you when this is over. Maybe otherwise, there'd have been a chance of you becoming a better person. Because…I do like you, Cass. I don't think you want to hurt people. It's just…you don't see the power you have. You don't see the damage you're doing. But now, you have a chance to undo all the pain you've caused Hector. Would you like that?"

I gulped, and felt a huge globby ball of snot and saliva run down my throat.

"If you tell me where the God Machine is, this could all be over before you know it. I'll take it, and get out of your life forever. And I'll leave you alive. You'll be able to tell whatever story you want to the police about what happened here. You'll be able to exonerate Foni and Hector completely. You'll be a hero."

I shut my eyes, and squeezed tears down my cheeks. I didn't trust myself to say anything out loud.

"But if you don't tell me…well, I'll nyx you, then I'll find another way back here. So will the Lyceum. So will your stupid, violent friends. Their parents too, I should imagine. It won't be long before the real SID start asking questions again." Hector smiled poisonously.

My throat had seized up. I could barely speak. My cheeks were damp with tears. "Fine," I whispered between heaves. "It's in the house."

Hector smiled and knelt to hug me. Foni let go of me and stood back. "Good girl. Lead the way."

"I can't." I shook my shackles at her.

"Of course." A set of keys appeared in her hand, which he used to free me from Sad.

I led Foni to the basement door. "After you," I said to her.

Foni looked at me suspiciously. Then she opened the door.

Behind it was nothing but darkness. Foni found a light switch. I braced myself for another deluge of insects. But only the normal number of spiders stood sentinel in each corner.

We walked down the stairs and along the booklined basement passage. The gentle smell of damp down here was almost nice after what I'd gone through upstairs. It felt like a long time since I'd been here last. But I still remembered where the secret handle was.

I stopped outside the door. Tears boiled in my eyes.

"Where is it?" Foni asked again, twitching.

With shaking hands, I found the secret switch at the back of the shelf. The door rushed open.

Foni gasped when I turned the chandelier on. Anyone seeing the place for the first time would.

Not much had changed since I was last here. The same antique equipment and furniture was dotted around the room, some of it under dust sheets. I saw the gramophone, the sofa bed, the giant insect-like machine at the back.

Just as Hector had promised, the last few books on the shelves were now gone. They were all completely empty, except for a corner which had a large collection of knickknacks.

Foni looked like a five-year-old in a toyshop. Her eyes flitted back and forth across the many wonders that the room contained. "So? Where is it?" she asked urgently.

"You promise to leave us all alone once you have it?" I asked. "To disappear, and never come back?"

"Absolutely! Once I have the God Machine, I'll disappear forever."

"Okay. It's that thing at the back." I pointed at the machine in the corner of the room.

Foni practically danced down the spiral staircase and into the room, gazing up at the floor-to-ceiling shelves on every side. She marvelled loudly at everything she saw on the way to the machine, picking up everything from a carved wooden cup to a rust-red rock, sighing with delight at each trinket. Finally, she laid her hands on the side of the machine and pressed her forehead rapturously into the metal.

I didn't hang around to see anything else. The second Foni touched the coiled-up machine, I stepped back out of the room and swung the heavy door shut. I scrabbled frantically for the handle and twisted it back to where it had started, listening for the smart clicks as the door locked into place.

The thick steel door blocked almost all the noise coming from that room. But it wasn't enough to block Foni's voice, shrill and confused.

"Cass? Cass, what are you doing?" She sounded like a lost child.

"Calling Mum," I shouted back, scrambling in my pocket for my phone.

There was a faint clanging of the spiral staircase, then a sudden thump against the other side of the door which sent me staggering back. It was more from the shock than anything else, though. The door didn't flinch. Then there came the desperate ratcheting sound of the useless door handle being pumped up and down.

"You sneaking, creeping, back-crossing double-stabber!" Foni screeched from inside. "You tricked me!"

"Now you know what it feels like," I said. My tears had already dried on my cheeks.

"But what is it?" Foni's voice had lost its cruel edge, becoming desperate and whiny. "Please. Just tell me. The God Machine. How does it work?"

"The God Machine is a stupid myth," I said.

I began to laugh.

The London Press

CURTAINS DOWN FOR CUTTLEFISH

Joost Meyer

The SID have today confirmed that a man arrested earlier this week has been formally charged with Cuttlefish's crimes. They are 'confident' that they have the right person this time.

Kaplan, 37, was apprehended during an attempted robbery of a home in Highgate. The police were tipped off by one of their own colleagues, DCI Helen Drake, who up until recently was a central figure in the Cuttlefish investigation.

Kaplan was arrested while trying to rob the home of Persephone Skeuopoios. He impersonated a police officer to gain access to her home, before magically killing her and her son. Also found in atroposy at the scene were six friends of

Persephone's son, who are believed to have stumbled into the robbery while it was in progress, as well as five unrelated individuals who have themselves been detained pending an investigation of their involvement with the case.

Ms Skeuopoios's husband Melanthios was accused of Cuttlefish's crimes many years ago, and killed during arrest in an operational blunder that haunts the Metropolitan Police to this day. Although Mr Skeuopoios was never charged with Cuttlefish's crimes, many continued to hold this belief. It is possible that Kaplan, believing that there was truth to this theory, suspected Ms Skeuopoios of possessing magical material. However, the SID are not treating Ms Skeuopoios as a suspect.

Until today, the SID had refused to confirm whether they considered Kaplan a suspect in the Cuttlefish cases. However, suspicion had been rife following eyewitness reports of the arrest, which claimed that the suspect was heard shouting "The great Cuttlefish has been brought down at last," "Cuttlefish will live to triumph another day," and "Yes, it is I, the one and only Cuttlefish," at the top of his voice as he was placed into the police van.

Following Kaplan's arrest, DCI Drake has returned to duty, where she remains in charge of the ongoing Cuttlefish investigation. Only a month previously, Drake had been suspended for her alleged mishandling of a previous Cuttlefish confrontation. Drake ordered the detention of hundreds of staff and pupils at Whittington School in order to conduct a systematic search for Cuttlefish within. Despite the considerable risks and strain this involved, no arrests were ultimately made, and Cuttlefish was thought to have eluded the manhunt. However, with this arrest, DCI Drake appears to have undergone a reversal of fortunes. Kaplan is expected to be brought to trial within the next two months.

Kaplan was an English teacher at Whittington School; the same site as the previous failed police action against Cuttlefish. Staff and pupils are said to be 'shocked' by the arrest of Kaplan, and describe him as 'always lively, funny…a born entertainer'. He had a special fondness for the dramatic arts, and was at the heart of the school's theatre programme. But it appears this love of performing had a dark side; the tendency towards high-profile identity theft for which Cuttlefish had become so notorious in recent months.

Whittington School has been temporarily closed pending a full internal review of its hiring and security practices. The chairman of the PTA, Anne Covley, told us, "Both the recent attack within the school walls and this shock arrest of a teacher lead us to believe that Whittington is not currently taking its security obligations seriously."

Cuttlefish: the criminal we loved to hate p. 49

THIRTY-THREE

KISMET

Mum was never completely sure why Benediktos Kaplan confessed to everything so easily. Nor why most of what he confessed to was total lies.

LIE 1
He confessed to all of Cuttlefish's crimes. True, he had committed the recent ones. But he confessed to *every* unsolved crime attached to Cuttlefish's name. Of course, it helped that they found all the Daedalus books in his house. Not just the ones he'd stolen, but the ones Foni had stolen over a decade ago – the ones Hector had given to him years later.

LIE 2
He confessed to killing everyone in the house. Including all my friends. And Baz, Yaz, and Hazza.

LIE 3

He confessed to being Cuttlefish. The one true Cuttlefish. Only Foni, Mum, and I knew the truth, that he was nothing but the copycat of a dead man who hadn't been Cuttlefish in the first place.

It didn't make a lot of sense to Mum that Mr Kaplan was so completely happy to cover up all of Foni and Hector's crimes. But it made sense to me. Mr Kaplan had finally got his kismet. His face was on the front page of every news site. Finally unmasked as Cuttlefish, Mr Kaplan was hated and feared by the whole world. And he couldn't be happier about it.

Mum explained all of Cuttlefish's lies to me a couple of weeks later. That's not exactly how she put it. She said there's been a few "irregularities" between Mr Kaplan's story and mine, but that she and her team weren't too worried about them as long as the main story was the same.

"They'll want to interview you soon," Mum continued cautiously. We were eating a huge brunch that Mum had made. It actually wasn't that bad, for Mum. "You won't have to testify in court, as you're too young. So whatever you say in the interview will be used as your testimony. Of course, you're free to give your side of the story in any way you want, but it might be worth thinking about…"

"You want me to agree with Cuttlefish's story."

"Not exactly. Not at all. Though given his story doesn't seem to implicate Foni or Hector at all, there seems no point in dragging them in, does there?" Mum gave me her biggest, cutest grin.

"How long have you known that Foni was Cuttlefish?" I asked in reply.

"Since before this started. I hope you'll forgive me."

"I do. I get it." I wasn't angry with Mum anymore. As soon as I'd found out the truth myself, I'd figured out that Mum knew it already. And Mum's lies and cover-ups had all made sense. She hadn't been trying to protect Foni because she was innocent. She'd been protecting her because she was *guilty.* It would have been an impossible choice to explain to me, let alone anyone else. But now, I'd seen for myself what Mum had known all along: whatever Foni had done in the past, she'd been punished enough.

The same went for Hector. I remembered what he'd done to my friends. I'd remember it for the rest of my life. But he hadn't meant it. Whatever powers Mr Kaplan had been teaching him, he wasn't in control of them properly. That's what he'd told me, anyway, and Hector was incapable of lying.

More importantly… He'd been punished since he was born for a whole bunch of things that he hadn't done, things that had nothing to do with him. I wasn't going to punish him any more.

Mum beamed with joy. "That's such a relief. I'm going to see Foni and Hector later. I'll tell them the good news."

"Why don't we invite them up here?"

I winced as the words left my mouth. I don't know where they came from. Certainly not me. They were not the words of a sane and rational person. But it was too late. I'd said them, and Mum's beam had just intensified by many thousands of lumens.

"That's a great idea! How about dinner?"

It was the first time the Skeuopoioses had set foot in our house. When Hector saw the piles of books in Mum's study, his eyes lit up. "Do you think your mother would let me alphabetize her books?"

I laughed. So did Hector, like he'd been funny on purpose. Obviously, he hadn't, but it was a step in the right direction.

Dinner was strange. Not the food itself – Mum actually knocked it out of the park for the second time running with a pasta bake. It was almost scary. Nor were Foni and Hector that weird. Away from the creeping mustiness of Omphalos, they could easily pass for a normal mother and son.

The strange part was that I ended up having to explain the entire evening of Cuttlefish's arrest to Foni and Hector, because neither of them could remember. At least, up until the part where Mum had got involved, which everyone knew.

Mum had been at home when I called her. She came straight to find me, as soon as she'd called in every favour she could from the people who still trusted her. On her orders, they dispatched about 1,000,000,000,000,000,004 police officers to Omphalos.

Mum didn't let them make any mistakes. While most of them guarded the door, a few of them stormed in, took Cuttlefish down with tasers, then arrested him and themselves to be on the safe side. The rest of the unit took them all away.

But Cuttlefish didn't even try to put up a fight. Apparently, he was puzzling over all the junk in the room when they went in, still hoping he could find the God Machine.

They had to arrest all the dead people too, of course. Just to be on the safe side. But sooner or later, they were all released. Including the Lyceum, much to Mum's frustration. When they woke up, they all started claiming that they'd been innocent passers-by, who'd heard shooting coming from the house and gone to investigate. Even though I knew the truth and did everything I could to prove it, the case against them got dropped. But "I know their names now," DCI Helen Drake told me darkly. "I'll see them again, sooner or later. Trust me."

Mum was in the news and on the TV almost as much as Cuttlefish himself. It was a great story: the heroic maverick detective who'd saved the day. Note to reader: what she'd actually done is turn up right at the end and take all the credit. But I honestly didn't mind. The internal investigation against her was dropped, and she went straight back to work crowned in everlasting glory.

Mum bookmarked all her favourite articles about DCI Helen Drake's swashbuckling arrest. *Curtains Down for Cuttlefish,* one of them read. In a way, it told a better story than the real one had been. A simpler and easier to understand story. Was it true? Well, it wasn't any less true than Cuttlefish's story to the police.

As for what I told Foni and Hector at the dinner table: that was true. Well, as close to the truth as I could get. It's not like I recited Mr Kaplan's horrific taunting of Foni or me word for word. Nobody needed to hear that. And I didn't tell Hector that I'd told him he was too stupid to live. What would have been the point?

When I stopped to think about it, a lot had happened that evening that only I would ever know about. So, as horrific as it had all been, it may as well have been a bad dream. Whatever story I chose to tell about it would replace the truth. Or maybe it would become the truth. I couldn't tell the difference anymore. I was the only survivor, and just like Cuttlefish had promised, that meant I got to decide what the truth was.

There were other things that Mr Kaplan had said that I still didn't understand, though. And now that Mum and I both knew the truth about Foni and Hector, and now that we all knew that we all knew, none of us needed to be guarded around each other.

"So...what is the God Machine?" I said cautiously.

"The God Machine? An old thought experiment of the Philosopher's," Foni explained enthusiastically, pouring cream on her chocolate tart (yes, Mum had made *pudding*). "The basic idea is that it's something which makes all sorcery *real*. Someone with the God Machine would have the total power to make anything they wanted come true. They would have the power of the gods, in other words."

I was aghast.

"A total myth, of course," Foni added. "The Philosopher only introduced the idea to demonstrate the limitations of sorcery. To show that sorcery, being an illusion by nature, could never really change reality – because if it *could*, sorcerers would basically have the powers of the gods. But hundreds of years later, people started to take the idea seriously. Daedalus – you've heard of him, right? – wasn't the first. He was just the most famous. After he vanished, rumours spread that he'd left behind coded messages in his books, or even enchanted the books themselves with the power of the God Machine. All total nonsense."

"I still can't believe you managed to persuade Kaplan it was in the house," Mum said. "You must have been extremely convincing. To be honest, I'm a bit worried!"

Everyone laughed nervously. To be honest, I was a bit worried too. It had been scarily easy for me to trick Cuttlefish.

"But how could anyone sane believe in something like the God Machine? No offence," I asked awkwardly.

"None taken," said Foni. "When you learn a bit of sorcery, you quickly discover that the boundary between reality and our collective perception of reality are not as distinct at they seem. At first, you might think a sorcerer is a bit like a storyteller, trying to convince people to believe their *story* instead of what's really there. But at a certain point, you realize that the reality they're trying to overwrite – the world all around us – is *also* a story. One that we ourselves have written, just by perceiving the world and trying to make sense of it through language and words. Once you realize how fragile our notion of reality is–"

"Thanks, Foni, but that's probably enough sorcery lessons for one meal," said Mum tartly. "I may be off duty, but…"

"Fair enough," said Foni, winking at Mum. Then to Hector, she whispered, "I think she's onto us."

We laughed, even though it was, for the record, too early to be joking about this. Like, 1000 years too early. Something else I'd discovered about Foni is that she had a very specific sense of humour. It was an extremely dry sense of humour that involved not doing or saying anything which gave away the fact that a joke had been made. To make the disguise even more complete, the joke itself was normally not very funny. It was very different from Hector's sense of humour, which involved accidentally saying something moronic and then pretending it had been deliberate once everyone started laughing. Unfortunately, this meant that Foni and Hector were never able to understand or notice each other's 'jokes', so they kind of needed other people around for them to work at all. Once I'd realized all this, I could almost tolerate their company.

After dinner, Hector and I left Mum and Foni to clear up the kitchen. In the sitting room, Hector took a deep breath and looked me straight in the nose. It was the closest to my eyes he'd ever reached voluntarily.

"I just wanted to say, thank you, Cassandra," he said hurriedly.

"For what?" I guessed it would be for saving him and his mother from both the Lyceum and Cuttlefish in a single day, which to be honest, he kind of owed me for.

"For being so kind to me today," he replied.

Kind? I'd barely even spoken to him, to be honest. We'd had a lot to talk about over dinner, so it hadn't been hard to keep up a base level of friendliness, and –

Oh.

That's what he thought kindness was.

"Er, yeah, no problem, Hector," I said graciously. "My…pleasure."

"And I'm sorry for committing sorcery. I know it's wrong, and I should never have done it in the first place."

"That's OK, Hector. I don't… I don't think it was wrong."

That hadn't been exactly what I was expecting to say, but I'd said it now.

"All I mean is…now that I know you and your mum a bit better, I get that not all sorcerers are bad," I continued. "And after everything that happened the other night…actually, there was something I wanted to ask you."

Hector gazed at my chin blandly.

"I just hated how *weak* I was the whole time. I had to be saved from Cuttlefish by your mum, and I had to be saved by *Cuttlefish* from the Lyceum, and…"

"You tricked Cuttlefish into locking himself up!"

I brushed him away. "I got *so* lucky. I just feel like I've spent too much time running away, and hiding, and keeping out of harm's way. You know?"

Hector gazed at me, not getting it. Of course he wasn't getting it. *Hector never got it.* Why had I not accepted this by now?

I took a deep breath. "Could you ever…teach me a little bit of sorcery?"

Please try to understand. I'm not a bad person. I'm not now, and I wasn't back then. I didn't want to become a sorcerer. I never wanted that. If I'd known what road I was going down, and where it would lead, I never would have taken the first step. It's just, after everything I'd been through…

"I want to be ready. If anything like this ever happens again, which obviously it won't, but if it does…I want to be ready for it. You know?"

"Yes. I know." Hector stared at my belly button and said nothing else.

"So will you do it?"

"Yes. I will." He smiled. "This is going to be fun."

THE END

THANKS FOR READING!

The Identity Thief is my debut novel, and the first in the God Machine series. The next books are going to take you deeper into the magical and murky world of the Lyceum, and their battle to bring sorcery into the light. I hope you'll stick around to read the next book when it comes out!

If you don't want to wait that long, you can hear Cuttlefish's story straight from his mouth. *I'm Nobody* catches up with the identity thief as he tells his life story to his prison psychiatrist. You'll find out how he mastered the art of mimesis, when he first crossed paths with Persephone Skeuopoios, and why he embarked on his quest to build the God Machine. All members of my Readers Club can download *I'm Nobody* for free – sign up on my website, **www.alexbryant.com**.

Once you're part of my readers club, you'll get to hear how the series is coming along, and of course be the first to know when the next book is released. You'll also be able to drop me a line with your opinions, thoughts on what should happen in the next books, etc. whenever you want!

If you enjoyed *The Identity Thief* and want to help me spread the word about it, there's three things you could do that would mean the world to me:

1. **Leave a 5 star review** on Amazon and Goodreads. Every 5 star review I get boosts my book in the rankings, so that more people find and read it. And needless to say, I personally read every review I get, and love to hear that people are enjoying it! (If you didn't like the book so much, you're welcome to leave a lower number of stars, of course. But weirdly enough, a lower number – even 4 stars – actually hurts my book's place in the rankings, so I'm actually better off receiving no review than a 4 star review!)

2. **Tell your friends** about *The Identity Thief!* Ultimately, the single most common way people find out about new books is from a friend. So a personal recommendation or shout out on social media would mean a lot to me. Don't forget to tag me in:
   Goodreads: **/alexbryantauthor**
   Instagram: **@alexbryantauthor**
   Facebook: **@alexbryantauthor**
   Twitter: **@alexbryantauth**

3. **Invite me to talk** at your school or reading group! If you're based in the UK and want me to come and say hi, just drop me a line: **alexbryant@km-books.com**.

HOPE TO HEAR FROM YOU SOON…

SO WHO'S ALEX BRYANT, ANYWAY?

Good question. As you've probably guessed (I'm incredibly unimaginative) I grew up and went to school in Highgate, North London, just up the road from Highgate Cemetery. I was much more of a Hector than a Cass, so I spent most of my school days choreographing elaborate magical fight sequences in my head. Eventually, I figured I may as well try and get them down on paper.

The very first germ of the idea for this novel came to me when I was 16 – I dreamt one of the scenes incredibly vividly, and it's survived almost unchanged into the final draft. (Guess which one it is! The answer's on my site…) So it's been a terrifying *thirteen years* of developing this world and filling it with characters – starting, of course, with shapeshifting, grandstanding maniac Cuttlefish. In fact, I wrote chunks of *I'm Nobody*, about Cuttlefish's time in Wandsworth Prison, before it occurred to me that I'd be better off going back and telling the story of what he did to wind up in prison in the first place.

As well as writing, I spend my time performing improv comedy. You can catch my troupe Hivemind on stage any time you're passing through London! More info on **www.hivemindimprov.com.**

Want to know more? Say hi:
Site: **www.alexbryantauthor.com**
Goodreads: **/alexbryantauthor**
Instagram: **@alexbryantauthor**
Facebook: **@alexbryantauthor**
Twitter: **@alexbryantauth**
Email: **alexbryant@km-books.com**

THANKS, EVERYBODY!

Behind any work of fiction stands an author. And behind that author stand a bunch of the author's friends who were forced to read their work of fiction before it was good, and who told the author how to make it better. In my case, those people are Ellie Griffiths, Inigo Lapwood, Su Laurent, Jesse Locke, Marcus Martin, Victoria Princewill, Edward Reader, Emily Reader, and Raven Undersun. I'm guaranteed to have forgotten exactly one person from this list. To you, I offer my deepest apologies.

Special thanks to my family for not just reading my novel in its many versions, but for being my focus group, brainstorming team, and production committee as required.

Thanks to Ivan Cakić and James Harding for a beautiful cover design that I fell in love with the moment I first saw it.

Finally, thank you for reading *The Identity Thief.* And for painstakingly getting to the end of the acknowledgements. Seriously, what kind of person does that? Are you sure there's nothing more fun you could be doing right now? Given that you're still, inexplicably, here, I'm always looking for advance readers to read my novels before they're published and give me feedback, write reviews, or give me cool ideas on what I should do next. I also need advisors to help me with designs and other plans. Do you think this could be you? Join the Readers Club at **www.alexbryantauthor.com** for more info!

Printed in Great Britain
by Amazon